By Christopher Dow

Fiction

Effigy
    Book I: Stroud
    Book II: Oakdale
The Books of Bob
    Devil of a Time
    Jumping Jehovah
The Clay Guthrie Mysteries
    The Dead Detective
    Landscape with Beast
    The Texas Troll Unlimited
    Darkness Insatiable
Roadkill
The Werewolf and Tide, and Other Compulsions

Nonfiction

Lord of the Loincloth (nonfiction novel)
Book of Curiosities: Adventures in the Paranormal
Occasional Pilgrimage: Essays on Film, Literature, and Other Matters
Living the Story: The Meandering, True, and Sometimes Strange
        Adventures of an Unknown Writer
    Vol.I: Growing Up Takes a Long Time
    Vol. II: Growing Old Takes Longer

Martial Arts

The Wellspring: An Inquiry into the Nature of Chi
Circling the Square: Observations on the Dynamics of Tai Chi Chuan
Elements of Power: Essays on the Art and Practice of Tai Chi Chuan
Alchemy of Breath: An Introduction to Chi Kung
Leaves on the Wind: A Survey of Martial Arts Literature (Vol. I–VI)

Poetry

City of Dreams
The Trip Out
Texas White Line Fever
Networks
A Dilapidation of Machinery
Puzzle Pieces: Selected Poems

Editor

The Abby Stone: The Poetry of Bartholo Dias
The Best of Phosphene
The Best of Dialog

DARKNESS INSATIABLE

DARKNESS INSATIABLE

Christopher Dow

Phosphene Publishing Company
Temple, Texas

Darkness Insatiable
© 2024 by Christopher Dow
ISBN 13: 978-1-7369307-9-3

Published by:
Phosphene Publishing Company
Temple, Texas, U.S.A.
phosphenepublishing.com

1.3

For Ditto Davis,
who made this and so many
other things better.

I

DOT COFFEESHOP WAS GUTHRIE'S FAVORITE restaurant in the area near his home, especially when he needed a substantial breakfast. It was Wednesday morning, and today, he did, having just come off a grueling case involving a vicious blackmailer. Thanks to his efforts, the guy was behind bars for extortion, battery, and murder and would be for a long time. Now, with spring edging into summer, the weather was beautiful, and for the first time in nearly a month, Guthrie had a chance to relax and eat some decent food. No sense in not starting with a hearty breakfast.

So there he was, sitting in a booth near the back, minding his own business and enjoying a Denver omelet with sausage links, hash browns, and coffee, when he saw a familiar figure through the wide windows that fronted the restaurant. The man entered, spoke briefly with the hostess, and pointed toward Guthrie's booth.

Damn, Guthrie thought, as the man turned toward him. Apparently, he'd become entirely too predictable. He seriously considered changing his choice of eating establishments but quickly dropped the idea. It probably wouldn't do any good. The old man would find him no matter where he was. He put down his fork as the man walked down the long aisle toward him, a whimsical smile teasing the corners of his mouth. He was of average height, lithe, and handsome in an ascetic way. His hair and smile were both gleaming white, set off against ebony skin that showed enough wrinkle to convey age but not enough to betray decrepitude.

"Hello, Mr. Guthrie."

"I haven't seen you in a while, Master Tereba," Guthrie said. "I thought you'd forgotten about me."

At least, he sometimes hoped the old man had forgotten about him.

"Nearly a year," Tereba said. "But I could never forget about you. Not after what we've been through together." Tereba waved toward the bench seat on the opposite side of the table. "May I join you?"

"Do I have a choice?"

"One always has a choice, though often between negative outcomes."

"Does that mean that instead of making me buy you breakfast, you've brought me a different negative outcome?" Guthrie asked as he waved to the seat on the opposite side of the table.

Tereba laughed lightly as he sat, teeth stark against his dusky skin. How the hell does he keep them so white? Guthrie wondered. Although Tereba looked to be in his late sixties, Guthrie knew he was probably the most ancient man on the planet. If there were others who were older, Guthrie didn't want anything to do with any of them. One Tereba was more than enough.

"So far, all your outcomes have been positive."

"You couldn't have convinced me of that at the time."

"I heard your last case was interesting."

"The blackmailer?" Guthrie shrugged. "It just took a little time is all. And here I was hoping I'd have the rest of the week off." He stared pointedly at the old man.

Kay, the waitress for the section where Guthrie usually sat, came over with a glass of water and a menu for the new arrival.

"Can I get you anything?" she asked Tereba.

"Just coffee."

As Kay left with the menu, Tereba gestured toward Guthrie's plate.

"Don't let me keep you from your meal. Go ahead and finish."

"Sure. I don't suppose I'll be doing much talking, anyway. What is it this time? Not some demon or troll or other fucked up thing, I hope." He lifted a forkful of omelet to his mouth and chewed while Tereba answered.

"Not one of those, I think, but certainly, as you put it, some fucked-up thing. I wouldn't need your expertise, otherwise."

"So you admit you only visit when you're asking for help? Does that mean you're nothing but a foul weather friend? Besides, I'm not sure barely surviving horrors of one sort or another qualifies as expertise."

"Nevertheless, once again I am asking for your help precisely because you *have* survived. I would call that expertise."

Kay returned with Tereba's coffee, and the old man went silent and gave her a bright smile before she left.

Guthrie knew that Tereba was a powerful perceptor of wrongness in the world, and if the old sorcerer had come to him, he would have to help in whatever way he could. Besides, he owed the old man his life and career. His sanity. Despite his sarcasm toward the old man and despite how harrowing the other cases he'd worked for Tereba had been, he had to admit that the idea of working another one got his juices flowing. Damn, he wondered. Am I becoming a danger junkie?

"Okay," Guthrie said. "Tell me what's going on."

"About three years ago, some of my colleagues in Baton Rouge and New Orleans became aware that a malevolent force had risen in the south Louisiana swamps. They investigated, but by the time they did, all they found were two small, deserted, and decaying villages. The force was no longer centered there."

"A malevolent force?" Guthrie said. "No better description?"

"We don't think it's a demon," Tereba said. His tone was hopeful, but a touch of uncertainty crouched in his tone. "It doesn't feel like that. At present, we simply don't have enough information."

Guthrie didn't bother to ask who Tereba's colleagues were. He figured that was above his pay grade. And truthfully, he didn't want to know.

"Thank goodness for small favors," he said. "But you don't know what it is or what spawned it?"

"My colleagues continue to investigate."

"You said they couldn't find it, whatever it is. What makes you think it didn't just disappear?"

"We think that's unlikely. From what my colleagues could tell, the force gained power in destroying one of the villages, then even more vitality after moving on to the other. We know it's dangerous and growing more so, and such things, once arisen, don't easily dissipate."

"And you want me to do something about it."

"There you have it, Mr. Guthrie," Tereba said, beaming a smile that was a little too deliberate. Was the old man actually concerned about him? "Intention is the mother of action."

He took a couple of sips of coffee then set the mug on the table.

"Do you have anything to go on?" Guthrie asked. "What this thing, whatever it is, looks like or where it came from or anything else?"

"While we might not yet understand how or where it originated, it imprints a noxious psychic residue on any environment where it remains. The villages it destroyed are not only rotting into the swamp before their time, they are imbued with a sense of pestilential corruption, though that is gradually fading. There is some evidence that, after leaving the swamp, it moved a couple of hundred miles to the northwest and settled for a time somewhere in eastern Louisiana. We don't know how it moved, but we don't believe that it has much motivational power on its own, at least for long distances, so it must have had help. Unfortunately, just as my colleagues were about to discover its new location, it vanished again. That was just a few days ago."

"Where?"

"I can tell you only this. A man who runs a small-time cartage business in Oakdale, Louisiana, disappeared mysteriously at the same time that the force vanished."

"So, a man who might have driven an unidentified malignant force of unknown composition or origin has disappeared. That's it?" Guthrie snorted and shook his head. "Not much to go on."

"I knew you'd appreciate the challenge," Tereba commented dryly.

"Oakdale's in Louisiana," Guthrie said. "I can't legally practice there."

"Oh," Tereba said. "But I believe you *are* licensed to practice in Louisiana as well as Texas."

The old man handed Guthrie an official State of Louisiana ID card—issued just the day before, he noticed.

"You did that?" he asked, staring at his photo on the card. Where the hell had Tereba gotten that? It wasn't either of the ones on his Texas driver's license or concealed carry license.

"It was necessary." Tereba shrugged. "Can't have you practicing illegally when you work for me."

Never mind all the illegal acts he'd done on Tereba's behalf, Guthrie thought. At least they'd all been directed at those who tried to use power to aggrandize themselves at the expense of others.

And there was the rub, Guthrie thought, slipping the ID into his wallet. He could turn down any client he wanted to for any reason. Maybe they wanted him to work a divorce case. He didn't do that. It brought up too many negative personal memories. Maybe they—or their cases—seemed too shady to take on. Or maybe they'd be trying to enlist him, unwitting, into some scheme or vendetta. But Guthrie wouldn't—couldn't—turn Tereba down. He knew from past experience that he might not live through an issue Tereba sent him to deal with, but he would go anyway. All the cases he'd sent Guthrie on had been consequential, and failure on Guthrie's part might have caused widespread harm and misery. Besides, he repeated to himself, he owed the old man. Big time.

"Or for your nominal employer," Tereba went on.

"My nominal employer…?" Guthrie began, but he was interrupted by his phone ringing. He stared at Tereba, mouth twisting sarcastically, as he dug the phone from his pocket. The old man smiled and nodded toward the phone.

"Your nominal employer, I believe," he said.

Guthrie glanced at the screen, which read, "Mutual Indemnity Insurance, Inc." He thumbed the answer button.

"Guthrie Investigations. Clay Guthrie speaking." He listened for several minutes, occasionally interjecting a "Yes" or "No."

"All right, Mr. Oliver," he said at last. "I'll be happy to take the case. I assume you know my rates. Okay. Email me the documentation, and I'll start immediately." He gave Oliver his email address then said, "That's right. Thank you. I'll keep you informed."

Guthrie hung up, laid the phone next to his plate, and stared at Tereba.

"Mutual Indemnity Insurance Company wants to hire me to investigate the disappearance of one of their policy holders. A man from Oakdale, Louisiana. They're paying top dollar. You did that, too?"

"Not me personally," the old man protested. "But my colleagues in Louisiana are concerned, even though the problem is now out of their jurisdiction, so to speak, and in mine. However, since the first lead is in Oakdale, that's where you'll have to begin."

"Mind if I finish breakfast before I begin?"

"By all means." Tereba took one last sip of coffee then stood. "You'll keep in touch?"

"Of course."

Tereba smiled, nodded, and headed toward the door. In moments he was outside, disappearing around the corner of the building. Was Li Wu waiting in the parking lot to drive Tereba home, or had the magical door to Tereba's home appeared in the wall around there? Maybe the old man was already sitting on the stool behind the counter of his apothecary shop. Maybe....

Fuck, Guthrie thought, staring at his half-finished breakfast and realizing he was no longer hungry. He pushed the plate back and waited for Kay to bring his check. While he did, he picked up his phone and punched in the number for Li Wu. Wu was one of Tereba's chief lieutenants, but he also was a deadly tai chi master. He'd become Guthrie's instructor, and over the past several years, Guthrie had learned a lot about the art from him. Wu answered on the second ring.

"Hi, Clay. Calling to beg off practice?"

"Hi Li. I wouldn't be if Master Tereba hadn't just collared me. Looks like I'll be out of town for a day or two."

"He told me. Call when you get back, and we'll resume practice."

"I will. By the way, did you just pick him up at Dot Coffeeshop?"

"Not me. I haven't seen him for several days. Until you called, I thought he was in New Orleans. Why?"

"Just wondering. I'll call when I'm done."

"Until then," Wu acknowledged, and they disconnected.

Guthrie pocketed the phone, envisioning Tereba sitting all nice and cozy in his apothecary shop while Guthrie prepared to risk his life once more for him. Kay brought his check, and he thanked her, left a nice cash tip, and went to the front to pay his bill.

At his office a short distance down the freeway, he reviewed the documents Mr. Oliver had sent, signing those that needed signing and printing those he might need in his investigation. Along with the name and address of the missing man—Norman Telfor—had come copies of three contracts from the insurance company. The ones for his Chevy van and home were both many years old, but the third—a hefty life insurance policy that paid double indemnity in the case of accidental or violent death—was dated just a couple of weeks prior to Telfor's disappearance. There was no policy for health, which was odd. Most people opting for either life or health insurance choose the latter.

The fact that Telfor was now missing might not entail his demise, but surely something was amiss, and Guthrie was immediately suspicious of Telfor's wife, Betsy, who was sole beneficiary of the life insurance policy. The vast majority of murders are committed by a so-called loved one or a friend or acquaintance, and the closeness in time of the institution of the life insurance policy and Telfor's disappearance was extremely suspicious. There might not be anything here, despite Tereba's story about some malevolent force, other than a simple murder for profit. Guthrie would have to question Mrs. Telfor to determine that for himself.

Guthrie folded the documents that had to be sent to Mr. Oliver into an envelope, then addressed and stamped it and dropped the envelope into the building mail drop. The other documents he slid into a manilla folder. Speaking of documents, he tugged out his wallet and slipped out the new Louisiana State PI license. The scrawl at the bottom was unmistakably his, though he knew he hadn't wielded the pen. How Tereba had managed that....

He dropped the thought, knowing too well that Tereba managed a lot of seemingly impossible things.

He replaced the license then drove home. There, he plotted a route to Oakdale on his map app. Although the town was only three hours away and he planned to return home after making his enquiries, he packed several changes of clothes, a kit bag, and his laptop in a small backpack. No telling what might transpire, and he preferred wearing clean clothes if he had to hang around for a day or two. You never knew, he reflected, what was going to happen when you worked for Tereba, and for that reason, he brought along his S&W M&P compact nine millimeter.

He locked the house, gave a farewell pat to the protective talisman Tereba had painted on his front door, then went to his Xterra and tossed the overnight bag onto the back seat. A moment later, he was backing out of the driveway.

2

GUTHRIE PULLED INTO OAKDALE JUST after noon. If there was any trail left by whatever had destroyed two villages and attracted the attention of Tereba's Louisiana colleagues, it would start here, where Norman Telfor lived and ran his hauling business. And disappeared. Guthrie didn't relish interviewing Betsy Telfor, but he had to.

Nor did he look forward to talking to anyone on the Oakdale's police force. Not that he feared or was intimidated by law enforcement. He'd once been an officer, himself, and he knew that law enforcement often demanded more control than he liked. And that went double for the kinds of cases Tereba sent him, which couldn't be explained at all. But he wasn't too worried. He hadn't yet encountered anything outré, despite Tereba's misgivings. He was just looking for a missing man and his van. And he had a legitimate reason thanks to his employment by Mutual Indemnity.

Oakdale was a nice-sized town that obviously had undergone recent growth and development. Several large subdivisions flanked the older part of town to the south and east, with a mall strategically placed among them. Probably logging and farming had been the original economic drivers, but a furniture factory, a warehouse distribution center for a major grocery chain, and a large metal fabrication plant, all new-looking, now sat along the highway into town.

Guthrie decided to visit Telfor's wife first, then the police. He needed to ascertain if the recent insurance policy might have prompted her to try to cash in at the expense of her husband. Spousal murder for insurance wasn't uncommon. If not, his employment on her behalf by the insurance company might incline her to trust him, and that trust might, in turn, become support when it came to dealing with the Oakdale PD.

Norman and Betsy Telfor didn't live in one of the new subdivisions. Their home was located in the older, poorer section of town that occupied a wide wedge to the north. The house was a small, shiplap-sided bungalow that once had been a hopeful light blue with darker blue trim, but the paint was fading and greening with algae along its lower margins. To its left sat a detached two-car garage in the same color scheme. Both pull-up doors were open, and from the sagging of the structure, it appeared they hadn't been shut in a long time. The bay on the left was empty, while a fifteen-year-old yellow Nissan pickup with a rusting bed sat in the bay on the right.

He parked along the curb, went up the cracked cement walkway to the front door, and knocked. The door opened a few moments later, revealing a tallish, robust-looking, and slightly overweight middle-aged woman in jeans and a loose, drab brown top. She'd never been especially pretty, and now anxiety and dull sorrow sagged her face. The eyes she raised to his own were lackluster and red-rimmed, barely roused with curiosity at the stranger on her stoop. Her whole being radiated genuine sorrow, allaying Guthrie's suspicion that she'd done something to her husband to collect the insurance settlement. Murderers don't fake deep sorrow when no one is watching, especially days later. Whatever he'd meant to her, Norman Telfor was gone, and she was feeling every moment of it. Guthrie told her who he was and that he represented Mutual Indemnity.

"Insurance?" she asked in a voice colored by a Cajun tinge. Only the barest hint of curiosity surfaced in her sad eyes. "You mean the car and house insurance? We don't have no other insurance."

That surprised Guthrie, but he didn't let it show.

"According to Mutual Indemnity, your husband took out a substantial life insurance policy about two weeks ago. You didn't know about it?"

"He never said nothin' to me. And I can't believe it. We ain't got money for nothin' like that."

"It's true," he told her.

Now Guthrie was suspicious of the policy itself. If Telfor hadn't taken it out, who had? Tereba and his unknown colleagues? It might be something they would do, post facto, to allow Guthrie to become involved from a legitimate angle. And maybe to help the grieving widow if something had happened to her husband.

"If you're here about life insurance," she said, suspicion darkening her brow, "does that mean you think my husband's dead?"

"We don't think anything, Mrs. Telfor. I was hired to look into your husband's disappearance. I certainly hope he's alive and well. That's what I'm here to find out. To find him. Do you mind if I come in so we can talk?"

"It's okay, I guess."

The living room had a sad, bedraggled feel, as if Betsy Telfor had lost interest in keeping it clean and tidy. She settled into a well-worn easy chair that roughly faced the TV. A matching chair sat next to it, a narrow side table cluttered with remotes, unopened mail, an empty drinking glass, and three beer cans dividing the two. A gilt-edged picture frame lay face down on the empty seat. The chair was probably Norman's, so Guthrie avoided it and sat on a similarly shabby but otherwise mismatched sofa. The whole house felt just as worn, but not as careworn as Mrs. Telfor.

"Is this insurance for me or some big company?" she asked, tone indicating she believed it would be for the latter.

"You, Mrs. Telfor."

"I still can't believe you got the right person," she said. "Norm don't got enough money to fix his van much less pay for some kind of life insurance."

"I have the right person," he assured her. He took a breath, then said, "I have to ask you some tough questions. Not because I want to, but because I have to understand what's going on."

She nodded.

"The police already asked me a bunch a questions, and they ain't done nothin'. And I don't think they're gonna. Might as well ask yours."

"I'm going to get to the bottom of this," Guthrie promised her, though assurances could only go so far in a case like this. "You have to be prepared for what I find."

"Norm's been gone near five days, now. The cops think he just run off, but I know somethin' bad's happened. I can feel it in my heart. Norm always said hope for the best but plan for the worst, and now I fear he didn't plan enough."

"You don't think your husband ran off?"

She snorted a bitter laugh.

"Not likely. Norm grew up here. He don't know nothin' else 'cept how to drive that van and carry stuff for people. His whole family's here. 'Sides, where would he go and what would he go with?" She waved around the room. "You can see we ain't got a lot, and the van needed a new transmission." She gave another bitter laugh. "He's a broke-down man with a broke-down truck. If he did run off, it wasn't far or fast. And if you're thinkin' another woman, hell, who'd want a broke-down, unshaven, middle-age man with a beer gut and no money?"

"His wife."

"Yeah." She looked into his eyes. "You gonna find him for me?"

"I will. But now, tell me about the day he disappeared. Who was he hired by?"

Now Guthrie was suspicious of whoever had hired Telfor, though he thought it unlikely he'd been hired to haul drugs or illegal immigrants for the cartels or anyone else. Not in a van with a failing transmission.

"It was some guy. I don't know who. Norm never said his name." She hung her head. "I just thought it was somethin' regular, so I didn't pay much attention. Like always. Norm don't tell me much about the business. Anyway, he was supposed to pick up a sofa somewheres in Airla. I ain't never heard of it, but Norm said it's a little town 'bout sixty miles north of here. The guy didn't want him to show up until near dark. I thought that was strange, but I didn't say nothin' to Norm about it."

"Maybe he couldn't meet Norm until then."

"Could be." She shrugged despondently.

"Did he say where he was taking the sofa?"

"Some town in Texas. He mighta told me the name, but if he did, I don't recall it. I wish I had. I told him that's a long way to drive on that old transmission, but he said it'd be all right and he'd be back by dawn." She sagged a little and stared at the floor. "When he didn't come home, I thought he mighta broke down. But if he had, he'd a called. But he didn't, and he never come back, and now it's been near five whole days."

She broke down, then, sobbing. Leaving her to her grief, Guthrie rose and picked up the empty drinking glass. He went to the kitchen, deposited the glass in the sink, then found a clean glass in a cabinet, filled it with water, and brought it to her. She was blotting her eyes with a tissue and took the glass after a moment, sipped, and set in on the side table.

"Thank you," she said, as Guthrie sat. "It's hard. I just wish he was here now."

"Yes," Guthrie said softly. "It's hard."

After a few moments and another sip of water, she said, "I think I can go on."

"The person who hired him must have paid a lot to do all that driving." Guthrie said.

"Norm never said what he was supposed to get. Alls he said was the pay was way more than expected—a real windfall. Enough to fix the van with some left over for us."

Betsy looked like she might be on the verge of breaking down again, and Guthrie didn't want to put her through any more grief than he already had.

"Please rest assured I'll find out what happened to your husband," he told her. "I hope the news will be good, but if it's not, the insurance settlement will help you financially. It's not much consolation, but it's all I can offer."

"That's more than the police is doin'. They just wrote off Norm like he wasn't nothin'. You can see what side of the tracks we live on. But you…." She peered intently at him. "I don't got much education, but I got a sense about people, and I think you're gonna do more than the police are."

"I'll do my best. Do you have a photo of Norm I can borrow?"

"The police took the good one I had in that frame." She pointed to the gilt-edged frame lying on the seat of Norm's chair. "Lemme find another."

She rose heavily, trod despondently across the room, and disappeared through a door. Guthrie heard some rummaging, then she returned, carrying a photo. She stared at it for a moment before handing it to Guthrie. It showed a slightly overweight middle-aged man in a Dallas Cowboys t-shirt, a big smile on his face and his arm draped around his wife's shoulders. She was smiling, too.

"That's a pretty good one," she said. "Our daughter took it right after the Cowboys won some big game or other last fall. Norm's a big Cowboys fan. Will you bring it back?"

"I will. Can you tell me what he was wearing when he left?"

"That same shirt that's in that picture," she said. "And jeans."

"Okay." He rose. "Thank you for your time. I'll do my best to find out what happened."

She simply nodded and showed him to the door. Guthrie got into his Xterra and sat there for a few moments, pondering what he'd learned. As far as Mrs. Telfor could tell, her husband had set off for work late Saturday afternoon and was never seen or heard from again. And if the job seemed off, the offer of some kind of hefty sum to a man near the bottom rung of society must have been like mana from heaven to Norm Telfor. Had that mana been laced with poison?

Guthrie started the Xterra and set off for the police station, where he was directed to a Detective Peters. Peters was a burly, florid-faced man with close-cropped blond hair and a blunt face that wore a serious demeanor. But he showed a pleasant smile after Guthrie showed him his credentials and told him he was working for the insurance company that had underwritten Telfor's policy. Peters led Guthrie to a cluttered desk among several in the squad room, and they sat, Peters behind the desk and Guthrie in the chair next to it.

"So, you're working the insurance angle?" Peters asked. "You think maybe Mrs. Telfor bumped off her husband to collect the insurance?"

"I had my suspicions on exactly that point. But I just visited her, and I'd say it's unlikely. She's definitely in grief, and when I queried her about the policy, she didn't seem to know anything about it. Even if we can't verify her story, I think it's true."

"If that's so, he should be home by now. Where is he?"

"That's the million-dollar question. While I'm sure this is a legit-imate claim, you can imagine the insurance company is reluctant to pay out without proof of death."

"Reluctant to pay out?" Peters' face hardened a little.

"Don't get me wrong, Detective. I can see Mrs. Telfor is up shit's creek without a paddle, and I intend to either give her a paddle or drain the creek. But I need to get to the bottom of Norman's disappearance. If he's alive, we need to find him and understand what's going on, and if not, finding him's the only way to help Mrs. Telfor collect the insurance. If there's anything you can tell me that might help help solve the case, we're all winners."

"Fair enough," Peters said. "I'm all about results. But after being a cop for more than twenty years, I can't say I've seen a whole lot of winners."

"Goes with the territory."

"You were a cop?"

"Once. Got wounded in the line of duty and was put out to pasture. Trouble was, I didn't much like the pasture, so here I am, trampling through other peoples' pastures."

Peters chuckled.

"Well, trample away. At least on this case." He shook his head. "I got nothing. Norm Telfor supposedly went to pick up a sofa in a small town north of here called Airla. To deliver said sofa to an unidentified town in Texas. In the middle of the night. Now, does that sound normal to you?"

"Not considering Norm is missing days after setting off on this non-normal trip."

"Mrs. Telfor came in late Saturday morning as soon as she realized her husband hadn't returned or called or answered her calls. I drove up to Airla right after she made the report, and there's nothing there."

"What do you mean nothing?"

"It's a ghost town. Nothing left, or at least not much. Maybe half a dozen buildings still partly intact, but everything there is collapsing and rotting away. A couple were burned. Weird. The whole place is a little creepy, too. It used to be a solid little community centered around a lumber mill, but I guess the mill went belly up and took the town with it. Tell the truth, I didn't even notice it was happening. Last time I was up that way was maybe five, six years ago, hunting with some buddies, and everything seemed normal." He shook his head. "Just goes to show what time can do, none of it good."

Guthrie tended to agree, though he couldn't help but think of Tereba, who seemed to defy time. But was Tereba good, or just Tereba? Guthrie probably would never know.

"My chief is writing it off as a cheating husband running out on his wife," Peters went on.

Guthrie shook his head.

"Not from what I can see. Norman just wasn't the type, nor does he have the resources."

"Stranger things have happened," Peters said. "But I think you're right. The chief has only been on the job a couple of years. His predecessor was involved in a real shit show, so he's not anxious to have unsolved cases hanging over his head. But I've been to Norm's house, and after talking to his family and friends, I doubt he'd be comfortable anywhere else."

Peters went silent for a couple of moments as he stared at Guthrie.

"I gotta say," he said at last, "I don't envy you. If he was taking the sofa to some town in Texas, hell, there are thousands of those. Without a name, that's kind of a dead end. Norman Telfor could be anywhere. How are you going to start?"

"Norm said he'd be back by dawn. That narrows the radius of the search."

"I hope you have a big budget and a lot of time," Peters said, handing Guthrie a business card.

Guthrie wasn't worried about the former, but he probably didn't have a lot of the latter. He thanked Peters and took his leave after securing the name of a good local restaurant, which he visited right after checking into a motel. It looked like his original plan to return to Houston tonight was off since apparently he was going to have to drive up to Airla and explore it before he could determine his next move.

3

AIRLA WAS ABOUT AN HOUR away, mostly on small state roads and winding parish lanes. He'd looked up the town on *Wikipedia* the night before, and the sketchy article, which was several years old, informed him it was an unincorporated township with a population of just over eight hundred. The sole industry was logging, and a lumber mill just north of town was the principal employer.

Detective Peters said the town was viable only five years ago but was now deserted. Deserted didn't half describe it. It had so shrunken into the surrounding pine forest that Guthrie almost passed it by. At first glance it seemed like just a couple of abandoned and collapsing homesteads nestled in the misty pine forest. But then he came across a small, burned-out general store and a decrepit gas station, pumps missing, awning toppled, and most of its glass broken out. The town didn't look like much, but the GPS on his phone told him he'd arrived even if his arrival sparked no interest among the citizens of Airla. There were no citizens. Apparently, *Wikipedia* needs to update its article, he mused, and he couldn't help but think of the two small villages a couple of hundred miles to the southeast that Tereba said had been destroyed by some unknown agency.

Eight hundred, he thought, looking around the decaying buildings. Where had they gone? What had happened to this little town to send it into such rapid decline? It certainly wasn't a lack of raw materials for the lumber mill. Dense pine forests stood all around. Airla should be the little town it once was, but now it was like a cancer patient, unable to maintain health and vitality and wasting away beneath the ravages of the disease. Hell, he thought after he parked and walked around the handful of overgrown streets, Airla looked like it had been abandoned thirty years, not two. But that probably was due as much to the humid forest encroaching on the town as to a lack of permanence of the human structures, though most of the houses were wooden and hadn't been of solid construction to begin with.

Several of the buildings had burned, including the single church, but most were just collapsing into the forest beneath time, weather, lack of maintenance, and their own weight. Not much was left inside any of the bare handful of partly intact buildings. The inhabitants had been poor enough, and they'd taken everything they could with them, leaving only an occasional piece of broken furniture to say that humans once made their lives here. Had their lives been as broken as the furniture they left behind? Maybe. The whole town had an oppressive sense of decay that went beyond the pervasive but not overwhelming odor of rotting wood, mold, and stale wet ash. Worse was the sense of eerie, vacant emptiness—a sense amplified by the complete lack of bird chirps and hum of insects. There were no birds skimming across open spaces, no squirrels leaping though tree branches. The entire forest around the town was still as death—an impression reinforced by lingering night mists clinging to the trees, brush, and remains of the structures.

But something was going on beneath the still quiet, though it might not have been visible among the remains of the town. At the outset of Guthrie's first case for Tereba, the old sorcerer had tattooed a protective talisman—the Armor of the Earth—on the skin beneath his navel. Over his power center, Tereba had said. It consisted of a quartered square depending four wavy lines, called a Kuei, surrounded by eight little stick-figure men representing Heaven. He'd etched them there without Guthrie's consent, and at first, Guthrie was angered by the unwanted mutilation. But over time, he'd become grateful for the talisman. It not only offered him a degree of protection from antithetical energies, the little stick-figure men seemed to twitch when supernatural danger was nearby. Even if they didn't actually move beneath his skin, they were his personal Geiger counter for the outré. And right now, the Kuei men felt like they were shaking a leg. Not much. Just a few weak and intermittent twitches, but that was enough.

The source of the itch remained directionless as he went from building to building. He wasn't really searching, just looking. He didn't know what to search for yet. None of the buildings yielded any useful information, but he did notice that the Kuei men's twitching was more evident on the north side of town, especially when he faced north. The only thing that lay in that direction was the sawmill, Airla Lumber Company, about two miles north of town, off a county road.

He returned to his Xterra and drove the distance to a sign at the mill entrance. Someone had splashed red and black paint on it. Down the overgrown, rutted, and pitted asphalt lane leading to the mill, small and medium-sized branches littered the pavement for as far as he could see. Obviously it hadn't had much traffic lately. The mists shrouding the marshy pine forest and carpeting the lane were thicker here than in town, giving the scene a dismal feel.

The Kuei men were kicking a bit stronger, now. After a moment of hesitation, he pulled into the lane, driving slowly, the Kuei men reacting more vigorously as he went. Though a few hardwoods grew along the sides of the lane and were scattered in the forest, most of the trees were pines, tall and jutting up on either side, making the lane seem like a narrow, claustrophobic canyon. The ditches on both sides were filled with dark, mucky water. Though none of the branches fallen on the rough asphalt were too large to drive across, Guthrie stopped at the first one, got out, and walked up to it. It was crushed in places where a vehicle's tires would pass. He looked ahead at the next few branches and saw the same thing.

This road might not be used much, he thought, probably because the mill was shut down, but someone had driven down here. Multiple vehicles from the look of things. And very recently, judging by the fresh wood gleaming whitely at the breaks. The question now was, had the occupants of the vehicles driven in and out, or were some of them still down at the mill?

Guthrie returned to the Xterra and proceeded with caution. He also made sure his pistol was readily accessible. After a couple of minutes, the road took a slight curve that ended in a large parking lot, crudely paved, clumps of weeds jutting here and there from the pitted, rutted, and cracked asphalt. Behind that sat the mill. Architecturally, it wasn't much to look at—just a large, boxy, cement-walled warehouse-like structure that appeared to have been built in stages.

The central and presumably original building was a simple large rectangle about a hundred and fifty feet long by a hundred wide. Three additional but somewhat smaller rooms had been added: one in the front and one at either end of the original structure. The front and smallest addition had a personnel door, but as Guthrie swung the Xterra around the parking lot, surveying the area, he saw big square openings in the outer walls at the ends of both side additions. Probably, he thought, to provide access for log and lumber trucks to enter and exit the mill. The place might once have been a bustling business, but now it hulked in its clearing in the trees, a dark mass devoid of activity, sunshine, and cleansing breeze.

Guthrie got out of his truck, opened the back door, and grabbed a pair of nitrile gloves from a box on the floor of the backseat. Stuffing the gloves into his pocket, he retrieved a hefty, extremely powerful flashlight lying next to the box—a souvenir of the last case he'd worked for Tereba the year before. Flashlight in hand, he approached the metal personnel door in the front addition. It was metal, skewed open about halfway and partly torn from its hinges, as if a battering ram had forced it. He pushed it as wide as he could, the rusted, twisted hinges squealing, and went inside.

A sense of oppressive, almost hostile breathlessness bore down on him as he stepped into the room. Guthrie had been in plenty of abandoned buildings in his life, but none as creepy as this. It was as if some overpowering stench of decay or the shadows of acts of mayhem and violence had only recently vanished. He wondered if there had been a body. Hell, maybe there still *was* a body. He drew his pistol as he shone the light around the space. The front addition clearly held the mill's offices. Broken and battered office furniture, overturned desks, and rusted filing cabinets were scattered around the open front area. Thousands of sheets of paper, greening with mold, lay spilled across the floor. It looked like a mob had torn the place apart. Several enclosed offices were toward the back, their doors broken open and holes smashed through their plasterboard walls. Guthrie checked each one, half expecting to find a corpse. The Kuei figures were dancing with danger, and he tamped down the sensation.

Once he cleared the front addition, he pushed through a pair of heavy swinging doors into the main building and stood there, waving his light around the interior. Several holes in the hangar-like roof admitted beams of light, dimly illuminating the huge space. Large square openings in the concrete walls at either end connected it to the slightly smaller spaces of the left- and righthand additions. Rusted remains of large saws, planers, and other milling machinery sat where they'd been abandoned, and the floor between and around them was littered with incomprehensible piles of rusting equipment, trash, and rotting pieces of lumber. Everything was covered by a thick layer of dust, and the sense of malignant decay was even more powerful than in the offices.

He stood there, reluctant for some reason to continue. And it wasn't just the dancing of the Kuei men that rooted his feet. Even without their warning, he could have sensed something wasn't right about the mill. A palpable sense of dread permeated the air, and he shone his flashlight beam over all the heaps of machinery and piles of debris, scanning for anything that might be a threat. But he saw nothing. There was only the persistent dread and the twitching of the Kuei men. But he was here, and he had to search the rest of the building. If he found Telfor's body, so be it. If he found something else, well....

He walked completely around all the piles of machinery and debris, making certain that the dread he felt didn't emanate from a direct threat hiding somewhere behind them. As he circled the main equipment, he noticed that most of it, like the front offices, had suffered damage. Keeping his pistol at the ready, he started toward the opening to the addition on the left. The Kuei men said there was less danger on this side, but he didn't want some lesser threat to creep up behind him while he was exploring the righthand addition.

This roof had holes, too, and it was lighter than the main room thanks to the outer opening in the far wall. As he expected, here the Kuei men were more subdued. The only equipment consisted of two large, rusting forklifts, one toppled onto its side. This room's floor was littered with trash and roof debris lying among skewed piles of warping lumber, but there seemed to be no direct danger. Time, he thought, to go toward the feeling of dread.

Stepping back into the main room, he wound his way across the littered floor until he reached the opening to the righthand addition, the Kuei men twitching with increasing intensity. This room, though it was somewhat larger than the one at the other end of the building, was devoid of old machinery except for a small crane with treads and a claw head. A nearby pile of logs indicated the room must have been a warehouse to hold logs before they were milled into lumber.

But if most of the logs were long gone, the sensation of malign oppression grew. Ignoring it, he gazed at the white Chevrolet van sitting off-center on the floor, passenger side toward him. The front door bore the words, "Telfor Hauling," crudely lettered in black paint flaking with wear.

Guthrie approached the truck cautiously, pistol up, and peered through the closed windows. The cab and cargo area were empty. Keys dangled from the ignition switch. Guthrie pulled out the nitrile gloves, donned them, and opened the door. When he did, a fetid, diseased odor wafted out, and he coughed and averted his face as he stepped back to catch his breath. Breathing shallowly, he leaned into the van again, fearing to see a body.

But the van was empty. More than empty. It was clean. Very clean. There was no litter of fast-food wrappers, gas receipts, or other items. Even the windows were polished. Looking around the cab and cargo area, Guthrie didn't believe it. A guy like Telfor might not have been a slob, but he worked out of this van. Lived out of it during the day. There was no way it would be this clean. Especially considering the nearly overpowering odor clinging to the interior.

He checked the glove compartment and console. Both were completely empty. No car insurance papers, no maps, no tire warranties, no tire-pressure gauge, no nothing. There was nothing under or behind the seats except for a tire jack, a lug wrench, and one crumpled foil gum wrapper that was caught in the mounting for the passenger seat.

Stumped, Guthrie sat in the driver's seat, staring around the cab. It was too clean. Obsessively clean. People who clean like that have a place for everything and expect everything to be in its place. That was enough justification for his hunch, and he flipped down the visor. People like that expect a visor to be a visor, not handy storage. A slip of paper tumbled into his lap. There was nothing above the other visor. The paper bore two handwritten addresses: one for Airla Lumber, though the company's name wasn't present, and one for an address on a county road in a town called Thorndike, Texas. There was nothing to indicate the nature of that address, either.

Guthrie decided not to give the paper to Detective Peters. He folded it and tucked it into his wallet. Texas was far out of Peters' jurisdiction, and Guthrie didn't want any inquiries the detective might make of local authorities in Thorndike to impede Guthrie's own investigation. If and when Guthrie resolved the matter, he'd let Peters know the outcome.

He pulled the truck's keys from the ignition and, holding them in his palm, peeled the nitrile glove down around them and off his fingers, leaving the keys untouched in their own little rubber bag. He didn't want anyone else to find the van and drive off with it and any evidence it might hold before he could report it to Peters—though that might not be much now that Guthrie had pocketed the Thorndike address. But there might be fingerprints, hair, or fibers. Maybe even some blood traces. He'd leave the discovery of those to Oakdale PD forensics.

Guthrie shut the van's door and exited the building through the wide opening in the end. It was the quickest way out. Despite the airy vacancy of the mill, its atmosphere had been oppressive, stifling, and almost oily with unknown residue, especially inside the van. Breathing deeply for the first time since he'd entered the mill, he walked back to his Xterra. He wanted to go to his motel room immediately and take a shower, but he had to visit Peters first.

"It was where?" Peters asked as Guthrie dropped the nitrile-bagged keys into his hand a little more than an hour later.

"The lumber mill about two miles north of town. Inside the addition on the right end of the building."

Peters looked a little crestfallen as he set the bagged keys on his desk.

"I didn't even think of looking there when I was up in Airla. Didn't think anybody would be moving a sofa from an old sawmill instead of a house. Did you see anything suspicious?"

"The cab was completely cleaned out except for the keys. I'd say that's suspicious."

"You think Telfor's body is somewhere back in those woods?"

"Could be, and you could mount a search, but I don't think so. Why would anyone kill him and drag him out into the woods but leave his van where it could be found? Cleaned out."

"You have any idea where he might have gone?"

"Not yet," Guthrie lied. "But I'm going to keep looking, even if there isn't really a trail."

"In Texas?"

"Yes."

"I'd appreciate it if you keep me informed."

Guthrie gestured toward the keys on Peters' desk.

"So far, so good."

After Guthrie left the police station, he went straight to his motel room and took a hot shower to wash off the oily sensation on his skin that seemed to cling like a bad odor that didn't stink. Food was next, and after that, he went back to the motel and reclined on the bed with his laptop.

Thorndike, Texas, *Wikipedia* informed him, was a small town with a population of a handful over eleven hundred—only a little more than Airla had boasted just a few years ago. Unlike Airla, Thorndike was incorporated, though it didn't have its own post office. Next, Guthrie checked the town on Google Earth.

It was located about equidistant—mostly on back roads—from the northwestern outskirts of Houston and Dallas's southeast side. If Guthrie divided the county, which was more rectangular than most Texas counties, into six equal-sized pieces, Thorndike was situated in the middle of the southwest sixth. Most of the county consisted of rolling countryside that rose quickly from the more-forested lowlands in the direction of Houston to hillier terrain toward the north and west. There, it was covered by farmland and tree-dotted pastures lined with narrow bands of forest. All of the roads around and through town were county roads except for a single state highway running along the western edge of town from the south toward the north and the county seat, which was thirty or forty miles from Thorndike.

The town seemed to be a minor hub for local ranchers and farmers and their employees. Its downtown consisted of six or so square blocks that blended in with a few surrounding neighborhoods. Those in turn faded into ranch and farm lands beyond. The satellite images showed that most of the land to the west, south, and east of town was open pasture or grazing land, while smaller farms predominated to the north. The several creeks and run-off gullies that crossed the area bore irregular outlines of riparian brush and forest, and all fed into the only named watercourse, Steele Creek, which passed about three miles south of town. Apparently, a quirk of the terrain there created a natural depression that the creek had filled with a large pond, its surroundings overlaid with a thick canopy of trees that was easily the largest forest for many dozens of miles around.

At last he shut down the computer. He'd be seeing the real thing soon enough.

4

THE DRIVE TO THORNDIKE TOOK slightly more than three hours. Just to cover all bases, Guthrie drove up to Airla and charted a route that he thought Telfor probably had taken. He didn't expect to find anything significant along the way, but there was no telling.

Like he thought, nothing was worth noting during the trip, though it was a pleasant drive, first through the east Louisiana piney woods, then through rolling countryside that gradually opened into farms and pastureland. But something definitely strange lay at its terminus. He actually arrived at the address on the slip of paper before he reached town because it was on the way in from the south, along the paved county road that bounded the east side of Thorndike. To his surprise, it was the location of the town dump.

Despite it being late weekday morning, an aluminum-barred gate was chained and padlocked shut across the entrance. According to the hours of operation posted on the sign mounted to the right of the gate, it should be open. And that raised another issue. Norm had driven here on Saturday night, and the posted hours indicated it would have been closed then. And on Sunday and Monday, too. The sign gave a number to call in case of emergencies, but Guthrie didn't figure this was an emergency yet, despite the oddness of the gate being locked during business hours on a weekday.

A dump. Surely Telfor hadn't driven all this way just to leave the sofa in an obscure town dump more than two hundred miles away.

There must have been a dump in Oakdale or Airla. Hell, Airla was dump enough. Maybe the client had just given Norm this address as a place to meet, from which he would lead him to the final destination. Guthrie supposed the backroads around here might be a bit confusing to a newcomer, especially at night. But surely Telfor carried a cell phone with a map app. He'd have to in his line of work. He was used to finding his way. Maybe the client didn't want any record of Norm's actual final destination. Right now, it was impossible to know. Not now, nearly a week after his disappearance. Not without asking him.

With little other recourse, Guthrie drove into town. It was a quaint-looking, simple little place, only slightly larger and better organized than Airla before it became a marooned wreck sinking into an ocean of pine. He drove its major streets, orienting himself to his memory of the satellite images he'd viewed the night before. It didn't take long.

The west side of town was bordered by the state road running north–south. Most of the town was east of that, though a scattering of businesses were situated on the state road, and several houses and farm buildings lay along a paved county road that angled off from it toward the northwest. Guthrie'd seen those on Google Earth, but he didn't bother driving up that way. He was more interested in the town center, which was located about a mile east of the state road. Thorndike contained one of each of the types of businesses necessary for small-town life: a mom-n-pop grocery, a hardware store, a bank, a cafe, and a Baptist Church among them. There were no lawyers that he could see. Presumably Thorndike wasn't large enough to support one. There was a doctor, though, who had a clinic in a two-story Victorian-style house facing Main Street at the edge of the better neighborhood, but Guthrie didn't notice a dentist office. Around the modest downtown lay open neighborhoods for a radius of less than a mile, and beyond those spread ranch lands and farms.

Notable was the Thorndike Police Department, located on a prominent corner in the middle of town. It was housed in an old two-story red-brick building that occupied most of the width of one block of Main Street, though its entry faced the side street. Obviously it hadn't been built as a police station. According to the emblem adorning the wall of the second floor, it had begun life as a Masonic Lodge. Thorndike might be small, but it openly advertised its adherence to law and order. Guthrie was curious about how they'd reconfigured the interior of such an old building to include secure cells. A one-story extension to the left side of the building, in the same red brick, housed Thorndike's city hall. It was pretty small for a city hall, but how many people could it take to run Thordike's city government?

A small, boarded-up tan brick building sat directly across the side street, and the remainder of the block down that side of the street was filled with two structures. The first was a cement-block building with a big, curving metal roof. The sign on the wall above its double garage doors and a personnel door read Eli Carlin's Auto Repairs. The second was a big sheetmetal quonset hut housing Ferris's Feed Store. The Baptist Church, which looked to be of mid-1980s design, sprawled across the entire block north of the feed store.

Next to the empty tan building along Main Street was a funeral home, then houses lined the street. Across Main from the police station was the grocery store, with homes on large plots occupying several blocks to the east. Heading west down the same side of the street lay the hardware store then the bank. All three were connected and looked to be built of the same red brick as the former Masonic Lodge, though the facade of the hardware store was painted battleship gray. The same side street running in front of the police station crossed Main to separate the bank from a two-story building featuring Leo's Corner Cafe. The homey curtains covering the upstairs windows indicated that Leo might live above it. Attached to the right side of the cafe was a smaller building with a barber pole rotating above the door. Both the cafe and the barbershop were of the same red brick as the police station and most of the other buildings clustered around the town center. Very possibly, they'd been sheathed a century ago by the same bricklayer as the others on Main, though similar red brick was common throughout the region's small towns.

Since it was now closing in on noon, the first place Guthrie visited was the cafe. When you need information, cafes and barbershops were the places it might be most freely bandied about, and he didn't need a haircut. But he was hungry. Good choice, he thought, after he parked on the side street and pushed into a pleasant odor of food.

The cafe's interior was old-fashioned without being either pretentious or decrepit. A high ceiling faced with old stamped-tin tiles painted a light blue gave it an airy feel, and several ceiling fans turned like lazy Mixmasters, blending the sundry odors of food and wafting them down upon the diners. Photos and trophies—mammal and piscine—were mounted on the walls. A counter with stools stretched in front of the kitchen, visible through a wide service window, and opposite, a row of booths lined up beneath the windows facing Main. Booths also lined the windows facing the side street, and about two dozen tables for four spread across the open floor.

Guthrie normally preferred a booth, but he perched on a stool at the counter instead. It was kind of hard chatting up a waitress from the distance of a booth but quite natural from the vantage of a counter.

Although it was nearly noon on a weekday, the place was only sparsely filled. Probably not quite lunch time. A middle-aged couple sat in one of the booths, and an older, unshaven man with a dejected look sat in another. Two men who appeared to be farm- or ranchhand types occupied one of the tables. Only one waitress was on duty, and the cook—a beefy, middle-aged man with short, crisp, salt-n-pepper hair—was visible through the service window behind the counter. Beyond him, her back turned to the window, a woman appeared to be chopping something on the rear counter. The waitress came up almost as soon as Guthrie was seated.

"Hello, sir," she said cheerily, putting a menu, a glass of water, and a paper napkin-wrapped knife and fork on the counter in front of him. "How's your day, today?"

"Just fine so far. How about you?"

"Me, too. Coffee?"

"Yes. Black. Thanks."

She brought over a mug and a steaming pot and poured.

"Do you know what you want?"

"I'll take a cheeseburger with fries. Mustard, but no mayo or ketchup." Almost always a safe choice.

"Coming right up."

She ripped off the slip on which she'd written his order, turned, and clipped it to a post just inside the service window.

"Order up, Leo."

While Leo fixed his food, Guthrie perused the waitress. She was in her mid forties, nice looking, slightly on the heavy side, and about five foot eight. Her dark hair was drawn into a bun, and the strands of gray lacing through it indicated she wasn't coloring it. She had a durable look about her, and a wedding band encircled her left ring finger. She didn't have on a name tag. Probably everyone in town knew her.

"Say," Guthrie said as she passed by him after returning from filling water glasses and coffee cups at the booths and table. "Mind if I ask you something?"

She eyed him with mock suspicion.

"I don't date strangers, even if they are attractive. Besides...." She held up her left hand to show him the ring.

Guthrie laughed and waved her protestation aside.

"Mrs. Leo?" he asked, and it was her turn to laugh.

"No. Mrs. Leo is in the kitchen with Mr. Leo."

"Well, anyway," Guthrie said, "nothing like that. I'm new here...."

"Coulda told you that already."

Guthrie chuckled.

"I might be in town for a few days. Is there a motel around here?"

"We aren't big enough for that," she said. "You'd have to go to the county seat to find a motel. That's about half an hour north."

"The reason I'm here is I'm trying to find this man." Guthrie showed her the photo of Norm Telfor. "Do you remember if he came in here, say last weekend?"

"Has he done something?"

"He's disappeared."

"Haven't seen him," she said, looking at the photo and shaking her head. "And I'd have remembered. We don't get many strangers in town. Our police chief, Bill Turner, might be able to help."

Behind her, Leo put Guthrie's plate of food on the window counter. "Order up, Bev."

The waitress retrieved the plate and brought it over to Guthrie.

"Beverly?" Guthrie asked.

"Bev's okay," she said, then she went to give the couple in the booth their check.

Guthrie ate, trying to decide what to do next. Norm's trail led to Thorndike, but surely he hadn't driven a sofa all the way from Airla just to leave it in the dump. There must have been dozens of other dumps along the way. Why the one in Thorndike? He finished his burger and coffee, and Bev came over to see if he wanted anything else. He told her no, and she ripped off his check and slid it onto the counter. He gave her a twenty and told her to keep the change.

"Thanks," she said. "You going to see Chief Turner about your missing man?"

"As soon as I leave here," he answered.

"You mind waiting just a second?"

Puzzled, Guthrie said okay, and Bev called through the window.

"Hey, Leo, let me have the chief's lunch."

Leo slid a styrofoam food container onto the window counter, and Bev brought it over to Guthrie.

"We always send over the chief's lunch right about now. Since you're going that way, I hope you don't mind taking it to him." A sardonic twinkle lurked in her eyes.

Guthrie laughed and picked up the styrofoam food container. It was warm, and steam and a pleasant odor leaked from the slit around its opening.

"I better get this over to him before it gets cold, or he might fine me. Or lock me up." He turned and headed for the door.

Even though the police station was just a short block away, he took the Xterra, both to get the food delivered warm and to have his vehicle on hand when he left. Flanking the City Hall addition was a moderate-sized dirt lot that held a new Ford Police Interceptor SUV, a new Ford Explorer, and an older Honda sedan. He parked, carried the food to the entrance, and went inside.

The interior was very simple. A counter with a swinging gate divided the narrow entry area from the back, and behind it sat two battered gray metal desks with gray formica tops, only one of which looked like somebody was using it. The back left corner was occupied by a small office with a glass half wall faced inside with Venetian blinds shuttered open. In the right wall was a barred door, but the angle was too acute for him to see past the bars. Probably the cell block. Between the office and the cell block were two doorways, one with a closed door and a sign reading, "Restroom," and the other with no door showing stairs leading to the second floor.

Two people were visible. A short, skinny middle-aged woman with bleach-blond hair in an attractive style sat behind the counter, nearly masked by the counter and radio console in front of her. The other was a man sitting at the desk in the small office. The glass obscured his features, but he appeared to be on the phone. The woman looked up as Guthrie entered.

"Can I help you?" she asked.

"I'd like to speak with Chief Turner."

"What's this about?"

"I'm a private investigator trying to ascertain the whereabouts of a missing man. His last known destination was Thorndike."

"Here?" She looked astonished, as if Thorndike had never been a destination for anyone.

"He was a delivery man," Guthrie explained. "He never made it home." He held up the food container. "I also have this. Bev at the cafe asked me to deliver it to the chief."

"Just a moment," the woman said, suppressing a smile.

She got up and skirted the desks as she made her way to the office door, which was open. Guthrie could tell that the man inside had hung up the phone and was already alert to Guthrie's presence and to the fact that something might be amiss. The dispatcher said something to him, and he rose and followed her to the counter.

The chief looked to be in his late forties. He was tall and rawboned, with a largish nose over a clipped gray mustache and graying but full hair swept back from his forehead. He wore jeans held up by a belt with a western buckle, a khaki button-down shirt, and worn but well-polished cowboy boots. He reeked of authority, even beyond the police shield fastened to the left side of his belt, the .40 Glock holstered on the right, and the shoulder-mounted mic. He looked exactly like the kind of man who'd be the police chief of some small Texas town. Given the circumstances, Guthrie wasn't sure if that was a good thing or not.

"Hello, Chief Turner. My name is Clay Guthrie." He showed his credentials. "I'm trailing a missing man on behalf of his insurance company and his wife. I wonder if I might have a few minutes of your time."

"Come on back," Turner said, eyeing the food container. "Is that for me?"

"Unless I'm mistaken," Guthrie said, holding out the container, "Bev at the cafe just called to let you know about the new delivery service. And the reason for my visit."

Turner's mouth twisted in a slight smile, and he took the container and gestured for Guthrie to push through the gate and follow him into the office. The office was neat and clean. Probably not a lot of crime here, Guthrie thought as Turner pointed to one of the two chairs in front of the desk and took his own seat.

"She told me you'd be bringing this over," Turner said, setting the container of food aside.

"Could be she just wanted to make sure I was sincere when I said I was coming to visit you."

"Could be. She also said you didn't try to hit on her and that you tipped well."

Guthrie chuckled.

"I guess there really are no secrets in a small town," he said.

"Don't bet on it," Turner said.

"Yeah, well, in any case, hitting hurts. I'm here looking for a missing man, not a quick roll in the hay."

"Good thing," Turner said, a twinkle in his eyes. "She and I've been married for twenty-two years, and I'd hate to lose her to some city slicker."

Guthrie had to laugh.

"I doubt if I'm slick enough for that, but if I'd known, I'd have tipped even better."

Turner smiled.

"So, what about this missing man?"

"Norman Telfor," Guthrie said, passing over the photo. "He's from Oakdale, Louisiana, and was hired to drive a sofa from a little town north of Oakdale to here. Or I suppose it was here. All I have is an address, but it happens to be the address of your town dump."

Turner looked up from the photo.

"The dump?"

Guthrie shrugged.

"I haven't seen this fella." He handed the photo back to Guthrie. "Course if he just drove up here, unloaded, and turned around and went back, it's possible nobody saw him except the people he was delivering to."

"How about that? Are there any new faces in town? Somebody who might need furniture moved."

"You can imagine we don't have a lot of new folks moving in around here except for migrant labor, though I don't suppose your man is part of that. But as a matter of fact, we do have a new man in town. I haven't met him, yet. What did you find out at the dump?"

"Nothing," Guthrie said. "It was closed."

"Closed?" Turner looked surprised. He got up, went to the door, and called out. "Hey, Tessa, you heard anything about the dump being closed?"

"I did, Chief. I got a couple of calls this morning from people who couldn't get in. I sent Emmet out, and he told me the gate was locked."

"Did he get hold of Freddie?"

"I don't know, Chief. He didn't say."

"Get him on the radio."

Turner walked over to her, and Guthrie rose and moved to the office door so he could hear the exchange. Tessa keyed the radio then spoke into the desk microphone in front of her.

"Emmet, come in."

"Emmet here," a voice came back.

"What did you find out at the dump?" Turner asked, taking the mic.

"Nothing, Chief. It was locked. I ran into Wally and Pete, and they said they had to unlock the gate themselves Wednesday morning during regular garbage pick-up, and they locked it again that night. They said they didn't see Freddie and figured he was laid up drunk."

"Did you find Freddie?"

"I went to his house, but his truck wasn't there, so I figured he wasn't home. Do you want me to go back there?"

"No. I'll check it myself. Stay on patrol. I'll get in touch if I need you. Out."

Turner set the microphone down and returned to his office. But he didn't sit down. Instead, he stood there staring at Guthrie for a moment. The stare wasn't intimidating, though Guthrie supposed it could be. It was curious. And a little excited.

"I guess you're going to stay around here for a day or two to see what happened to your man," he said.

"Yes." Guthrie nodded. "If anything happened at all. If you don't mind."

"What do you plan on doing first?"

"My only lead is the address for the dump, so I'd like to check it out as soon as it's open."

The chief stepped to his desk, slid out a drawer, and pulled out a ring of keys.

"What are we waiting for?" he asked, removing one of the keys and tossing the ring back into the drawer. "I have the key right here."

"Don't you want to eat first?" Guthrie gestured toward the unopened container of food.

Turner looked at the container then back at Guthrie.

"What you're doing sounds a little more interesting that handing out speeding tickets, quashing domestic arguments, or tossing drunks in a cell overnight. Or eating another umpteenth meal from Leo's. Let's go."

Turner paused only long enough to grab a well-worn, narrow-brimmed tan Stetson from a coat rack beside the door before he headed across the main room toward the station's front entry, Guthrie following.

"We'll be back later, Tessa," Turner said to the dispatcher. "Put my lunch in the fridge, will you? Mr. Guthrie and I are going dump diving."

"I think it's called dumpster diving," she corrected.

"Looks like it's bigger than that," Turner said as he went through the door, into the noon sunshine, Guthrie on his heels.

5

THEY TOOK CHIEF TURNER'S FORD Police Interceptor SUV. It looked practically brand new. Guthrie figured the older Honda sedan next to it must belong to Tessa, the dispatcher. He wasn't sure about the Explorer.

"Nice vehicle," Guthrie commented.

"You should have seen what I *was* driving," Turner said, buckling his seatbelt. "An old-school Crown Vic. I made them buy this and another for my officer last year."

"That's Emmet?" Guthrie asked as Turner fired up the engine.

"Emmet Taylor. He's been with me for about six years."

"He's your only officer?"

"My only one. At least until we get these Interceptors paid for. So far, you've met two thirds of the Thorndike Police Department, counting Tessa. The town isn't big enough to warrant more, and if we need help, the state police barracks are right up the state highway near the county seat. But we never do. Thorndike is usually quiet except for regular weekend brawls down at the Lazy Q. That's our local roadhouse," he clarified. "Being a Thorndike police officer doesn't pay much, but any steady job around here that isn't being a ranch- or farmhand is hard to come by."

Turner pulled out of the parking lot.

"I thought we'd go over to the old Chaney place and have a talk with the new owner first," he said, scratching his cheek. "He's the only person who's moved here recently."

"Seems logical the sofa might belong to him."

The old Chaney place lay nearly three miles south of downtown, about half a mile from the northern edge of the forest surrounding the large wetlands Guthrie had noticed in the satellite images. Turner talked while he drove there, east along Main Street until it intersected the paved county road that was Thorndike's eastern border, then south, in the direction of the dump.

"Until a couple of months ago, Jim Chaney lived his whole life in the house we're going to," he said. "Ownership of the ranch goes back to his great-great-grandfather, who was one of the first settlers in this area right after the Texas Revolution. Course, the house isn't that old. Jim's grandfather built it to replace the original cabin. Their place was really something back then. They employed a dozen regular hands and a bunch of extras during roundup and so forth."

"You said, 'until a couple of months ago.' He sold the ranch?"

"He did." Turner shook his head. "And it hasn't been pretty."

"What happened?"

"I guess it was a confluence of things. There's a big marsh south of town. An extremely valuable resource. It used to be part of Jim's ranch, but now it's all he still owns. Steele Creek comes out of the northwest about three miles south of town. A dip in the terrain there made a small marsh before the creek runs southeast toward the Navasota River. Back when Jim's grandfather was running the spread, he dammed the outlet to make the pond larger. Now the pond is ten to fifteen acres in size, depending on the season and weather, with lots of arms going into the surrounding forest where there used to be gullies carrying runoff from the prairie. The marsh around the pond is maybe another sixty or seventy acres, and it's surrounded by an oak forest with a scattering of other trees. All told, he still owns approximately eleven-hundred acres. As you can imagine, that was a tremendous resource of water and shade for the Chaney herds."

The creek and marsh, Turner went on, though diminished in years of little rain, kept the forest, and the Chaney herds, intact, even when the herds of the other major ranches sometimes suffered significant losses from exposure to the sun during intense summers and dehydration in years of drought. Backed by that resource, the Chaney spread grew to be one of the most prosperous in the county.

"It would have continued to rival the others, even though some were larger," Turner said with a shrug, "but unfortunately, Jim wasn't the rancher his forebearers had been. It wasn't so much he was lazy, but he grew up more interested in being the high school stud than in learning from his parents how to run the ranch. And later, his interest in appearances caused him to spend a whole lot of money and influence convincing the county to expand and improve the dirt roads south of town to give him better access.

"Most folks around here resented that, but the repercussions for Jim proved to be drastic. He put too much faith in the marsh and forest to protect his herds and neglected spending on things that really need attending to, such as building more barns for his stock. He always said that cows wear leather coats, but leather coats and trees can protect cattle only so much. His mismanagement during a winter of several sudden and prolonged freezes followed by a summer of severe drought killed off two-thirds of his herd and even damaged the marsh and forest around it. Originally, the Chaneys owned a considerable amount of acreage west of the state road and south of Steele Creek, but to keep himself solvent, Jim was forced to sell that to Chuck Willis, who owns the big spread over that way. All that began Jim's economic downfall. And his fall from grace in the eyes of the community."

"It's hard to imagine economic hardship becoming a fall from grace."

"It was a steady downward progression. After Jim lost the majority of his herd and a significant chunk of land, he changed. I guess that would be a lot to bear without something happening to a person—especially someone with Jim's background. It was like he'd betrayed his ancestors as much as himself. Before his losses, he was fairly well respected for his temperament, but afterwards, he turned bitter and volatile. And the bitterness ate away at him, just as his mismanagement ate away at his family ranch. And then his wife, Enid, quit coming into town and even stopped going to church. Didn't take long for folks to figure Jim was taking out his anger on her." Turner shook his head. "Too bad, too. Enid was one of the bright lights of our town when she was young. The princess of the high school and ever popular at church socials. She never said a word about the abuse, though everybody knew. She just stopped being part of the community, and now, she can't."

"She died?"

"Less than two years ago. Ovarian cancer. She's buried in a small old cemetery about a mile from the house, just past the east end of the marsh. Jim was shook, even if he'd treated her badly during their marriage. They never had kids, so she was his whole life. Her and the ranch. Both abused. After she passed, Jim lost interest in keeping things up. Maybe he just gave up hope. He gradually lost all his hands as his operation went downhill. He was getting on, barely, but in the end, I guess losing her was the last straw since he finally sold out."

"Sold to the man we're visiting?"

"The house, barn, and about twenty acres," Turner said, shaking his head. "What he did with the rest was give the whole town a slap in the face. That's the biggest part of his fall from community grace."

"How so?"

"You have to understand the political and economic situation here."

Turner told Guthrie that the Chaney Ranch was one of five major family-owned ranches surrounding Thorndike. Two—the Carpenter and Willis Ranches—were west of town, across the state road, separated from each other by Steele Creek. Bart Kopecky's ranch was east and southeast of town. The Chaney Ranch lay immediately south of Thorndike, and south of that was Leland Fuller's ranch. They'd all been family owned until Bart Kopecky died. His heirs didn't want to keep on ranching, so they sold the property to Grant Industries, a huge ranching and farming corporation with land holdings all over the state.

"That must have impacted the traditional ranchers here," Guthrie commented.

"Big time. The main problem is that Grant utilizes a lot of mechanization, and what isn't mechanized is mostly handled by imported migrant labor, not by locals. As soon as Grant bought out Bart's spread, at least two dozen people were instantly out of full-time work, and a bunch of part-timers, too. That's a lot of people in a town as small as Thorndike. And the few who managed to hire on with Grant are getting paid less."

"Can't be good for the local economy."

"It wasn't," Turner said, "and most everybody around here thinks so, too. No sooner was the ink dry on the Kopecky sale than Grant Industries turned its corporate eye on the the other four big ranches."

The problem was, none of them wanted to sell. The Chaney and Fuller properties were contiguous with its main property, so Grant Industries focused on them. Regular as clockwork, a Grant representative contacted Jim and Leland to see if they'd changed their minds about selling. Both resisted, and even though his ranch was failing, Chaney held out for as long as he could.

"After Enid died, I guess he kinda gave up hope and went ahead and sold out to them, except for the marsh," Turner said. "As for Leland, he's already bought up a bunch of smaller ranches next to his own, and except for the Grant Ranch, his is the biggest spread around. He's working on building his own ranching empire. He already owns a small regional stockyard that he plans on expanding, and he's got construction of a meat processing plant in the works. He calls himself the Meat King of Texas."

"Grow 'em, stow 'em, and pack 'em up," Guthrie said, and Turner chuckled.

"Something like that. But when Jim sold his spread to Grant Industries, that really pissed off Leland since it put a damper on his plans. Thing was, he wanted Jim's pasturage, but he covets the marsh even more. He can do without the acreage, but getting hold of the marsh would have been a real coup since his property borders its southern edge."

"But Grant Industries didn't get it, either."

Turner shook his head.

"That's the rub. They coveted the marsh as much as Leland did, but they had to be satisfied with the pasturage because Jim refused to sell the marsh. That almost put the kibosh on the deal, but Grant knew Leland would buy the acreage if they didn't, so the deal went through. Grant bought what it could except for about twenty acres around the old house and barn because Jim was still living there. Keeping that last remnant gave him the illusion of still being a viable rancher, I suppose. At least for a time."

They hadn't gone as far as the dump when Turner swung the SUV right, onto a well-graded dirt county road. The forest surrounding the marsh spread to the left of the road, about half a mile away.

"Grant and Fuller were both pretty unhappy,"he said. "Steele Creek is the boundary between the two ranches, and they have to share the water. Personally, I think Jim refused to sell the marsh out of guilt as much as out of spite. About eight years ago, Enid made

Jim build her a cabin down in the marsh, and she moved there permanently. It was afterwards that nobody in town saw much of her. After she died, Jim continued to live in the house until he sold it to this fella we're visiting a couple of months ago and moved permanently to the cabin."

"If selling his acreage to Grant Industries was sure to upset the town, why didn't Chaney sell to Fuller?"

"Truth is, Jim would never have sold even a cow pie to Leland. But Leland wasn't the only one upset by the sale. In fact, the whole town is pissed at Jim, even beyond him abusing Enid. Whatever else Leland Fuller might be, he's still a local boy as well as a major employer, and most folks think Jim should have put his enmity behind him and sold to Leland for the good of the town. But he didn't, and now they consider him a turncoat. Around here, that's worse than being a stranger. The sale became a serious economic issue for the smaller ranchers and farmers. They're always stuck between bills and uncertain income, and on top of that, they can't compete with the corporate farm, so they feel forced to sell out, too, just to salvage something. Some have sold to Fuller or Grant, and a lot of them, right or wrong, blame Jim for their troubles.

"Plus, like I said, everyone knows Jim abused Enid. Since she died, Jim's become even more reclusive, taciturn, and generally unfriendly. As far as most people in town are concerned, he's a pariah." Turner shook his head and sighed. "It's tough to see someone who had everything lose it all."

"Seems like there's bad blood between Jim and Leland."

Turner told Guthrie that Jim Chaney and Leland Fuller were the same age, and like Chaney, Fuller was the inheritor of a family ranch operation that was as old as the Chaney Ranch. The Chaneys and Fullers had a long-standing feud over the property line between them. The Fullers claimed the northern edge of the marsh belonged to them and they should have access, but the Chaneys had a deed that gave them legal right to the entire wetland.

"Maybe because of that, Jim and Leland have hated each other since high school. Probably before, since their parents hated each other. They were always rivals—in school, in sports, in their teenage society, and later in life, in ranching. I was too young to know about all of that at the time. They're about fifteen years older than me, and my parents weren't really caught up in any of it since Dad was the foreman for the Carpenter Ranch and never worked for the Chaneys or Fullers. But just about everybody knew about their greatest rivalry, who was Enid Kellmann."

"That would be Jim's deceased wife?"

"That's right. She was a year younger than them. Her parents weren't ranchers or farmers. Her dad worked for a local oil drilling supply company, and her mother clerked in the feed store, so they didn't have the kind of money the Chaneys and Fullers had. But Enid did have one attribute that was hard to beat since she was the most beautiful girl in town. She could have had anybody, but around here, that meant either Jim or Leland. The nature of the rivalry couldn't be ignored since the two of them sometimes came to blows over her."

"But Jim won out."

"He did, and everything seemed fine until it wasn't. And when it was suspected that Jim had been abusing her, he and Leland came to blows again, though I don't know why since Leland had long since married and had kids. I actually had to lock both of them up overnight once when they started fighting at a town council meeting. Two older men brawling isn't a pretty sight, I can tell you, and they spent half the night yelling at each other through the bars. That was before Enid died, but she was already living at the cabin, and I don't know if she even knew about it."

The county road had run straight for about a mile and a half between tree-dotted pastures then meandered around a pair of lazy curves before Turner pointed ahead.

"There's the Chaney place."

Guthrie saw an old-fashioned, two-story ranch house in faded white with green trim. It had seen better days, as had the detached two-car garage next to it, its doors closed. A hundred feet away hulked a large wooden barn peeling dark red paint, flanked by a chicken coop and a pair of sheds. Off to one side was a pump house, and near that stood an old stone-rimmed well with a little, weather-worn, shingled roof peaked over the opening, which was covered with a square of warped and rain-darkened plywood. An air of dilapidation hung around the buildings, as if their better days had seen better days themselves. The one incongruous element was a new black Audi A3 sedan parked on the curving dirt driveway in front of the house.

"That's an expensive car," Guthrie commented. "It looks like the new owner has some bucks. Maybe he'll restore the house to its former glory."

"I'll just be glad if he doesn't turn out to be some rich guy out to take over and rule his own small town."

"From what you say, Leland Fuller already has that goal in mind."

"Not really. He's working on an empire, all right, but the town of Thorndike is only peripheral to that. He grew up around here, and he's not about to mess with the status quo since he already has top status."

They got out of the SUV and went up creaking steps to the wide covered porch. Turner rapped sharply on the door. A few moments later, it opened, revealing a white man in his late thirties. He was average in every way—looks, height, build, coloration. His hair was medium brown, and so were his eyes. He wore slacks, a button-down shirt, leather shoes that looked expensive, and a patrician air.

"I'm Chief Turner of the Thorndike Police Department. Mind if I ask you a few questions?"

"Not at all," the man said. "What's this about?" His voice sounded puzzled, but the eyes that moved to Guthrie then back to Turner were shrouded and didn't hold any questioning. Guthrie noticed he had a Louisiana accent, though it wasn't pronounced.

"This is Mr. Clay Guthrie," the chief said. "And you are…?"

"George Rand," the man said. He gestured back into the house. "Unfortunately, I'm a little preoccupied with painting. Do you mind if we talk on the porch. I'd hate for you to stain your clothes."

He stepped onto the porch and pulled the door to behind him before Guthrie got more than a glimpse of an entryway with an empty old-fashioned farmhouse coat and umbrella rack. There wasn't a drop of wet paint in sight—certainly not on Rand's pricey clothing—and no odor of it in the air. But there was a faint smell of disinfectant and bleach.

"Mr. Guthrie is in Thorndike investigating the disappearance of a man a few days ago. He was delivering a piece of furniture to some place in Thorndike, and…."

"And since I'm the only new resident in town, you naturally thought he might be delivering it to me." Rand gave a short little chuckle and shook his head. "He wasn't. I bought this house fully furnished and only brought my clothes and some personal items."

"Do you mind looking at his photo, anyway?" Turner said. It was a question, but it sounded like a command.

"Not at all." Rand took the photo that Guthrie held out and gave it a good look. Nothing registered in his eyes or in his body language, but was it possible that Guthrie saw a negative register, as if Rand hadn't reacted enough? As if he was too controlled? Too incurious?

Rand passed the photo back and shook his head.

"Sorry, gentlemen. Never seen him before. Maybe he was delivering the sofa to someone already established here."

"How'd you come be in Thorndike?" Turner asked.

"That's quite simple. Over the past decade, I made quite a bit of money in real estate and the stock market, but the lifestyle I was living was killing me. I finally realized I had enough money to comfortably retire somewhere away from the fast-pace life I'd been living. I liked Thorndike because it's small and quiet, yet if I have to do business in the big city, both Houston and Dallas are only a couple of hours away."

"Do you mind telling me where you were last Saturday and Sunday?"

"I was in Houston most of last week and only arrived home this morning. I stayed in the Hilton Americas, if you need to check."

"That won't be necessary," Turner said. "You live here alone?"

"Never married," Rand responded.

That wasn't strictly what Turner had asked, Guthrie thought, but Turner didn't seem to notice.

"Well, welcome to Thorndike, Mr. Rand. I hope you find your stay here pleasant."

"I'm sure I will, Chief. I look forward to meeting people in town."

"Thanks for your time," the chief said, and Rand nodded at him, then at Guthrie, eyes lingering. For just the barest moment, some sort of recognition flickered there, but it was quickly shrouded.

Rand reentered the house and closed the door, and Guthrie and Turner returned to the SUV.

"What do you think?" Guthrie asked.

"His story seems plausible enough."

"But you don't like him."

Turner stared at Guthrie for a moment, jaw clenching slightly.

"You're right," the chief said at last. "I don't like him. But that's not an indication of guilt."

"Maybe not," Guthrie said. "But he said he was painting, and there was no paint on his clothes or odor of it in the air. And there's something else. He said that Telfor must have delivered the sofa to someone else in Thorndike."

"And?"

"You only told him Norm was delivering a piece of furniture. How did Rand know it was a sofa?"

Turner's eyebrows went up.

"Indeed," he said. "It would seem that something's not quite right with him."

Yes, Guthrie thought. Something definitely wasn't right with George Rand, even beyond his shrouded eyes and prevarication. But he couldn't tell Turner that the whole time they'd talked to Rand, the Kuei men on Guthrie's belly had been twitching.

"Shall we go dump diving?" the chief asked.

6

CHIEF TURNER STEERED THE INTERCEPTOR down the dirt county road toward the paved one leading to the dump in one direction and town in the other, dust pluming from his tires.

"I know you said the dump was locked up earlier," he said, "but we'll check it, anyway. Hopefully Freddie'll be there now, and we can ask him if he saw Telfor or let him in."

"Freddie?"

"Freddie Jensen. He manages the dump. He's a little more than five years older than me. I can't say we were ever friends, but he's a good sort even if he is a bit troubled."

Like every able-bodied male teen going to Thorndike High School, Turner told Guthrie, Freddie had played football and was a running back.

"He was a good one, too, and helped put our little school near the top in the region. He wanted to go pro, but he couldn't get into college to improve his skills in college ball and get noticed by the leagues, so that was the end of his glory days. After that, his teenage party drinking became habit drinking, even after he secured a job at Dixon Resources, a now-defunct sand and gravel quarry in the next county, about twenty miles southeast of here.

"They trained him to operate a bulldozer and other heavy equipment, and he worked there until Dixon shut down a little more than twenty years ago. Freddie isn't the most proactive sort, but he was smart enough to buy a backhoe with a front-end loader from them, so he wasn't left totally in the lurch. Back then, his drinking problem wasn't so bad he couldn't function, and he did okay for a while, hiring himself out to local ranches and farms. Sometimes he dug ponds or irrigation ditches, sometimes holes for septic or fuel tanks, and sometimes he demolished small houses or outbuildings. He was even hired to dig graves for livestock that died before they could be led to slaughter. In fact, he helped Jim Chaney bury his herd after they died from exposure. Anything anybody might need a backhoe for, Freddie was their man.

"But most of the larger places eventually bought their own heavy equipment, and only a few of the smaller local ranchers could afford to hire him, and finally even that dried up. The last person who hired him regularly was Jim Chaney, who he worked for for several years. But when Jim sold out to Grant Industries, that was gone, too. Freddie was living on the edge for a while. On charity, really. The only thing that saved him was he owns the house he lives in, which was left to him by his parents, so at least he has a roof over his head. But around that time, the town needed somebody to manage the dump, so I convinced the town council to give Freddie the job."

Guthrie chuckled at that.

"Don't laugh," Turner said. "Somebody has to collect the dump fee and regulate what comes in. You wouldn't believe what the people around here'll try to dump out there. The worst of it's the dead bodies of large animals like cows and pigs. Even horses. A lot cheaper than hiring Freddie to bury them and easier than burying them themselves. If we let folks dump bodies there, the place would be half a mile high with rotting carcasses by this time next year. Somebody's got to keep them out."

"And that's Freddie."

Turner nodded.

"But there's more to the job than that. Maintenance requires the use of a bulldozer, which Freddie can operate. So far, his drinking hasn't affected his work, and he's usually there during the day. When he's not operating the dozer, he hangs out in a small shack near the entrance, collecting fees and drinking. He's supposed to open up at seven, so it's odd the gate was locked when you came by."

At the intersection with the paved county road, Turner steered right and drove south another mile and a half before slowing at the entrance to a nondescript dirt track that wound out of sight to the left, around a low wood of scrub oaks. A battered and askew black mailbox stood sentinel, its mouth gaping open.

"Freddie's house is back in those trees," Turner said, waving down the track. "But let's go on to the dump and see if he's there."

Moments later, the entrance to the dump came into view on the left. Turner pulled up to the gate, which was still closed and chained shut.

"Now that's peculiar," Turner said, glancing at his watch. "Maybe Freddie's sick."

"Or drunk?"

"Probably not drunk yet, though he's undoubtedly been drinking." Turner handed the gate key to Guthrie. "Mind doing the honors? Just leave it open after I drive through."

Guthrie got out, expecting a strong odor of rotting garbage, but the tepid breeze wafting over the dump bore no taint. He went to the gate and reached for the lock linking the chain. And paused. There were two locks, on opposite sides of the loop of chain: one old and weathered, the other new enough to still have its sheen. He tried the key in the new lock, but it didn't fit. The older lock took the key, and Guthrie snapped it open, draped the chain around the gatepost, and swung the gate wide. Turner pulled through then immediately to the right and parked beneath a big spreading oak growing beside the front hurricane fence. Before he got out, he laid on the horn, sending a long blast over the mounds of trash, junk, and dirt.

"I guess he isn't here," Turner said after he got out and came up to Guthrie. "His truck's not here, and he'd have heard that for sure. Dump's only a little more than half a square mile, though we have room to expand at the back." He snorted and chuckled at the same time. "Let's hope it doesn't come to that."

"It's best to keep things quiet and simple," Guthrie agreed as he handed over the gate key. "Your town has both right now, and it sounds like even Leland's plan to become the Meat King of Texas won't impact that very much."

"I hope not," Turner said. "Let's have a look in there."

He headed toward a weathered wooden shack standing twenty feet behind and to the right of the gate. A small bulldozer sat beneath a metal awning behind the shack. The shack had a window on the front above a narrow counter, but the window was shuttered with a piece of plywood hinged at the top. Tacked beneath the counter was a sign, black letters hand painted on a dingy white background reading, "Honk Loud!" The door was in the right side wall, and it was unlocked. Turner pulled it open, and Guthrie stared past him into the dim interior. A small, scarred wooden desk and a worn office chair occupied most of the space, which smelled of stale cigarette smoke with an undertone of whiskey.

"Not here," Turner said, closing the door. "Let's go to his house and see if he's there."

"Let's take a look around here, first," Guthrie said.

"I'm not sure why," Turner said. "If Freddie's truck isn't here, then he isn't, either."

Maybe not, Guthrie thought, but something definitely was in the dump. Some wrongness. Even if he couldn't see it, the Kuei men were twitching. But he couldn't tell Turner that.

"Humor me," he said.

"You looking for something in particular?"

"Not really," Guthrie shrugged. "I'd say we were looking for something that's out of place."

"So," Turner said laconically, mouth wrinkling slightly, twitching his mustache. "We're looking for something out of place in a dump, where everything finally ends up out of place?"

Guthrie chuckled, and the two began walking through the dump, initially following the main dirt track between the surrounding mounds. As they moved deeper into the dump, only the slightest odor of garbage tinged the air.

"I have to say that Thorndike has one of the cleanest dumps I've ever seen," Guthrie said. "I've been to one of the landfills in Houston several times, and you could smell it miles away. Each time, I wanted to shower immediately afterward."

"I don't imagine that folks in Thorndike are any cleaner than folks anywhere else," Turner said then sniffed the air. "But if you mean this place isn't stinking all that bad, you're right. I guess Freddie's been burying the garbage like he's supposed to."

Guthrie couldn't imagine what they might be seeking, but after they'd explored the front half of the dump as thoroughly as they were going to in their present attire, he realize that the twitching of the Kuei men increased the deeper he and Turner wound between the mounds.

Just like a uranium prospector following the increased clicking of his device, Guthrie followed the Kuei men's more energetic twitching.

"Let's look down here," he suggested at last, pointing along an obscure track that led toward the rear of the dump.

The chief, who so far had been following along tolerantly but not expectantly, had a puzzled look on his face.

"You seem to know where you're going," he commented.

"Not really. I just have a feeling something's down this way."

Turner looked skeptical, but he gestured down the track.

"After you."

The track wound through a couple of curves between the mounds of debris then angled straight to the dump's rear, eight-foot cyclone fence. Normally, there'd be nothing to see but the sparse woods past the fence and open Grant Industries land beyond. But now, an old Dodge pickup partially blocked the view. Its formerly brown paint was faded, chipped, and splotched.

"That's Freddie's truck," Turner said.

They walked forward but paused to stare at three items lying on the dirt track about forty feet from the truck. They were two heavily scuffed pull-on work boots and a pair of stained bluejeans, a worn leather belt threaded through the loops.

"Now those are definitely out of place." Turner said.

The Kuei men on Guthrie's belly were kicking now. Whatever he was looking for was close by.

"Quiet, now," Guthrie muttered, massaging his belly with his palm. The twitching subsided but did not entirely vanish.

He glanced at Turner. He'd been around the chief for less than an hour, and initially Turner had seemed rock solid, loquacious, and laid-back. But now he looked taciturn and tense, and Guthrie saw his hand drift unconsciously to the butt of his pistol. No wonder, Guthrie thought. Even discounting the warning of the Kuei men, he could feel a greasy pressure that was something other than physical closing in and depositing itself on the surface of his skin. It was the same sensation he'd felt just the day before in the Airla Lumber mill, and nearly as strong. Whatever it was, obviously it was affecting Turner, though the chief might have chalked it up to little more than his own cautious misgivings. But Guthrie had no misgivings. He knew they were zeroing in on something. But what?

Raising his hands beside his mouth in an impromptu mega-phone, Turner yelled, "Freddie! Freddie!"

Only silence answered. And now, Guthrie noticed just how complete the silence was. No birds chirping, no insects buzzing, and both should have been abundant around a dump. There wasn't even the obscure sound of a rodent scurrying through the debris or squirrels in the nearby trees. There weren't even any flies in the air. It was the same kind of dead quiet that surrounded Airla.

"You hear anything," he asked Turner, who cocked his head.

"No," he said. "Nothing unusual."

"No insects? No birds? I haven't even seen a rat or mouse. I'd say it's unusual not to hear or see those in a dump."

"You're right." Turner shook his shoulders, unconsciously bracing himself against the greasy pressure. "Let's look over the truck. Don't touch anything."

Guthrie didn't need the warning. The Dodge's windows were open, and though the engine was off, the keys hung from the ignition, as if Freddie had stepped out only briefly and planned to return soon. Turner reached inside and pressed on the horn. A nasal blast tore the silence, which snapped back in place as soon as Turner let up.

"Nothing," Turner said.

The man might have been the chief of police and a stalwart guy, but there was something lost in his voice, as if the encroaching silence and aura of dread had leached out his determination. Even if not consciously, surely he was feeling, like Guthrie, the profound sense of oppression that hung over the back of the dump—something that penetrated deeper than bad odors and dragged at the spirit.

They walked around the truck, examining but not touching anything or marring any of the footprints or tire tracks.

"Freddie sometimes finds things people have tossed out that he can fix up and sell at Marnie's Resale Shop," Turner said. Speaking the words seemed like an effort. "That's probably what he was doing back here. Looking for stuff to fix. But where is he, now?"

Guthrie turned three hundred and sixty degrees and felt the Kuei men kick up more strongly when he faced the last mound at the right of the dirt track.

"Let's check over there." He gestured to the mound. Turner looked puzzled then nodded almost absently. Guthrie wished he could be more circumspect in approaching the danger indicated by the Kuei men, but the matter was too urgent. If Turner wanted to know what led him to whatever it was they were about to find, Guthrie would just pass it off as a guess or instinct or some such thing.

He approached the pile of refuse and peered at it. Whatever was causing the Kuei men to act up was in that pile. But it couldn't be. The refuse in front of Guthrie had been there a long time. Mixed in with dirt, it had compacted into a mass that was obviously undisturbed.

Refusing to give up, Guthrie walked around the end of the mound, between it and the fence, and that's when he saw a sofa sitting near the back of a forty-foot-wide open area enclosed by mounds of debris on three sides and the fence on the fourth. From what he could see of the ends protruding from beneath the two heavily stained blue moving quilts covering it, it was some kind of green velour, filthy and greasy with age and use. The quilts were lumped up from beneath, as if refuse had been piled on the cushions before the quilts were laid over them. A greasy pall of nastiness hung around the thing, which, even at a distance of thirty feet, stank of filth, moldy decay, and old rot that had lost its pungency.

He took a few steps toward the sofa and stopped, halted by an almost palpable sense of dread. The Kuei men were kicking so much that he had to take a moment to quiet them. They'd led him here and warned him of danger, and now he needed to dampen their distracting squirms.

He glanced back at Turner, who looked tense and was holding back.
"You okay, Chief?"
Turner shook himself and braced his shoulders.
"I'm fine."
He didn't look fine.
"There's something in there," Guthrie said. "We have to take a look."
"Maybe," Turner said. "But I don't like it already. Wait."
He turned and strode hurriedly back the way they'd come. Only a few minutes passed before Guthrie heard the sound of the Interceptor rolling down the track between the mounds of debris, but the pervasive dread made the wait seem far longer. The SUV stopped some distance behind the Dodge, and a few moments later, Turner, visibly forcing himself forward, came around the mound to where Guthrie waited.

"We need to wear these," the chief said, handing over a pair of nitrile gloves. "Even if it isn't a crime scene." He stared at the sofa while he snapped on the gloves, then shook his head and heaved the kind of sigh a person gives before undertaking something extremely unpleasant. "Jeez, this thing reeks." This time, he shook his whole body as he braced himself. "I guess we'd better check it."

He didn't sound enthusiastic, but he bent to the task, body language saying he hated touching the sofa or blankets, even through the protective layer of nitrile. Guthrie understood perfectly. Breathing shallowly, they each grasped one of the quilts and dragged them off the too-lumpy, too-thick cushions. As the quilts came off, the noxious odor and sensation of dread seemed to billow into the air like an unseen smoke signal. They stepped back, almost choking. But that wasn't what sent a jolt through Guthrie, and Turner even gasped.

A body lay on the sofa. What was left of a body. It was somewhat flattened, as if dried out, and it appeared to have lain there for a very long time. There weren't any flies or maggots, just a husk of sere, darkened skin stretched over dried flesh, muscle, and bone. Weirdly, none of the visible skin was broken or torn open as with other old corpses Guthrie had seen. This one looked more like a completely intact mummy than anything recent. The corpse was wearing a Dallas Cowboys t-shirt, a large, dark stain spread across the front, right over the heart.

"Jesus," Turner said. "You don't think that's your boy, do you? I mean, this thing must have been here for months or more. Hell, there isn't even a ripe smell of rot, just this…." He shook his shoulders as if shrugging off a heavy weight. "Your boy disappeared, what? A week ago?"

"That's right," Guthrie said. "It's not Freddie?"

Turner reluctantly focused on the corpses and shook his head.

"Definitely not. Freddie's bigger and has a bushy gray beard, and this man doesn't. And Freddie doesn't dress like that." Turner gave Guthrie an appraising stare. "When we came to the dump, you didn't know he was here, did you?"

The statement could have been accusatory, but Turner's voice was too unsteady to hold any threat.

"No, I didn't."

"But when you got near it, you knew something was off and you zeroed right in on it."

"Luck of the draw, Chief."

"Yeah." Turner shot him a jaundiced look. "Well, we'd better back off. This is a crime scene, and I don't have the qualifications or personnel to look into something like this."

They went to Turner's SUV, Guthrie, for one, glad to be out of the malignant pall that suffused the air around the sofa, though it could still be felt here, more than sixty feet away despite the intervening mounds of refuse and dirt. The chief radioed Tessa and had her patch him through to the state police barracks and the county sheriff's office. He also told her to send Emmet Taylor to the scene.

Taylor arrived in ten minutes, parking his Interceptor behind Turner's. When he got out, Guthrie was surprised to see that he was black considering the part of the state where Thorndike was located. The officer looked to be in his mid thirties and was a little taller than Guthrie and definitely bulkier, all of it solid muscle, as if he worked out regularly. Unlike Turner, who favored jeans and a plain khaki shirt, Taylor was in a full uniform of dark blue, and his black lace-up boots with the cuffs tucked in were worn but polished.

"Emmet, meet Clay Guthrie. He's a PI who came into town this morning looking for a man who disappeared over in Louisiana, and we think we might have found him back there."

Turner waved toward the last mound of dirt and refuse as Guthrie and Taylor shook hands. The officer's grip was like a vise.

"Want me to watch over the body?" Emmet asked, eyes drifting unconsciously in the direction Turner indicated. Despite his solid grip, he didn't seem anxious for Turner to say yes.

So, Guthrie thought. He can feel it, too, even this far away, even if he doesn't realize it.

Turner shook his head.

"I don't think you want to be back there. I called the sheriff, staties, and coroner. Let them do the dirty work. Why don't you man the front gate and direct them back here?"

Emmet nodded, eyes unconsciously grateful. He got into his vehicle, backed down the track to the first junction, and drove off toward the front gate. Turner also backed his Interceptor down the track to the junction and parked there to give the soon-to-arrive law enforcement access. The first DPS troopers showed up inside twenty minutes and the sheriff soon after, but it took another half hour to get the crime scene investigation team on site. Once they'd started their work and Turner and Guthrie had told what they knew to the sheriff and DPS captain, Turner slapped Guthrie on the arm.

"They don't need us around here at the moment," he said. "Come on."

"Where we going?" Guthrie asked.

"To find Freddie."

7

CHIEF TURNER SEEMED TO BRIGHTEN as soon as they got into his Interceptor and left the dump, though his serious demeanor remained. Guthrie wasn't surprised. He, too, felt the diminishing of the pervasive oppression, and the Kuei men stilled as soon as the SUV drove through the gate. But now matters appeared more serious than before. Turner drove to Freddie's driveway.

"Freddy's property also backs up to the Grant Industries spread," he said as he swung the SUV past the battered mailbox. The box was empty, but maybe it always was.

A hundred yards beyond stood a small, dilapidated bungalow that once had been white but now was mottled with patches of faded, peeling paint against the steel gray of weathered wood. The brown-shingled roof was threadbare and liberally spotted with repairs of splayed tin cans embedded in tar. An unkempt vegetable garden lay on the right side of the house, and on the left stood a small pole barn with corrugated tin sheathing on the roof and three sides. Inside was a backhoe with a front-end loader, sitting on a trailer. Next to the barn were the hulks of two forty or fifty year-old rusted-out cars and an almost equally decrepit black Chevy pickup, half masked by weeds and brush that had grown up around them and encroached on what formerly was yard. A large, greasy bare patch marked the spot Freddie parked his truck, and a well-worn path of dirt led from the parking spot to the front door.

"It isn't much," Turner said as he stopped on the greasy bare patch. "But it's something."

They got out of the Interceptor and walked up to the front door. It still bore traces of green paint, but less after Turner banged on it with his fist and a few flakes loosened and fell to the cement pad in front of the threshold.

"Freddie!" Turner yelled, and he pounded and yelled Freddie's name again, but only silence and falling flecks of green answered.

Turner looked at Guthrie, shrugging as his face made a sour expression, then he turned back to the door.

"Freddie!" he yelled. "Come open the door!"

"You don't think he's passed out drunk in there, do you?" Guthrie asked.

"Could be," Turner said. "Freddie's got a lot of faults and weaknesses, chief among them drink. But probably not, since his truck's over at the dump."

He turned back to the door, and this time, he didn't knock but tried the knob. It turned, and he pushed the door open.

"I guess he's not big on security," Turner said.

"You sure you want to go inside without a warrant?" Guthrie asked.

"Probable cause since a body was found near Freddie's truck, and Freddie has disappeared," Turner said and led the way inside. "Freddie!" He yelled. "Freddie, it's Chief Turner! We're coming inside!"

There was no response, and the place felt empty to Guthrie. Empty of people, that was, but not of objects. A lot of objects. The interior was a hoarder's paradise. Every available space was piled high with old furniture, cardboard boxes filled to splitting, used and abused appliances, and assorted junk. Narrow lanes wound from one jam-packed room to the next. The smell inside was intense, but after the corrupted atmosphere around the sofa that had seemed to creep into the spirit, Guthrie barely noticed.

"I guess Freddie isn't big on housekeeping, either," Turner commented dryly.

"Was he always like this?"

"Can't say. I've driven him home a few nights after he's had one too many at the Lazy Q, but he never invited me in, and I never had a reason to enter before now." Turner stared down an aisle leading toward a hall and the back of the house. "Maybe he's passed out on his bed. Or he might be hurt."

What the chief didn't say was that Freddie might be lying dead on his bed. A single alcoholic male in older middle-age and living in poverty and squalor.... It wouldn't be surprising if his body had given out. Or maybe simply his will to live.

But there was no fetor of death in the house, only the odor of dust and uncleanliness with a heady tang of rat urine. Guthrie followed Turner down the hall, half the width of which was taken up with piled boxes, until they came to a dead-end in a bedroom that was clear enough—at least in the middle—to accommodate a beat-up wooden bed. Dirty rumpled sheets and blankets lay atop the mattress, but not Freddie. The closet was filled with boxes, and a pile of clothes lay in one corner. It was hard to tell if they were dirty or clean.

Guthrie and Turner retraced their steps past a dilapidated bathroom to a second bedroom. This one was so completely filled that the door would open only halfway.

"If Freddie had any incentive," Turner said, peering through the gap, "he'd fix up all this stuff and have Marnie sell it."

"We each do what we do, Chief, and that's what we do."

Turner gave him a jaundiced look and shook his head.

"We've been this far," he said. "We'd better check the rest."

They stopped at the bathroom on the way back. A dirty glass with a toothbrush propped inside sat on the worn formica counter beside the sink, a partially flattened tube of toothpaste next to it. The bathtub was dry, as was the towel that hung from a nearby hook. No Freddie in the kitchen, either, and no signs of disturbance or violence. The sink was filled with dirty dishes, and the closed cabinets revealed little besides a few pots and pans, dishes, canned and boxed food, and three bottles of cheap bourbon. The fridge was equally uninformative, holding a bare minimum of staples. In a couple of minutes, they were outside, breathing fresh air.

"We probably ought to check out the barn, too," Turner said.

They went to the pole barn, but all that was in it was the backhoe and racks of tools above a workbench along the rear wall. The tools were all neatly arranged, and Guthrie noted that the backhoe, though well-used, seemed to be in good condition.

"Freddie's managed to maintain that," he commented, nodding at the machine.

"That backhoe represents the best time of his life. I guess he maintains it because he's always hoping someone will hire him and bring back his glory days." Turner stepped out of the barn, and Guthrie followed. "Now where would he go?" Turner mused, staring aimlessly around the clearing in which the house sat.

"He have any friends he might go see?"

"Not that I can think of. Just about everybody in town knows who Freddie is, and Freddie knows a lot of folks, but there's nothing like friendship there, only acquaintanceship. Besides, it's four miles to town, and it's not likely he'd walk there without his jeans and boots. And he'd take his truck."

"Well, he's not here, and his clothes and truck are at the dump. Who's within walking distance that he might go to in an emergency?"

"I guess that'd be Jim Chaney. Like I said, Freddie worked for him a spell before Jim sold his spread, and he helped Jim bury all those cows. Jim's cabin is down in the marsh, about a mile from his old house. It's about three miles from here driving but less than half that if you cut straight across the pastures. Freddie might go over there, but I can't think why he'd leave his truck and clothes at the dump and walk."

"We know his truck was parked close to the sofa with the body," Guthrie pointed out.

"You're not suggesting that Freddie had anything to do with…."

"Certainly not. He's probably just an innocent bystander. It seems to me something spooked him before he knew a body was there. It was still covered up and undisturbed when we found it. The only way to know is to find him and ask. Let's talk to Jim Chaney then go back to town and see if anyone's seen Freddie there. Maybe go to Leo's first. Waitresses in small town cafes know just about everything that goes on. If he's been there today or there's any new gossip around town, surely your wife will know it."

Turner shot him a bemused look.

"Surely," he said. "Bev knows just about everything that goes on in Thorndike."

The drive to Chaney' cabin was nearly the reverse of the trip from his old house to the dump and Freddie's, the only difference being that Turner drove a quarter of a mile past the long curving driveway to the house and its new owner. There, the county road stopped at the entrance to a narrow dirt lane that went off to the left. The lane, bordered by ditches and barbed-wire fences strung from cedar posts, ran straight across a grassy pasture for nearly half a mile then entered the oak forest ahead. Fifty or sixty feet outside the edge of the forest, a rusty iron gate interrupted another fence that stretched across the grasslands on either side, separating them from the trees.

"This is the edge of the marsh and Jim's property," Turner said. "Jim keeps the gate locked, so we'll have to walk from here. It's about three-quarters of a mile to the cabin."

They got out of the SUV, climbed the gate, and began walking down the lane. The narrow track, turned sinuous beneath the trees and still bordered by ditches, wound through a quickly thickening understory. Soon, it was impossible to see more than a hundred and fifty feet in any direction except ahead and back along the track. Beneath the trees, the temperature dropped several degrees, and the air was moist. Even at this late hour, a low, vague mist twisted through the foliage.

"Kinda chilly in here," Turner noted. "I wonder if we're going to have an unseasonable cold snap."

Some kind of snap, Guthrie thought. The Kuei men were twitching, though only subtilely. Something was in the woods, and it wasn't very nice. But the sensation faded the farther they walked.

At first, Guthrie didn't see any of the pond Turner had described, but soon he spotted glimmers of water through the trees on either side. Somewhere off to the left, something large and unseen splashed in the water. A raccoon scurried out of sight to the right. Squirrels ran through the trees and leapt from branch to branch, and a pair of birds foraging for bugs on the open track ahead suddenly flew off, disturbed by their approach.

"I can see why Fuller and Grant Industries were upset not to get this," Guthrie said, waving around. "Jim could have sold this to either for a fortune."

"I guess he couldn't bear to part with it since it was where Enid spent her last few years. If I didn't know different, I'd almost believe she grew up in southern Louisiana. There's no way Jim was going to let either of them despoil it for profit. They might squabble over it after Jim passes, but until then, it's all his."

They rounded a final curve, and the track widened into a grassy somewhat flat area some forty or fifty feet across. On the side closest to the cabin sat a Ford 150 pickup that was at least ten years old. Sixty feet or so past that, down a grassy slope with a well-worn path, was the cabin.

"That's a long way to carry sacks of groceries," he said.

"Jim eats a lot of his meals in town these days," Turner said, heading down the path to the cabin's front door. "I guess he isn't much of a cook."

"Is he a drinker?" Guthrie asked as he followed, glancing down the wide grassy slope to the pond. It was flanked on the right by the cabin and, behind that, the end of a deck stuck out over the water. A dented, eight-foot long flat-bottomed aluminum boat painted dark green lay face down on the bank next to the deck, just above the waterline.

"Never known him to be, though he's gotten a bit peculiar since Enid died. But that's probably just old age and loneliness. He keeps himself pretty isolated down here."

The cabin was a simple wooden structure about forty feet wide and thirty deep, painted forest green with light brown trim. It was built on a rise in the land that overlooked the wide pond that was the heart of the marsh. The main body of water spread across several acres, though the cabin blocked sight of most of it. The part Guthrie could see looked beautiful, edges shaded by the surrounding trees, center filed with light that sparkled on the water's gently ruffled surface. Birds and insects flitted over it, chasing and being chased, and the water was dimpled by fish rising to eat insects fallen into it. It was a truly bucolic scene, and Guthrie had a hard time imagining a more peaceful setting for a retirement home.

"Yo, the cabin!" Turner yelled out as they approached. "You in there, Jim? It's Chief Turner!"

The door, set near the front left corner, opened just as they reached it, and an older man stepped into the opening. From what Turner told Guthrie, Chaney was in his mid sixties, but he bore no traces of decrepitude. He was a little shorter than Guthrie and stocky in the way that lifelong laborers get in older age. His thinning hair had once been dark brown but was graying, and gray stubble darkened his cheeks and chin. To his surprise, Guthrie actually recognized him as the older man with the taciturn expression who'd been sitting in a booth at Leo's Cafe when he'd eaten there earlier. Turner had said Chaney ate many of his meals in town.

"Chief Turner." Chaney opened the door wide and stepped onto the small wood-plank porch. "What brings you down here?"

"This is Clay Guthrie. He's a private investigator from Houston. He's searching for a man who disappeared up this way, and we think we found his body this morning in the dump. Freddie's truck was there, but there's no sign of Freddie. Have you seen him?"

"As a matter of fact, I did. Couple a days ago. Lemme think.... Tuesday evenin', it was. He came down here just after dusk. Stumbled down here, really." Chaney chuckled. "At first, I thought he was drunk as a skunk. He wasn't wearin' any pants or boots. But then I thought he wasn't. He was all panicked about somethin'. I tried to calm him down and find out what happened, but all he said was somethin' chased him outta the dump."

"He wasn't wearing any pants or boots?" Turner asked, glancing at Guthrie. "Did he say why?"

"Alls he said was they got stained with some kinda black evil, and he had to leave 'em behind. But askin' more just got him more upset, so I quit askin'."

"Did he say what chased him out?" Guthrie asked.

"I couldn't make hide nor hair of it. If you know of somethin' with a body made of fog and a thousand black fingers, then you know more about it than I do."

"Fog?" Turner asked.

"That's what he told me, but like I said, I couldn't make much sense of it. I mean, we always got night fog this time of year, 'specially south of town, here. In fact, by the time he got here, it was pretty thick in the woods. He was plenty scared, but I just passed it off as drunken ravin's." He peered at Turner and then at Guthrie. "But now you say you can't find him?"

"We haven't been looking long." Turner said. "Where did he go then?"

"He didn't leave right away. He was too scared. I let him spend the night and give him a pair of pants and old boots. He left first thing in the mornin'."

"Did he say where he was going?"

"I thought he was going to the dump to get his truck."

"Can you think of any other place he might have gone?" Guthrie asked.

"His house, the dump, or town. Or maybe the Lazy Q. Can't think of anyplace else unless he got a handyman job somewhere around here. If he did, he didn't mention it to me."

"You have a beautiful place," Guthrie said.

Chaney was quiet for a moment.

"My wife loved this marsh," he said at last. "I always feel surrounded by her spirit down here."

Guthrie reflected on that. Could the spirit of an abused and painfully deceased woman be at peace?

"Do you ever see her? In more than spirit, I mean."

"Like a ghost?" Chaney stiffened and snorted. "Whoever heard of such a thing?"

I have, Guthrie thought, but he didn't press the matter.

"Have you noticed any changes in the marsh since Freddie left?" he asked.

"What kinda changes?" Chaney' brow wrinkled in puzzlement.

"I don't know. Something like what Freddie described or anything else that seems unusual."

"You mean have I seen a creepin' fog with a thousand black fingers out to get me? The answer is, no." The puzzlement darkening his brow turned a bit nasty and defensive. "Can't see why you might be askin' that or about ghosts. Freddie was ravin'. That's all."

"I didn't mean to offend you, Mr. Chaney," Guthrie said.

"Okay, Jim," Turner said in a soothing voice. "Thanks for your help."

"Sure thing, Chief. Let me know when you find him. He worked for me for a long time on and off, and I'd hate to hear somethin' bad happened to him."

Chaney retreated into the cabin, and Guthrie and Turner walked up the path, past the truck, and along the dirt track. They didn't speak for a couple of minutes, but Guthrie could sense that Turner was puzzled. At last, the chief broke the silence.

"You want to tell me what's going on?" he asked. "You asked Jim some peculiar questions."

"I was just wondering about the state of the marsh," Guthrie answered. "He's been around it his whole life, so he should know best."

"I might leave it at that," Chief replied. "But Jim didn't react well, and I should know since I've been around him my whole life."

"He lost his wife. His whole life, almost, counting his ranch. I guess anybody might react poorly to a stranger questioning him."

Turner gave him an appraising look.

"Kinda sounds like bullshit to me," he said. "And I've lived around cows long enough to know bullshit when I smell it. You know something you're not telling me?"

"You know as much about this case as I do" Guthrie said, despite the increased twitching of the Kuei men the farther they walked. "I don't even know if that body we found is the man I'm looking for. Considering the shape he's in, it's not likely."

"Maybe not," Turner said. "But we still have a body that's obviously a homicide. And we found it on a sofa, which is what your boy was hauling. And it was wearing a t-shirt just like the one in the photo you showed me. There hasn't been a homicide here since Bruce MaCabe shot Eustace Smith in the parking lot after a brawl at the Lazy Q. That was more than five years ago."

By now, Turner's Interceptor had come into view, and as they stepped out of the shaded coolness into the sun, the Kuei men relaxed. Guthrie followed Turner over the gate, and they got into the SUV.

"Where now?" Guthrie asked.

"Let's go to Leo's," Turner said. "Like you said, waitresses know everything. Besides, I missed my lunch, and all this excitement has got me pretty hungry. And it's sure to be a long night."

At Leo's, they went inside and sat in a booth.

"Hi, Bill," Bev said, bringing over water and menus. "Tessa said you didn't eat your lunch."

"Something came up," Turner told her. "This is Clay Guthrie. Mr. Guthrie, this is my wife, Beverly."

"Pleasure to re-meet you, Mrs. Turner." Guthrie shook her hand.

"You just keep calling me Bev," she said. "Nobody calls me Mrs. Turner except our daughter's friends."

"Well, call me Clay," he told her. "You, too, Chief."

"All right," Turner said. "He's working with me on a case."

"That man you were looking for this morning?" she asked Guthrie. "I hear ya'll found him in the dump."

"I swear to God," Turner said shaking his head but smiling. "The only thing faster than the speed of light is the speed of gossip. Speaking of gossip, you seen Freddie today or heard anything about him?"

"Freddie?" Her eyes looked thoughtful. "No. Last time I saw him was on Saturday, when he came in for his regular burger."

"Did he seem off to you?"

"It's hard to tell if Freddie's off or just being himself. But no, can't say he seemed any different than usual."

They ordered, and Bev left.

"You have a daughter?" Guthrie asked.

"Emily. She's a senior. And a son, too. Ethan. He's a sophomore at Texas A&M." Turner paused, giving Guthrie an appraising look that meant he was about to change the subject to something Guthrie would have preferred avoiding.

"I think we need to have a frank discussion, Clay."

"Okay, Chief. What do you want to discuss?"

"What the hell is going on. You say Telfor disappeared only a week ago, but the corpse we found—*you* found—hasn't been there that short a time. More like months. Especially stuffed in that sofa and covered up."

"Maybe he's not Telfor."

"But you don't think so."

"No. You noticed the t-shirt, and Mrs. Telfor told me Norm left wearing that shirt. But I can't explain his odd state of decomposition. Or lack of."

"Yeah. I couldn't even smell any animal decay, though that sofa has to be the most nasty and foul item I've ever encountered, even without the body." Turner peered intently at Guthrie. "So what led you to it? It's almost like you knew something was back there."

Kuei men dancing, Guthrie thought.

"I don't know," he said. "Instinct?"

Turner gave him a flat, penetrating stare.

"Is that a question?"

"Okay," Guthrie admitted. "You could say I have a sort of sixth sense. Something that alerts me to the presence of…certain types of things."

"Like dead bodies?"

"More like things that shouldn't be like they are."

"Wish I had an instinct like that."

"No," Guthrie said. "You probably don't."

Turner looked like he wanted to ask more, but their food arrived, and Guthrie, thankful for an excuse to terminate the interrogation, dug into his meal as Turner did likewise. When they were done, Turner apparently forgot to ask more about Guthrie's "instinct."

"What now, Chief?" Guthrie asked.

"I need to go back to the dump to see what's going on. I'd like you to stay in town for a few more days until we get this sorted out."

"I was planning on staying, anyway," Guthrie replied, thinking that the sorting out might be a little more difficult than finding the body. "Bev told me there isn't a motel in town, but there's one in the county seat. Is that close enough?"

"I think we can do better than that. Let's go." Turner stood, put his hat on his head, and turned toward the door.

"What about the check?" Guthrie asked.

"Bev'll take care of that." Turner waved at his wife, who was standing behind the counter, and called out, "Don't expect me until late."

She waved back, then Turner led Guthrie out of the cafe to the Interceptor. He drove to the police station and pulled up next to Guthrie's Xterra.

"Follow me," the chief instructed. "There's a trailer park out on the state road going north." He grinned. "You could call it Thorndike's northernmost suburb. It's not bad as trailer parks go. About fifty mobile homes in all. Most of the people who live there work on Miss Agnes's ranch. That's Agnes Carpenter. You haven't met her yet, but I'm sure you will. She owns the big spread west of the state road and north of Steele Creek. In fact, the trailer park is ten acres carved out of the flank of her property, but she doesn't own it. She sold it to Warren Evers, who used to work for her and her brother, Ed, before Ed died. The sale puzzled folks for a time until Warren started putting mobile homes on the plot, and it quickly filled up with some of Miss Agnes's employees. Mostly those who don't have the skills to move up to one of the houses in town or its outskirts." Turner shrugged. "I'm sure you know it isn't the fate of everyone to be capable of achieving what they aspire to."

Guthrie wrinkled his mouth and nodded sadly then got out of the Interceptor and into his own vehicle. He pulled out after the chief, who drove down Main Street to the state highway then turned north, toward the county seat. But they didn't go far. A little less than two miles farther on was Evers Trailer Park. Guthrie had noted it while perusing the satellite images of Thorndike.

Turner pulled in and drove up to a well-kept double-wide with a flower garden around its perimeter that sat prominently to the left. The rest of the trailer park looked pretty well maintained, too, with many of the homes bearing flower gardens and lawn furniture. Here and there, thirty-year-old oaks stood between the mobile homes, and half a dozen women were visible, sitting together in the shade, watching their children play. The place was more like a neighborhood than a way station for the transient.

Guthrie parked next to the Interceptor, got out of the Xterra, and followed Turner up to the door, where the chief rapped sharply. The door opened a few moments later, revealing a middle-aged man with a thick middle covered by a faded blue Led Zeppelin t-shirt. His stubbly gray hair and short gray beard gave his head the appearance of a large, fuzzy burr.

"Chief." He seemed surprised.

"Hi, Warren. Meet Clay Guthrie. He's working with me on a case. Clay, meet Warren Evers. He owns the trailer park."

"What can I do for you, Chief? It's not about that murder over at the dump, is it?"

"Not as far as you're concerned," Turner assured him. "Mr. Guthrie needs a place to stay, and I thought you might have an empty you could rent him for a few days at a reasonable rate."

"Sure," Evers said, coming down the steps and waving toward the rear of the park. "Got one right over there at the back. Folks moved out last week. I got it cleaned up, but nobody's moved in yet. Mr. Guthrie can stay there, if he likes."

"Clay?"

"It's okay with me," Guthrie said.

"Good," Turner responded. "Then I'll leave you two to negotiate. I need to get to the dump."

8

WARREN EVERS HAD LOANED GUTHRIE a set of bedclothes, a pillow, and a towel, but the pantry in the mobile home's kitchenette was bare, so as soon as Guthrie got out of bed and cleaned up the next morning, he drove into town. His first stop was Leo's Cafe. Seven other people were in the place in various stages of completing their meals. Neither Chief Turner nor Jim Chaney were among them. Guthrie took a seat at the counter, where Bev greeted him warmly.

"I want to thank you, Clay, for bringing this case to my husband," she said when she brought over a glass of water and a cup of coffee. "We both like the slower lifestyle here, but I confess Bill sometimes longs for a little action." She chuckled. "More action, at least, than the weekend fights down at the Lazy Q."

"It wasn't me who brought the case," Guthrie said, wondering if she'd still appreciate him later, when everything came to a head. "I just followed it here."

"That may be, but that body might have gone permanently undiscovered if you hadn't found it."

Considering the palpably foul odor and sinister aura that surrounded the sofa, Guthrie doubted that.

"Speaking of your husband, did he say where he'd be?"

"The dump. He said to tell you to go out there if I saw you."

"Thanks. I'll have two eggs over medium, sausage, grits, and whole wheat toast."

"That's the Number Three," she said. "For future reference."

She took his order to the kitchen service window, behind which Leo was busily attending to his griddle while his wife bustled about, cutting, chopping, and frying. After that, she toured the room with a pot of coffee and a pitcher of water, replenishing empty mugs and glasses. His food was ready in about ten minutes, and he tried to eat without wolfing it. He was anxious to get to the crime scene.

When he did, he found a woman state trooper guarding the gate.

"Sorry, sir," she said as Guthrie pulled to a stop beside her and rolled down his window. "The dump is closed until further notice." Her expression was businesslike, but it relaxed when Guthrie spoke.

"My name is Clay Guthrie. I think Chief Turner is expecting me."

"That's right, sir. Come on through, but you're going to have to park over there and walk in." She waved toward the wooden shack where half a dozen law enforcement vehicles, Turner's included, were parked.

"Thanks," Guthrie said as the trooper stepped back and touched the brim of her hat.

Guthrie parked next to Turner's Interceptor and got out, not bothering to lock the door. What was the point with a state trooper on guard not fifty feet away? He set off down the track that led to the back of the dump, passing two more troopers stationed along the way.

Usually law enforcement officers hang around crime scenes, maybe to try to spot something or just out of curiosity or routine. Or habit. But not here. Not a single one of the cluster of eight state troopers and sheriff's deputies was even as close as the CSI van that had backed down the track. Nodding as he passed, he noted their curiosity, but none said anything. They seemed subdued, and no wonder. Even from here, Guthrie could sense the edge of the malignant aura surrounding the sofa. The officers were unconsciously keeping on its periphery.

He skirted the van and came upon the pickup, a crime scene tech in a lightweight hazmat suit going through it. Then he saw Turner. The only law enforcement officer actually on the scene. He was standing near the back fence, just past the end of the last mound of refuse. The Kuei men were registering strongly, and the aura infusing the forty-foot clearing was palpably and uncomfortably foul. Guthrie was shielded from the worst of it by the Kuei men, but Turner wasn't. He looked tense, and on edge, but he didn't look like he was going anywhere.

He's a brave man, Guthrie thought, wondering how the chief was rationalizing the pervasive and invasive sensations. Probably just as extremely foul odor, which certainly was an obvious component.

Turner spotted him and waved him over. From his position, he could watch what was going on yet be out of the way. Portable lights used to illuminate the area while the techs worked through the night, now extinguished, stood around. Only four crime scene techs labored around the area: two over the sofa, one sifting through debris near it, and the last taking tire and shoe impressions from the margin between the last mound of debris and the hurricane fence. The corpse had been lifted off the sofa and was now encased in a black bodybag on top of a blue plastic tarp. Guthrie wished he could get a closer look, but the body bag was zipped shut. The two blue moving quilts, neatly folded but not yet bagged, lay on the tarp beside the bodybag.

"Anything?" he asked.

Turner shook his head.

"No wallet, phone, keys, or anything else. All they can say is he appears to have been in his forties."

"You're sure it's not Freddie?"

"They brought me over for another look as soon as they laid him out," Turner said. "It's definitely not Freddie. He does resemble the photo of Norman Telfor you showed me, but the condition of the body makes it hard to be sure from a simple visual examination."

One of the people working the scene—a tall man with a medium build—straightened and came over. He pulled off his face mask, revealing a middle-aged, saturnine face with a serious, almost pained, expression topped by graying hair cut short.

"I have to say, Bill, Thorndike must have the cleanest dump in the county. I expected this corpse to be half eaten-up by insects and other scavengers, but I can't say I've seen a single insect, birds, or rodent here. Not much stink, either, at least until you get close to that thing." He threw a wave at the sofa. "Y'all spray this place regularly with Lysol?" He looked at Guthrie. "Who's this?"

"Clay, this is our county medical examiner, Dr. Robert Latimer, more popularly known as Dr. Bob. Doc, this is Clay Guthrie, the PI I told you about."

"Well, Mr. Guthrie," Latimer said. "You've sure given us a puzzle. And a nasty one, at that." He shook his head as if to clear it. "I've seen a lot of crime scenes over the past twenty years, and this has to be the most unpleasant despite the lack of blood and gore." He shook his head again. "I don't know what it is, but it's almost like the nastiness is more than decay, which, I'm sure, you've already noted the lack of. This body desiccated, almost like all the moisture was sucked out of it. Fairly quickly, I'd say, but not quickly enough to cause hemorrhaging anywhere if you discount the chest wound. But even if he'd bled out completely, he wouldn't have turned into that." He gestured toward the body bag. "Thank goodness we have these hazmat suits, but even so, the air around the body and the sofa is pretty hard to bear."

Guthrie knew what he meant. With the quilts and body removed, the sofa exuded an effluvium that wasn't just odor but a sense of corruption and dread that suffused the atmosphere around it. Even at thirty feet, the sensation was strong, but his Kuei men were no longer twitching as much as they had when he and Turner first discovered the body. It was as if unveiling the corpse and sofa to the air and light of day and separating them was dissipating the corruption, albeit slowly. Maybe the Kuei men were reacting to some sort of residue that clung to them and was gradually evaporating. That meant that neither the body nor the sofa were the main source of infection, merely repositories, though definitely the sofa was far more contaminated.

But what, exactly, had been the source of the contamination, and where was it now?

"Bill says you think he might be the man you've been looking for," Latimer said.

"That's right."

Latimer shook his head.

"I don't see how that's possible. Your man disappeared, what, only a week ago? Considering the condition of the body...." He shook his head, a perplexed expression on his face. "I don't know what to think. I've never seen anything quite like it."

"Chief Turner says the body was stripped clean of identification and personal items."

"Not entirely. Whoever searched him missed this." Latimer pulled a small, sealed, clear plastic baggie from his pocket and held it up. "It was around his neck, under his shirt."

Guthrie peered at the contents of the bag and saw that it was some sort of small gold pendant on a lightweight gold chain. The pendant was spotted with dried blood.

"It's a Saint Christopher's medal," the ME said. He shook his head again. "It didn't give much protection to this traveler."

"Speaking of his shirt, Norm Telfor's wife said he was wearing a Dallas Cowboys t-shirt when he left."

"I'm sure you noticed the deceased is wearing one, too," Dr. Bob said. "That's one indication he's the man you're looking for."

"Any cause of death?" Turner inquired, and that gave Latimer something to work with other than his puzzlement and discomfort.

"My preliminary examination shows he was shot once in the chest at close range. From the amount of blood, the bullet probably pierced his heart. Most likely he was dead before he was placed on the sofa, but not long before since there's some blood on the quilts and sofa cushions. Not much, though. He was definitely dead by then. There should be a lot of blood where he was shot. I'll be able to tell you more after I get him on the table." He glanced over his shoulder at the tech processing the sofa. "I'd better get back," he said. "I don't want to leave David alone with that thing. I'll call you as soon as we have a complete report."

"Here's the detective in charge of the case in Oakdale, Louisiana," Guthrie said, passing over the business card Detective Peters had given him. He'd already plugged the detective's number into his phone. "He can probably arrange to have some genetic material couriered here. That way we'll know for sure if it's Norman Telfor or not."

"That would help," Latimer nodded."

"Thanks," Turner said, and Latimer returned to his colleague.

"What now?" Guthrie asked. "Freddie? He must have something to say about this. If he's alive."

"I have a bunch of local men combing the area around here and his house to see if a body turns up, but so far, nothing. If he's out there, the buzzards will let us know pretty quick. But I can't look for him right now. I need to go on patrol since I sent Emmet home to get some sleep. You can ride along, if you want. If you're still with me, that is, until we're sure we found your boy."

"I am."

What Guthrie didn't say was that he had to find out what was behind Telfor's disappearance and death. Tereba had sent him here to deal with something out of the ordinary—something that had apparently destroyed three towns—and, if possible, eliminate it. And because of the strange location and condition of the body— and especially because of the strong twitching of the Kuei men around the sofa and, to a lesser extent, in the woods in Jim Chaney's marsh—he knew it wasn't a case of simple murder.

As they walked toward the front of the dump, Turner told Guthrie he'd done a background check on George Rand the night before but hadn't found anything criminal on him in the Texas law enforcement databases.

"He has a Texas drivers license issued two years ago, and he owns a townhouse in Dallas as well as the old Chaney place, but other than that, he seems clean."

Considering the squirming of the Kuei men when he'd been around Rand, Guthrie doubted the man was clean.

"You suspect him of something?" Guthrie asked.

"Nothing I can pin any facts on. But you didn't like him, and neither did I."

"Do you want to question him again?"

"About what? We need more information."

They reached the vehicles, and Turner suggested that Guthrie follow him into town and park at the police station. After that, Turner would do the driving. They followed the plan, and inside of fifteen minutes, Guthrie was seated in the Interceptor as Turner pulled out of the parking lot then turned left on Main Street.

9

"THAT'S WHERE BEV AND I live."

Turner pointed to a 1960s-era red-brick ranch-style house on Main Street, just east of the police station. A newer red brick than covered many of the older buildings in town. Two legs of the town's water tower were located on the back corner of the lot, the other two at the rear of the police station.

"The good news is that Thorndike mows my yard, and I have the best water pressure in town. The bad news is my office is practically next door, and nobody around here seems to understand the difference between it and my home."

The chief drove on, pointing out various features. Guthrie had driven a lot of backroads in Texas during his life and seen a lot of little towns not too different from Thorndike, but he'd never really done more than drive through or past them. The tour Turner took him on really fleshed in the life that kept Thorndike viable.

They started by driving the town's southeast quadrant. It was residential, but only two of the six streets running north–south were paved, the rest and the few connecting side streets were composite dirt and gravel. The lots tended to be a third of an acre or more, though many were empty and overgrown, particularly the larger ones toward the southern periphery of the neighborhood, giving the area a threadbare appearance.

Modest houses, ranging from solid brick to ramshackle wooden structures, were the norm along the streets closest to Main, but a large number of the outlying lots held mobile homes. Only a handful of the houses seemed newer than forty years. Driveways of the same composition as the streets ended in small garages, prefab metal carports, or often, nothing at all but bare, greasy patches on the ground. A lot of the properties had small metal buildings, barns, and pole barns, making it appear as if their owners had once operated businesses out of them, but most now seemed like overgrown rural homesteads. Or maybe a disused and overgrown pole barn or shed was de rigueur in a small town like Thorndike.

A modest wooden church built on a pier and beam foundation and surrounded by old oaks sat toward the southern edge of the neighborhood, and Turner waved toward it as they passed.

"That's the Methodist Church. You probably saw the Baptist Church in the next block over from the police station. It's the biggest, and the smallest is an Assembly of God out on the state road going north."

"I saw that on the way to the trailer park. No Catholic Church or synagog? No mosque?" Guthrie asked.

"There's a Catholic Church and a synagog up in the county seat, but you'd have to go to Houston or Dallas to find a mosque. You can imagine folks around here aren't too fond of Islam."

"You seem at least tolerant." Guthrie was thinking as much of Turner hiring a black officer as he was of religion.

Turner shrugged.

"I was in the Army," Turner said. "Did one tour in the Middle East and another in Europe. You learn a lot in the military, especially serving overseas. Some of it isn't about warfare and killing, especially when you find yourself immersed in another culture." He shrugged. "I can't say I'm fond of Islam, but I met a lot of nice Muslim folks in the Middle East, and they all hated the terrorists as much as we do. Besides, these days it seems that every country and religion has its terrorists. What about you? How'd you become a PI?"

"It's not a long story," Guthrie said. "I was a Houston cop and was wounded in the line of duty. I was too young to grow old and fat behind a desk, so I took a disability pension, though it wasn't much. Barely enough to survive. Over the next couple of years, I found I was eating myself up with bad memories, and I realized I had to do something to get myself out of the despondency I'd sunken into. Policing was all I'd wanted to do, but with that taken away, becoming a PI was the next best thing."

"It gets in the blood," Turner said, nodding.

After a few more turns, he drove across Main Street, into the neighborhood in the northeast quadrant of town. The houses here were more substantial and newer than on the south side, though a lot of them also had metal buildings or secondary structures on their large lots. But unlike those to the south, several of these housed viable businesses. The doctor's office was there, as well as Marnie's Resale Shop, a beauty salon, and a small-engine repair shop. Thorndike might be modest, Guthrie thought, but it had all the basics.

Thorndike's school sat on a substantial plot a couple of blocks north east of the police station and Baptist Church. It consisted of two main buildings, one old, one of recent vintage. The older building was a simple, rectangular, two-story brown brick structure with lots of large, white-framed sash windows facing an empty square asphalt parking lot in front. The newer one sat to the original building's left, and it looked like it might hold a gymnasium. Four temporary classroom trailers stood to the right of the original building, and the grounds behind were taken up with playground equipment and playing fields.

"You're looking at the entirety of Thorndike's school system," Turner said. "First through twelve. Classes ended for the year about two weeks ago. They used to combine the first three grades into one, but they trucked in those temporary classrooms a few years ago, and now each grade has its own teacher. The original building was built after the war." He chuckled. "World War Two, that is. The newer one holds the gym. Wish we'd had it when I was going there. We can thank Miss Agnes for that since she donated the money. In fact, we can thank her for saving the school. For a time, the town council thought it'd be cheaper to bus our kids to the county seat, but Miss Agnes put a stop to that by setting up a trust fund for the school."

"You mentioned her earlier."

"Yeah. Agnes Carpenter. My dad was her foreman for most of the time I was growing up. You'll meet her soon enough, I suppose. She likes to keep her finger on Thorndike's pulse. Most folks consider her the queen of our town. She has some economic and political power but even more social influence. You could say I owe a lot of my tolerance to growing up around her."

After cruising by the school, Turner swung left, down the street that went past the Baptist Church, which sprawled across the entire block just north of and across the street from the police station. He drove by the feed store and auto repair on the right and the police station on the left then turned right on Main Street and headed west. Past the funeral home on their right and Leo's Cafe on the left, the downtown ended, and well-kept early twentieth-century homes strung along the roadsides for a quarter of a mile. The homes on the left continued, but the lots on the north side were replaced by larger plots of land. First came a large square holding the city park. A spare scattering of playground equipment and picnic tables were thoughtfully placed beneath a canopy of half a dozen spreading oaks, and several women, children, and young teenagers were there, taking advantage of the nice weather.

"We don't have much going on in the park most of the time," Turner said. "During the school year, the kids are too busy, and in another month, it'll be too blasted hot. The only real activity there in the summer is the Fourth of July picnic."

The next plot on the right held Stansic Oilfield Services. The company was, Turner explained, Thorndike's largest business aside from the ranches. The company consisted of an old white bungalow close to the road, with three medium to large sheetmetal buildings filling up most of the remainder of the property. Racks of drill pipe were next to one of the buildings, and a couple of trucks with stainless-steel tank trailers hooked to them stood on the dirt and gravel parking lot in front.

'That's where Enid Chaney's dad worked, but that was back when Floyd Stansic owned the place. His son, Dale, runs it now. He and his wife lived in the house, but Bev tells me she's pressuring him to move into our better neighborhood."

Spread across a broad, bare field behind the oilfield services company was Thorndike's cemetery.

"Yeah," Turner said when Guthrie commented on the size of the graveyard. "Some years we have more deaths than births, though that's starting to change. There's another cemetery south of town, just off the east end of the marsh, but it's a lot smaller and older and isn't used much anymore. Mostly old settlers and their families are buried there, including Jim Chaney's parents and all the rest of the Chaneys.

Enid's buried there, and I guess he's got a plot, too." He shook his head. "The last of the Chaneys. Hard to believe."

The houses on the left side of the road ended right across the street from the oilfield service company, where the final lot was occupied by a well-kept bungalow with a new blue metal roof and a flowerbed in front of a concrete slab porch. To the right of the house sat a wide and neat tan metal building, a sign in front proclaiming it was the home of the Canine Cottage.

"That's our vet, Dr. Hughes," Turner said. "He and his wife, Mabel, also breed Great Pyrenees. They're great herd watchdogs, big enough to take on coyotes." He gave a short chuckle. "Kind of an odd business for a town like ours, but people come here from all over the state to buy them."

Ahead, past several large vacant, grassy areas on either side, Main Street ended at the state road. Easily visible less than a quarter of a mile to the right was Thorndike's only gas station: the Pit Stop.

"Not much up that way you haven't seen," Turner said. "Just the Assembly of God and the trailer park. How are the accommodations?"

"It's a trailer," Guthrie said, "but Warren loaned me some bedding, so it's comfortable enough. Thanks. I wouldn't mind having an internet connection, though. Think you can arrange it?"

"I'll give Warren a call," Turner said then steered south on the state road, pointing out more features, such as Johnson AgLime, Thorndike's second-largest company, which comprised two older sheetmetal buildings flanked on the left by a mobile home that served as the office.

"They mine and crush limestone into a powder that farmers spread on fields to improve soil structure and crop productivity. Some of the ranchers use it in animal pens to help keep the ground dry. Kinda like kitty litter. It's owned by Gary Johnson. He used to work out at the same quarry where Freddie worked, but he managed to make more of himself than Freddie did after the place shut down."

The third-largest company—one that repaired and sold used farming equipment—was a quarter of a mile farther down the road and on the other side. The hulks of rusting tractors, plows, harvesters, and other farm machinery in the overgrown grassy lot said this business wasn't as profitable as the others.

"That's Al Henley's place," Turner said when he saw Guthrie staring. "He ekes out a living repairing equipment for the smaller farmers and ranchers, but even that business is drying up. He's in his late six-ties, now, so it probably doesn't much matter to him anymore."

The last call they made was to Thorndike's roadhouse. Facing a wide dirt and gravel parking lot, it looked like it might once have been an old country store. The big, square false front above a shallow cov-ered veranda was painted light gray and bore the inscription, "The Lazy Q," in blocky black letters. Simple wings with sloping corrugated tin roofs added to both sides had more than doubled the interior space of the original structure. Standing off to the left of the building was a long, narrow, crudely built house sheathed with wooden siding painted in the same light gray as the roadhouse. The paint on both buildings was dingy with age, but the roof on the house was newer tin in an off-white. A satellite TV dish was mounted on one end. Instead of driving by, Turner veered into the parking lot.

"If some towns have a wrong side of the tracks," he comment-ed as he parked in front of the building, "this is one all by itself, even if Thorndike doesn't have any tracks." He switched off the SUV. "This is a likely place that Freddie might come. Let's go in and see if Frank's seen him. Frank Orman," he clarified at Guthrie's puzzled look. "He owns the place."

Guthrie followed the chief up the steps, across the narrow cov-ered veranda, and through the front door. Inside, the place was not substantial, but it was dim and cool. The air had a yeasty smell. At the back of the addition on the left side, a low bandstand presided over a modest dance floor surrounded by red formica-topped tables with tubular metal frames and matching chairs with padded vinyl seats and backs. The righthand addition had more tables except for a cleared area at the back that held two pool tables. The original, central structure contained the bar, behind which were racks of liquor and a door into a back area. Office and storage, Guthrie sur-mised. A chunky middle-aged man with longish but thinning blonde hair going gray and gathered into a skimpy ponytail stood behind the bar, and even at this relatively early hour, six patrons were in the place: four men sitting together at a table and a couple of others perched on barstools.

The murmur of conversation in the room evaporated as soon as Guthrie and Turner entered, and Guthrie thought he caught a flash of hostility from the men at the table. Turner ignored them as he stepped up to the bar.

"Hi, Frank," he said as the bartender came over to them. "How's business?"

"What you see is what you get," Frank said tersely. He didn't seem especially pleased to see Turner. "Something I can do for you, Chief?"

"Mr. Guthrie, this is Frank Orman. Frank, meet Mr. Guthrie. He's working with me on a case."

"The dead man out at the dump?"

"We're looking for Freddie Jensen. Have you seen him in the last couple of days?"

"Can't say so," Orman said. "Is he involved?"

"When was the last time you saw him?"

"Maybe a week ago. Before last weekend. He don't come in here much when we got a crowd."

Turner surveyed the room.

"How about any of the rest of you? Anybody seen Freddie Jensen?"

"Ain't seen him recently," came a voice from the table, rising among mutters of denial from the others. The speaker was a big man with a head of brown hair and a seriously thick and dangling Fu Manchu mustache. "He's probably lying out somewheres in the dump, drunk as a skunk."

"How about you, Will?" Turner said to one of the men at the bar. "He hires on with the Fredericks sometimes, and you work for them. Freddie been out there the last few days?"

"I ain't seen him recently."

"You looking to arrest him?" asked another of the four men at the table. He, too, was big and had a long, square-cut full beard and a shaved head. His voice was nearly a sneer.

"Relax, Wiley. Nobody's arresting anybody, at least until the next time you get drunk and start a fight. We just want to ask him a few questions. Tell him I'm looking for him if you see him."

This last was directed at Orman but said loud enough for everyone in the place to hear. Then Turner headed for the door.

"Kind of a hostile group in there," Guthrie said when they emerged into the sunlight.

"I suppose so." Turner chuckled. "Even Frank doesn't like me much, but he tolerates me because I break up the fights that happen here almost every weekend before they break up his bar. But I guess almost all the others like me a whole lot less since I've hauled every one of the men at the table to jail more times than I care to count.

The one who spoke up first is Lonnie Sanford, and the others with him are his older brother, Wiley, Johnny Miller, and Rob Fitzgerald. If you haven't guessed it already, they're the main troublemakers, and they like to fight, especially with folks smaller and weaker than them." He shook his head. "It's weird how misbehaving people always get mad at the ones calling them out on their misbehavior."

"Ain't that the truth," Guthrie said.

They got into Turner's SUV.

"Where to now, Chief," Guthrie asked. "I think you've just about showed me the whole town."

"Well, the Lazy Q is Thorndike's southernmost building. But let's go on down a bit, and I'll show you where Steele Creek runs under the road. You can see the western edge of the marsh off to the side."

Steele Creek was about a mile farther on, and after they passed over it, Turner U-turned, pulled onto the bridge, and stopped so Guthrie could see the creek as it meandered off into the thicket of the marsh. He couldn't see very deeply into the wetland, but he did notice well-worn tire tracks running off the road and down the embankment.

"People fish down there?" Guthrie asked.

Turner laughed.

"Some people fish down there, but there's not a whole lot to catch. Not this far out of the marsh. You'd have to go in deeper, and all that's Jim Chaney's posted land."

His radio crackled to life.

"Chief Turner," Tessa's voice said. "Come in, Chief."

Turner lifted the mic.

"Turner here."

"I think you need to come into the station, Chief. The ME called to say he's taken the body to the morgue in the county seat, but now a couple of FBI agents are here and want to talk to you."

"I'll be there in about ten minutes," Turner said, and he replaced the mic in its holder.

"The FBI," he said, a certain amount of resignation in his voice. "I guess they had to show up considering the interstate aspect. I suppose they'll want to talk to you, too."

"Let's get it over with," Guthrie said, and Turner pulled off, heading back to town.

10

THE FBI AGENTS INTRODUCED THEMSELVES as Laura Wilson and Charles Aznar, stationed out of the Dallas office. Wilson, a black woman in her early forties, was the lead. Aznar, Hispanic, looked a handful of years younger.

"Sorry to barge in on your case, Chief," Wilson said after they'd all settled into chairs in Turner's office. There were three chairs in front of the desk, so Tessa must have brought in one from the outer office. "But it looks like we have a possible interstate kidnapping."

"Dr. Latimer says there wasn't much blood on the sofa and he must have been killed elsewhere," Turner said.

"There's every indication that's so, but the Bureau likes to cover all the possibilities."

"Has there been a ransom demand?" Guthrie asked.

"No," Wilson said, looking at him. "You're the person who led Chief Turner to the body?"

"Clay Guthrie. That would be a mischaracterization. I was hired to look for Mr. Telfor and enlisted Chief Turner in my search. We discovered the body purely by chance."

Guthrie saw Turner give him the evil eye, but the chief said nothing.

"You're a PI?" Wilson asked.

"That's right. Licensed in Texas and Louisiana."

He explained that he'd been hired by Mutual Indemnity to find out what happened to Telfor, and the search that began in Oakdale ended in Thorndike.

"Chief, you want to tell us what happened?"

Turner did, beginning with Guthrie walking into the police station around noon the day before and ending with the discovery of the body.

"Any news from the coroner's office?" Turner asked. "Are we even sure it's Norman Telfor?"

"A little," Aznar said after getting a nod from Wilson. "Genetic material from Telfor's wife arrived by courier only about an hour ago, and it'll take several days to process, so we won't know for sure until then. But we do have a good indication. As you already know, the body was stripped of everything that could readily identify it, but one item was left behind."

"The ME showed us a Saint Christopher medal," Turner said.

"Whoever searched the deceased must not have noticed it beneath his shirt," Aznar said. "We sent a photo of it to Detective Peters, and he showed it to Mrs. Telfor, who positively identified it as belonging to her husband. We can't be absolutely sure until the fingerprint evidence or genetic sequencing come in, but it looks like the body is definitely Norman Telfor."

"Betsy Telfor told me that Norm left wearing this Dallas Cowboys t-shirt," Guthrie said, pulling out the photo of Norm with his wife and passing it to Wilson.

"That's what was on the body," she said, glancing at the photo before handing it back. "That helps lock in the ID."

"What did you do with the sofa?" Guthrie asked.

"The sofa?" Wilson looked puzzled for a moment then understood. "Oh, that. God, what an awful thing that is." She shook her head as if to clear cobwebs from her thoughts. "It's almost impossible to believe Mr. Telfor could have driven all the way here with that in the back of his van. I don't think I could stand to be around it for more than a few minutes. It's been hauled up to the coroner's office for further examination, along with the truck that was found at the scene. From what I hear, the forensics team doesn't even want to go near it without full hazmat suits, and you know how tough those people are. But so far, it's a blank. A filthy, nasty blank. In more ways than one. Apparently, the body didn't suppurate the way most corpses do, so all that filth on it didn't come from Mr. Telfor's decay but was there before he was placed on it."

What decay? Guthrie thought as she focused on him.

"Any idea why Telfor might have been hired to drive that sofa to a dump more than two hundred miles from home?"

"I was going to ask exactly that if I found him."

"Well, nobody's asking him anything now." She directed her attention to Turner. "The forensics team has wrapped up at the crime scene, so we're releasing it to you. Since it's in the town dump, you might want to open it up, but I advise keeping any incoming refuse from that area."

"Thanks," Turner said. "Let me know if you learn anything else."

"We'll do that," Wilson assured. "We'll be looking into this for a couple of more days, but unless something shakes loose, we'll be sent on to another assignment. Since Mr. Telfor and the van were stripped of everything, it's reasonable to assume that robbery was the motive and that his death was a consequence of that. So, it looks like there hasn't been a kidnapping, here, just a simple robbery and murder."

Or not so simple, Guthrie thought. Apparently the agents didn't think that Telfor's body being found in Thorndike and his van in Airla was an issue. Or the condition of the body and the sofa. He didn't bring up any of that.

"You're probably right," he said. He wanted the agents to believe they understood the whole matter. That would leave the case to the local authorities. And him. Even if the agents were sincere, they'd never understand what might be going on in Thorndike. He was going to have a tough enough time convincing Chief Turner that their enemy might not be conventional. Or natural.

"I guess that hands jurisdiction back to you, Chief," Wilson said, rising. Aznar followed. "We'll be in touch if something comes up. I trust you'll do the same?"

"I will," Turner said, ushering the agents to his office door. "Thanks." Guthrie thought he caught a touch of sarcasm in that last word.

When the agents were gone, the chief turned sardonic eyes on Guthrie and twitched his mustache.

"Did you hear that? 'I advise keeping any incoming refuse from that area.' No shit. Condescending, aren't they?"

"I guess you don't think they'll be forthcoming."

Turner gave a laughing snort.

"Did you hear them call this a simple robbery and murder? Does it look simple to you, even if there wasn't a kidnapping? Why'd Telfor's body end up here and his van in Airla? And foremost, if your goal is robbery, why rob a man who apparently had very little to steal except his van, which technically wasn't stolen? And why did Norm have the address of our dump?"

"My thoughts, exactly," Guthrie answered, glad that Turner didn't ask where he'd obtained the address. "There are still too many unanswered questions. If the motive of the man who hired Telfor was robbery and murder, he probably would have been from Oakdale since nobody was in Airla and nobody here knew Telfor."

"Maybe a jealous lover in Oakdale hired him on the sly and lured him out to Airla, where he knew there'd be no witnesses," Turner ventured. "Maybe the robbery aspect is just to cover up the real motive."

"Norm Telfor was philandering, lured out of town, and killed by a jealous lover then driven hundreds of miles to Thorndike?" Guthrie shook his head. "Besides, like Betsy Telfor told me, who'd want a broke and broken-down middle-aged man with a broken down truck and a beer gut? Besides her?"

"Maybe *she* didn't, anymore. Maybe it was *her* jealous lover, and they both killed him to collect the insurance. One of them drove his body to our dump where it wasn't likely to be discovered or identified, then drove the van back to Airla to pick up their own vehicle."

"Not her. She's genuinely in grief, and she didn't seem to know about the insurance."

Probably because Tereba and his colleagues had arranged it to give Guthrie a legitimate reason to seek out Telfor. One more thing he couldn't tell Turner.

"Besides," he went on, "why bother driving all this way? They could have killed him in Airla and just left him there. Betsy could have said she didn't know where Norm had gone, then she and this purported lover wouldn't have had to create a fiction about Airla and some unidentified Texas town. Which turned out to be real."

"Yeah," Turner nodded. "That sofa certainly isn't fiction, either. That's another stick in the craw. Literally." He grimaced. "We know Norm was picking up a sofa in Airla and delivering it here, and we found him on one, covered with moving quilts, probably his own. It must have come from Airla. But why would someone looking to dump the body where it wasn't likely to be discovered or identified bring the sofa, too?"

Because, Guthrie mused, Norm Telfor was just peripheral. It was his van that counted—an obscure means to get the sofa from one place to another. What really counted was the sofa. Or something that had ridden on the sofa. Something that had ingrained its being into the fabric, padding, and ticking and clung there long enough to make the journey from Airla to Thorndike. Something that had destroyed two villages in southern Louisiana before laying waste to Airla. And as Agent Wilson noted, it would be very difficult for a person—a normal person—to remain for long in an enclosed space with the sofa. Certainly not long enough to make the drive to Thorndike. Even protected by the Kuci men, Guthrie didn't believe he could, which made him certain that Telfor hadn't done the driving but had been killed in Airla and brought to Thorndike with the sofa. But who had done the driving, and why bring Telfor's body along? Who could stand to be in an enclosed space with that thing for that long? And why Thorndike?

Then it struck him that maybe whatever the rider on the sofa was, it had been given Telfor's body to feed off of during the trip. That might account for its bizarre condition. Guthrie didn't know what the rider was or where it might now be, but he knew one thing for sure: There was no way he could broach any of this to Turner. Not now, though perhaps that time might come.

"Good question," was all he said.

"You don't think someone here killed him?"

"No. The van was in Airla, and if the killer lived here, how would he even know what or where Airla is or that the lumber mill was abandoned? Telfor's driver's license would have showed he lived in Oakdale. Besides, Dr. Bob thinks he bled to death somewhere else. Probably Airla."

"I guess that's right. It makes more sense that he was killed there and his body taken far away to avoid identification. That would explain the van." Turner didn't express it much, but he visibly brightened. "So that would mean the body's here purely by chance. It could have been any dump anywhere. It just happened to be here."

Events like that don't just happen, Guthrie mused, but he was saved from commenting by a sudden subdued rumble sounding from the chief's side of the desk. It was the chief's stomach growling, and he looked a bit embarrassed.

"I guess it's a little past my feeding time," he said. "I've been up since before dawn, and goin' and blowin' ever since. What say we visit Leo's?"

"I ate before I went out to the dump," Guthrie said. "I think I'll go over to the grocery and get some supplies. I'll check in later."

Nodding, Turner collected his Stetson, and he and Guthrie left the station. Outside, they split, Turner heading toward the cafe while Guthrie walked across the street to the small grocery store—Chaloupek Grocery. There, he loaded a cart with some essentials to stock the trailer's empty larder, including a small drip coffee maker, then rolled the cart to the checkout counter. The clerk was a woman in her early-thirties, mousy brown hair cut short and ragged and tattoos on her arms. Her face was fairly attractive except for the sour look on it, the wrinkles around her eyes and mouth indicating the expression was habitual. The name "Hetty" was printed on the tag perched crookedly on her pneumatic chest.

"I guess you can tell I'm new in town," Guthrie said conversationally as she rang up his purchases.

"I guess," she replied, avoiding eye contact.

"I'm working with Chief Turner on the case involving that man who was found in the dump."

"I guess I heard about that," she said, eyes on her work.

"Have you happened to see Freddie Jensen in the last few days?"

"Is Freddie involved?" She looked at him for the first time, curiosity damping down the sullenness in her eyes.

"Probably not directly, though he might have seen something."

"Most everbody thinks he's dead." She stopped shuffling groceries across the scanner, and the gleam of curiosity in her eyes took on a knowing edge.

"We have no reason to believe that," Guthrie told her, noticing the look in her eyes. "What about you?"

"Well," she said reluctantly. "I guess I know he ain't 'cause he come in yesterday and bought a bunch a canned goods."

"Did you see how he got here?"

Her face twisted into a frown for a moment before returning to its sour mode.

"Mister, I'm inside the store. How you think I can tell how people get here?"

"Did he say anything to you about the dump or where he might be going?"

"If he did," she said huffily, "I don't remember. He's a stinkin' drunk, anyway, and you can't believe a thing he says. 'Sides, I ain't got nothin' to do with him or that body at the dump, and that's all I gotta say."

She went back to ringing up Guthrie's purchases, tight lips and sullen posture signaling she was done talking about Freddie or anything else. Guthrie paid, left the store, carried the four plastic sacks of groceries across the street to his Xterra, and piled them on the back seat. Then he went to find Turner. He walked to Leo's and glanced through the front window, but apparently the chief had finished eating lunch and returned to the station. Guthrie walked over and went inside.

"Back so soon?" Turner asked, looking up as Guthrie entered his office.

"I have something to report. The checkout clerk at the grocery, told me Freddie came in yesterday and bought some canned goods."

"Hetty Mruska," Turner snapped, slapping his desk top. "Goddamnit, she should have told me. We might have been able to catch up with him."

"At least, we know Freddie was alive as of yesterday."

"There is that," Turner acknowledged.

"Unfortunately, he didn't tell her where he was going."

"There's that, too." Turner rose, stepped to the hat rack, and picked up his Stetson. "Or maybe he did, and she just didn't want to say. I'm going over there and chew her out."

"I think I'll pass on that visit, if you don't mind."

"No problem. I want to talk to the Chaloupeks, anyway. Maybe they saw something or know something Hetty doesn't. Or won't say."

"She was pretty cold to me," Guthrie said. "Is she a problem?"

"Not really unless you count a generally bad attitude as a problem" Turner said as they left his office and headed toward the front door. "Remember Lonnie Sanford from the Lazy Q? The one with the bushy Fu Manchu?" Guthrie nodded. "Well, she's his girlfriend, so you can imagine what she's like when she's not at work. A lot of weekend nights, she's down at the Q, drinking it up with the boys and triggering fights, though she rarely gets physically involved. She lets Lonnie and Wiley finish up what she started, which they're only too happy to do."

They left the station and went their separate ways, Turner striding purposefully across the street toward the grocery store. Guthrie got into his Xterra, pulled onto Main, and drove west.

At the trailer, he put away the groceries then gathered his dirty clothes and took them to the small, cement-block laundromat that sat amidst the mobile homes, wishing he'd brought more. With the few he had, he'd be washing them every couple of days. While he was waiting, Warren Evers came in.

"Saw you was in here, so I thought I'd bring this over." Evers handed Guthrie a slip of paper. "That's my wifi code and a temporary password. Chief Turner said you might need 'em."

"Thanks," Guthrie said. "I appreciate it."

"No thanks necessary. I worked for Miss Agnes for a long time, mostly under Grady Turner, and he was always fair with me. Can't do no less for his son, 'specially if it helps that murder investigation."

After the clothes were clean and dry, Guthrie returned to the mobile home and stowed them in the closet. Then he sat down at the dinette table, laptop opened in front of him, and input the wifi code and password. Guthrie was grateful. The trailer didn't have a TV, and the wifi gave Guthrie access to media as well as communications. Later, tired from the long day, he fixed a simple meal then settled down to the laptop to try to relax and wait for sleep to shuttle him to tomorrow.

II

SUNDAY MORNING'S DAWN WAS OBSCURED by an overcast sky. Guthrie ate a bowl of cereal and fixed a short pot of coffee. From what Chief Turner told him the day before, nearly the whole town would spend much of the morning in one of Thorndike's three churches. Even Leo didn't open his cafe until eleven to take advantage of the after-church crowd. Guthrie phoned the police station, and Tessa informed him that Turner was in church with Bev and their daughter, Emily, and would be back in the office afterward.

Not wanting to spend the morning surrounded by the mobile home's cheap paneling and intensely minimalist decor, Guthrie locked the trailer, got into his Xterra, and drove south. He didn't turn toward town, though, but continued on past the Lazy Q. The twinging of the Kuei men when he and Turner visited Chaney's cabin had made him curious about the marsh. He knew he could park off the shoulder where Steele Creek ran under the road, and he wanted to see if he could explore the marsh from there.

He was surprised to find two vehicles already parked on the shoulder by the bridge: an old brown Ford Ranger and a full-size, two-tone blue Chevy pickup, also old. Somebody must be fishing down in the creek, he thought. He parked on the grassy margin next to the shoulder and walked down the embankment to the the water. The creek bed and the woods beyond were partially obscured by the residue of nighttime mists, but then, Jim Chaney had said it was often foggy down here, south of town.

Guthrie didn't see anyone, but he did spot a well-worn path beside the creek leading into the mist-shrouded marsh, so he cautiously headed down it. The Kuei men weren't acting up, but the forest was thick and silent over the flowing stream, and the mists lent a somber feel despite the frolicking of a pair of squirrels in an oak, the bright hum of insects, and birds flitting from tree to tree.

Thirty feet from the state road, he encountered a barbed-wire fence. A sign on a fencepost read, "Posted, No Trespassing," but the wires were cut where they crossed the path. Somebody besides Jim Chaney, he thought, is familiar with this place.

A couple of hundred feet into the forest, the shape of a man resolved out of the low mists. He was sitting on a camp stool and wearing khaki pants, a blue shirt, and an old blue baseball cap. Even from behind, Guthrie could tell he was Hispanic. He was set up where the creek finally widened into a true pond, though this far upstream, the pond was still narrow, with banks that wound along the tree lines on either side as they expanded eastwardly, in the direction of Chaney's cabin. Guthrie estimated that the cabin was probably half a mile away though it was masked by the bank's curves and the trees, brush, and weeds growing nearly to the water's edge.

Two metal fishing rod holders were jammed into the ground, one on either side of the man, the right one empty, the left one full, and he gripped a second rod in his right hand. Guthrie's sneaker soles were silent on the soft, damp earth of the path, and the mists muffled the sounds of his approach. As he neared, he could hear the man humming tunelessly as he twitched the lure on the end of the line. The man finally heard a footfall when Guthrie was about twenty feet from him and just about to speak. He jolted to his feet, dropping the rod into the water, and spun, body stiff with fear, fists clenched.

"Fuck!" The word almost choked out of the man's throat. "What the fuck, man? Why you sneaking up on me?"

"Sorry," Guthrie said, holding up his hands. "I didn't mean to startle you."

"Well, you scared the crap outta me."

The fear of surprise relaxed from the man's face, replaced by another fear—that of bigotry and violence. The man cast his eyes around, searching for anyone accompanying Guthrie.

"I'm alone," Guthrie said. "And I mean you no harm. I just want to ask you a few questions."

The man appeared to be in his mid-fifties. He was a little shorter than Guthrie's own medium height and was stocky. His shock of black hair bore traces of gray.

"Okay," the man said, giving a hangdog look. "You caught me fair and square stealin' Mr. Jim's fish."

"Are they good fish?"

The man looked startled by the question.

"Good? Good to eat, you mean?" He nodded cautiously. "Yes, sir. Good to eat."

"Then you better pick up that rod you dropped and get back to fishing. You were humming when I came up, so I assume you can talk while you fish."

"You mean you ain't here about me fishin'?"

"No." Guthrie was here to ask about the marsh, and that now seemed even more important because as he'd walked deeper into it, the Kuei men had started squirming. Not much, but enough to warn Guthrie of nearby, if faint, danger.

The man gave a nervous chuckle then bent to retrieve his rod. But instead of continuing to fish, he simply reeled in the line and inserted the rod into the empty holder before turning back to Guthrie, wiping his hands on a cloth that hung from his belt. His body language was subservient, but his eyes held an independence that said any subservience had been forced on him.

"If you ain't here about me fishin', what you want?" The man's tone wasn't belligerent, exactly, but there was a subtle challenging undertone.

"My name's Clay Guthrie. Mind telling me yours?"

"Why? So you can report me?"

Guthrie waved his hand as if casting something away.

"If I wanted to report you, I'd just tell Chief Turner the make and model of your pickup. I bet he knows who you are. But relax. I told you I don't care about your fishing."

"Segundo Yanez," the man said after a long pause. He didn't look relaxed.

"I suppose you heard about the body they found out at the dump."

"Who ain't?"

"I'm working with Chief Turner to find out what happened to him."

"What's that got to do with me?"

"Nothing. But I'm new around here, and I'm curious about this marsh. From the look of things, you come down here a lot."

"Not so often…," Yanez began, but Guthrie cut him off.

"Often" he corrected gently. "The path down here is well worn."

"I ain't the only one," Yanez said defensively. "Jeff Mayfield's down there, right now." He waved toward the path as it wound deeper into the marsh around the sinuous periphery of the widening pond.

"Relax," Guthrie said again. "What I'm interested in is the marsh, and since you spend a lot of time here, I thought you might be able to tell me something about it."

"What's there to tell? It's wet and got fish."

"And nothing else?"

"Like what?" The man's tone was direct, but something furtive glimmered in his eyes, and his shoulders remained tense.

"I don't know. Like anything strange."

"I don't know what could be strange."

"But there is something, isn't there? Something different."

"It's been pretty foggy the past couple a days," Yanez said, scratching his ear. "But that ain't all that unusual this time a year."

That was an easy answer, but it didn't roll easily off Yanez's tongue and sounded more like a rationalization than a reason.

"Is there something else?" Guthrie pressed. "You've been coming down here a long time. Surely you know what it feels like. Has that changed any?"

Yanez gave him a wary look, and his body language grew even more defensive.

"You sound crazy to me, mister."

"So, nothing?"

"Nothing."

Yes, Guthrie thought, taking in Yanez's body language, the agitation radiating off of him. Something. Maybe it was too subtle for him to associate it with anything other than his own paranoia about Guthrie catching him poaching. But inside, he knew something was different, even if he didn't consciously recognize it. Guthrie certainly did, thanks to the twitching of the Kuei men, but he let it go.

"You catching anything?" he asked, changing to subject to something that wouldn't further alienate Yanez.

Yanez gestured to a stringer in the water, two fish squirming on it.

"Got a couple. Dinner for tonight."

"Well, nice meeting you," Guthrie said. "I think I'll explore a little more."

"Don't you sneak up on Jeff, like you did me," Yanez said. "He's got a pistol on him."

"Thanks for the warning."

Guthrie moved off down the narrow path skirting the edge of the rapidly widening water, his movement swirling the mists. The first bend took him out of sight of Yanez, and a couple of hundred feet farther on, he spotted the second poacher. He was standing beside the pond, legs shrouded by mists, holding a rod and reel. He was African American, a little taller than Guthrie, fairly well-built, and looked to be in his mid-forties. His hair was cut short and showed gray among the black, and he was dressed in jeans and a faded black t-shirt. The man hadn't yet seen him, so Guthrie thought he'd better call out a warning as he neared.

"Coming up behind you," he said.

The second poacher spun, dropping his rod and reel and reaching for an old S&W .38 Special stuck in his waistband.

"Whoa, there," Guthrie said, holding up his hands. "I'm unarmed." That wasn't true, but no sense in making the man more anxious than he already was. "I'm not here about you fishing. I just want to ask you a few questions."

"Questions about what?"

"My name is Clay Guthrie, and I'm helping Chief Turner look into that body found in the dump a couple of days ago. I'm sure you've heard about it."

"I heard," the man said, relaxing enough to let the hand hovering over the pistol drop cautiously to his side. "But I don't know why you're down here askin' me about him. The dump's three or four miles over thataway." He waved carelessly toward the east.

"Mind if I ask your name?"

"Jeff Mayfield," the man said without hesitation. "And let me tell you, I don't give a shit if you report me to Mr. Jim. He told me he don't care if I fish down here."

"I assure you I don't care if you're poaching or not," Guthrie said amiably. "I doubt if Jim Chaney needs to keep all the fish in this pond to himself."

Mayfield gave Guthrie a sharp look then laughed.

"I like that one," he said. "I'll have to remember that. So why you down here, scaring off my fish?"

"Well, I'm not very familiar with this area, so I thought I'd check out the marsh while everybody else is in church."

The man laughed again, this time with more than a trace of derision.

"Church," he said, contempt in his voice. "Hell, half the people in Thorndike don't belong in no church."

"I take it you're not a religious man."

"I ain't a church-goin' man, if that's what you mean. This fishin' spot is all the church I need."

"So, you come down here often?"

"Every few days," Mayfield said. "Sometimes more, 'specially when the fish are bitin' like they are today. It feeds me regular."

Guthrie glanced in the five-gallon white paint bucket sitting next to Mayfield's green tackle box. It was half filled with water, two fish inside feebly waving their fins.

"Looks like you're having some luck."

"More than usual considering I been here less than half an hour. Seems like all the good fish are up this way, today. But you didn't come down here to ask me about fishin'. And I don't know nothin' about that body that got found."

"Didn't think you did," Guthrie said. "I just got curious about the marsh. It's a beautiful place."

Another lie. His Kuei men were squirming more than they had back at Segundo Yanez's fishing spot. Especially when he faced the direction of Jim Chaney's cabin.

"Most of the time," Mayfield replied. "Kinda feels dismal, today. Maybe it's the overcast and all this fog."

"Is it dismal down here very often?"

Mayfield gave him a curious look.

"Could be." He shrugged. "I don't pay much attention to anything but my fishing." He shrugged again. "If it is, maybe it's just me, since I ain't been feelin' too good lately."

"Sorry to hear it," Guthrie said. "But at least you have a good catch."

"Yeah, not bad."

"Mind if I ask you why you're packing that .38?"

"Is that any of your business?"

"Probably not, but it's pretty peaceful down here."

"Maybe if you're white."

"So, you have some bigots harassing or threatening you?"

"Bigots," Mayfield snorted. "The Lazy Q's right up the road, and my pickup's the only one like it in town. That's reason enough."

"I take it you're talking about the Sanfords."

"You know 'em?" Mayfield bristled a little.

"No, but I encountered them yesterday. They don't seem like very pleasant people."

"You fuckin' got that right," Mayfield said. He relaxed some, but not a lot. "They come down here every so often to harass me and Segundo. I gotta do something to defend myself."

"Let's hope it doesn't come to that."

"If it does," Mayfield said, patting the butt of the revolver, "they better watch out."

"Well, thanks," Guthrie said, sensing that he wasn't going to get much more from Mayfield. "I think I'll go on down the path a little ways."

"Be careful down there," Mayfield cautioned. "The cabin's only a little farther on, and Mr. Jim don't like trespassers. He might take his shotgun to you."

"I'll watch out for him."

He'd watch out for something, for sure, since the Kuei men twitched more when he faced the direction of the cabin, even if it was still out of sight around bends and curves. After Guthrie waded through the mists for another few hundred feet, the path took a final bend, opening the view into the main body of the pond. Out in the middle of the water, the mists were wispier, though they still clung to the trees and brush all around.

At the apex of the bend, he stopped and peered around a bush. The cabin was visible ahead, maybe two hundred feet away, though most of it remained obscured by tree branches, foliage, and the pervasive mist. The deck he'd glimpsed on his visit with Turner was the width of the cabin and cantilevered over the water's edge. It bore a tin roof and was surrounded by a wooden railing. Sitting on it was the figure of Jim Chaney, staring across the hazy water.

Apparently he's not much of a church-goer, either, Guthrie thought, keeping behind cover as he perused Chaney and the cabin. Maybe he should have been because what also wasn't obscure was the Kuei men's increased kicking. The scene spread out before Guthrie might appear serenely placid, but beneath its surface, hidden within the mists, lurked something as sinister as it was unseen and unknown.

Guthrie wanted to talk to Chaney again, but he decided against approaching the cabin from the path. That would seem too much like trespassing, and while Guthrie couldn't actually see a shotgun on the deck, that didn't mean Chaney didn't have one. No, he thought. Best to approach the cabin by the road as he and Turner had done on Friday.

He eased backward on the path so his movement wouldn't attract Chaney' attention. When he was completely out of sight, he strode toward the second poacher's spot. In the short time Guthrie had been up the path and back, Mayfield had packed up and left. So had Yanez. At the bridge, both trucks were gone. Maybe they'd caught enough fish, or maybe they just didn't want to talk to Guthrie any more. Or maybe it was something else.

Guthrie got into his Xterra, pulled out onto the road, and drove toward town. He turned onto Main Street and eventually headed south along the paved county road to the dirt lane that led to Chaney's cabin. When he arrived at the metal-barred gate blocking entrance to the marsh, he got out, climbed it, and started down the track.

12

WITHIN SECONDS, GUTHRIE WAS BENEATH the canopy of trees. The overcast of the early morning had broken by now into scattered clouds, but despite the sunshine and the fact that the daytime temperatures were comparable to the last couple of days, Jeff Mayfield was right. The marsh's shaded cool seemed sharper than it had when he'd come down here with Turner only two days before. Almost chill. And the mists still clung to the foliage back in the forest and lightly carpeted the track. Suppressing a shiver and calming the twitching of the Kuei men, which, from this angle of approach, seemed to be reacting to something in the woods to the left instead of from the direction of the cabin, Guthrie followed the track's gentle S-curves.

The activity of the Kuei men increased the deeper the road wound into the forest and picked up even more after he spotted slender fingers of water groping among the trees to the left. But soon after, the twitching subsided, though it didn't entirely cease. By the time he reached the cabin, it was much diminished, as if whatever caused it remained in the forest behind him.

Figuring Chaney would still be on the back deck, Guthrie hailed him as soon as he was close enough.

"Mr. Chaney! It's Clay Guthrie! I was down here with Chief Turner the other day!"

A moment later, Chaney's head protruded from the back left corner of the cabin where the entrance to the deck was. He stared at

Guthrie for a moment as if focusing, then he stepped fully into view as Guthrie walked toward him. He was still unshaven and dressed in the same clothes he'd worn two days before. Either that, or his wardrobe was monotonous.

"I hope I'm not disturbing you," Guthrie said.

"Everybody disturbs me," Chaney snorted. "But you're here, now. Might as well get done what you came to do."

He beckoned then disappeared around the corner, and Guthrie followed. On Guthrie's previous visit, he and Turner had talked to Chaney at the cabin's front door, but now, as Guthrie rounded the back corner and stepped onto the deck, he got his first real view of the deck and pond. Except for the gap at the corner where he'd entered, the deck was surrounded by a wooden rail. The cabin had a back door, but it was closed. Overhead was a corrugated metal roof —not that it was needed for shade, even when the sun was high. Not here beneath the thick tree cover. But it obviously helped keep the deck clear of debris and out of the weather. Guthrie could easily imagine sitting out here in a rain storm, sipping a cup of coffee and contemplating the splashing of the raindrops on the surface of the water.

The spot was gorgeous. Here, the body of the pond was some two hundred feet or more across, and it extended far enough around the bends and curves to either side that it seemed to go on forever. This early, out in the middle, the surface gently steamed as the water released heat from the day before into the cool air above. Because of the steam rising from the pond, the mists along the banks were higher than in the forest and clung like Spanish moss to the lower branches and foliage of the surrounding trees.

The forest on the other side of the pond didn't extend as far as it did on the road side of the cabin—maybe a hundred yards. Despite the mist, a broad, sunlit pasture was visible through gaps in the trees and foliage. More sunlight played over the quiet water. Insects flittered over it, and birds occasionally swooped down, harvesting their insect meals. Fish harvested from below, too, snatching any bug that fell into the water, dimpling its surface. Anybody standing here would admire the beauty of the scene, and Guthrie wished he could, too, but the Kuei men reminded him of the business at hand.

"Mind if I sit?" he asked.

"Might as well," Chaney said, gesturing to a heavy wooden chair, its padded floral seat cushion worn and faded, as he settled into an even more worn wooden rocker.

Guthrie sat, and the two of them were silent for a moment as they stared over the pond's placid surface.

"It's very nice here," Guthrie said, the subdued twitching of the Kuei men saying it wasn't so.

"My Enid loved this spot," Chaney said, rocking softly back and forth. "She used to sit in this very chair for hours on end."

"Chief Turner told me your wife died recently and that she spent a lot of time down here."

Chaney gave him a narrow sidelong glance before answering.

"I don't know what that whippersnapper told you, but don't nobody know nothin' about it."

"Want to tell me?" Guthrie asked, trying to imagine the tall, rawboned Turner as a whippersnapper.

"Why should I?" Chaney said, bristling.

"Because something isn't right down here."

"What do you mean by that?" Chaney leaned forward almost belligerently in his chair, the rockers creaking on the deck boards. "What would you know? A stranger."

"I don't know. That's why I'm asking."

"What's it to you? I thought you was investigatin' that murder over at the dump. What's that got to do with me or my marsh?"

"Probably nothing," Guthrie said.

"If it's nothin', then nothin's keepin' you here."

Chaney rocked back and deliberately turned to stare over the pond, shutting out Guthrie.

"Thanks for your time, Mr. Chaney."

Guthrie rose, walked to the edge of the deck, and turned the corner. He was just beyond the front of the cabin and heading up the slope to Chaney's truck when Chaney's voice stopped him.

"Come on back, Mr. Guthrie. I been feelin' a bit anxious and low lately, but it ain't right I was so rude. We can sit a spell and talk."

Chaney was at the back corner of the cabin, beckoning. Guthrie reversed his steps, and in a few moments, both were settled into their chairs.

"Tell the truth, I ain't had many people to talk to since Enid died," Chaney said after a long silence. "Maybe not even before that. Folks around here just don't cotton to me. Not for a long time. I used to be somethin', but now you'd think I was as much a stranger as you. Or worse. I guess I lost the knack of socializin'."

"I often feel the same," Guthrie said.

"I guess I don't mind, much. Now that my ranch is gone, there ain't much for me to do 'cept sit down here and watch over this place. You ought to see it beneath a thunderstorm. Beautiful. No wonder Enid loved it. Not that there weren't other reasons…."

He shook his head sadly, and Guthrie couldn't help but wonder if he preferred not to think of those other reasons—perhaps the real reasons—Enid lived here alone, apart from him. But even if that was so, now that Chaney had started talking about her, he couldn't stop. As if he was a dammed-up marsh just itching for release.

"What I want to remember is her pure spirit." Chaney paused again, pain clouding his brow. Then he looked up at Guthrie, eyes filled with guilt. "I gotta admit I crushed that right outta her. It wasn't right, and I got no excuse. It was like I was sick in the head. Sick in my heart. Sick, cruel, and careless. I suffered losses and didn't take 'em well." He shook his head again. "No, that ain't right. I took them out on her. I guess she felt safe enough distancing herself from me, even if she was too afraid to actually leave. And where would she go? Leland had long since married Beth Mislowski, and they were happy and had their own kids. Leland had a whole new life without Enid, and there was no place for her to fit into it." He paused, looking at Guthrie. "You know who Leland Fuller is?"

"Chief Turner told me about the different ranches around town and some of the history. I know your wife was considered the princess of the high school, that you and Leland vied for her hand, and that you won."

"Yes," Chaney said sadly. "I won. Ain't it funny how things turn out? The man who got the princess is livin' alone in a cabin in a marsh, while the one who didn't is surrounded by family and about to own a quarter of the whole county." He gave a sarcastic snort. "Tell the truth, I spent most of my life wonderin' why she never left me. Was it she had faith I'd eventually change? Or was it pride? Could she admit she'd chosen wrong?" He stopped and stared at Guthrie again, eyes wells of pain and guilt. "I don't know why I'm tellin' you all this. I never said any of it to anybody. But I ain't felt right the last couple a days, and I feel like I gotta tell somebody or I'll bust open."

"You're telling me because I'm a stranger and have no pre-judgements about you or any stake in the game."

"I guess that's right, though ain't that a pitiful situation? But I guess it's no more pitiful than my past." Chaney paused for a moment, collecting himself. "I admit now it was all my fault. I lost myself somehow, and took out my anger on her. I never beat her," he said hastily, shaking his head. "I know folks around here think I did, but I could never do that. But I was unkind. Cruel. Unfair and cruel." He hung his head for a moment, then looked at Guthrie. "You see, Enid was barren. That wasn't her fault, but I blamed her. My ranch was prosperous, but that was all appearance. Success hadn't brought me and Enid happiness, only comfort and resentment. Once she told me, 'I just feel so bad, Jim. All this work your family did makin' the ranch one of the best around here, and I never gave you someone to pass it to.'

"Well, hell," Chaney said sadly. "That stabbed me worse than any knife coulda since bad luck and my own mismanagement nearly destroyed everythin' else I had. I told her we got each other, and the way I reckoned, that was plenty. But it wasn't plenty for her. She had the mother instinct ingrained deep in her soul, and there was no one to lavish it upon."

Chaney knew it was customary to blame a wife for a couple's childlessness, but he'd gone to school, read the newspaper, and watched the news and other programs on television. He knew a man might be shooting blanks just as easily as there being no target to shoot at. He went to the doctor, was tested, and was told there was nothing wrong with his ammunition.

"I didn't tell Enid but kept up the pretense I was likely the blame, but she always saw through that. Knew deep down I blamed her. I told her we could adopt. Lots of times. But she always said no. She wanted true flesh and blood, and that was somethin' her own flesh and blood couldn't produce. Nothin' I said could stop the darkness growin' inside her. Or my growin' resentment of it. My ranch was five generations old, but I had no one to leave it to when I'm gone. That ate at me for a long time. Too long. She always knew what was what, and it finally drove her away from me."

To escape him during those years of bleakness and turmoil, she spent more and more time beneath the shielding branches of the marsh's forest and on the banks of the pond.

"She came down here so much she wore a path the cows adopted for their own," Chaney said with a faint smile. "It was a long walk from the house—more than a mile each way—so I made that little road where the trail was so she could drive down here whenever she wanted. That ended up being most all the time. Just to keep away from me." Chaney shook his head sadly, mouth crinkling with disgruntlement. "She even thought about approaching Agnes Carpenter. She'd have taken her in and made her feel safe. You met Agnes?"

"Not yet. I understand she's a force to be reckoned with."

"That she is," Chaney said with a nod. "She and Enid were best friends when they were young, but that's one more thing I took away from Enid. Agnes's brother died a few years before Enid did, and Enid figured she could help her with chores around the house while Agnes managed her ranch. But I guess Enid had too much pride for that. When they were friends in high school, Enid was top dog and Agnes was her homely handmaiden. Could be Enid couldn't stand their roles reversed. Didn't want Agnes to see her troubles. She might not have been about to leave me, but she quit talkin' to me, acted like I wasn't even there or was a hired hand. She was like a ghost hauntin' the house. My fault. All my fault, though I didn't see it like that back then.

"Finally, she came to me one day and said she wanted me to build this cabin for her. I didn't want to. I didn't want to lose her. But I knew I already had, and this was the only way to keep what little was left. So I went ahead and built this cabin, and it was the best and maybe the only really good thing I ever did for her. She said it wasn't gonna to be permanent, just a place to go when she was feelin' low. But she started spendin' more and more time down here 'til it was her permanent home. I came down several times each week to check on her and bring her supplies, and she always said she'd be comin' home in a few days, but I knew it wasn't so. The cabin was her home by then, and any vow to return home was a determination to stay put."

Living in the marsh, away from him, Chaney said, she regained some of her old self. And no wonder. Down in the cool, misty calm beneath the trees, enchantment lay—at least for Enid. It was the most peaceful place on the whole ranch, Chaney said. Maybe the most peaceful place in the whole county.

"Course, by then, it was too late," Chaney said bitterly. "Ovarian cancer, it was. The very womanly organs that failed her also took her life. It was like a spit in the face from God." He stared at Guthrie, eyes glaring fiercely. "You want to know why I ain't in church today? That's why."

The darkness growing in her soul began to grow in her body. She became thin, wan, and pinched with pain. Time after time, she refused to let him take her to the doctor, but at last the pain was too great. He bundled her into the truck and took her to County General Hospital in the county seat. The whole way, she lay slumped against the door, face white, fingers clutching a heavy scarf draped around her neck.

"The people at the hospital took over after we arrived, and all I could do was sit in the waitin' room while the doctors examined her. At last they told me there was nothin' they could do about it 'cept make her comfortable as possible. She went into the hospital, but she'd never leave."

She didn't, and somehow, a part of him didn't, either. He took her body back to Thorndike and had her interred in the small cemetery near the eastern end of the marsh, where his forebears were buried. Next to the empty plot that would eventually be his. A handful of mourners showed up, but none except the Turners and Freddie Jensen spoke to him, not even to express their sorrow, not even Miss Agnes. And then he went home, back to his house. Even though Enid hadn't lived there for years, she'd been just a five-minute drive away anytime he wanted to be with her. But now she wasn't even there. She'd been his whole life, and now there was nothing.

"At least she got to spend her last few years in peace. Personally, I think bein' in the hospital, away from her home with no hope of return, was the final straw. You know what I mean?" Chaney gave a sardonic laugh. "Sometimes I think she only married me for the marsh, not for myself."

Chaney fell silent, then, as his gaze drifted across the water, his voice came again, soft.

"You asked me the other day if I ever see her, and I said no. But that ain't true. Sometimes, I fancy I see her spirit driftin' along the paths like a ghost, at ease with her surroundings but not at peace with herself. 'Specially the last couple a days. Or maybe it's just me —my own lack of peace as I sit here, wonderin' how things went so wrong with our lives. My life. How? What evil quirk of my being made me into such a beast to my own wife that she had to get away from me?"

Guthrie had no answer for that, only his own guilt.

"Look through those gaps, yonder across the pond." Chaney pointed, changing the subject. "That sunshiny land you can see out there past the trees on the other side? That's Leland's north pasture. Son-of-a-bitch schemes and dreams every night about gettin' my marsh. He used to drive his truck down the track along his fence line, peerin' through the forest at what he hopes will eventually be his. To gloat about the disasters that befell me. But he almost never comes up this way now. I guess he finally got it through his thick head I ain't sellin' this marsh to him or anybody else. I got bigger plans for it. And don't ask me what they are. That's for me to know, and others to find out."

"Can you tell me anything about the man who bought your old house and barn and the property around it?"

"Him?" Chaney snorted. "Rand, or somethin' like that. My real estate agent took care of the sale, and I never even met him before yesterday. He came down here, saying he wanted to be neighborly." Chaney's nose and upper lip wrinkling with distaste. "He didn't seem all that neighborly, and I can't say I liked him much. Asked if I'd consider sellin' my marsh to him. I told him no. He can have the house. I don't care about that. It quit bein' a home after Enid left. It was just a place where my own weakness destroyed everything I had. But I ain't sellin' the marsh to him or anyone else. It's hard goin' on sometimes, but keepin' watch over what Enid loved is the best thing I can do."

"I'm glad," Guthrie said. "It's good that you have something to keep the darkness at bay."

Chaney nodded, peering at Guthrie.

"I think you know about that, and then some, by the looks of it."

"I've had my share of troubles," Guthrie admitted. "Now I'm trying to help others."

"Well, I ain't sure I need all that much help, but I appreciate you thinking of me."

The tension in Chaney's body belied the first part of that statement, but Guthrie didn't press the issue. Figuring he'd learned about all he was going to at the moment, he rose.

"Thanks you for your time, Mr. Chaney," he said. "Do you mind if I visit you again."

"I suppose not," Chaney said, shrugging. "If you do, you'll be the only person 'sides Freddie Jensen who visited me down here more than once or twice. Including that whippersnapper police chief."

"Speaking of Freddie, have you seen him?"

"Not hide nor hair. You don't suppose somethin' happened to him, do you?"

"I don't know, but he was seen a couple of days ago. Chief Turner and I are looking for him, but so far we haven't found him."

"I'll let the chief know if I see him."

"Thanks again," Guthrie said. "I'm sorry for your troubles."

"They're troubles, all right," Chaney said, then he turned his attention to the pond, rocking gently back and forth.

Guthrie left the deck, went around the cabin and up past Chaney's truck, then started down the dirt road toward the gate. He hadn't gone more than a hundred yards before the Kuei men started acting up again. The whole time he'd been at the cabin, their activity had subsided to twitching, but now, the farther he walked, the stronger the sensation became. The mists blanketing the forest floor suddenly seemed shades darker, and the atmosphere grew oppressively still and heavy, as if the barometer abruptly registered a zone of negative pressure. The sensation wasn't physical, exactly, though he could feel his skin tighten at its touch.

"What the hell?" he thought as a sudden wash of the malign pressure made him stagger.

He'd been walking along the righthand track, and the stagger sent him toward the ditch on that side, almost into the shallow water at the bottom. But his tai chi training gave him the reflexes to react and send him wobbling back onto the track, leaving him with a feeling of repulsion at the dark decay that filled the ditch.

His scuttling steps had taken him almost all the way across the narrow track, but he managed to stop himself from stepping into the ditch on that side. A quick glance showed him that the lefthand ditch looked as normal as the righthand one looked diseased. He cautiously approached the righthand ditch and peered into it. The lefthand ditch had an equal amount of water, but the plants in it were green and vital, while those on the other side were dead, dark gray-green and umber mush that stank of rot. The feeling of oppression was greater on that side, too, as if effluvium from the blight lay over the forest behind it.

Those sensations had not been so pronounced when he'd walked down the track only half an hour before. And now the Kuei men were squirming. Guthrie found a stick and dragged it through the diseased ditch, trying to lift some of the dead foliage in it for a better look, but everything in the water was so rotted that it disintegrated to slime at a touch. Guthrie tossed the stick aside, moved to the left side of the track, and hurried on. He wanted out of these woods, and the sooner the better.

At last, he reached the sunlight at the edge of the forest, and the oppression eased, though even here, the righthand ditch was filled with rank rot. He got into his Xterra and drove off slowly, pausing periodically to examine the ditches on both sides of the track, then the dirt county road, and then, when he reached it, the paved county road leading north to town and south to the dump. The entire distance, the righthand ditch held diseased water, while the one on the left remained clear of blight.

Guthrie turned right and followed the road to the dump, monitoring the righthand ditch. It was diseased all the way to the dump, but not beyond, and this far from the marsh, the sensation of oppression had long vanished, as had the twitching of the Kuei men.

He got out of the Xterra and examined the ditches, only then noticing for the first time a wide swath of rot marring the underbrush and weeds between the dump and the road. It was as if some pestilence had flowed out of the dump, into the ditch on that side of the road, then over the road and into the ditch on the other side. There, it hadn't run far to the south but only toward the north, that direction leading to the marsh. He didn't remember the swath of destruction from his previous visits to the dump, but those times he'd been focused on the dump's entrance, not its margins or ditches.

But what was it? Certainly plant pathogens existed, but to have them attack the plants in the ditch on one side of a road but not the other seemed unlikely. Puzzling over that, Guthrie got back into the Xterra and headed toward town.

13

THE HOUR WAS APPROACHING NOON, and Guthrie's stomach was beginning to growl. Leo's Cafe would be open by now for the after-church crowd, so he headed that way. He hoped Turner might be there for lunch, though he spotted the chief's SUV in front of the police station as he looked for a place to park. There was nothing along the street for two blocks around, so he just left the Xterra in the station's lot and walked to the cafe. Inside, it was crowded with families and small groups of adults, and the air was filled with the sound of happy people talking.

He quickly scanned for the chief but didn't see him. No matter. He'd be going to the police station after lunch, anyway. Leaving the few empty tables and booths for larger groups that might arrive after him, he headed for one of the three empty stools at the counter. Since the chief wasn't here, he hoped he'd get a chance to talk to Bev. She might know something and even be willing to tell him. He was disappointed again. Bev was working the tables and booths, and a teenage girl was behind the counter. When she brought him water, silverware, and a menu, he saw her name tag read, "Emily."

"You must be Emily Turner," he said, and she smiled.

"And you must be Mr. Guthrie."

"I am. You look just like a younger version of your mom."

"Thank goodness. Can you imagine if I looked like Dad?" Guthrie laughed.

"You said it, not me. I'll start with coffee."

She left to get it while he perused the menu. He'd only eaten here a few times, but everything so far had been good. It better be, he thought. Leo's clientele were country folk used to hearty, solid, good-tasting food. Leo would quickly go out of business if he slacked off on quality or quantity. But the pleasant hubbub of the patrons in the room said that probably wasn't going to happen.

Even though it was lunchtime, Guthrie's eyes gravitated to the Country Breakfast with what was billed as a slab of ham. Okay, he thought, but before Emily Turner came back, Bev stepped up behind the counter.

"Bill said he told you who Agnes Carpenter is. Miss Agnes, most people call her."

"He said a little about her."

"She's in the back booth and asked me to invite you for breakfast."

Guthrie glanced toward the back of the cafe. In the last booth next to the windows facing Main sat an older, gray-haired woman. She was looking his way.

"How did she know who I was?" Guthrie asked, turning to Bev.

"She knows everybody in town, but she doesn't know you. Who else could you be? Besides," she smiled, "she asked me."

"Your husband practically called her the queen of Thorndike, so I guess it's an honor to dine with her."

"Let's call it a distinction," Bev replied, the smile turning quirky. "You can tell me later if it was an honor."

"Okay. I'll visit with her. But I don't want her paying for my meal." He took out his wallet and handed her a $20 bill. "That should cover my food and a tip. I'll have the Country Breakfast, eggs over medium, whole wheat toast." He nodded toward Emily, who was returning with his mug of coffee. "I'd hate to see a mom steal a tip from her daughter."

"I'll be the one bringing the food to your table," she said. "But Emily will get all the tip."

"Sounds good," Guthrie said, and he rose and walked toward the back of the cafe, carrying his coffee mug, while Bev explained the situation to Emily.

The woman watched him approach. Her gray hair was pulled back in a bun from a square, somewhat fleshy face, but since she was behind the table, Guthrie couldn't see her whole body. He had the impression of a robust, stocky build with small breasts and larger but not heavy hips—the figure of a woman used to a lifetime of hard work with body language that projected authority. She was encased in a very nice but subdued dark blue dress speckled with tiny white and yellow flowers. The narrow lace collar and narrower lace cuffs did not make her look prim. Guthrie doubted that Miss Agnes was ever prim. Proper, perhaps, but not prim.

Her face was impassive as he neared, neither genial nor severe, her eyes steady, watchful, and perceptive. His sixth sense told him she was every bit the local powerhouse Chief Turner made her out to be. He didn't need a sixth sense, though, to feel the eyes of almost everyone in the room watch him walk to the queen's booth. Clearly, she was holding court and everybody in there wondered what she wanted to talk to the stranger about. The stranger who had brought death into their little community.

"Hello, Mr. Guthrie. I'm Agnes Carpenter."

"Yes, Ms. Carpenter. Pleased to meet you."

"Beverly told you I invited you for breakfast?"

"She did, and I appreciate the offer."

"But then I saw you order and pay for it with a twenty-dollar bill. My invitation included the meal."

"You have excellent eyesight, Ms. Carpenter. But since I'm visibly aligned with your police department, I really shouldn't let you or anyone else buy my breakfast, except maybe Chief Turner. That wouldn't be proper. However, I'd be happy to join you while I eat if your intention is conversation."

Miss Agnes nodded and waved to the seat opposite.

"I hope you don't mind eating in a booth." She smiled in a slightly self-deprecating way that seemed genuine. "Leo reserves this one for me. I am a slow eater, and more to the point, the benches are softer than the seats at the tables, and my backsides aren't as cushioned as they used to be."

Guthrie set his coffee mug on the table and slid in opposite her.

"I prefer booths, myself," he said.

Clearly she'd already finished eating, and only a half-full mug of coffee sat in front of her. Bev came over with fresh water and silverware for Guthrie and a coffee refill for Miss Agnes. She gave her a fresh mug instead of pouring coffee into the old one.

"So," Miss Agnes said after Bev left, leaning forward on sturdy elbows, "you're the big city detective who brought Bill Turner the big case all small-town law enforcement dream of."

Guthrie had to laugh.

"Has Chief Turner been telling tales out of school?"

"Bill wouldn't dare not to tell me anything I want to know. I've known him since he was born, and his daddy worked for my family nearly all his life. But I would never think of trying to influence him."

"I hope you're not blaming me, Ms. Carpenter. When I came here looking for Mr. Telfor, I had no idea we'd find him like that."

"Strikes me I'd blame you if you hadn't uncovered him as soon as you did. That killing took place in our town. Who knows who might have done it or what might have happened if you hadn't found it out. And call me Miss Agnes. Everybody does, so you might as well, too. Ms. Carpenter sounds too formal."

"Thank you, Miss. Agnes. Why don't you call me Clay? But surely you don't think any local people are involved."

"We're a good, God-fearing little town, Clay. But that doesn't mean we don't have our bad apples."

She gave a sideways glance, and Guthrie saw she was looking at a table where Lonnie Sanford sat with Johnny Miller. Clearly Sanford had been watching them, but he quickly averted his gaze when Guthrie looked at him. Miss Agnes's eyes returned to Guthrie, and she lifted her coffee mug, took a sip, and stared at him over its rim for a moment before setting it back on the table.

"You seem like a straightforward man."

"I try to be, even if it doesn't always work out."

"Bill tells me he checked into your background. You were once a police officer. You were wounded in the line of duty and now operate a small detective agency."

"Small is the operative word," he said. "I only have a few clients."

"Yet one is a large insurance company whose case leads you right here, to a mysterious homicide."

"I certainly didn't expect the homicide," Guthrie said.

"I think you did," she said then quickly held up her hands. "I phrased that wrong. I don't mean I think you had anything to do with the murder, only that I think you suspected something wasn't right even before you came to Thorndike."

Bev came over to the table with his order. It arrived more quickly than Guthrie thought it would considering the crowd in the cafe —perhaps another sign of Miss Agnes's status. Guthrie thanked her, and she left.

"A man disappearing might not indicate anything criminal," Guthrie said as he salted and peppered the eggs. "Lots of people vanish without foul play. But when a man with no reason to disappear—or the means to do so—vanishes while on a job, it's not a good sign."

He picked up his fork and attacked the food.

"Bill said that when you went to the dump, you seemed to know right where the body was."

"Not exactly. I didn't know anything. I just had a hunch."

"A hunch." Her mouth wrinkled slightly. "Bill said you told him you had some sort of sixth sense."

"I guess he really does tell you everything."

"He also told me Freddie Jensen's truck was left at the scene and the two of you went looking for him but didn't find him. Do you think he might be involved?"

"If he is, it's probably only peripherally. As a witness. We won't know until we find him. We're still looking."

"Poor Freddie," Miss Agnes said, leaning back with a sigh. "In many ways, he's just a lost soul with no direction. But I can't see him hurting anyone, much less being able to kill a grown man younger than him for no good reason before running off and leaving behind everything he ever had."

"From what Chief Turner told me and what I've seen of Freddie's life, I agree. But we still need to find him. He was closest to the scene. We'll find him eventually. He doesn't have his truck, and he can't have much money. And Thorndike's all he's ever known."

"Do you think you can't find him because he's dead?"

Guthrie shrugged.

"Hard to say. We know he was alive the day after he left his truck at the dump. If he's dead, it happened at least twenty-four hours after the other death. Probably days after. And I think we'd have found his body by now. Search teams have combed the areas around the dump and his house, and they've come up with nothing. Besides, if the person who killed Mr. Telfor killed Freddie, too, we'd probably have found his body along with Mr. Telfor. But without further information...." He shrugged again, and took a bite of ham. It really was a small slab, and it was tasty. Maybe even from a local producer.

"I notice that you're not wearing a wedding ring," she said.

Guthrie managed not to do more than pause in chewing at the abrupt change of subject.

"An interesting, handsome man like you with a good income," she went on. "Seems like you would have found someone by now."

"I was married once," he said after he swallowed. "She left me."

"Left you? Was that before or after you were injured in the line of duty?"

"She left while I was in the hospital."

"That was cruel of her."

"No," he said. "It wasn't. She should have left. I was in a bad place."

"And now you're not?"

"No. I'm not in a bad place. At least, not the same bad place." He chuckled. "I'm trying to help solve a mysterious homicide, and some might think that's a pretty bad place to be."

"So, no girlfriend?"

"Maybe. When I have time."

"We never have time," she said. "Look at me. People all around here look up to me, but what am I, really, but an old maid with no one left?"

"The heck you don't have people left," Guthrie said. "Look around. All these people looking up to you are who you have left. You have a whole town left, and that's a big family. More of a legacy than most folks can ever dream of."

"Bill warned me there's more to you than meets the eye."

"Isn't that true of most of us?"

"No, it's not," she said, eyes steady on his. "And Beverly thinks so, too. She deals with all sorts of people in her job, and she's a smart gal. I put a lot of stock in what she says."

"I wish I could convince you...."

"Oh, you've convinced me, all right." She snorted a laugh. "I've been around enough years and hired enough people to know what kind of person is sitting across the table from me." She leaned forward, small breasts pressed against the table's edge. "You don't have to tell me your secrets, but promise me you'll stay and help Bill work through this thing."

"I fully intend to do just that, Miss Agnes," he assured her. "Mind if I ask you some questions?"

"Am I under suspicion, too?" She said it lightly, but a hardness lurked underneath.

"Of course not. But I'm a stranger here, and I need to get a sense of Thorndike's dynamics."

She gave a short laugh.

"Not much dynamic going on around here."

"It seems to me there is. For one thing, there's the issue of Jim Chaney's unpopular sale of his ranch and his ongoing ownership of the marsh."

Miss Agnes snorted, her brow clouding.

"He's only down there hiding from the rest of the town, too cowardly to face us after the way he treated poor Enid." She didn't seem to question that Guthrie might not know who she was talking about. "She was my best friend growing up, but after she married Jim, she changed. Or he changed her. Now she's dead, and he barely comes into town. Does his shopping up in the county seat where nobody knows him. He could die down there in that cabin, and nobody would even know."

"Until tax time," Guthrie said.

Miss Agnes laughed at that.

"Chief Turner also told me a faction of the town is interested in turning Thorndike into a bedroom community," Guthrie said. "That has to raise some hackles here and there. And your name has come up as a potential major player in that game. A player who still holds a hidden hand."

"You certainly are a forward fellow."

"Isn't that what you want me to be? That's what it's going to take to find out what's behind the murder."

"Yes, you're right. All right. Yes. I have a large ranch. My brother, Edward, and I inherited it from our parents. But Eddie died of pancreatic cancer nearly seven years ago, leaving it all to me. I've run it best as I could, but you can see I'm not a young woman. And neither Eddie nor I ever got married and had kids. All we had was the ranch, and I guess that was enough. Our one big kid that constantly needs tending. Now that Eddie's gone and I'm getting on in years, it's as much a burden as it is a source of pride of accomplishment."

Her eyes grew distant for a moment, remembering her deceased brother, perhaps? Or her own impending retreat?

"Anyway," she continued, "folks around here are wondering what I'm going to do with the ranch. I'll have to sell it, of course. Everybody knows that, and that's the issue. Just who am I selling to?"

"So you haven't taken sides yet?"

She stared at him for a long moment then said, "Perhaps I have, but as you say, I still hold a hidden hand. I'm not ready to reveal it."

"I don't play poker," Guthrie said, "But I've heard good poker players play the other players as much or more than they play their hands."

"Indeed." Her eyes were steady on his.

By now, Guthrie had finished his meal, and less than a minute after he pushed his plate aside, Bev came to collect it and to bring both of them fresh cups of coffee. She was instantly attentive to Miss Agnes, Guthrie noticed, and he surreptitiously glanced around the room to see if the other diners resented the extra attention. None seemed to notice, or if they did, they took it as a matter of course. Whatever the people might think of her personally, Guthrie reflected, Miss Agnes truly was the queen of Thorndike.

"There is something else I want to talk to you about, Clay," she said, leaning forward and speaking in a confidential tone. "Something quite disturbing."

14

"DOES IT INVOLVE YOU PERSONALLY?" Guthrie asked.

"Yes, me, but certainly others," Miss Agnes responded.

Now the strength in her eyes was undermined by something that seemed a mixture of trepidation and disgust. Guthrie was shocked to see that coming from a person of such substance, but then he saw a strain of anger running through them as Miss Agnes's staunchness returned.

"What's the problem?"

"Somebody has been writing poison pen letters to various people in town, telling lies shouldn't be told. But since the lies are embedded in true things, they might be taken for the truth."

"They're actual letters? Through the mail?" he asked, and she nodded. That made sense, he mused. It was difficult to remain completely anonymous online but easier through snail mail. "When did they start?"

"A few days ago. Maybe a week."

"Are you a direct victim?" Guthrie asked. "Have you received one of these letters?"

In answer, she dug in her purse and pulled out an envelope that she handed to Guthrie.

"This is the first one."

The postmark was from the the county seat, and the envelope wasn't addressed to Miss Agnes but to someone named Bridget Hansen.

"Who's Bridget Hansen?"

"She's the wife of the Baptist Minister. Don't worry. I didn't steal it. She gave it to me. And if you're wondering, the return address is a phony. I drove up to the county seat myself to check."

The addresses weren't handwritten but had come from a printer. Smart, Guthrie thought. No handwriting to analyze.

"Go on," Miss Agnes said, nodding toward the envelope. "Open it up and read it."

Guthrie extracted the paper and unfolded it. The letter also was printed, in an outsized font below a business-style letterhead, but this was no ordinary business letterhead. It consisted of an extreme close-up color photo of an eyeball staring at him. It had a brown iris, and though it looked feminine, there was no makeup on the lashes or eyelid, and it could have belonged to a man or a woman. Next to the eye, set in a ragged, threatening red font, read the words, "Eye See U."

He scanned the message printed below the letterhead. It was brief and to the point.

"Im watchin everone," it read. "I know all about Agnes and Ed Carpentr. Fuckin insest perverts. No wonder hes dead. She probly killed him. Im gonna to expos and destroy her."

"Whoever sent this isn't strong on grammar or spelling," Guthrie commented as he refolded the letter, inserted it into the envelope, and handed it back to her.

"There's another." She handed him a second envelope. This one was addressed to Mildred Brooks and had the same bogus return address. Mildred's the wife of the Methodist minister," she said before he could ask. "She got this this next day. She and Bridget assured me they didn't believe a word and would never say anything about them."

The paper inside was the same as the first, and so were the eyeball letterhead and threatening message.

"Any others?" Guthrie asked, putting the letter back into the envelope and handing it to her.

"One more." She passed it over.

It had the same letterhead, but this message was directed straight at Miss Agnes.

"You nasty disgustin old bag," it read. "Even as I write your decayin. Ever time I see you I see you decay. I smell it. Nothin can save you from retribution."

Sighing, Guthrie refolded the letter, slipped it into its envelope, and gave it back to Miss Agnes.

"There are others," she said as she put all three letters into her purse. "Not sent to me, but several other people have gone to Bridget to confide that they've received similar letters, all with the same eyeball but different messages. Not always about me, though. About different people in town. There may be more I don't know of."

"Are you coming to *me* for advice?"

"Who else can I talk to about this?" she asked. "You're the only stranger in town. You're the only one who can't know us well enough to write such trash. Everyone else is suspect."

"Even Chief Turner and Bev?"

Miss Agnes's shoulders slumped.

"No. Not them. But Bill has his hands full, and I don't want to burden Bev with any of this."

"She isn't one of the victims who approached you?"

"No."

"That doesn't mean she hasn't received a letter."

"I can't bring myself to ask her," Miss Agnes confessed. "What if she doesn't know? I don't want to tell her about it." She hesitated, brow troubled. "I guess it's my damned pride. You have to understand how difficult this is for me, Mr. Guthrie. Those letters contain a disgusting innuendo that implies an unspeakable relationship between me and my brother. It's not true, but even so, some people will believe it because they'll want to."

"I won't even entertain the possibility."

"Eddie had a few girlfriends here and there," she went on. "People get natural impulses just like livestock. Sometimes you have to satisfy them even if you don't intend to breed. But nothing permanent ever worked out for him."

"Boyfriends for you?"

"I used to get natural impulses, too," she said with a wan smile. "I may never have been a looker, but I had a couple of boyfriends over the years. Broke up with the last one when Eddie got sick. He lived up in the county seat, but I had to take care of Eddie, and afterward, there just didn't seem to be time enough to run the ranch and run up to see him every week, and that was that."

"Nothing to write home about? Or a poison pen letter?"

"Not if you're writing the truth. But lies can taint lives ever after."

"I'll look into it, if I can, but I think you should let me tell Chief Turner. He's in a better position to think about who might be responsible. Do you have any suspects?"

She shook her head.

"All I can say is it must be a longtime resident since whoever it is knows a lot about Thorndike." She leaned back and gave him a long stare. "A mysterious death," she said at last. "A corpse in an unusual state. A disappearance. A poison pen letter writer. All at once. And then you arrive, saying you work for an insurance company."

"Freelance," Guthrie corrected. "I'm not on their payroll."

"Still, it doesn't add up. I think Bill's right. There's more to you than appears on the surface."

"As I said, I'm only here...."

"Save it, Clay. I know my Ps and Qs, Ps being people and Qs being questions. Something is going on in Thorndike that isn't good. I can feel it in my bones, and now I see evidence of it with my own eyes. I'm a God-fearing Christian woman, but the first time I saw a two-headed calf born in our herd, I realized that not everything is covered in the scriptures. Some things are just out of the ken of most of us. But not you. I think you're here to help us with something we can't help ourselves with."

"I'll do my best, Miss Agnes," Guthrie assured her, wondering just what that best might be and what it might require. "I hope you'll pardon me, now. I have something to discuss with Chief Turner."

"Thank you for talking to me, Clay," she said as he rose. "Please visit me anytime you feel like it. Bill can tell you where I live."

"I will, Miss Agnes. Until then."

Guthrie walked to the police station and went inside. Turner glanced up and waved him in from behind the glass.

Guthrie pushed through the gate and went to the office.

"Anything new?" he asked as the chief gestured toward one of the two chairs in front of the desk. Tessa must have moved the third chair back to the outer office.

"Nothing yet. Dr. Bob said he'd call when the autopsy is complete.

Guthrie intended to tell Turner about the rot at the margin of the dump and all along the ditches to Chaney Marsh, but before he could, a sudden knock at the door stopped him. Tessa leaned inside.

"Chief, you better get over to the Chaloupeks," she said. "There's some kind of emergency."

15

"I'M ON THE WAY," TURNER said as he rose and went to the hat rack for his Stetson.

"Mind if I tag along?" Guthrie asked as he stood.

"Don't see why you need to," Turner said. "But come along if you want."

In a moment, they were heading across the street to the grocery store. The owners were out front, Mr. Chaloupek's face twisted in rage, his wife's white with shock. With them were the cashier, Hetty Mruska, her face as sour as the first time Guthrie had seen her, and another employee, a slender, mid-twenties man with a shock of blonde hair. Guthrie had seen him the day before, stocking shelves.

"What's going on, Todd?" Turner asked. "A burglary?"

"Worse," Chaloupek said. "We opened up as usual, right after we ate at Leo's, and…. You'll have to go in and see for yourself." He waved toward the sliding front doors. Turner went inside, followed by Guthrie and Chaloupek. Mrs. Chaloupek and the other two waited on the sidewalk.

At first, nothing seemed amiss, but as soon as they passed the two checkout counters, the problem became obvious. The first sign was the sound of a box falling off a shelf somewhere in the middle of the store. As they entered the aisles, they saw boxes and plastic bags and pouches of food strewn on the floor, contents spilling through ragged holes. By then, the cause was obvious. In the first minute, Guthrie must have seen two hundred rats and mice scurrying around and scaling the shelves, eating what was spilled or chewing holes in formerly fresh containers. The only items that seemed unscathed were canned and non-food goods, such as paper towels and trash bags. The three hurried through the store, seeing destruction and ruin on almost every aisle.

"What the hell am I going to do?" Chaloupek's tone was almost a moan.

"First off, you need to get rid of these rodents," Turner said. "There's an exterminator in the county seat. I'll call him so he understands it's an emergency. Hopefully, he can do something to drive them out right away."

He radioed Tessa, explained the situation, and assigned her the task of contacting the exterminator. "And get Wally and Pete over here with the garbage truck. They can't do regular pickup until we reopen the dump, so they might as well do something to earn their pay."

He signed off then turned to Chaloupek.

"I've never seen a single rat in here," he said. "How'd they get in?"

"No idea, Chief. As soon as I saw the mess, I called you. I haven't had time to go through the store."

"Why don't you take a rough inventory of the damage while Mr. Guthrie and I look around?"

Chaloupek didn't seem enthusiastic about walking around a store with hundreds of scurrying rodents, and Guthrie wasn't, either. He remembered all too well his narrow escape from a horde of rats intent on eating him alive during the first case he'd worked for Tereba. But those rats had been aggressively focused on one object: him. These didn't seem aggressive at all but more like a lazy. Hungry crowd invited to a free lunch. Chaloupek nodded and began gingerly walking the aisles, surveying the damage.

"All these rodents didn't come in through some small rathole," Guthrie said.

"Wouldn't seem possible," Turner agreed. "Or at least likely."

A short search later, they found the point of ingress. The door to the alley that ran behind the grocery, hardware store, and bank stood wide open. A few stragglers were scurrying across the threshold, and more rats and mice milled around on the alley's dirt and gravel surface. Turner examined the door before he shut it.

"No signs of forced entry," he mused. "The Chaloupeks must have left it open."

"I can see them forgetting to lock it, but leaving it wide open...." Guthrie let the sentence hang.

"You think somebody deliberately opened it?"

"Seems a possibility."

"An unlikely one," Turner said. "The only people who have access are the Chaloupeks and their employees."

"Anybody in the store could come back here if nobody was watching. With only four people working here, it's not likely they'd constantly keep watch for people going into the back who shouldn't."

"I guess that's right," Turner said, then shook his head. "This is crazy." He looked like he was going to say more, but at that moment, his shoulder mic squawked. "What is it, Tessa?"

"The exterminator will be down in about an hour," she told him.

"Thanks."

As soon as Turner ended the call, Chaloupek appeared and came down the hall toward them. He stopped at a double-door set in one of the walls, opened one side, and cautiously stared around the interior. Then he shut the door, heaved a large sigh of relief, and looked at Guthrie and Turner.

"The storeroom was shut tight, thank God," he said, "so nothing was damaged back here. I won't be able to completely restock, but there's enough to keep me going for a few days until I can get a shipment from the supplier in Houston. But those damn rats fouled all the produce and all the meat that wasn't in the walk-in. I'm going to have to throw it all out. I can't afford any of this. Even if the insurance does pay, it'll be weeks before they'll cut me a check. This isn't just a blow to me, but to the whole town. Even if shoppers do come back. I've always kept a clean store, but nobody'll trust us now."

"Relax, Todd." Turner waved toward the back door. "Someone left that open last night, and that's how the rats got in."

Chaloupek stared at the door, mouth ajar. Then his jaw snapped shut, and he shook his head.

"I could swear I locked it up before we left."

"This is some sort of accidental occurrence," Turner went on. "Nobody's going to hold it against you. The exterminator says he'll be here in an hour. I'll see if I can get some people to help you clean up after he clears out the rodents."

"That'll be great, Chief. I can't pay them, but tell anybody who'll help I'll give them a big discount next time they shop. But what'll I do with all the refuse with the dump closed?"

"We'll make an exception in this case. Wally and Pete are coming over with the garbage truck, and they'll help you clean up and haul everything out to it. They have a key to the dump and can unload away from the crime scene."

Leaving Chaloupek in the store, Guthrie and Turner went outside, where Turner assured Laura Chaloupek that everything would be taken care of.

"We found the back door wide open," the chief said. "That's how the rodents got in. Any of you know anything about that?"

"The back door?" Laura looked puzzled. "I'm pretty sure I checked it shortly before we closed yesterday."

Turner looked at the young blond clerk.

"How about you, Kevin?"

"I didn't go back there for maybe an hour before we closed. I was working the vegetables."

Turner didn't have to query Hetty.

"I think it was him," she spat without preamble, jabbing a finger at Guthrie. "He was in yesterday. He could a done it when nobody was watchin'."

Turner looked half surprised, half bemused.

"Why him?"

"He's the only stranger in town. Maybe he's tryin' to mess with us."

"He's not the only stranger in town," Turner said.

"Well, I don't know nothin' 'bout that," Hetty groused. "I still think it was him."

"All right. Duly noted. Now, maybe you ought to go inside and help your boss clean up."

"I ain't goin' in there with all them rats," she snapped.

"You can go home," Mrs. Chaloupek told her. "You, too, Kevin."

"I ain't afraid of no rats," Kevin said.

He headed into the store while Hetty went to an old blue Nissan Sentra parked a block down the street.

"She have something against you?" Turner asked as she drove off.

"Seems like," Guthrie said, "though I've only seen her once. When I checked out yesterday. Maybe she's mad I told you she'd seen Freddie."

"I better go in there, too," Laura said unenthusiastically.

Guthrie's eyes followed as she went through the sliding doors. Dimly past the front windows, he could see Todd and Kevin rushing about with brooms, trying to herd the rodents toward the rear of the store and out the back door.

"Where the hell did they all come from?" Turner wondered.

It was a rhetorical question, but Guthrie answered, anyway.

"Remember how clear the dump was of rodents?"

Turner gave him a look that was both startled and skeptical.

"You're not suggesting all the rats and mice in the dump suddenly left and came into town to raid the pantry, are you?"

Guthrie shrugged.

"No rodents in the dump and suddenly a rodent invasion in the town's only grocery store."

That didn't seem to convince Turner. Guthrie figured he just thought it was some happenstance. Maybe it was, Guthrie thought, but still, it was strange.

They returned to the station, where Turner told Tessa to phone around to find volunteers to help the Chaloupeks restore order to their store. Then he turned to Guthrie.

"We need to deal with the situation in the grocery," Turner said. "Don't see why you need to hang out around here. I'll call if something comes up."

Guthrie nodded, thinking he'd tell the chief about the rot in the ditches later. It wasn't going anywhere, anyway.

He left the police station and drove to his trailer to file a report with Mutual Indemnity.

16

GUTHRIE ROSE WITH THE DAWN and, after breakfast, sat at the kitchenette table with a mug of coffee and his laptop, a low-altitude Google Earth image of Chaney Marsh on the screen. The twitching of the Kuei men when he'd visited the marsh the day before plus the rot in the ditches leading into it concerned him, and he wanted to fix its parameters in his mind. But there really wasn't much to see except for thick tree cover surrounding an irregular glimmer of water at the center of the pond. Only one corner of Jim Chaney's covered deck was barely visible.

He closed the laptop and was just about to leave for the bridge over Steele Creek and reenter the marsh from that angle to see if the Kuei men would still react, when the phone rang. It was Turner.

"Mind coming to my office?" the chief said. It was a question but sounded more like an order.

As soon as Guthrie entered the police station, Tessa gestured toward the chief's office. The Venetian blinds over the window were down and closed, so he couldn't see who was inside, but Tessa clarified.

"He's with those FBI agents," she said, thin lips pursing and nose wrinkling.

As Guthrie pushed through the swinging gate and started toward the office, Tessa pointed to the rolling chair tucked into the knee well of the empty desk.

"You might want to take that."

Guthrie gripped the back of the chair and steered it toward the office door. Inside, Agents Wilson and Aznar already occupied the two chairs in front of the the chief's desk, so Guthrie pushed his chair off to one side so he wouldn't be flanked by the agents. They and Turner all wore serious expressions.

"Thanks for joining us, Mr. Guthrie," Turner said. Guthrie assumed that the formality was due to the presence of the agents and not because he was under suspicion. At least not by the chief. The agents were another matter.

"I have to tell you, Mr. Guthrie." Wilson said, "that you and the chief have stumbled on a most peculiar case."

"It seems so."

"We're curious about your involvement and would like to ask you a few questions. If you don't mind."

"Go ahead."

"You say you were hired by Mutual Indemnity Insurance Company to look into the disappearance of Mr. Telfor."

"That's right."

"Only one glitch," Aznar said.

"Glitch?"

"Yes. Your assignment to the case came after another investigator had already been assigned but was bumped to put you in place."

"I'm working freelance for Mutual Indemnity," Guthrie said, shrugging. "I know nothing about the company's internal bureaucracy or how they assign cases." Perhaps he did: Tereba's influence?

"Well, the guy who got bumped was a company employee," Wilson said, "so it's curious they hired a freelancer. In fact, you never worked for Mutual Indemnity before, so why now? All of a sudden. On a case where a missing man turns up dead two hundred miles away and in a different state from where he disappeared, not to mention looking like he's been dead for months, not days."

"I don't know why they hired me. They didn't say. I received a call last Wednesday offering me the case, and I took it. Maybe the office guy had a full caseload and needed someone else to work this one. Maybe he's a bad investigator. Or maybe I'm better suited for field work than the office guy. You'd have to ask Mutual Indemnity. I was hired by a Mr. Oliver there."

"Who hired you just a day after you obtained a Louisiana PI license."

"Beginner's luck, I guess."

"Luck?"

"Maybe somebody recommended me. I've worked for other insurance companies. You'll have to ask Mr. Oliver."

"Still," Aznar put in. "You have to admit the optics are off."

"Are they? I was hired to find a man, and I followed his trail to Thorndike. I didn't expect to find him at all, much less dead, but that's the way Chief Turner and I found him. I don't know what happened to him, and I have no idea why the body is in that condition. And I'm just as anxious as you to find out."

More so, he thought.

"Isn't your case for Mutual Indemnity finished, now that we've found and positively IDed your guy?"

"Technically, I suppose," Guthrie said. "But I'm not working another case at the moment, and I'm willing to help out here. Besides, finding the body doesn't bring closure for Telfor's wife. She'll want to know what happened, and so do I."

"Finishing what you started?" Aznar asked, tone vaguely accusatory.

"You're not suggesting I brought murder with me to Thorndike, are you?"

"No," Aznar said. "It's almost certain that Telfor was killed in Airla. Oakdale PD found his blood in the sawmill where you found his van. Enough to suggest he was shot and died on the floor there and was transported here after he was killed."

"Why bring his body here?" Turner asked.

"Bodies aren't easy to get rid of. We believe the killer drove the body here to the dump, thinking it wouldn't be discovered. And if it was, it was two hundred miles from the scene of the murder and in a different state, so it would be more difficult make a connection with a man who disappeared in Airla."

"That raises another question, Mr. Guthrie," Wilson said. "How did you track him here in just one day since nobody knew where he was going or even which direction?"

Damn, Guthrie thought. Here it comes.

"I knew he'd been hired to pick up a sofa in Airla and deliver it to a town in Texas'" he stalled. "I didn't know he was killed there and his killer made the delivery for him."

"You think that's what happened?" Aznar asked.

"He was hired to deliver a sofa, and you say he was killed in Airla. He sure didn't drive himself and the sofa to Thorndike."

That raised Aznar's hackles, but Wilson interrupted before he could say anything.

"Let's cut to the chase, Mr. Guthrie. Chief Turner says you knew the delivery address. How? Even his wife didn't know that."

"Okay," Guthrie admitted, not wanting to get into a deeper quagmire. "I found the dump's address written on a slip of paper tucked over the van's visor. It was the one thing missed by whoever cleaned out the van."

Turner stiffened and gave him the evil eye.

"And you didn't think to share that with Oakdale PD?" Wilson demanded. "Withholding evidence is a crime. We ought to arrest you right now."

"It wasn't strictly evidence at the time since no one knew a crime had been committed," Guthrie replied. "Oakdale authorities just believed Telfor had run out on his wife and were already dropping the investigation. For all I knew, I was chasing a cheater, which is bad but not criminal. Besides, if I'd given it to Detective Peters, would that have made any difference? Thorndike's out of Oakdale—and Louisiana—jurisdiction, and I believed time was of the essence, so I came straight here."

"You have the paper with the address?"

Guthrie pulled out his wallet, extracted the folded slip of paper, and passed it to her. She unfolded and glanced at it.

"This has the address of the sawmill, too," she commented, refolding the paper and slipping it into her jacket pocket. "Don't think we didn't do a little checking on you," she said, expression severe.

"I'd be surprised if you didn't."

"All that stuff you told Chief Turner about being a cop checks out. As does your detective agency. Such as it is."

"Just me. That's the best way to keep everything confidential."

"Let's keep it that way," she said. "Everything about this case is screwy, and don't think we don't consider you part of the screwiness."

"What about the sofa we found him on?" Guthrie asked, as much to turn the tables as to get an answer.

"Are you trying to change the subject?" Aznar asked, an undertone of belligerence in his voice.

"I'm trying to get to the bottom of this case," Guthrie said flatly, staring right at Aznar, who bristled. "And let me remind you, without me, there wouldn't be a case at all."

Aznar looked like he might get up out of his chair, but Wilson quickly inserted herself into the conversation.

"There may be some sort of chemical contamination," she said as Aznar settled tensely into his seat. "We sent some samples of the fabric to the lab in Dallas and should hear back in a couple of days."

"That's not what I meant," Guthrie said. "If the only purpose in bringing Telfor's body to Thorndike was to dispose of it, why bring the sofa, too?"

"Who knows why murderers do what they do?" Wilson said. "Maybe there was no sofa to be delivered, and the killer simply used one already in the back of the dump as a convenient place to hide the body. Just coincidence." She glanced at her watch. "This is all very interesting," she went on, "but it doesn't get us closer to the hows and whys. Agent Aznar and I are going to Oakdale to talk to Detective Peters then to Airla to see the sawmill where you found the van. We'd prefer you didn't leave Thorndike until we come back."

"I wasn't leaving, anyway," Guthrie said. "Like I said, I want to help bring closure to Mrs. Telfor."

"Right," Wilson said, tone skeptical. Then she looked at Turner. "We'll be in touch."

She and Aznar got up and left the room. Turner followed them to the door and shut it then turned his gaze on Guthrie. He didn't look happy.

"They don't sound convinced about any of this," he said, taking his seat. "Or about you."

"I think that's a perennial condition for FBI agents."

"And for police chiefs," Turner said. "Why didn't you tell me about the address?"

"Where I got it is irrelevant, and like I told the agents, there was no indication at the time that a crime had been committed."

"There was every indication. I don't like you withholding information from me."

Guthrie didn't know what to make of this turn, but he resolved to be as forthcoming as he could given the circumstance. How much he might be able to divulge depended on what kind of information Turner might be able to absorb without rebelling.

"I apologize, but would it have made any difference? What was important was the address and what it led us to."

"Yeah, that." Turner didn't seem mollified. After a pause, he said, "What the agents didn't tell you is they also checked into your financial records. It seems that most of your work is fraud, corporate espionage, or blackmail cases, often for insurance companies and sometimes other sorts of companies. From the look of your bank statement—and yes, they showed me that, too—all of that pays pretty well."

"You just can't believe what hard work it is, sitting all day in a car outside some guy's house, waiting for him to come out seemingly fit as a fiddle when he's suing for a debilitating injury. The bladder ache alone is...."

"Save it," Turner interrupted sharply. He tented his fingers and stared at Guthrie over them. "What about these three other deposits, all correctly reported as income, but whose source is traceable only to a single law firm? Who isn't talking."

"I've twice tracked down stolen artworks for wealthy clients. Naturally, such clients don't want any sort of publicity, especially any that might hint at weaknesses in their security." Guthrie wasn't about to launch into a true and detailed history of his past. Turner wouldn't believe it, anyway.

"And they both had the same law firm?"

"I was hired by that firm," Guthrie shrugged. "I can't tell you about its relationship to the clients since I don't know."

Turner's jaw clenched, but he managed to keep his tone level.

"All right, be that way. Can you at least tell me what sort of art?"

"Once a sculpture, once a painting."

"Did you find them?"

"I did."

"What about that third large deposit?"

"It was a missing person case."

"With the same law firm?"

Guthrie just shrugged and held his hands palm up. Turner didn't seem pleased with the response.

"Did you find him? Her?"

"Him. No." Guthrie sure wasn't going to tell Turner that Buddy Horton had ended up as a pile of troll shit.

"But you got paid, anyway. By the same law firm."

"He was murdered, and we had an eyewitness to the act, but the body disappeared before the authorities arrived. The remains were later found and identified though DNA. But my work led to the uncovering of an international smuggling operation that was using the U.S. rail system to move contraband." All that was true enough. Mostly. And verifiable.

"I remember reading something about that last year, only I don't remember your name. It was some other fellow."

"Gilbert Espinoza. He was the railroad employee who witnessed the murder. He hired me to help him. If you have any doubts, call him and ask about me."

"Why you? Why not tell the cops or a supervisor or someone higher up?"

"The cops wouldn't have believed him, and his supervisor was part of the smuggling ring." Guthrie shrugged. "Maybe the higher-ups, too. Who could he trust except for an outsider?"

"How did he find you?"

"The law firm recommended me."

"Jesus Christ, Clay. Would you be straight with me for one fucking second?"

Guthrie could have prevaricated further, but Turner would have seen through that, and it would have erected even more of a barrier between them than already was building. Not of hostility, exactly, but of distance and mistrust. That wasn't what Guthrie needed right now. He needed Turner on his side, all the way. He had to take a chance and tell Turner at least something true about his background, even if he only scratched the surface.

"Okay, Chief. I'll be as straight with you as I can. Most of the time, I'm a regular detective, but sometimes, something abnormal happens, and I'm sent out to deal with it."

"Just who sends you?"

"A man," Guthrie said. "I won't reveal his name." Whatever he told the chief, he wasn't about to tell him that Tereba might be a thousand years old and possessed sorcerous power. Would Turner believe him if he did? Could he? Most of the time Guthrie barely believed it himself.

"Government?"

"Not officially." Guthrie had come to realize that Tereba was just one member of a network of men and women of similar abilities—though perhaps not longevity—living here and there around the world. And who knew? They might actually be affiliated with some government somewhere. "I can't say because I don't really know."

"So you aren't here by accident."

"He would say there is no such thing as an accident."

"You believe that?"

"Let's just say I've learned to believe some things I never would have when I was younger."

"You're saying you take abnormal cases on the word of a man whose backing you know nothing about except he doesn't believe in accidents?"

"I didn't say I know nothing about him. I know he's powerful and connected. And he saved my life, and I saved his. I work for him mostly because the issues he sends me to resolve would have had dire negative consequences if they'd continued."

"So this is a good guy trying to rid the world of evil, and you're helping him? How do you know that's what he's doing? He could be leading you on."

"This isn't your garden variety evil, like murder, rape, torture, or even corporate greed and malfeasance, evil as all that is. And I know because of my personal involvement."

"You think that's what's happening here in Thorndike? Some kind of evil?"

"We've all noted the condition of the body in terms of timing and other characteristics, such as the lack of insects and decay. But there's more. Didn't you feel bad and anxious around that old sofa? Bad in a way that wasn't just dirty on the outside? And so does the coroner and his team, and apparently, even Wilson and Aznar. What do you make of the rats, and what about Freddie? Why has he disappeared after claiming that something evil tainted his pants and boots?"

"If we have some abnormal thing going on in Thorndike, what is it?" Turner asked cautiously, looking and sounding both skeptical and interested.

"Finding out that will be half the battle."

"And the other half?"

"We'll have to eliminate it."

"As in kill? Remember, this is a law enforcement officer you're talking to."

"And if that law enforcement officer encounters a rabid dog in the street, would he hesitate to kill it?"

"Killing a rabid dog isn't the same as killing a person."

"Not even if that person is about to shoot you or someone else?"

"Okay, okay." Turner held up his hands. "We can go back and forth with this sort of stuff all day and get nowhere."

"If it makes you feel better, Chief, the objects of my searches have rarely been human, though they had human aid."

"Not human. Like animals?"

"No, not animals."

"What else could it be but human or animal? And what about this human aid? Did you shoot them?"

"Even humans can be mad dogs under the right circumstances. The men and women I've had to confront were, in every sense of the term, enemy combatants. Power-hungry enemies of humanity." He shrugged. "But really, I only shot those who shot at me first, and I didn't kill every one of them. Most of those no longer with us are that way because they were ground up in the machinery of their own schemes, not because I personally did something to them."

"Want to tell me about those circumstances?"

"They're not easy to talk about and certainly nothing to brag about. Maybe later, when this is all over and you have a better idea of just how screwed up reality can get."

"You seem to think it *will* be all over."

"No sense in going into things with a defeatist attitude."

Turner's stare was opaque, and Guthrie couldn't tell if he'd convinced him of the necessity and urgency of taking direct action against an unknown and invisible foe about which they knew nothing.

"Okay," Turner said at last. "Personally, I think all that non-human stuff is full of crap. But Miss Agnes called me last night. She's pretty taken with you and says it's smart to pay attention to a man who practices lateral thinking, whatever the hell that means. She also says you know more than you can say, and I guess I have to agree with her. As usual. She says to trust you, and her word means a lot to me." He shook his head slightly. "Can't say you've given me much of a handle to grab on to, but I'll grab. For now."

"Better grab tight," Guthrie said. "It's probably going to be a rough ride."

"You know you sound batshit crazy. I'm sure there's a rational explanation for everything."

"Let's hope so. But let me show you something that might help convince you something's going on that's both unseen and tangible as well as not very good."

"What?"

"Best to show you. Telling won't do the trick."

Before they could leave, though, they were interrupted by Tessa knocking on the door.

"Yes?" Turner called out, and Tessa cracked the door and stuck her head inside.

"Dr. and Mrs. Hughes want to talk to you, Chief."

"What about?"

"They won't say, but they're pretty upset."

17

"I'LL BE RIGHT WITH THEM." Turner looked at Guthrie and said, "Mind waiting with Tessa while I talk to the Hughes?"

"I'll be in the front office."

Guthrie rose and left, taking the chair he'd brought in with him. He passed a casually but well-dressed middle-aged couple as they headed for the chief's office. Turner ushered them in and closed the door. Guthrie pushed the chair over to the empty desk and sat.

"Who are they," he asked Tessa.

"Dr. Hughes is our town vet."

"The Canine Cottage?"

"That's them."

"Did they say what's wrong?"

"Not to me. They only wanted to talk to the chief." She shook her head. "Thorndike hasn't seen this much excitement for, like, ever."

"Too bad it's the wrong kind of excitement," Guthrie answered.

"Amen to that," she said, casting her eyes toward the chief's closed and shuttered office.

The Hughes conferred with Turner for about fifteen minutes, then the door opened and they emerged and headed for the outer door. Mrs. Hughes eyes were red and tearstained, and Dr. Hughes wore an expression of subdued fury.

"We'll find out what's going on," Turner promised as he came out after them, and then they were gone, the outer door swinging shut behind them.

"What's that about, Chief?" Tessa asked.

"Can't say right now," Turner said, then he looked at Guthrie. "There was something you wanted to show me?"

They left the station and went to Turner's SUV.

"Where to?" the chief asked as they settled into their seats and buckled up.

"The dump."

Turner heaved a disgruntled sigh.

"Not again. I swear I've stunk like garbage since we first went out there."

"Don't worry. We're only going to the entrance."

Turner pulled off and drove east on Main, toward its intersection with the county road leading south.

"What's going on with the Hughes?"

Turner hesitated, then said, "They showed me letters someone sent to three local farmers and ranchers who have herds of sheep and who bought Great Pyrenees from them, accusing them of animal cruelty and improper breeding practices and threatening to expose them."

"Is it true? The abuse, I mean."

"Not so far as I or anyone else knows. The Hughes would call themselves God-fearing folk, and if any sort of abuse is going on, Thorndike's small enough that everyone would know." He shrugged helplessly, then said, "I suppose the truth doesn't really matter, does it? Once a lie takes hold, it's hard to shake it off, and if this one gets out and people believe it, it'll damage them for sure."

Guthrie thought he heard Miss Agnes's influence in Turner's words.

"Don't tell me," he said. "Each letter was prefaced by a closeup photo of an eyeball and the words, 'Eye See U.'"

Turner's jaw nearly dropped.

"How do you know that?" he demanded, looking sharply at Guthrie.

"The Hughes aren't the only ones," Guthrie said.

"What?"

"When I talked with Miss Agnes yesterday morning, she showed me two similar letters slandering her that were sent to the Baptist and Methodist ministers' wives and a third threatening her directly. She says others have received letters, too. Several, and I don't think she knew about the Hughes."

"Why did she tell you instead of coming to me?"

"She said it's because I'm a stranger and so couldn't have been the one to write the letters. It has to be someone who lives in Thorndike and knows the people here. Personally, I think she's too embarrassed to approach you directly."

"Embarrassed?" Turner snorted. "Miss Agnes?"

"You might be, too, considering what the letters said."

"What was that?"

"I promised not to say. You'll have to ask her."

"This job." Turner shook his head. "As if I don't have enough to worry about with a homicide and Freddie missing, we got to have some jerk sending poison pen letters." He glanced at Guthrie. "You don't think the messages are connected to the murder, do you? I mean, how could they be?"

"Best not to form theories just yet, Chief. Let's gather the evidence and see where it leads."

During the rest of the drive to the dump, Guthrie told Turner how he'd spent Sunday morning.

"I was curious about Chaney Marsh," Guthrie told him. "So I went back there."

"You talked to Jim again?"

"Not at first. I thought I might get a different perspective on the marsh, so I went to the bridge over Steele Creek."

"You seem mighty interested in that marsh."

"I am. When I got there, a couple of pickups were parked on the embankment: an old brown Ford Ranger and an old two-tone blue Chevy."

"The Ranger belongs to Segundo Yanez, and the other is Jeff Mayfield's. Both of them fish down in the creek a lot."

"They told me their names, but I have to tell you they weren't fishing the creek. I found both of them in the marsh. Yanez was where the creek widens into the pond, and Mayfield was down around a couple of bends toward Jim Chaney's cabin."

Turner shook his head and chuckled.

"Yeah, I should have said poaching. Both of them go down there all the time. I guess the fish are fatter in the pond than in the creek. I asked Jim if he wanted to lodge a complaint, but he said no, he already knew about it and didn't care. I guess he recognizes a couple of other needy souls. Did either of them have anything to offer?"

"Not really, but they seemed antsy. At first, I thought it was because I'd caught them, but then it seemed more than that. I went a little farther up the path, and when I came back, both of them were gone."

"I know where we can find them if we need to," Turner said. "Segundo is one of the janitors at the school, and Jeff works at Jack Herwitz's lumberyard."

"It was after I saw they were gone that I visited Jim again."

"And?"

"He was in a melancholy mood. Maybe he's always like that, but there was a change since our last visit. He seems to believe that something might be threatening him. And he said George Rand paid him a visit and tried to buy the marsh."

"The threat he was talking about is probably those high school kids. There's a group of four or five of them who are constant troublemakers. They like to party down to the marsh near where Segundo and Jeff fish. but so far, they've done nothing worse than trash up the place. Jim's complained about it, but I don't often catch them in the act."

"It's probably not the kids, then. Or at least not just them."

"What, then?"

"I can't say," Guthrie shrugged. "But something is wrong down there. I can feel it."

"Your sixth sense?"

"Maybe, but it strikes me that Jim and Segundo are sensing it, too."

"But not Jeff?"

"He seemed very defensive, and that interferes with accurately assessing sensation. Maybe he's always that way. He was packing a .38."

"Can't say I blame him considering his skin color. Still lots of bigotry around here." Turner shot Guthrie a sideways glance. "So what's going on at the dump. More evidence?"

"More like an indication. I want to get your impression."

The two fell silent until the SUV reached the dump. The gate across the entrance was locked, yellow crime scene tape festooning its top rail.

"Pull in and stop," Guthrie instructed.

When Turner had, they exited the vehicle. Almost immediately, the chief noticed something he hadn't before.

"Did this have two locks the other day?" he asked, lifting the loop of gate chain to show two padlocks, one old, one new, each on opposite sides.

"It did," Guthrie said, examining his memory of the visit when they'd discovered Telfor's body. "Shouldn't it?"

"No."

Turner pulled out the key for the gate, which fit into the old gray-steel lock, but he didn't have a key for the new brass one. He shrugged and let go of the chain, which rattled against the metal gate.

"Maybe Freddie lost his original key and just replaced the lock," he mused. "He knows Wally and Pete would have a key to the old one."

"Shouldn't he have told you?"

"Yeah, but we're talking about Freddie. Not the most attentive person I've ever known."

"Cutting out a link and replacing it with a lock would give an alternate key-holder easy access to the dump any time he wanted."

"Could be," Turner acknowledged. "We won't know until we find Freddie."

"How long will the dump be closed?" Guthrie asked.

"Freddie or no Freddie, we're reopening tomorrow. Wally and Pete will trade off supervising until we find Freddie. People are starting to complain about trash and garbage piling up at home, and if we don't open it, they might start throwing it in the ditches."

"Funny you should say that. Come over here and take a look at this."

18

GUTHRIE LED TURNER TO THE road and about twenty feet north. He stopped and waved an arm across the trees that masked the dump from the road. Nothing seemed wrong with the trees, but as Guthrie had noted earlier, the grass, weeds, and underbrush along a twenty-foot wide swath had wilted to a diseased brown.

"What do you make of that?" he asked.

Turner stepped to the shoulder and peered across the ditch at the swath.

"I don't know. It looks like some sort of blight." He looked at Guthrie. "Why didn't we notice it earlier?"

"We were concentrated on the body on the sofa. And it might not have looked this bad a few days ago."

"This is what we're here to look at?"

"Just the start. Look in the ditch."

The swath continued into the ditch then seemed to widen a little along both sides of the trench for about twenty feet in either direction.

"Whatever it is," Turner said, "it didn't get far."

"No, Chief, it did. Over here."

Guthrie walked across the pavement and pointed into the ditch there. Every plant in the ditch above the shallow waterline was sere, and the ones in the water were wilted wet rot. Dead frogs, tadpoles, insects, and even a couple of birds floated in the stinking muck.

"See," Guthrie said. "The blight spilled across the road then went north along the ditch, but not south."

"That way's downstream, so to speak," Turner said.

He squatted beside the ditch, searching it with his eyes. Then he stood and looked at Guthrie.

"What's this mean?"

"Let's drive a little more," Guthrie suggested.

They returned to the SUV, and Guthrie directed Turner toward the graded county road to the former Chaney property and Chaney Marsh.

"Drive on the left side," Guthrie said, "and keep track of the ditch."

Turner did, slowly, until they reached the graded road.

"The blight runs down this way, too," Turner said after he'd turned left.

"Park, and let's check the other side," Guthrie directed.

"Nothing," Turner said when they were standing over the north ditch. "What's it mean?" he asked again.

"I noticed it on Sunday," Guthrie said. "I don't know what it means, but the blight runs all the way down this ditch. Most blights are species specific and don't cause this kind of wholesale extermination. This one looks like it's killing animals, too."

"Maybe you think it isn't natural, but there must be a scientific explanation. I have to work from facts."

"Let's drive on, then, and you'll see one important fact. The blight doesn't affect any other ditches, only the one that runs from the dump to Chaney Marsh."

"I'll need to see that."

In the SUV, Turner pulled off, driving slowly and staring into the ditch as much as he looked at the dirt road ahead. As they passed Rand's house, Guthrie saw that the Audi wasn't in front. When they reached the dirt track leading to Chaney's cabin, he turned down it and crept forward until he stopped at the gate. The blight continued down the lefthand ditch as far as they could see, which was the first bend in the track, some hundred feet beyond the tree line.

"I didn't notice it until I was half way back to the gate," Guthrie said, "so I'm not sure if it goes all the way to the pond or not."

"If it gets in there, it might cause Jim some problems," Turner said, staring down the ditch. He turned to Guthrie. "I have to admit it's peculiar, but I don't know what to make of it. You?"

Guthrie hesitated. If he said what he was thinking, Turner might not believe him. But if he didn't and the chief suspected he was holding back, he'd shut Guthrie out.

"I think whoever brought Telfor's body to Thorndike," he said at last, "also brought something else. Something unnatural that was riding in that foul sofa, and this is the trail it left from the dump to the marsh."

"What?" Turner looked unbelieving. "Like some sort of ghost or evil spirit?"

"Yes. Maybe that's why the sofa is so nasty. Whatever it is fed on Telfor's body and the rot in the dump to grow stronger before it came out and flowed down the ditches. Maybe partially carried by the night mists. Remember, Freddie told Jim that whatever chased him out of the dump was like a creeping black fog that tainted his pants and boots with evil."

"That sounds completely nuts."

"Does it? You know that sofa is so contaminated it's almost impossible to be around. And it's not just tangible filth. Something caused the contamination, and it wasn't Telfor's body. Whatever did is probably why the body is in such a strange state."

"But what the hell could do that?"

"That's for us to find out, Chief."

"And you think it—whatever it is—is down there in the marsh?" He waved across the forest spread before them.

"If it hasn't taken hold already, it soon will."

"You know, Clay, I ought to run you out of town right now. If you start talking about an unnatural invisible horror lurking in the local swamp, you're gonna upset a whole lot of people."

"That's why I'm talking only to you about it. I don't need to convince everyone. Just you, because the two of us are going to have to find out what we're dealing with and how to eliminate it."

"Even supposing I believe you, which I don't, how could we do that?"

"I'm not sure since we don't know what it is."

"You want to go down to the cabin and talk to Jim again?" Turner asked, casting worried eyes down the track to the cabin.

"I don't think that'll do much good right now. I'm more interested in talking to Yanez and Mayfield. They're familiar with the marsh and don't have an emotional attachment to it like Jim does. But the real key is finding Freddie Jensen. He must have been there when the sofa was dumped, or at least soon after. If anybody knows who dumped it, it's him. He saw something, and we need to know what that was."

"Unfortunately, nobody's seen him since Hetty checked him out at the grocery," Turner said. "Frankly, I'm running out of options. I'm beginning to think he might be dead, too."

"He's not dead. He's hiding out somewhere. Would he have left the area?"

Turner shrugged.

"Not without his truck. The county seat is the closest town, and that's way too far to walk. Besides, there's nothing up there for him. I'm baffled," he admitted. "Freddie's such a fixture in town that I confess I don't know a single thing about any family he might have elsewhere."

"We have to work on the supposition that he's alive and has information that'll be valuable for us. We have to find him."

"Let's go to his house and see if he's come back."

"I'm at your disposal, Chief." Looking for Freddie would give Turner something practical to focus on and help restore his equilibrium.

Turner backed down the dirt track to the dirt county road, then drove to the paved road and the turn off to Freddie's house. When they reached the dilapidated structure, nothing seemed different than on their previous visit except that the crime scene tape Turner had strung across the door now lay on the ground beside the meager concrete porch. Obviously someone had entered the house.

Inside, Guthrie didn't spot any changes in all the clutter in the living room, but water puddling the stained tub showed the shower had recently been used. The bar of soap was missing, and so were the toothbrush and toothpaste that had been on the counter. The hook where the towel had been hanging was vacant, and in the bedroom, the pile of clothing that had been lying in a corner was gone, too, and so were the blankets. Several kitchen cabinet doors stood ajar that before had been closed, and all of the non-perishable food stuff had vanished. When Guthrie opened the refrigerator, he saw that a carton of eggs, a loaf of bread, and some other items also were missing. Notably, the three bottles of whiskey that had been in one of the cabinets now lay jumbled in the sink. They were empty, and the sink smelled of alcohol, as if the booze had been poured into it.

"Someone's been here," Turner said.

"Someone who was dirty and hungry. Freddie?"

"I don't see who else would use his shower and take his food and clothes. I guess that's some sort of evidence he's still alive."

"And that he hasn't gone to family," Guthrie said. "If he had, he might have come back for his clothes and toothbrush, but he wouldn't have taken soap, food, and blankets. He's holed up somewhere. He'll surface after his food runs out."

"I hope you're right," Turner said. "I hate to think something happened to him. He could be hiding in any abandoned barn or shed around town, or even under some bridge."

"Yes, but where? We still need to find him."

"We will," Turner said, though his tone held doubt. "Let's check Chaloupeks Grocery to see if he's been there again."

They left the house, closing the door behind them. Turner didn't bother to rearrange the crime scene tape but simply scooped it up and tossed it onto the SUV's backseat floor. After that, he drove to town, where he stopped at the grocery store.

"You don't need to come in," he told Guthrie. "I'm just going to remind the Chaloupeks and their help to let me know immediately if Freddie shows up."

Turner left the SUV running while he went into the grocery store. He was gone about fifteen minutes—longer than Guthrie expected.

"The Chaloupeks are still cleaning up in there," Turner said after he returned. "They haven't seen Freddie since Hetty checked him out the other day, but they'll let me know if he comes in. They did tell me something disturbing, though. They've received complaints that suggest their scales are rigged and that all the rats in the store proved it was filthy. When they questioned the complainers, they were shown some of those 'Eye See U' letters."

"What about the clerks. Hetty? Or Kevin?"

"Both denied receiving any letters, but a lot of folks might do that if the messages embarrass them." Turner passed a weary palm across his face, then he glanced at his watch. "It's already almost five. Let's call it a day."

19

WHEN GUTHRIE WOKE ON TUESDAY morning and looked out the trailer windows, he saw an overcast sky. Not threatening, just a nearly uniform leaden gray that dimmed the landscape. Whatever he did today, it probably would have to do with Chaney Marsh, which had become, he felt, the repository of whatever malign force had infiltrated Thorndike. But there seemed to be no point in visiting the marsh immediately, so he drove to the police station.

Turner's SUV and Tessa's Honda were in their usual spots, as was the Explorer, which Guthrie had learned, belonged to the mayor, who he'd not yet met. Guthrie picked a spot of his own and went into the station. Tessa glanced up as he entered and nodded her head toward the chief's office.

Guthrie pushed through the swinging gate and went over to Turner's door. The Venetian blinds were again levered open, and the chief saw him and waved him in.

"Good thing you're here. I'm headed up to the county seat to get a full report on the autopsies and other evidence. Want to ride along?"

"I do."

"It's only about forty minutes from here, and I'm not due up there until one. We can sit here on our asses until then, or we can do something constructive. Let's talk to Miss Agnes about the letters."

The chief rose, collected his hat, and headed toward the front door, Guthrie close behind. They got into the Interceptor, and

Turner pulled off, heading toward the state road, where he turned north. But almost immediately, he swung the SUV left, onto the road that angled off to the northwest. This was new territory to Guthrie, who hadn't been up this way, though he'd looked at the road on Google Earth. The drive was short. After less than a mile, they came to a cluster of structures set several hundred feet from the left side of the road: a large, two-story farmhouse; a second, smaller house, also two-story; a large metal barn; and several smaller outbuildings, including sheds and a chicken coop at one side of a large, fenced-in chicken yard. The entire property was neat and clean, providing a sharp contrast to the properties in the southeast quadrant of town.

Both houses were sheathed in shiplap, and the larger one was faced by a wide veranda trimmed with touches of gingerbread. They were a similar age to Jim Chaney's old house, but these homes had been kept up and sported coats of white paint and tasteful gray trim that couldn't have been more than a few years old. Two young Hispanic boys were playing in the yard of the smaller house, and they looked up, grinned, and waved as Turner steered the Interceptor down the sweeping dirt and gravel driveway to the larger house. He waved back.

"That's where I grew up," he said, nodding toward the smaller house. "My dad was Miss Agnes's foreman, and we lived there almost the entire time he worked for her. He only stopped after his stroke. Miss Agnes would have made sure he was comfortable even if he couldn't do work for her, but by then, I'd come home to take care of him. Her new foreman, Jaimie Hernandez, lives there now."

Apparently, Miss Agnes heard the SUV crunch up the long dirt and gravel driveway, and she emerged from the house just as Guthrie and Turner reached the steps to the veranda. When Guthrie met her on Sunday, she'd been sitting behind a table, dressed in church clothes, gray hair in a bun. Today, her hair was gathered loosely at the back and falling to her shoulders, but he saw his impression of her had been correct. She wasn't a tall woman, but her solid body, currently encased in a green plaid shirt and worn blue jeans tucked into pull-on work boots, radiated command and awareness. And something else. It took Guthrie a moment to realize it was affection for Chief Turner akin to the pride of an aunt in the accomplishments of a favorite nephew.

"Hello, Bill," she said, smiling as they mounted the steps. "Clay." She stared at Guthrie for a moment then said to Turner, "I suppose your colleague has told you about the eyeball letters."

"You should have come to me about that, Miss Agnes," Turner chided. "Mind if we come in and discuss it?"

In answer, she stepped across the threshold and waved them inside.

Guthrie couldn't see all the way into the house, but the three rooms he could were filled with antique furniture, though the sofa and chairs in the parlor were of modern vintage. The room had a vacant feel, as if it wasn't used much. Miss Agnes waved Guthrie and Turner to the sofa and took a chair roughly facing them.

"I don't know what I can tell you that I haven't told Clay. I have these three nasty and disturbing letters. I suppose he told you the contents."

"He didn't."

"Thank you for your discretion," she said to Guthrie, "though I don't suppose that matters now." She looked at Turner, "I know of three others in town who've gotten letters, also."

"There are more, Miss Agnes," Turner said. "Several attacking the Hughes and Chaloupeks, and there might be other victims we don't know about. Mind showing me the ones you have?"

"I'll be right back."

Miss Agnes rose and left the room, but she returned in less than a minute, three envelopes clutched in her hand. She passed them to Turner, who stared at the eyeball and "Eye See U" letterhead on the first letter for a moment before reading the message below. After scanning the other two letters, he sighed and looked up at Miss Agnes.

"Do you recognize the eye?"

"No," she said. "It could be anybody with brown eyes."

"Mind if I keep these for the time being?" he asked. "They might yield some clues."

"I certainly don't want the nasty things," Miss Agnes snorted. "Just don't show them to anyone."

"I'll have to show them to Tessa since I'm going to have her investigate the source. But we'll keep the contents confidential. And I'd appreciate it if you told anyone else who's received one of these to let me know, too."

"I will, but what if these lies get out? No telling what damage they can do."

"I don't think you need to worry too much. Slander against one person might stick, even if it's a lie, but not this kind of wholesale slander. It looks too much like a deliberate attack on the whole town instead of somebody revealing supposed individual corruption. And if there are enough of them out there, people are going to realize that if what was said about them isn't true, then the rest of the allegations probably aren't, either. In this case, we can rely on safety in numbers."

"I hope you're right," Miss Agnes said. "Have you made any progress on the murder?"

"Not much. We're still looking for Freddie Jensen."

"I sincerely hope nothing's happened to him," Miss Agnes said. "He's a poor soul who doesn't need extra trauma in his life. I always thought he needed a second chance, and now I only hope he's alive to get it."

"We have evidence he's alive," Guthrie told her. "He's obviously been back to his house to clean up and get food. He's probably holed up somewhere."

"But why?"

"That's what we want to find out," Turner said. "We believe he saw something that spooked him, but we won't know until we locate him."

"I'll keep my eye out," Miss Agnes said, then she blanched and gave a sour chuckle. "Damn, after those eyeball letters, I'm going to have to watch my language."

Both men laughed briefly then rose.

"I'll let you know what's happening," Turner promised.

"I know you will."

She escorted them to the door and out to the front yard.

The two boys who'd been playing in front of the other house saw them emerge and yelled out, "Chief Bill! Chief Bill! Come over!"

"Excuse me," Turner said with a wry smile, handing the letters to Guthrie. "Duty calls."

As he walked toward the boys, Miss Agnes chuckled.

"They think he's an Indian chief. They don't know about the police chiefs and crime, yet."

"They seem to like him."

"They've known him since they were born. He's like an uncle."

They watched Turner play catch with the boys for a minute, then Miss Agnes touched Guthrie's arm. He faced her, and she stared intently into his eyes.

"You keep him safe, you hear?" She said, voice low but forceful. "He might have been his momma's boy, but he's also the closest thing I ever had to a son. I watched him grow up, then leave. I tried to get him to stay, but I finally understood the ranching life isn't for him. Then he came back to protect us." Her eyes dropped momentarily before returning to his. "But something…something in my bones, tells me he's gonna need protecting most of all. You promise you'll help him. You promise me, now." Her voice wasn't pleading, despite the tone of entreaty.

"I promise," Guthrie said sincerely. He intended that, anyway.

She nodded, then turned her eyes toward the chief and watched with Guthrie as Turner and the boys tossed the ball a few more times. Finally, he waved goodbye and walked toward the Interceptor, waving again, this time at Miss Agnes.

"I'd better get going," Guthrie told her.

She smiled and nodded as he went to join Turner. A couple of minutes later, the chief was steering the SUV onto Main Street. He glanced at the clock on the dash.

"We still have an hour before we need to leave for the coroner's," he said. "Let's grab a bite before we head out."

20

TURNER DROVE THEM TO THE cafe and parked in front, and they went inside. At this mid-morning hour on a weekday, only the older couple Guthrie had seen here before were in the cafe. He and Turner took a booth beside the front windows, away from the couple. Bev must have seen them park because she was at the table almost as soon as they were seated, bearing water, coffee, menus, and silverware. She took their orders, went to the service window to clip the order slip inside, then returned to the booth and slipped in next to Turner.

"I just served the Baxters their food, so they won't need me for a little while," she said. "I'll take a quick break until your food's ready."

"So, while we wait, tell me about you two," Guthrie said. "High school sweethearts?"

"No" the chief said. "She was four years behind me in school, and I didn't even notice her back then. I met her right here soon after I came back to help tend to Dad. She's worked at Leo's since she graduated."

"Now don't you try to tell Clay you were the one to step up to the plate," Bev said. "The truth is, he gave me the eye for a few weeks but just couldn't work up the nerve to ask me out."

"It wasn't that. I just couldn't believe she wasn't attached."

"Is that a polite way of saying I was an old maid?" she asked, then she gave Guthrie a sardonically haughty stare. "I'll have you know I had plenty of suitors, just none who were suitable. Until this lanky man starts coming into Leo's. Like I said, he kept giving me the eye but doing nothing. So, one day while I was refilling his coffee cup, I mentioned there was a movie I wanted to see playing at the theater in the county seat. Even so, it took him another two days to ask me to go."

"It's the truth, Clay. I was a dumb rooster who needed a little prompting to crow. But when I had the chance, I jumped at it, and we've been together ever since."

"I met Emily on Sunday, but isn't there another?"

"Our son, Ethan, goes to A&M," Bev said, pride in her voice. "He's studying engineering."

"No law enforcement for him?"

"Definitely not," Turner said.

"So how'd you come to be police chief?" Guthrie asked.

"When I graduated high school, my best prospect was to hire on with Miss Agnes and try to work my way up to foreman. That's what my dad did, and he had a good job with her—at least for these parts —and she always treats her help well. But I watched my dad work hard for his pay, and decades of that just wore him to a nubbin. I didn't want that for me or any family I might raise.

"So I looked at my only other options, those being college or the military. I wanted to go to college, but it was too expensive for a poor boy like me, and I couldn't qualify for any scholarships. You might think Miss Agnes could have helped me out like she's done so many others, but back then, she couldn't. All those freezes and droughts that killed off most of Jim Chaney's herd did a lot of damage to all the ranchers around here, including the Carpenters.

"All that took place during a critical time for me, so with few other options, I went into the Army and did one tour in the Middle East, with a second in Europe as an MP. When that was over, I knew the Army wasn't for me, either, though I'd liked being an MP. So when I came back to Texas, I enrolled in the police academy in Dallas. I was with Dallas PD for about four years, and I'd probably still be there if Dad hadn't had his stroke. I resigned and came home to help Mom take care of him. By then, Miss Agnes had recovered financially, and she very generously paid some of Dad's medical expenses. But he and Mom had to move out of the house to let the new foreman move in, so we moved to a smaller house in town. Not the one, we live in now, though. Bev and I bought that after we got married so we'd both be close to work."

"That must have been hard on your parents."

"Hardest on Mom, who'd made that house her home, but Dad was pretty debilitated and didn't seem to care where he was." His lips tightened with thought. "He didn't last long after that. Maybe six months. And right after he passed, Mom came down with liver cancer, and she was gone by the end of the next year. I think she missed Dad so much she just had to follow him. So there I was, high and dry in Thorndike without a job. I wanted to stay here because of Bev, and I could have hired on with Miss Agnes, but I still didn't want to do that kind of work. Plus, I just didn't know the business. I'd been in the Army and the DPD while many of my high school peers were learning how to run ranches and farms. I reapplied to the DPD, and I even applied to the Houston PD, but luckily, Thorndike's previous chief, Gary Withers, got funding to hire an officer. He knew me from before I left and appreciated my military and police background, so he offered me the job. When he retired seven years ago, I was hired to replace him. Anyway, after I got the job, I hired my own officer."

"Order up, Bev," Leo called out, and rose to get it.

"I'd say Emmet is a brave choice," Guthrie said.

"Not brave. Practical. Like me, he grew up in Thorndike in a good family. He has roots here and knows a lot of people. And he served a couple of tours in the Army in the Middle East before he came back."

"How do the locals take to being policed by a black officer?"

"He is fairly well respected among the black and brown residents, and most of the whites. There's a few who don't like it, but the badge gives him some protection as well as authority. He saw combat, and you've probably noticed he's pretty tough. Not many around here would mess with him. He and I are the law here, and the hard-core bigots know I can make things difficult for them if they disrespect him."

Bev returned with their meals, set the plates in front of them, then excused herself.

"Break's over," she said. "I have to finish up with the Baxters and help get ready for the lunch crowd."

She left and went to the table where the older couple sat.

"And how come a country boy from Thorndike didn't become a bigot, too?" Guthrie asked as he attacked his food.

"I guess growing up around Miss Agnes gave me a perspective I might not have had otherwise. She and Ed had a big library, and she encouraged me to read. That's one way to travel the world and experience all sorts of people and history. And the Army and my time in the DPD taught me a lot of things I never could have learned in Thorndike or from books. One of them was to live with and get along with just about every color person you can imagine. And religion, too." He shrugged. "Lots of folks who hold bigotry in their hearts only find reasons to sustain it, but after a time, I just found myself looking at people, not colors or symbols. You don't need those to tell the good from the bad."

Guthrie gave a short laugh.

"I'm surprised they still have you as chief."

"Gary Withers managed to keep folks in line because he believed in diplomacy first but decisive action when needed, and everybody around here knows I'm the same. The truth is, most of that decisive action is keeping the brawls at the Lazy Q from becoming murderous, and Emmet and I exercise that duty frequently. But more importantly, I placate the various factions in town. I can do that because they know I won't take sides and can't be bought. Nor can Emmet. I keep them from each other's throats. But eventually, one of them will develop a bite big enough to swallow them all."

"What then?"

"Hell, I just hope I can snatch my arm away before it gets chomped off." He shrugged. "If that happens, I guess I'll just retire. It all depends on what happens and when and how."

Then both went silent as they ate their meals. After they were done, Turner glanced at his watch.

"Enough grub and gab. Time to visit Dr. Bob."

2I

IN TEN MINUTES, THEY WERE on the state road, heading for the county seat. When they arrived at the medical examiner's office, which occupied a building set apart from the county sheriff's office, they were greeted by a crime tech who led them to the autopsy room, adjacent to the morgue. They followed the tech through a pair of swinging doors, into the autopsy room's chill, then the tech left.

Five people besides Guthrie and Turner were present, though only two were alive: Dr. Bob Latimer and another tech. They each wore a gown and face protector as they stood over the autopsy table in the center of the room, working on a body whose chest was splayed open. Not the one found in the dump, but an older man with a thick middle, sagging flesh, and gray hair going white. To the right were stainless steel carts holding trays of surgical equipment, and more equipment was stored in glass-front stainless steel cabinets against the nearby walls. Off to the left, four gurneys were arrayed, two of which were occupied by bodies—one sheet-covered and the other in a zipped-up black body bag. A faint scent of decay hung in the air despite the chill and chemical odors. Dr. Bob saw them come in.

"Close him up," Latimer said to the tech, then he came over to Guthrie and Turner, tugging the mask from his face and setting it on a table. He stripped off his rubber gloves, dropped them into a trash bin as he passed, and flapped his hands in the air.

"Thank goodness for a chance to take off those damn things and let my skin dry out," he said, "Pleased to see you, again, Mr. Guthrie." Latimer stuck out his hand, and Guthrie shook it. It was warm and damp from being in the rubber glove. "Maybe I should rephrase it to say that you've presented us one hell of a body. None of us has ever seen anything like it. The closest anybody's gotten is that Mr. Telfor somehow turned into a dried-out version of those bog mummies occasionally found in the United Kingdom and Europe. But those took a couple of centuries to form, and from your investigation, it seems Telfor became like that in a matter of a few days. While lounging on a sofa."

"Can we see him, Dr. Bob?" Turner asked.

"If you must," Latimer said heavily, his wrinkled upper lip and nose uncharacteristic on the face of any coroner. "He's not in here. We might know what killed him, but we sure as hell don't know what turned his body like that. Even though the FBI toxicology lab says there's nothing obvious to worry about, I'm not taking any chances. He's in the coolers. We've got the temperature turned down so low he's just about frozen solid. Not that it's helped much." He jerked his head toward swinging double doors in the far wall. "This way."

Latimer led them through the doors, into the morgue. Drawers lined the back wall like a bank of filing cabinets for the dead. Or maybe huge safety-deposit boxes for some kind of afterlife. Latimer went over, tugged out a drawer, and pulled down the sheet that lay over the body. The man beneath the sheet did, indeed, resemble a dried-out bog man. His torso was flattened beneath the huge, Y-shaped autopsy suture, and his skin looked like dark leather, a uniform muddy brown that appeared simultaneously desiccated and damp. It showed none of the normal signs of decay.

Bad as Telfor looked, that was the best of it. The corpse still exuded an aura of foulness that went beyond decay. Guthrie's Kuei men had been twitching since he'd entered the morgue, though not as much as he'd expected. Latimer stared down at the body, nose wrinkling again, and Turner seemed reluctant to lean over it. Guthrie didn't blame them.

"Okay," Latimer said. "Norman Telfor. Positive ID. Cause of death was a single gunshot wound to the chest that penetrated the heart." He pointed to a small hole that seemed almost inconsequential next to the autopsy incision. "We retrieved the bullet. A .380. It's fairly intact, so if you find the weapon, we can do a ballistics match. Death would have been almost instantaneous. No signs of alcohol or drugs in his blood or tissues, though from the condition of his liver, I'd say he was a moderately heavy drinker."

"No time of death, I assume," Turner said.

"I understand he was shot in Airla, so we can infer that the time of death occurred sometime between six and nine PM the Saturday before last. That's what I'm putting on the report, but to tell the truth, it could have happened many hours later. His blood was on the cushions and moving quilts, so we know he was placed on the sofa and covered up after he was shot. But it wasn't a large amount. He clearly died in that sawmill. Otherwise, a lot of our forensic tools are useless in this case. Often we can use the degree of rigor or decay or the life cycles of insects feeding off a corpse to roughly determine how long the victim has been dead, but this corpse shows no signs of normal decay and there are absolutely no larvae." He shook his head, looking almost distraught at the thought. "No larvae, no ants, no nothing. Impossible, especially considering the environment in which the body was discovered, but true. Even the organs haven't deteriorated normally."

"When you examined the jeans and boots that were lying on the ground," Guthrie asked, "was there any sort of black stain on them?"

"What sort of stain?"

"Freddie Jensen ran to Jim Chaney for protection," Turner supplied after a glance at Guthrie. "He told Jim that something black and oily stained his jeans and boots."

"The jeans and boots were definitely not the cleanest I've ever seen," Latimer responded. "But there wasn't anything unusual. Nothing that wouldn't be there considering Mr. Jensen worked in a dump." He stepped to a nearby cabinet, opened it, and pulled out a plastic bag containing a wallet, a pocketknife, and some loose change. "These were in the jeans' pockets," he said, handing the bag to Turner. "I didn't bother including the handkerchief since it was pretty used. You might want to give them back to Mr. Jensen when you find him."

"Okay," Turner said, taking the bag.

"Would you mind sending a copy of the report to the insurance company?" Guthrie asked, passing Latimer a slip of paper with the contact information for Mr. Oliver at Mutual Indemnity. He knew that the policy covering Telfor would pay double-indemnity if the cause of death was murder. He hoped that would help Betsy Telfor since nothing else about this case could.

"Sure thing. I just hope you guys solve this case ASAP. The sooner we get rid of that body, the better. If nothing else is needed, we're releasing him to his wife in a couple of days, and that can't come soon enough. I don't know what it is about him…. He's just repellent, somehow. Don't ask me more, or I'll start sounding like some sort of crank. There was a case some years back—the mid-1990s, if I remember correctly. A woman suffering from a terminal cancer collapsed and was rushed to the ER. Her heart stopped, so naturally, they defibrillated her. An oily sheen then appeared on her skin, and almost immediately, the doctors and nurses attending her began to experience nausea and lightheadedness. Several even passed out, and a couple had to be hospitalized themselves. It turned out she'd been chronically lathering her body with an over-the-counter analgesic containing dimethyl sulfoxide to combat the pain caused by her cancer. Her skin was suffused with it. Normally, dimethyl sulfoxide is benign, but when the ER team administered the electric shock, it broke down into dimethyl sulfate, which is a nerve gas that's been used in warfare." Latimer shook his head. "We just don't know, sometimes."

"I think we both understand perfectly," Turner said, not mentioning that it was highly unlikely Norman Telfor had been using some pain-relieving cream in excess.

"Yes" Latimer said. "You found him. I think he was worse, then. It's probably some sort of off-gassing, like that woman, though we can't detect any toxic substances. We even checked for radiation. Maybe the body will eventually rid itself of whatever it is, maybe not, but I'm going to recommend he be cremated rather than buried. Certainly there shouldn't be a public viewing. Not that anyone would want to look at that." He gestured to the body lying in the drawer.

"Would you convey that information to Detective Peters?" Guthrie said. "He'd be in a better position to convince Mrs. Telfor to follow your suggestion."

"I'll do that, of course."

"What about the sofa?" Guthrie asked.

"Normally, we store larger items in a metal building out back," Latimer said. "But the sofa was simply too foul. Far worse than Mr. Telfor. That damn thing contaminates everything it touches. In fact, it's entirely possible that whatever is contaminating the sofa transferred some of that contamination to Mr. Telfor's body after he was laid on it. We didn't want it spoiling any evidence not related to this case, so we bought a small shed to store it in. As far from everything else as possible." He chuckled sourly. "We'll probably tear it down and dispose of it along with the sofa when the case is closed. Preferably by fire." He shook his head, an expression of confusion on his face.

"What?" Guthrie asked.

"I don't know," the coroner demurred. "But it's something more than the physical contamination. None of us can stand to be around it for any length of time, even with the hazmat suits. Some of us get headaches, some nausea, some vertigo." He shook his head again. "Like the body, it's probably off-gassing a toxic substance, even if we can't detect what it is."

The words sounded reasonable coming out of his mouth, but some sort of doubt lingered in his eyes.

"There's something more, isn't there?" Guthrie pressed.

Latimer hesitated a moment then said, "Clearly the sofa is a nexus of contamination, even if it's not the original source. If I had to characterize it, I'd say it's not just filthy, foul, and contaminated; it's loathsome. That's the worst of it, and I can't explain it. The hazmat suits protect us from the physical filth and contamination, but the sofa is very difficult to be around, and the suits are no help. I can't tell you what it is." He shrugged. "It just feels like, like…." His voice dropped off as words and concepts failed him.

Guthrie knew the feeling the coroner was talking about. He'd managed to dampen down the twitching of his Kuei men, but he could sense the malign exudations from the corpse, and the sofa had been worse. Both Turner and the coroner were edgy and getting more so the longer they stood over Telfor's body, but Guthrie agreed with the coroner that whatever outré contamination had engulfed Norm was slowly fading.

He asked where Freddie Jensen's pickup was, and Latimer told them it was parked next to the shed holding the sofa.

"Speaking of vehicles," the ME said, "we sent images of the tire impressions at the dump to the Oakdale PD, and they confirmed they were definitely made by Mr. Telfor's van. So we know his van was in the dump despite where it was found."

Abruptly, Latimer hunched up his shoulders and shivered.

"Let's get out of here," he suggested, and he pulled the sheet over the body and slid the drawer shut before leading them back to the autopsy room. Turner was obviously relieved to be leaving the body behind, and so was Guthrie.

"What's with the guy on the table?" Turner asked.

"Local resident. Heart attack. His wife said he refused to take his statins for years, and his arteries and veins are just about solidly packed with cholesterol. The other two are less prosaic."

He led them over to the sheet-covered body and pulled the cover down to reveal a man's torso. He was a tough-looking Anglo male, but the three gunshot wounds to his chest had been tougher.

"The results of a barroom brawl last night," Dr. Bob said, shrugging. "If there's anything that'll kill you quicker than cholesterol build-up, it's getting shot in the chest." He glanced at Turner. "Seems like we had one of these down your way a few years back."

Turner nodded as Latimer pulled the sheet over the body and turned to the body bag.

"This is our latest," he said. "A John Doe. He just came in this morning, so we haven't had a chance to unwrap him. The body was found in a ditch off a county road northeast of town. He was stripped naked, and there was nothing on his person to identify him. His fingerprints aren't in AFIS, and so far, the police haven't managed to locate anyone who knew him, and no one matching his description has been reported missing."

Latimer glanced at Guthrie and Turner as he reached for the body bag's zipper.

"It isn't pretty," he warned as he unzipped the bag.

22

THE UNZIPPED OPENING REVEALED THE naked corpse of an African American man. A through-and-through gunshot wound, back to front, had wrecked his right shoulder, and stab wounds and gashes too numerous to easily count were slashed everywhere across his face, chest, arms, and legs, leaving ugly, pale gaping mouths. His eyes were puffed shut, contusions splotched his face, bruises marred his chest and abdomen, and ligature marks darkened his wrists and ankles. Worst of all, he was castrated. Guthrie felt Turner start as the man's face came into view, and despite the disfiguring wounds, Guthrie instantly recognized him, too.

"You can give him a name," Turner said. "That's Jeff Mayfield. He lives—lived—in Thorndike. I'll send up the particulars after I get back to the office."

The coroner gave him a sharp look.

"What the hell is going on down there, Bill? Two murders in less than two weeks. That must be some kind of record for Thorndike."

"Not one I relish," Turner said. "At least Telfor was actually killed in Airla."

"I haven't fully examined Mr. Mayfield," the coroner said, "but certainly he was shot from behind. None of the knife wounds are particularly deep, so call it a death of a thousand cuts. Those contributed to his death, but he bled out mostly from the castration and gunshot wound."

"He was tortured?" Turner asked, though it sounded more like a statement.

"It's likely. It took some time for him to die, so it was painful. Deliberately painful. In a practiced way. Both of his Achilles tendons were slashed, making it impossible for him to escape from his attacker, even if shock from the gunshot didn't disable him. We don't have the bullet since it went all the way through, and we have no idea where to look for it, but the wound looks like it was made by a medium-caliber handgun round. Based on my preliminary examination, it appears that at least two, possibly three, different knives were used. And obviously, he was severely beaten before he was castrated and died. There might have been multiple attackers, considering the differences in the wounds."

"Was he killed where he was found?" Guthrie asked.

"Definitely not. The body was dumped. He was killed elsewhere, and wherever it was, there'd be a lot of blood."

"Well, I can't say this has been a productive visit," Turner told the coroner. "I came up here for answers, but all you've given me are more questions and another murder."

"This one might not have taken place in your jurisdiction, either," Latimer pointed out.

"Even so, Jeff is one of the citizens I swore to serve and protect."

"It's strange Jeff was murdered like that," Guthrie said after they were in the Interceptor and Turner had steered onto the road. "He had a revolver on him, and he almost pulled it on me when I surprised him. He was wary of trouble and was big and fit. He wouldn't have been easy to take down."

"Unless it was a sneak attack," Turner said. "Possibly by multiple attackers, according to Dr. Bob. Since he was shot from behind in the right shoulder, he probably couldn't have drawn his gun. Or maybe he didn't have his gun on him at the time." He sighed. "Could be any damn thing."

During the drive to Thorndike, they discussed the various ramifications of the case. They now knew Norman Telfor had died in Airla, but who had driven his body and the sofa to the dump? Had Freddie let the van into the dump, or had someone else used a key to the second lock on the dump gate? Why were Telfor's body and the sofa brought all the way to Thorndike's dump from a dead small town in Louisiana? Where was Freddie? And did Jeff Mayfield's death have any connection to any of the rest of it? Most of all, Guthrie wondered what the hell was now lurking in Chaney Marsh.

When Turner finally pulled into the parking lot next to the police station, a sparkling clean black Chevy Silverado HD with lots of chrome was parked next to Guthrie's shabbier Xterra.

"Now what does he want?" Turner muttered.

"Who?" Guthrie asked.

"Leland Fuller."

No sooner had Guthrie and Turner gotten out of the Interceptor than an older, well-built man with a patrician air emerged from the door to City Hall. He was dressed in a light-gray western suit that looked expensive, and his head was topped with a wide-brimmed, snow-white Stetson One thing was certain: If he and his rival, Jim Chancy, were the same age, Fuller had beaten Chancy at the aging game. And maybe every other game except winning the hand of Enid Kellmann. He spotted Turner and Guthrie as he came down the steps and strode over to them.

"Hello, Chief," Fuller said jovially.

"What can I do for you, Leland?" Turner asked without obvious enthusiasm, but Fuller didn't seem to notice the question. Instead, he turned to Guthrie and looked him up and down.

"You must be that city slicker detective who found the body in the dump. Just so's you know, I don't give detectives much never-mind. No offense intended, son. Hell, I barely tolerate Bill, here."

Hard to take that kind of thing without offense when one is wearing a badge, but Turner just ignored it.

"And you must be the Meat King of Texas," Guthrie said.

Fuller puffed up a little and seemed to regard Guthrie in a more favorable light, apparently not noticing the slight sarcasm in Guthrie's voice.

"You heard that right, son," he said.

"I wouldn't underestimate Mr. Guthrie," Turner said.

Fuller gave Guthrie another appraising stare then looked at Turner.

"What can I do for you?" Turner repeated.

"Not what you can do for me," Fuller said. "What I can do for the Chaloupeks. I heard about their problem, and that's a problem for Leo, too, since he gets all his supplies from them. And the whole town. I've been over to the store, and to Leo's, and just now to Mayor Acuff. Since you're here, I might as well tell you the good news."

"Good news would be welcome, today," Turner said.

"I can't do anything about all the spoiled produce, but I'm donating enough meat to restock the grocery. Free of charge, mind you."

"That's mighty nice of you," Turner said. "I'm sure the Chaloupeks will appreciate it."

"Hell, the whole town will appreciate it," Fuller beamed. "Even your city slicker detective friend knows I'm the Meat King of Texas. It's not like I'm hurting for supplies. 'Sides, I can't have folks in my town starve, 'specially since half of 'em work for me." He leaned forward and said in a conspiratorial voice that retained its joviality, "Between the three of us, I'll just raise the price of everything going out a few cents to cover it."

Fuller straightened and touched two well-manicured fingers to the brim of his hat.

"Got to get back to the ranch now and make sure that order arrives first thing in the morning."

With that, Fuller strode to the Silverado, got in, cranked the engine, and roared out of the parking lot.

"Generous of him," Guthrie commented as the dust settled.

"Not really," Turner responded. "It just puts the town more in his debt." He sighed wearily. "It's been a hell of a day, and I need to go in and send a report on Jeff Mayfield to Dr. Bob."

Since the hour was edging into late afternoon, Guthrie left the chief and drove to his trailer. That night, he dreamt of monstrous saurians rearing out of primeval swamps.

23

IN THE MORNING, GUTHRIE DROVE to the police station, but Turner wasn't there.

"He said you'd probably come by," Tessa said, "but he's across the street at Eli Carlin's Auto Repair investigating a break-in. Somebody stole a bunch of his tools. I don't know how long he'll be. He would have sent Emmet, but he was already on another house call. Some kind of domestic disturbance." She hesitated for a moment then said, "He told me about Jeff Mayfield." Her gaze was steady, but her lips were tight, and her eyes held sorrow and fear in equal amounts. "It's terrible. We never had this kind of stuff happen here, and now it's all sorts of crazy. What's going on?"

"I wish I could tell you," Guthrie said sincerely. But he couldn't. He didn't have enough information to tell anybody anything, and even if he did, could he tell anyone other than, perhaps, Turner?

"Anything you want me to tell the chief?" Tessa asked.

"I'll be back," he intoned in an Arnold Schwarzenegger voice, and that brought a short laugh from her, though her eyes remained tense.

Outside in the sunshine, he pondered what to do next. There was, he realized, only one thing to do, and that was visit the marsh again. Everything about this case reinforced his opinion that an unknown something had ridden into Thorndike on the sofa and now was taking root in the wetland. He wanted to see it again, feel it again to discover if the sensations from his previous visits remained or were any different.

He drove to the bridge over Steele Creek. The shoulder where both poachers' trucks had been parked was empty. Guthrie pulled onto the grass, got out, and walked down to the creek. The creek, path, and surroundings looked the same as when he'd come this way two days ago: shaded, misty, and chilly. At the time, there'd been no activity from the Kuei men this far upstream, but today, their twitching told him something was different. Whatever had flowed down the ditches from the dump had definitely become stronger.

He moved cautiously along the path, legs swirling the low mist, to where the creek widened into the pond. The place where Yanez had been fishing was trampled, numerous sneaker footprints impressed into the damp soil, some of which Guthrie recognized as his own. The others, all the same, must have been Yanez's. Leaving Yanez's fishing spot behind, Guthrie walked down the trail beside the pond toward the place where he'd met Jeff Mayfield, the Kuei men's antics increasing the farther he went. When he reached Mayfield's spot, he saw the bank there also was trampled with footprints, but something about them made him bend and bat the mists aside for a closer look.

At least five different shoe impressions were pressed into the damp dirt. A few were his own sneaker treads from his previous visit, but the other four were clearly made by different shoes. Most of the prints undoubtedly belonged to Jeff Mayfield, but what about the others? Segundo Yanez? Guthrie would have to compare these prints to the ones back at his fishing spot, but he didn't think so. Both Mayfield and Yanez had been wearing old tennis shoes, and three sets of prints had been made by smooth soles and heels. The two larger sets seemed to have wide, heavy heels and probably had been made by work boots, while the heels of the third, smaller, set were much crisper and shallower, as if from a lighter man wearing street shoes. All the sets overlapped one another in confusion, nearly obliterating Guthrie's tracks from his previous visit, as if there'd been a struggle.

Then, as Guthrie straightened, he saw what he'd missed, partly because of the mists and partly because he'd been so focused on the footprints. The undergrowth beside the path was trampled and beaten down, and the foliage was spattered with what looked like blood.

Despite himself, Guthrie backed up a step, instantly convinced Jeff Mayfield had been attacked—and possibly died—on this spot.

But how did his body end up forty miles away, northeast of the county seat? And what happened to his clothing, truck, and fishing gear? Guthrie cast around with his eyes, but there was nothing in the brush or on the path that wasn't natural. Then, almost incidentally, his eyes caught a dim shape in the murky water, and he bent for a closer look. It was a fishing rod and reel. It looked a lot like the one he'd seen Mayfield using.

Guthrie left the rod and reel where they were and glanced up the path toward the bend that concealed Chaney's cabin. Footprints were there, too. Two sets—both going and coming back. One was clearly his own tracks from his earlier visit, and the other resembled the prints left by Mayfield's sneakers. Walking beside the path so he wouldn't leave additional prints, he went down it and cautiously approached the last bend, the Kuei men's activity increasing as he went. He halted behind the bushes at the apex of the bank's curve and peered through them. Jim Chaney was sitting on the covered deck, staring out across the water. It was as if he hadn't moved since Guthrie had last seen him. He even seemed to be wearing the same clothes.

Guthrie backed away and returned to the state road, paying attention to the footprints along the path and wishing he'd noticed them before he'd trampled them. He could tell that all the ones with the heels had come from the state road and returned in that direction. As he walked, the kicking of the Kuei men decreased but didn't quite vanish, even after he reached the Xterra. He sat there and considered calling Turner, but he knew the chief was preoccupied with the burglary, so he decided to drive into town to report the scene in person as soon as the chief was done with Eli Carlin.

His immediate plans changed as he approached the Lazy Q. Although it was before noon on a Wednesday, a large, recent-model, jacked-up four-wheel-drive white Chevy pickup, two American pickups—one a fairly recent blue Chevy, the other a battered red Ford—and a vintage gray Ford sedan were scattered around the dirt and gravel parking lot.

The one incongruous vehicle was a black Audi A3.

Guthrie doubted that there were two such cars in Thorndike, so it could only belong to George Rand. That made him wonder why Rand was here. He wore expensive clothes as comfortably as he did his patrician air, bragged about having money, and said he wanted to make acquaintances in town. But the Lazy Q's clientele certainly wasn't

Thorndike's upper crust, and drinking with the local riff-raff before noon on a weekday seemed a little out of his comfort zone. The temptation to find out why Rand was here was too strong to resist, so Guthrie swung the Xterra into the dirt parking lot. The crime scene he'd just left had waited this long. It could wait another few minutes.

Most of the vehicles were parked close to the building, so Guthrie pulled into the empty road-side of the lot. Before getting out, he unholstered his pistol and locked it in the glove compartment. Then he strode across the lot, went up the three steps to the veranda, and pushed into the building. The jukebox was playing a country-western song, but nobody was out on the spare dance floor. There were no women in the place to dance with. Two of the tables scattered around its margins were occupied—one by two middle-aged men drinking draft beers and playing dominoes and the other by five men, also drinking beers—theirs from a pitcher on the table. Three empties sat next to it.

Guthrie recognized four of the men from his previous visit with Chief Turner: the Sanford brothers and their two cronies, Rob Fitzgerald and Johnny Miller. The fifth was George Rand, and they all looked buddy-buddy.

Guthrie's goal wasn't about confrontation but about intelligence gathering, so instead of approaching the table, he walked over to the bar where Frank Orman stood. Rand's appraising stare as Guthrie crossed the room turned into a sly but icy smile.

"I'm Clay Guthrie," he said to Orman. "I was in here the other day with Chief Turner."

"I remember," Orman said. "What can I get you?"

"I'll have a draft," Guthrie said, though he had no intention of drinking it. Alcohol wasn't in his diet any more. But it was polite—perhaps necessary—to order something.

"Frank, right?" Guthrie asked when the bartender set the mug of beer in front of him on a round cardboard coaster.

"Must be," Orman said, starting to move away.

"Stay for a minute, will you?" Guthrie said. "I'd like to ask you a few questions."

Frank gave him the evil eye, and his jaw hardened.

"More questions about Freddie Jensen?"

"Just wondering if you've seen him."

"No."

"How about Jeff Mayfield or Segundo Yanez?"

"Don't know 'em."

Guthrie guessed he could try greasing Frank's palm with a twenty, but already he didn't like the guy.

Guthrie turned around and called out to the other occupants of the room.

"Any of you guys know Jeff Mayfield or Segundo Yanez?"

"Frank already told you," said one of the men sitting with Rand. Wiley Sanford. His shaved head gleamed in the light, and his full beard jutted forward aggressively. His tone was belligerent. "Ain't no Mayfield or Yanez around here. We don't let niggers and wetbacks drink with decent white folk."

"That's funny, Wiley. Decent white folks don't engage in bigotry. But apparently, you do. Jeff Mayfield told me you and Lonnie sometimes go down where they fish and hassle them."

"They's trespassing on private property."

"And you aren't when you go down there to harass them?"

"Jim Chaney told me...."

"Jim Chaney didn't tell you anything," Guthrie said. "But he did tell me he doesn't care if they fish the pond."

"Well, who gives a shit what you say?"

"Chief Turner might since it looks like Jeff was murdered down there. Where you go to harass him. You've heard about that, I'm sure."

They couldn't have, yet none of them seemed surprised. Rand leaned over to Wiley and whispered something. Wiley smiled, nodded, got up, and came over to the bar. Close up, he looked to be in his late thirties and was big, meaty, and tough looking, though a beer gut was beginning to spill over his belt. His thick forearms each had a tattooed snake that twisted around the arm from elbow to wrist. He was in a need of a bath, too, Guthrie thought, noticing he was wearing smooth-soled pull-on work boots, small clots of dried mud clinging to the sides of the soles.

Behind him, still at the table, Rand was giving a subdued smirk, though calculated curiosity lurked in his eyes. The other men at the table perked up as if eager to view some excitement.

"Lonnie seen you in Leo's, talking to that old bag, Agnes Carpenter," Wiley said. "Why don't you ask her? And now, you need to move. This end of the bar's mine."

"Okay." Guthrie picked up his beer and moved to the other end of the bar.

Wiley followed.

"This end's mine, too."

"Two ends?" Guthrie said with a faint smile.

"That's right."

The exchange had lasted less than a minute, but already Guthrie'd had enough. If there was anything he hated, it was a bully, so he decided to do a little bullying of his own.

"I guess you need that much room to hold your fat ass."

"What the fuck did you say?" Wiley's shaved cranium flushed, and his beard and mustache twitched as his face screwed with anger.

"Or maybe you just have two assholes."

The words were designed to provoke, and they did.

"You must want your ass kicked real bad," Wiley growled, thrusting his beard forward threateningly.

"That's right, Wiley," Fitzgerald chirped up. "You tell 'im."

"Okay," Orman said harshly to Guthrie. "I'm gonna have to ask you to leave. Now."

"Why, sure," Guthrie said pleasantly.

"Pay for your beet, first," Orman said.

"Sorry, but it's Wiley's bar, that it must be Wiley's beer. Make him pay for it."

He headed for the door, hearing footsteps follow behind him, and beyond that, chair legs scraping the floor. He was already down the steps and out into the parking lot when he heard Wiley bark behind him.

"Hey, you! Where you think you're goin', faggot?"

Guthrie turned. Wiley was in front as his brother and the two men with them came through the door and down the steps. The leader, Guthrie thought. Lonnie was only a tad smaller. The other two were about Guthrie's height, Fitzgerald heavier and Miller lighter, and Guthrie judged that neither of them had the balls to start a fight, though they might participate if they thought they would win. The dominoes players also emerged, but they stayed on the porch, onlookers to possible mayhem. Rand came out, too, and stood behind them, watching with intent curiosity.

"You talking to me?" Guthrie asked blandly.

"Who the fuck you think I'm talkin' to?"

Guthrie pulled out his phone and speed-dialed Turner's number.

"Who you callin', faggot?" Wiley demanded, taking an aggressive step forward.

Turner came on the line.

"I know you're busy this morning," Guthrie said, "but you better send an ambulance to the Lazy Q."

"You hurt?"

"No, but somebody is about to be." Guthrie hung up and slipped the phone into his pocket.

"You're gonna need that ambulance," Wiley sneered.

"Get 'im, Wiley!" Johnny Miller yelled, and Wiley, uncharacteristic of his name, obeyed and waded in, clearly considering the smaller Guthrie easy pickings.

Most guys throwing an initial punch will aim at the head, and Wiley's strategy was no different. But a head can bob and weave, and his first punch went sailing by as Guthrie swerved left and circled his arms up to ward off the blow. In an instant, he was perpendicular to Wiley's angle of force and had him twisted sideways across his own center. He gave the upper arm and shoulder a sharp, surging upward shove that launched Wiley off his feet and sent him crashing to his side on the oily dirt. Something Guthrie had learned early in his tai chi training was that there's no more solid and powerful a fist than Earth. Slam somebody onto the ground, and it hurt them without hurting you.

Despite the shock, Wiley was up in a moment, obviously as groggy from the beer he'd been drinking as from the impact. He turned on Guthrie, face a red mask of anger and embarrassment. He swaggered forward and tried another punch at Guthrie's head, completely exposing his torso. He might have thought his stomach muscles and beer gut would absorb any blow, and they might have. But not his solar plexus. A hard, snapping punch with the first two knuckles driven into the solar plexus will make any man's legs melt right out from under him, and a really powerful blow there could freeze the diaphragm, sealing the breath with potentially fatal consequences.

Guthrie didn't want to kill Wiley, only disable him, so he ducked under Wiley's swing and drove his knuckles into Wiley's solar plexus. Using the recoil of the punch, he danced back as Wiley grunted. For a split second, a look of contempt crossed Wiley's features, but it instantly faded into shock as he tried to take a breath. He groaned and crashed to his knees in the dirt, clutching his middle and gasping for air.

"Get up, Wiley!" bellowed his brother. "Get up!"

Wiley did, leaning heavily on his knees, gasping, before straightening with obvious effort. He shook his head and focused on Guthrie, face twisting with rage. His brute instinct told him to charge and throw another punch, which is exactly the wrong thing to do against anyone at all adept at tai chi. As his blow launched, Guthrie simply sidestepped and hooked the wrist of the incoming fist in the gap between his left thumb and forefinger. His right forearm came up beneath Wiley's forearm, locking the elbow straight between Guthrie's forearms. Then using Wiley's forward momentum, he pulled the punch back, simultaneously spinning on his axis and twisting Wiley's arm. The leverage, twist, and spin, applied to Wiley's momentum but at an inopportune angle, caused him not only to sail by Guthrie with his feet in the air, it flipped him over and sent him crashing onto his back eight feet away.

When he didn't get up, Lonnie decided it was his turn. He wasn't quite as big and strong as Wiley, but he was big enough and maybe a little quicker. But he was drunk enough that he was clumsy. He, too, came on strong, punching at Guthrie's head. Some people never learn, Guthrie thought as he sidestepped to the left, behind Lonnie's forward leg, snatched the incoming wrist with his right hand, and whipped his left arm under Lonnie's armpit and across his chest. Then he turned sharply left on his axis, throwing Lonnie over his left leg, onto the ground behind him. Lonnie landed on his upper back with a heavy thud and a woof. He started to get up, but Guthrie grabbed one of his dangling mustaches and jerked it one way while kicking Lonnie's supporting arm out from under him the other way. Lonnie collapsed, unable to clutch his shoulder and nurse his raw face at the same time, but fully capable of groaning curses.

Guthrie turned to Miller and Fitzgerald, but they just shook their heads and backed off. Then he strode to the bottom of the steps and looked up at Rand, who didn't seem cowed but stared back, eyes calculating.

"I have your number now, Rand. It's only a matter of time before I learn enough to come down on you. Hard."

"Not if you're no longer around."

At that moment, Orman pushed through the front door, holding a sawed-off pump shotgun. Behind him, Rand stared with great intensity at the back of his head, a twitch of gleeful anticipation marring the dead line of his mouth.

"He's trouble," Rand said to Orman. His voice was soft, but it held a note of command. "We don't want him around."

"I don't think you'll be needing that, Frank," Guthrie said.

"Maybe I will," Frank said, raising the barrel.

"And how will you feel when Chief Turner bakes your ass for murder of someone investigating a crime with him? You'll lose your bar, you'll go to prison, and you'll regret your actions for the rest of your life."

"I got witnesses'll say you attacked me."

"They'll all lie?" Guthrie gestured to the two dominos players.

"If you really have my number," Rand said, "you know they'll say whatever I want them to say."

Guthrie looked at Orman and waved at the two men groaning on the ground.

"If I attacked you, Frank, you'd be down there with them."

"All the same...." As Frank leveled the barrel at Guthrie, Rand's dark eyes bored into the back of his skull.

24

AT THAT MOMENT, FLASHING LIGHTS and a hooting siren approached from the direction of town. Seconds later, Turner's SUV spun into the parking lot in a clatter of gravel, and Turner got out. His sharp eyes instantly took in the situation.

"Put down that fucking gun, Frank."

"This bastard's on my property, causin' trouble."

"Trouble is the Lazy Q's middle name. That's because you give assholes like Wiley and Lonnie free rein to do whatever they want, but I never see you pointing that fucking gun at them. Put it down, or I'll arrest you and shut you down for good. Now!"

To emphasize the command, he laid his hand on the butt of his pistol, and Frank reluctantly lowered the shotgun.

"Tessa," Turner said into his shoulder mic. "Cancel that ambulance." Then he called out to the two men who'd been playing dominoes. "Chuck," he ordered. "You come down here. Skipper, you bring me that shotgun."

One of the men reluctantly and gingerly took the gun from Orman's grip and came down the steps with his partner. He handed the weapon to Turner, who jacked out its shells and tossed it into his SUV.

"Don't you know it's a felony to carry a weapon into a bar?" he said to Orman. "I could arrest you right now for that."

"I gotta be able to protect myself and my business," Frank complained. "I wouldn't a used it."

"Then why did I just witness you raising it at one of my officers?"

"Fuck!" Orman spat. "This guy is one of your officers? Since when?"

Yeah, Guthrie wondered. Since when?

"Since I said so," Turner said. "From now on, he asks you a question, you answer just like it was me asking. And if I hear of any more shit from you, I'm going to shut your place down."

"You can't do that...."

"I can do any fucking thing I want in this town," Turner grated. "And I have plenty of reasons where the Q is involved. You understand that, don't you, Frank?"

Orman just stood there, tight lipped, face red with rage. Turner scanned the others. By now, the fallen men had struggled to their feet with the assistance of their two companions. "You get that, Wiley? Lonnie? This man is my employee, and if you fuck with him, you're fucking with me. You hear me?"

The two smaller men nodded reluctantly, but Wiley and Lonnie just glared, the latter gingerly massaging his shoulder. The skin beneath the mustache Guthrie had jerked looked red and raw.

"Good, then," Turner said, and he waved toward the vehicles in the parking lot. "Get in your trucks and go home. And be glad I don't arrest you for DUI. Now. Don't come back here tonight. You two wait here," he told the dominos players.

"They ain't paid for their beers, yet," Orman complained.

"Tough shit, Frank. Go back inside and close up. You're done for the day."

"You can't do this," Orman snarled, but after only a slight hesitation, he went inside and shut the door. A moment later, they heard the sounds of the front bolt being shot home, and right after, Wiley and Lonnie's big, jacked-up white Chevy roared out of the parking lot, followed by Miller and Fitzgerald in the blue Chevy pickup. As if that was a signal, George Rand stepped down from the veranda and started toward his Audi, but Turner stopped him.

"Not so fast, Mr. Rand. I need a statement from you, too."

"Of course, Chief." Rand said.

"Wait where you were," Turner ordered, pointing, and Rand went back up the steps. He didn't seem to like being ordered around.

"Okay, Chuck," Turner said to the domino players. "You saw it go down. What happened?"

"This fella here," Chuck waved at Guthrie, "was just askin' Frank about Freddie Jenson and Jeff Mayfield and Segundo Yanez, and Frank was bein' his usual asshole self. And I guess Wiley and Lonnie didn't like him askin', either, and got ornery. You know how they are, 'specially when they're drinkin'."

Turner nodded slightly, expression saying he knew all too well.

"What then?"

"They told him they didn't know Jeff or Segundo, which you know ain't true. Then Wiley went up to the bar and told this fella all the bar stools was his. Then this fella asked Wiley if he needed all the stools because he has a fat ass or because he might have two assholes."

Chuck snickered, and at his side, Skipper tittered then quickly suppressed it. Turner shot a sidelong look at Guthrie, who simply shrugged.

"Well, then," Chuck went on when Turner looked back at him. "Frank told him to leave, and he did, but Wiley and his boys followed him out into the parkin' lot. But he didn't start the fight. They did. Come out after him and threw the first punches."

"You shoulda seed it, Chief," Skipper put in. "This fella," he gestured to Guthrie without looking at him, "used some kinda magic karate stuff on Wiley and Lonnie. Throwed 'em all over the place like they wasn't nothin', and them a lot bigger than him, too."

"That's what he did," Chuck affirmed. "It was all over before I could even blink."

"All right," Turner said. "You two can go home."

The dominoes players went to their vehicles and drove out of the parking lot. Turner looked at Guthrie.

"Some kinda magic karate stuff?" he asked.

"Not karate. Tai chi. A style of kung fu. I occasionally find it handy in my line of work."

"Obviously. Where'd you pick it up?"

"A friend taught me."

"A good kind of friend to have."

"The best."

"Wait here," Turner said, and he walked to the veranda where Rand stood. They spoke for several minutes, then Turner waved toward the Audi, and Rand went to it, giving Guthrie a flat stare. A moment later, he drove off.

"What did he say?" Guthrie asked after Turner came over.

"He pretty much corroborated what Chuck and Skipper said, but he spun it a little different. In his version, you were the aggressor."

"You believe that?"

"You did tell Wiley he had a fat ass with two assholes."

"Seemed appropriate at the time."

"So, now you've had your first up-close encounter with Wiley and his crew."

"The usual troublemakers?"

"They're oilfield roughnecks who work for Stansic Oilfield Services. The whole town avoids them whenever possible, as you can imagine, having just met them. But they don't tend to give me much trouble, even when they're down here brawling. They know I can do something besides toss them in jail for a night or two. If Dale Stansic learns they're making trouble beyond the usual drunken brawls, that won't go over well with him, and they could lose their jobs, so it's kind of surprising they tried to come down hard on you right off."

"I think Rand had something to do with encouraging them to attack me."

"Why would he do that?"

"I'm not sure. Maybe to test me. There's something about him that's off, and he knows I see it. I think he realizes I'm a danger to him."

"You're sixth sense?"

Guthrie shrugged.

"Maybe he did," Turner said, "but that would be hard to prove. It's all over now, anyway."

Guthrie stared at Turner for a moment, then said. "About that officer thing...."

Turner laughed.

"I just said that to shake their tree. But we could make it official, if you want, especially since you were with HPD. Gives you a little more clout, but don't expect me to pay you anything. We don't have the budget for a second officer."

"I'm already getting paid by the insurance company," Guthrie said. "But I wouldn't mind the clout. Before we make it official, I need to show you something."

They drove their separate vehicles to the bridge over Steele Creek, where they parked. Guthrie led Turner down to the creek, where he stopped.

"Why's it still foggy down here?" the chief wondered aloud.

Guthrie had no answer.

"We need to walk off the edge of the path from here on," he told Turner. "We don't want to mess up any shoe impressions. I've already done enough of that. See?" He pointed as they started down the path. "There are six types of prints going and coming: three different tennis shoes, two smooth-soled work or cowboy boots, and shoes with regular heels. One of the sneaker prints is mine, and the other two are from Jeff Mayfield and Segundo Yanez. It's the ones with heel marks that interest us."

They followed the prints to the spot where Yanez had been fishing, and now that he was paying attention, Guthrie could see that Yanez had walked toward Jeff's fishing spot and back one time.

"Let's go on," Guthrie said. "Jeff Mayfield was fishing just up ahead."

All the sets of prints continued to Mayfield's fishing spot. When Guthrie and Turner arrived, Guthrie pointed out the trampled confusion of prints on the bank and the submerged rod and reel, then the possible scene of Mayfield's murder in the brush behind them.

"I take it you think this is where Jeff was killed." Turner was thoughtful for a moment. "There doesn't seem to be enough blood, but he might have been attacked here."

"He told me the Sanfords sometimes come down here to harass him and Segundo."

"That sounds like them. You think they did this?"

Guthrie merely shrugged.

"You touch anything?" Turner asked.

"Nothing."

"What about those tracks?" Turner pointed to the prints on the path leading toward Chaney's cabin.

"One set appears to have been left by Jeff, and the other is mine. I left it the first time I talked to Segundo and Jeff. I think Jeff left his tracks after my first visit. I went up the path again a second time after I found the blood, but I walked off to the side. I wanted to get another look at the cabin."

"What did you see?"

"Jim Chaney sitting on the back deck, staring out across the pond. He was in the same chair and wearing the same clothes as when I talked to him on Sunday morning."

Turner nodded up the path.

"Let's take a look."

The chief led the way, walking stealthily to the left of the path. At the final stand of concealment, they stopped and peered through the foliage. Guthrie could have been looking at a photograph. Jim Chaney was sitting in the same chair, wearing the same clothes, and staring across the pond. A deathly quiet hung over the unnaturally smooth water, almost as if time had stopped beneath the thick tree cover over Chaney Marsh.

"Are we going up there?" Guthrie hissed. The words were a harsh vibration in the inert air, but vibrating no more harshly than the Kuei men.

"Not from this angle" Turner backed away and led Guthrie toward the bridge. "We need to bring in the coroner again. Something screwy is going on with Jim, but he's not going anywhere. Right now, let's go to the office and call Dr. Bob and make your deputizing official."

They drove to the police station, where Turner had Tessa call in Officer Taylor, who was on patrol. After he arrived a few minutes later, Turner explained the situation to him and Tessa. Then he made a phone call.

"It's Chief Turner, Mayor," he said after a moment. "Would you mind coming over to the station for a few minutes? Yes, it's important. Okay." He hung up.

"I think I can deputize you on my own, but it would be better if Mayor Acuff approves the move." Turner chuckled. "Mayor Lloyd Acuff, that is. He says he's a distant cousin of the old country-western singer Roy Acuff. Personally, I doubt it, but he probably won a few extra votes by making that claim."

"If he mentions it," Tessa warned, "just nod and smile like it's obviously true, or he'll go on and on about the familial connections."

"You don't want to hear it," Taylor affirmed.

Mayor Acuff arrived just two minutes later. He was a slightly overweight, fifty-something man of medium height, with thinning dark brown hair a couple of shades lighter than his three-piece suit. He seemed to take his job seriously, and thankfully he didn't mention familial connections. Turner explained the situation to him.

"Another one?" Acuff shook his head sadly. "I didn't know Mr. Mayfield, but still, his murder is a shock on top of the other one." He stared at Guthrie with eyes that held a mixture of sadness, worry, and calculation. The calculation won out. "Can you help Chief Turner solve these murders?"

"I don't know," Guthrie admitted. "But I think the chief needs all the help he can get."

"And you're not asking for pay?"

"I'm being paid by the insurance company. I'm staying to help bring closure for Mr. Telfor's wife."

"Then you have my blessing. But I think Thorndike needs to pay you something to make your employment legal."

"If you have a one dollar bill," Guthrie said, "I'll take that."

Turner pulled out his wallet, extracted a bill, and gave it to Guthrie.

Then, with the mayor, Emmet, and Tessa as witnesses, Turner swore in Guthrie and handed him a badge he pulled from a desk drawer.

"Now you're officially on Chief Turner's payroll," Acuff said, "but don't expect a raise or retirement package." The attempt at humor fell flat, and the mayor glanced at his watch. "Well, if you'll excuse me, Janie is expecting me home for lunch."

"What the hell is going on around here?" Taylor asked dejectedly after the door shut behind the mayor. "Not that I'm not glad to have you on board." He stuck out his hand, and Guthrie shook it. "Almost too much is happening for me and the chief to keep up." He glanced at Turner. "You want me down at the bridge?"

"We'll take care of it for now. Go back on patrol, but keep extra watchful. No telling what's going to happen next."

"Can't do anything else the way things are," Taylor said, and he left the station.

Turner called Dr. Bob, the DPS barracks, and the sheriff, then he and Guthrie left for the bridge to wait for them to show up.

25

TWO STATE TROOPER CRUISERS, EACH with two officers, arrived at the bridge about fifteen minutes before the coroner. The sheriff showed up fifteen minutes later.

"What the hell's going on down here, Bill?" Latimer asked as soon as he walked up to Guthrie and Turner, three crime scene techs trailing behind him.

"Seems like everyone's asking that same question, but I'm just as puzzled as you, Dr. Bob."

Turner laid out the situation, including Guthrie's two previous visits, all the various sets of shoe prints, the rod and reel in the water, and the blood in the brush where a struggle seemed to have taken place.

"After that," he finished, "he brought me to the scene, and I called you. We'll supply you with samples of our sole impressions later. And now," he waved toward the path down to the creek, "it's all yours."

"What about Jim Chaney?" Latimer asked. "Is he involved?"

"Clay and I are going to talk to him right now, but on the surface, it's not likely. Whoever slashed up Jeff would be covered with blood, and we went down the path far enough to see Jim. He seems to have been wearing the same clothes for several days, and it doesn't look like there's blood on them. Besides, what motive could he have? But we'll approach the cabin from the front, not the path. Don't want to mess up your crime scene any more than we already have. Oh, by the way, Clay has agreed to stay on as one of my offi-cers for the duration of this case."

"Bill told me you used to be with HPD," Latimer said, turning his eyes on Guthrie. "Welcome back to law enforcement. I have every confidence in Bill and Emmet, but even in a big city, this would be a puzzling case." He looked at Turner. "I can tell you the sheriff is keeping his eye on it, and so is the district attorney. But they all know it's your jurisdiction. They'll stay out of it as long as you make some progress, so I'm glad you're getting a little extra help. Well...." He swiveled his head and stared down the path to the creek, then into the woods. "Lot of mist down there for this late in the day."

"It's been like that a lot here, lately," Turner replied. "But it's not too bad at the crime scene. Just be glad the damp preserved those shoe tracks."

"Small favors," Latimer said, then he shrugged his shoulders as if preparing to do something unpleasant. "I guess we'd better get to it."

He started down the bank, followed by his small gaggle of techs.

"Let's go talk to Jim," Turner said tersely.

"Segundo Yanez, too. He might have seen something."

"Jim first."

"How do you want to play this?" Guthrie asked as Turner drove the roads to Chaney's property.

"Tell the truth, I'm not really sure." Turner said. "I've known Jim all my life, and while I can't say I particularly like him, it's tough to confront someone you know about a murder."

"We don't know Jim even knows about it. From what I've seen, he's practically catatonic on that back deck."

"That doesn't mean he didn't get up and do it."

"What about the clothes? You saw how Jeff was hacked up. If Jim did that, his clothes would be covered in blood. They aren't today, and they're the same clothes he was wearing when we came looking for Freddie. Besides, Jeff was shot with a slug, not a shotgun. And if Jim did it, how'd he get Jeff's body up to the county seat, dispose of his truck somewhere that nobody's found it, and get back here, all by himself? And what about all those other shoe prints?"

"I hope you're right, but for all we know, Jim has a closet full of the same shirt. I don't think I've ever seen him dress much different. And he might have a rifle and pistol as well as a shotgun. As for the body, truck, and shoe prints...." He shrugged and let the sentence hang.

"Do you make him for a psychopathic murderer?"

Turner just drove on without answering, and a short time later, he pulled into the dirt road that led to Chaney's gate.

"Last time we were down here, we were looking for Freddie," he said. "That seems like a lifetime ago. Now I don't know who the hell I'm chasing." He shrugged. "Freddie'll just have to go on the back burner until we get some of the current mess straightened out."

"This current mess is happening because of something Freddie saw. It's critical we find him."

"Tomorrow," Turner said with a sigh. "Right now, we have to talk to Jim. The murder happened on his property and within a ten minute walk. Jeff was shot, and he probably made a lot of noise while he was being attacked. Even if Jim doesn't know what happened, if he was sitting on that deck doing nothing, surely he'd have heard something."

"Surely," Guthrie agreed.

Turner pulled up to Chaney's gate and parked, and they got out.

"Remember what I said about him having that shotgun close by," Guthrie warned as soon as they'd climbed the gate and were walking down the track.

"We'll give him a holler as soon as he can hear us," Turner said.

All too quickly they were beneath the canopy, where the hazy day dimmed almost to twilight, giving the woods an ethereal feel deepened by the pervasive mists clinging to the foliage and carpeting the ground.

"See?" Guthrie said, gesturing to the lefthand ditch.

If anything, the disease at the bottom had increased and was overtaking the upper edges, contaminating the surrounding grass and weeds with dry rot. He glanced at the ditch to the right and saw that it still looked normal. For how long?

Turner stared into the gray-green and umber slop at the bottom of the ditch then straightened and hiked up his shoulders.

"It's getting chilly."

Guthrie agreed, privately trying to suppress the increased twitching of the Kuei men the farther he and Turner walked. Usually, he had no trouble keeping the sensations to a minimum, but that wasn't so easy right now. The only good thing was the talisman provided him a measure of psychic protection. And he needed it. He could feel the oppressive effects of whatever it was that now lay in the marsh, almost like a pressure pushing at them, impeding their progress. For Guthrie, the sensation was more an irritation than a direct impediment, but Turner was growing visibly itchy and anxious the farther they went.

"You okay, Chief?"

"I don't know what it is," Turner said, "but this place is giving me the willies. It stinks, too. What the hell is that smell?"

Indeed, the still air was redolent of vegetable rot, mold, and small animal death.

"You hear any birds?" Guthrie asked. "Insects? Any squirrels in the trees?"

Turner held still for a moment, concentrating.

"Nothing. Like the…."

"Like the dump," Guthrie finished for him.

Turner rubbed his arms.

"I don't feel right."

"Stay strong, Chief. I feel it, too. But we have to go on."

Turner took hold of himself, and they forged ahead, Guthrie in the lead. By the time they came in sight of the cabin, they were forcing themselves forward. But then the ennui suddenly slipped away as a strong, pervasive odor replaced the stink emanating from the forest.

"What's *that* smell?" Turner asked, sniffing.

"Garlic. Look. He's got cloves of it hanging all around the eves and windows."

"You mean like to ward off vampires?"

"To ward off evil," Guthrie responded.

Turner shot him a skeptical look before yelling out, "Yo, the cabin! Jim Chaney! It's Chief Turner!"

A moment later, Chaney stepped around the corner, bearing an over-under double barrel shotgun at port arms. He looked haggard, and his cheeks were grizzled with a week's growth of beard. He stared at them for a moment then lowered the shotgun so its barrel pointed at the ground.

"Might as well come around since you came all the way out here."

He waved them forward then disappeared behind the corner. Guthrie and Turner approached and rounded it to see Chaney propping the shotgun against the wall beside the back door. Chaney noticed Turner eyeing the weapon.

"You never know who might come callin'," he said.

Chaney looked more wan and stressed than the last time Guthrie had seen him, and he gazed at them from sunken, bloodshot eyes.

"Has someone come calling?" Guthrie asked.

"That Rand fella. Every damn day. Wants to buy my marsh, too, but I ain't sellin', and I told him so in no uncertain terms last time he was down here. He didn't much like that and got kinda testy."

"I hope you're not planning on shooting him," Turner said.

"Might do if he comes down here again." Chaney wrinkled his upper lip. "Bastard gets under my skin." He sat in his rocker and gestured to the other two chairs. "Might as well sit and tell me what you got to say."

"What's with all the garlic?" Turner asked, declining to sit. Guthrie remained standing, too.

"Lot's of stink in the marsh," Chaney said. "The garlic keeps the air fresh 'round the cabin. You know, like those fancy air freshener things but better. Enid always said garlic will cure just about anything, so I thought I'd try it." He chuckled. "I musta bought every bit of garlic for a fifty miles. I even bought all the garlic powder and sprinkled it on the ground all 'round the cabin. Been eatin' it, too. I'm pretty sick of the stuff, but the feelin' ain't so bad, now, so I guess she was right."

That seemed to take Turner aback, but he recovered quickly.

"I need to ask you a few questions, Jim. Can you tell me where you've been for the past two days?"

"I guess I been right here most of the time 'cept when I went into town and up to the county seat and a couple other places day before yesterday to buy the garlic. Yesterday, I went to the grocery stores in Twin Oaks and Barton. 'Sides that, seems like I ain't been off this porch in days. I just don't feel right bein' anywhere else but here or inside."

"So you haven't gone down the path around the pond toward the state road any time lately?"

"Ain't been down there in a spell. Maybe a couple of months. Bunch a those delinquent teenagers like to park up by the bridge and go down there. They get drunk and smoke dope and who knows what-all. Alls I know is they leave a mess. When I hear 'em, I like to sneak up and let loose a couple of blasts from my shotgun. Into the ground, mind you, but it scares 'em off right quick" He gave a chuckle.

"Have you heard them or anyone else down there, lately?"

"No, but I know Jeff Mayfield and Segundo Yanez fish down that way. I caught 'em a couple a times, but that don't bother me none, and I told 'em so. They're both poor, and I ain't eatin' all the fish."

Guthrie smiled to himself.

"So you didn't hear any sort of unusual commotion down there in the last couple of days?"

"No, but like I told you, I ain't been here the whole time. What's this about?"

"You mentioned Jeff Mayfield. His body was discovered just northeast of the county seat yesterday morning. He was murdered."

"Murdered? Jeff?" Chaney shook his head, eyes registering disbelief. "But what's that got to do with me?"

"We think he might have been attacked and possibly killed where he was fishing."

"Down there?" Chaney looked shocked. "Jeff Mayfield murdered? How?" He rose to his feet. "I need to see."

"You stay right there, Jim," Turner ordered. "It's an official crime scene, and the coroner and the crime techs are down there right now."

Chaney hesitantly subsided into the rocker, but he wasn't relaxed, and he leaned forward anxiously.

"You don't think I had anything to do with it, do you, Chief? I ain't go no reason to hurt Jeff."

"When was the last time you had a bath, Jim?" Turner asked.

"Bath?" Chaney sat back, looking surprised at the question. Then a bit dumbfounded. "Hell, I don't know. A few days ago. Maybe a day or two before you and him first came down here together. I don't rightly remember. What's that got to do with anything?"

"You have a rifle or pistol?"

"No. Alls I got is my shotgun. Why?"

"Mind if I look at the bottoms of your boots?"

Chaney seemed peeved at the request, but he lifted one leg then the other for Turner's inspection. He was wearing work boots with waffled soles, not smooth-soled Western or work boots or shoes with heels. There was no trace of mud on them.

"I told you I ain't been down there in months," Chaney said. "I sometimes go down the other way to visit Enid, but I ain't done much walkin' around anywhere the last week. Every time I leave the cabin, I don't feel so good. It's like Enid's keeping me here. I swear to you, Chief. I may be guilty of killin' her spirit, but I never laid a hand on Jeff Mayfield."

"I didn't think you did, Jim," Turner assured him. "Mr. Guthrie and I are going now, but I want you to hear two things. First, Mr. Guthrie is now officially one of my officers. And second, you are not to go down the path toward the crime scene. Not one step down that path. You understand?"

"You telling me I can't go where I please on my own property?"

"I'm telling you to stay away from the crime scene until I tell you otherwise. You said you hadn't been down that way in months, anyway. Walk the other direction if you have to walk somewhere. Go visit Enid."

"And for how long is this goin' on? I seen a bunch a dead fish in the water, and I got to figure out what's killing 'em."

He waved toward the pond, and Guthrie's eyes followed the gesture. The broad surface might have been hazily sunlit out in the middle, but despite that, the whole scene seemed dreary—wholly unlike the last time he'd seen it. More than a dozen fish floated belly up on the surface, the spaces between them speckled with the bodies of thousands of insects. The dead-still water looked scummy and was shot through with narrow streaks of diseased green, while shreds of mists coiled through the foliage all around.

"See all that green shit?" Chaney went on. "I think Chuck Willis or Agnes Carpenter must be usin' some kinda poison chemicals and pollutin' the water upstream. I gotta take samples up there before the creek runs into the pond."

"Look, Jim," Turner said, softening a little. "It's a crime scene, and we can't have you messing it up. It won't be long until you have it back. If you really need to take samples, take them on the west side of the bridge."

"Well," Chaney said reluctantly. "All right. I'll do that."

"Don't you think you'd be better off living in town?" Turner asked. "It's not safe out here, and you're isolated…."

"I'm not isolated," Chaney bristled. "I have Enid. I can feel her. She's always with me."

"All right, Jim. But I'm just a phone call away if you need me. If you remember anything at all, let me know. And do me a favor, will you? Take a bath and change your clothes. You're starting to smell like a wild boar."

Chaney's eyes widened a little in surprise, then he barked a laugh.

"Okay, Chief. Next time you or your new officer come visitin', I'll be all gussied up for you."

"Goodbye, Jim," Turner said, and he pivoted and walked toward the corner of the house.

Before Guthrie followed, he looked at Chaney.

"The garlic is good," he said. "Burning sage might help, and cinnamon, clove, and ginger are good, too."

Chaney gave him a blank stare for a moment.

"You trying to pull my leg, young feller?"

"No," Guthrie said. "I'm trying to increase the number of your weapons."

"'Preciate the advice." Chaney gestured toward the chief's retreating back. "Don't you think you need to catch up to your boss?"

Guthrie smiled and nodded at him before following Turner around the corner.

"Somebody slashed Jeff Mayfield," Guthrie said as soon as they were out of earshot, "but it sure wasn't Jim Chaney."

"Agreed. One whiff of him, and I knew he hadn't changed his clothes since we were first down here."

As they headed up the path to the track and emerged from the cloud of garlic odor, the outré pressure resumed. Guthrie also noticed that the rot had now infiltrated the lower reaches of the ditch on the west side of the track close to the cabin. That faded after a couple of hundred feet, though the ditch opposite looked more diseased than ever. But the feeling of oppression in the atmosphere beneath the mist-shrouded tree cover remained strong. When they'd approached, it had seemed as if they'd had to fight an intangible pressure hindering their progress, but now it was at their backs, almost pushing them along. Pushing them away. Guthrie suddenly realized that both of them were hurrying like they had somewhere important to be. Or somewhere important *not* to be.

He forced himself to slow to a normal walk, and after Turner surged ahead dozen feet, he stopped and glanced back, fidgeting while Guthrie caught up, eyes nervously scanning the marsh around them.

"Slow down, Chief," Guthrie said as he came abreast of Turner.

"Jesus," Turner said, shaking his head then glancing at the dark woods on either side. "What the fuck is going on? I feel like I've got a tailwind."

"It doesn't want us here," Guthrie said.

"It?"

"Whatever is now lurking in the marsh. We had to buck its pressure coming in, now it's pushing us out."

"If you were anybody else and this was any other situation, I'd say you're crazy." Turner bunched his shoulders like he was preparing for a fight. "Let's get back to my vehicle."

They hurried on, the intangible pressure remaining steady at their backs. After what seemed like forever, they emerged into the sunlight, where the sensation ceased. They climbed the gate, went to the Interceptor, and slid inside, but Turner didn't start the engine right away. Instead, he stared for a long moment into to woods beyond the fence.

"You felt it, didn't you?" Guthrie asked.

"I don't know what I felt. Seems to me it's nothing supernatural. Just the rot you found in the ditches contaminating the marsh and fouling the air. What with the stink in the woods and all that garlic around the cabin, all I feel is a headache. Maybe I'm coming down with something. You think we ought to call in the EPA?"

Having the FBI and other law enforcement hanging around was bad enough, Guthrie thought. We don't need another federal agency involved. Tereba had sent him here to deal with the situation, not make a public spectacle of it.

"I don't think that's a good idea," was all he said.

Turner was silent for a few moments.

"You think Jim's all right down there?"

"The garlic seems to help," Guthrie said. "The feeling wasn't as bad around the house."

"I don't know if I can take any more of this weird shit right now," Turner said, truncating further discussion of sensation. "I need something concrete to wrap my head around." He reached down and twisted the key in the ignition. "Let's go talk to Segundo."

26

SEGUNDO YANEZ LIVED IN A MOBILE home, but it wasn't located in Warren Evers' mobile home park. Instead it sat along one of Thorndike's dirt streets seven blocks southwest of the downtown grid, close to the southern edge of the town's neighborhoods. On the drive there, Turner reiterated that Yanez was employed as a janitor at the school.

"You get him the job?" Guthrie asked, remembering that Turner had gotten Freddie Jensen the job managing the dump.

"No, that was Miss Agnes's doing."

"She's quite the grand dame, isn't she?"

"She's out to make Thorndike a more modern place, and there's some who support that, but others don't want change and are against her. It's probably evenly split, but she's got resources and clout a lot of the others don't. And business savvy."

In short order, Turner pulled up in front of Yanez's mobile home, which was tucked beneath four thirty-year-old oaks that looked like they'd grown up around it. Indeed, it appeared to have been there longer than the houses on either side. It was old but looked well maintained beneath its light gray paint and was a lot cozier than Guthrie's own temporary quarters. Comfortable. Lived in. Loved.

A one-car metal carport had been added to the mobile home's left end, and inside it sat Segundo's brown Ford Ranger. A small, tan metal shed stood at the other end, and more than half the mobile home's front was masked by a corrugated tin-roofed deck that was faced with white lattice panels to cut the glare and heat of the afternoon sun. A flowerbed stretched across the front of the deck, and between it and the dirt street lay a small, neatly mown front yard. Modest as it was, the home obviously received a lot more personal care than Freddie Jensen's more substantial structure had.

The chief led the way up the steps at the left end of the deck and past three green plastic outdoor chairs and a cluster of empty plastic flower pots. The door opened a crack at his knock, and a small, chubby Hispanic woman peered out with frightened eyes.

"Hello, Marielle," Turner said, removing his hat. "This is my new officer, Clay Guthrie. Is Segundo home?"

"Yes, Chief Turner," she said hesitantly, opening the door wider. "Has my Segundo done something wrong?"

"Why do you ask?"

"I am frightened for him," she admitted. "He has been very nervous since we heard about Jeff Mayfield."

"We don't think he's done anything," Turner assured her. "We just need to ask him a few questions. Maybe he saw or noticed something."

Mrs. Yanez stepped back to let them in. The exterior of the mobile home might have been showing its age, but the interior was as neat and tidy as the small front yard. Well, Guthrie reflected, Segundo has something Freddie doesn't—a wife. That brought a pang of regret, but now wasn't the time to contemplate that particular hole in his life.

"Segundo," Mrs. Yanez called out as Guthrie and Turner entered. "Chief Turner is here. He wants to talk to you."

A moment later, Segundo emerged from the back of the trailer, eyes furtive when they weren't downcast.

"Come on," Turner urged. "Let's sit down and talk."

The three of them settled at the small table adjacent to the kitchen area while Mrs. Yanez took a chair in the living area, attentive to the conversation.

"I think you know why we're here," Turner said.

"I didn't have nothin' to do with Jeff Mayfield bein' dead, Chief Bill," Yanez said, the words spilling out of his mouth. "We known each other a long time and was fishin' buddies. I'd never hurt him. I'd never hurt anybody."

"Relax, Segundo. I know you didn't hurt Jeff. We're just trying to find out what happened to him, that's all. I know you were his friend. Maybe his only real friend. So you have to tell us what you do know."

"Alls I know is I ain't seen him since the mornin' after he," Segundo nodded toward Guthrie, "caught me and him down there. I swear it, Chief Bill. That's all I know." Yanez hung his head.

"But you did see Jeff down there on Monday morning?"

"Yeah, but I wasn't there long. I had to leave. I told him not to stay, but he just wouldn't listen. Said all the big fish was up where he fishes, almost like something drew them there, and he was gonna catch as many as he could."

Not drawn, Guthrie thought, recalling the dead fish floating in the pond. Driven.

"Why did you have to leave, Mr. Yanez?" he asked.

"I just had to, that's all." Yanez lowered his eyes.

"Look at me, Segundo," Guthrie said, and Yanez reluctantly did. "You do know something. Something that isn't right. You can tell me. Look at me, and say I won't understand."

"You gotta tell them, Segundo," Mrs. Yanez said, anxiously leaning forward in her chair. "You gotta tell them."

"I tried to warn him," Yanez said plaintively. "I should a made him pack up with me and leave, but he wouldn't, and I couldn't stay. Not after what I seen."

"What was down there, Segundo?" Guthrie asked. "What did you see?"

Yanez's shoulders stiffened, and he rubbed a weary palm over his face.

"You ain't gonna believe me," he said, resignation weighing his voice.

"Tell them, Segundo," Mrs. Yanez urged. "Tell them."

Yanez lifted fear-filled eyes to stare into Guthrie's own.

"La Llorona was down there," he said in almost a whisper. "I seen her over on the other side of the pond, floatin' through the woods toward me. I was scared, but when I went to tell Jeff, he wouldn't listen. Just laughed at me." His shoulder slumped, and he shook his head sadly. "Poor Jeff. He ain't laughin' now."

"You saw La Llorona in the marsh?" Guthrie asked.

"I seen her," Yanez insisted. "Clear as I see you. But I don't 'spect you'll believe me." He looked at Turner. "You said I didn't do nothin' to Jeff, Chief Bill, but you're wrong. I knew what was down there, and I shoulda made him leave, but I'm a coward." His head hung lower than ever, and he rubbed a palm across his face again. This time, it came away damp, and his shoulders shook.

"Did you see any other people down there?" Turner asked after Segundo composed himself. "Jim Chaney, for example? Or the Sanfords?"

"No," Yanez said, looking up at Turner. "I didn't see no human person but Jeff. When I went over to warn him, he thought I was talkin' about Mr. Jim, but he said he went up and saw Mr. Jim on his back deck, watchin' the pond. Do you think he was looking for La Llorona, too?"

"I think he's wishing his wife was still with him," Turner said, and Yanez glanced at his own wife, the fear in his eyes softening with care.

"You didn't see anybody else?" Guthrie pressed.

"No, sir. Nobody. I left right after."

"Okay, Segundo," Turner said, rising. "That's all for now, but we might have more questions for you later. In the meantime, your old fishing spot is a crime scene and off limits. You are not to go down there for any reason. If you have to fish, find another place."

"Don't worry, Chief Bill. I ain't never goin' down there ever again. There's no way La Llorona's gonna kill me an' eat my soul."

"Okay," Turner said, and he moved toward the door, nodding to Mrs. Yanez on the way out.

"We'll get this sorted out, Marielle," he assured her. "Don't you and Segundo worry."

Then they were out the door, heading for the Interceptor.

"What the hell is La Llorona?" Turner asked as soon as they were seated.

"You ever hear of the water nymphs of Greek myth?" When Turner nodded, Guthrie said, "Well, La Llorona is something like those combined with a ghost. Supposedly it's the spirit of a Mexican woman who drowned her children and who has haunted shaded bodies of water ever since."

"You think some mythical Mexican spirit is behind all this?" Turner's voice was skeptical.

"No. I think what Segundo saw was simply an image he was familiar with and fearful of. He saw or felt something in a woods next to a water source, and the superstitions he grew up with kicked in. It could be that whatever is causing our problems has the ability to appear in different guises, or maybe people just respond to its presence by seeing what they want to see."

"That's crazy." Turner said.

"Then what did he see?"

"I don't know." Turner shrugged helplessly. "I'm voting for nothing,"

"Jim Chaney insisted that Enid is always with him at the cabin," Guthrie reminded him.

"If he's not just speaking metaphorically and really thinks he sees her, well, yeah, that's kind of like this La Llorona. You think the two are linked?"

"I think they're both manifestations of the same force or presence."

"Ten days ago, I'd have said you were crazy and run you out of town," Turner said, shoulders sagging. "Today, I'm looking to you for help."

"We'll help each other, Chief. That's what it's going to take."

Turner started the engine and began angling through the streets toward the police station, when his radio hissed and Tessa's voice came over the speaker.

"Chief Turner, do you copy?" She sounded a little breathless.

"Turner here," the chief said, lifting the mic to his mouth.

"Jerry Cantu called. Three guys just held up the Pit Stop."

27

"HE SAYS THEY LEFT DRIVING north," Tessa said.

"I'm on my way. Contact DPS and let them know there's a runner coming their way. Have Emmet meet me at Jerry's."

Turner replaced the mic and glanced at Guthrie.

"You're gonna have to ride along."

"I'm now one of your officers," Guthrie reminded him as Turner pressed on the accelerator. "This happen often?"

"We've had a few burglaries but never an armed robbery. First time for everything, I guess."

In moments, he was steering the Interceptor down a road leading to Main Street, lights lit and siren hooting. As they raced along, Guthrie couldn't help but think that if the perps were heading north, they'd have had to pass by the edge of the marsh just three miles south of the Pit Stop—and through the field cast by the presence now residing there. Had its corrupting influence helped spur them to commit a violent crime just minutes later?

A block before they reached Main, Officer Taylor's SUV roared past, heading toward the state highway, lights flashing. Turner made the corner moments later and raced along in Taylor's wake. A mile later, both vehicles tore around the corner onto the state road going north. The Pit Stop was just a hundred yards ahead on the right, and in seconds, Taylor whipped his cruiser up to the door and emerged, hand on the butt of his pistol though he didn't draw it. A slight, middle-aged Hispanic man was standing in front of the doors, pointing frantically up the state road toward the county seat.

Turner squealed to a stop behind Taylor's cruiser, and he and Guthrie piled out.

"They went that a way, Chief!" the Hispanic man yelled, voice shrill with excitement. "They're in a black Camaro!"

"Calm down Jerry," Turner soothed. "The state police are waiting for them up there." He turned to Taylor. "Go after them, at least as far as the town line, just in case they try to run back this way. If they do, call me immediately. And tell the staties the make and color of the car."

"Chief," Taylor nodded, ducked into his Interceptor, and pulled off, lights still flashing, heading north.

"Who's this?" Jerry asked.

"Clay, this is Jerry Cantu, owner of Thorndike's only gas station and convenience store. Jerry, meet Clay Guthrie. He's temporarily serving as one of my officers."

"Your officer, eh? Seems like the more officers you get, the more crime we have. I ain't never been robbed like this. Worst I usually get is kids and teens pilfering the candy section."

"Okay, Jerry," Turner said. "Let's go inside, and you can tell me about it."

It had been a typical day, so far, Cantu said. All his customers had been locals except for a guy driving a box truck who'd pulled in to gas up, use the facilities, and buy a small sack of snacks and a couple of bottles of soda. But that had been mid-morning, and after that, it was just locals again until the three punks showed up. Jerry knew they were trouble right from the start, and he'd have stopped them cold with his .357, but they all had guns and got the drop on him.

"I'm glad they did, Jerry," Turner said. "Just think of the mess you'd have to clean up. All that blood and tissue. If you'd lived, at all, that is. It could be Lucy cleaning up your blood. I've told you not to keep that thing in here."

"What if I'm robbed?" Cantu said, exasperation in his voice.

"You just told me this is the first time you've been robbed."

"That's right."

"So, in the past, you never needed a gun, but all that time, it was clearly within reach of all those kids and teens pilfering candy."

"Well…," Cantu sputtered.

"And now, the only time you've been robbed, it didn't do you any good, did it?"

"I guess not. But if I'd been faster…."

"If you'd been faster, they might have shot you, and instead of talking to you right now, we'd be telling Lucy that you're dead and we're taking your body to the county morgue. I've got enough of those, already."

"I'm sorry, Chief."

"Okay. Tell me the rest of it."

There wasn't much. The three punks pushed Jerry around and punched him a few times before emptying the register and stealing several bags of snacks and a couple of cases of beer. One of them hit him on the head before they left, but he managed to ward off the blow a little and didn't completely lose consciousness, though it was a couple of minutes before he could get himself together and call the police.

"What about the safe?" Turner asked. "They didn't try to get you to open it?"

"They did, but I told 'em only the owner has the key."

"You're the owner," Turner said.

"Wanna bet? Lucy pulls all the strings in my house, and she's the one with the key. That way I can tell the absolute truth when I say I don't have it."

"Smart thinking," Turner said with a chuckle. "All right, Jerry. Officer Taylor will stop here later and take your statement. In the meantime, you can resume business."

"You mean you ain't gonna shut me down and put up that yellow tape?"

"That wouldn't be good for business, would it?" Turner said.

"Neither is gettin' robbed."

"Maybe not, but as soon as everybody learns what happened, I'll bet nearly every single one of them comes by, hot to hear all about it, and they'll be buying gas or snacks while they're here. The next two days will probably be the best your business has ever seen."

"Well, hell, Chief," Jerry said, brightening. "You just might be right."

"Okay, Jerry," Turner said. "Now put that revolver in the back somewhere and take it home with you tonight and don't bring it back. If I find it here again, I'm gonna take it away from you. You hear me?"

"Yes, Chief."

Even before the doors had shut behind them, Cantu was on the phone, letting people know he'd been stuck-up. As Guthrie followed Turner out to the Interceptor, the chief's shoulder radio hissed and Taylor's voice came over.

"DPS has them in custody," the officer said. "You were right. As soon as they saw the state police coming toward them, they turned and tried to run back this way. I just blocked the road right at the town line. They tried to run around me, but you know those ditches along there. Too deep to drive through. They just crashed into one, and the car turned onto its side. It was pretty comical. No serious injuries. By then, we had 'em surrounded, and they surrendered. The car crashed outside the town limits, so I just let DPS take them into custody."

"That was the right thing to do. They'll be tried up in the county seat, anyway, and now we don't have to take care of them in our little jail until their arraignment. Come on back after the staties mop up and take Jerry Cantu's statement. Then you can resume your patrol."

"Copy that, Chief. Out."

Guthrie got into the Interceptor while Turner went into the station to tell Cantu the good news that the perps had been apprehended and he'd get back his money and property.

"What now?" Guthrie asked after Turner returned and slid into the driver's seat.

"Let's check out Jeff Mayfield's home."

Mayfield also lived in a mobile home, the last domicile at the far southeast corner of town except for the house where Freddie lived, which was a couple of miles farther down the county road. Beyond to the east and south lay the massive Grant Industries property. Despite the similarities in their homes, Mayfield's was a far cry from the Yanez's cozy, tree-nestled domicile. Mayfield's was in stark sunshine and not well maintained. As with almost every lot south of Main, discarded automobiles, machinery, and junk protruded from the heavy growth of brush and weeds. The trailer was in need of paint, and the tiny air conditioner in one of the windows didn't look at all adequate to cool the interior, especially since the trailer lay completely exposed to the brutal Texas sun. It probably wasn't pleasant in winter, either. The only nod to modernity was a satellite TV dish mounted on one corner of the roof.

"His truck's not here," Turner commented as he parked in the dirt driveway.

"They'll probably find it in the county seat," Guthrie said.

Turner nodded, and the two of them got out and walked up rickety wooden steps to the front door. It was shut and locked, but Turner retrieved a pry bar from the toolbox in the back of the SUV.

"I'll get a warrant later," he said as he levered the door open.

The interior of the mobile home was a slobby mess, but the mess looked indigenous, not as if the place had been ransacked. It smelled of sweat and old food grease, and dirty dishes filled the sink. Turner poked around a little, and Guthrie followed his example, but they didn't find anything that might help identify Mayfield's killer. In fact, there was nothing at all to indicate that Mayfield was dead except for his absence. But his .38 wasn't there.

After half an hour, they left, and Turner shut the door. Then he went to the Interceptor, got out a roll of crime scene tape, and strung an X of it across the doorframe.

"I've had this since I've been chief," Turner said as he finished, holding up the roll of tape, "but if this shit doesn't let up, I'm going to have to buy more."

"Obviously the attack took place in the marsh, even if the killing didn't," Guthrie said. "I doubt it had anything to do with Jeff's life, per se. He died because of where he was, not because of who he was or anything else about him."

"It all goes right back to Chaney Marsh, doesn't it?" Turner said.

"That's where it goes."

After they left Jeff Mayfield's mobile home, Turner drove them to Leo's.

"I haven't had anything to eat since breakfast," he said. "My brain's starting to get fuzzy."

"You got no complaints from me," Guthrie said. His stomach had been growling on and off for the last hour.

Bev brought them coffee, water, and silverware, but no menus.

"The Blue Plate Special is really good today," she said. "Chicken-fried steak, mashed potatoes, your choice of a side veggie. Just the thing for two hungry men."

"That sounds good to me," Turner said.

Guthrie nodded in agreement.

"Better make it fast, or we'll start on the napkins."

She laughed and went to place their order. The food came quickly, but not quickly enough to prevent Turner's radio from interrupting the meal before they'd barely begun.

"What?" Turner asked, keying the mic.

"Mrs. Slansky just called," Tessa answered. "She says her husband's trying to kill her."

28

"TELL EMMET WHAT'S GOING ON so he'll be up to speed if I need him," Turner said into the mic. "Clay's with me. He can help out." He signed off, glancing ruefully at the barely begun food then up at Guthrie. "Okay, let's go stop Mr. Slansky from killing Mrs. Slansky."

Turner signaled to Bev to preserve their meals, then he hurried out the door, Guthrie in his wake. The other customers in the cafe stared after them, worry on their faces. Even the average Thorndike resident was anxious these days.

"Is this a common occurrence in the Slansky household?" Guthrie asked as they slipped into the Interceptor.

"Not at all. As far as I know, they get along well. They're even in the same business. He's the town barber, and she runs a beauty parlor out of the remodeled garage next to their house."

Turner started the SUV and pulled off, reaching for the switch for the flashers and siren. But he pulled his hand back.

"Enough shit's been going on," he said. "No need scaring folks more than they already are."

Considering the concerned expressions of Leo's patrons when they'd hurried out, Guthrie had to agree.

Turner drove fast. In less than two minutes, they arrived at the Slansky residence in the northeast quadrant of town—a simple bungalow sheathed in tan aluminum siding standing in a neat yard, the beauty parlor in a detached garage next to it. Seconds later, they were at the front door. It was shut but not locked, and Turner cautiously twisted the knob and pushed the door wide. The living room, visible through the opening, was in shambles. The coffee table in front of the sofa was overturned, its contents of magazines and other items strewn on the floor. Shards of broken dishes and glasses were scattered over the other debris. A lamp lay on the floor behind an overturned end table, and it looked like half the mantle above the simple gas fireplace had been swept clean of photos and knickknacks.

"It's Chief Turner!"

"Back here!" came a woman's panicked voice. "Careful! He's got a bat!"

Slansky was indeed holding a baseball bat at the ready position. He was at one end of the dining room table, a scowl twisting his forty-something features, snarling wordlessly at his wife. She was at the other end of the table. Blood welled from a cut above her left eye, and she clutched her left arm against her side. Her sleeve masked any damage, but the way she winced every time she moved, the arm was clearly injured.

"There he is, Chief," she said, nodding toward her husband. "You stop him, now, and keep him away from me. He already punched me in the head and busted my arm with that bat."

"Larry," Turner said. "I need you to put that down."

"I ain't puttin' down nothin'," Slansky ground out. "Not 'til she admits what she done."

"But I ain't done nothing, Larry," she said. "Can't you get that through your thick skull?"

"I know you done," he insisted. "I got proof." He let go of the bat with his left hand, picked up a piece of paper lying on the table, and shook it at her. "I got proof right here. What you got to say to that?"

"Proof of what, Larry?" Turner asked.

"That she's a pillandering whore."

"What?" The question sounded like a grunt of laughter coming out of Turner's mouth. "You think Frannie is cheating on you?"

"I got the proof!" Larry shook the paper again, this time in Turner's direction.

"Let me see that," Turner said. He reached out, but Guthrie stopped his arm.

"I'll get it for you, Chief," he said.

He stepped toward Slansky, reaching for the paper. Slansky held it out suspiciously and raised the bat a little. As he did, Guthrie surged forward and twisted the bat out of his grip.It clattered to the floor, the paper fluttering down next to it.

"Why you...," Slansky snarled, and he took a clumsily poke at Guthrie's face. That was all Guthrie needed to tie him up in a joint lock.

Turner picked up the bat and retrieved the paper.

"Hell, Larry," he said after looking at the paper. "Don't you realize this is complete bullshit?"

"But it says right there...."

Turner held up the paper so Guthrie could see what was on it. An eyeball at the top with the words, "Eye See U." Beneath was a slightly longer bit of text saying that Frannie had enjoyed sex with just about every man in town, including Turner and Mayor Acuff.

"*Who* says?" Turner demanded of Slansky. "Do you even know who sent this letter?"

"No," Slansky admitted reluctantly. "I guess I don't."

"No. You don't. You're our barber. You hear all sorts of gossip. Is all of it true?"

"I guess not."

"But you believe this?" Turner shook the paper. "A letter that's not even signed? You believe Frannie and all these men, including me, have something going on with her on the side? That's just ridiculous."

Guthrie felt Slansky sag a little at the truth that he'd reacted with total belief and rage to something that was a total lie. He loosened the joint lock and stepped back as Slansky angrily shrugged him off and straightened.

"That hurt," he said, massaging his shoulder.

"Now look, Larry," Turner said. "Nobody around here wants your wife except you. You're not the only person in town to get a letter like this, and they're all nothing but a bunch of lies. You hear me?"

"I guess so, Chief." Slansky slumped and hung his head. "I guess I just.... I don't know. I just lost it. I never done nothin' like this to her before. Have I, honey?" He looked at his wife, desperation in his eyes. "Never once before."

"That's true," Frannie said, looking at Turner, her anger softening beneath the pain. "He never hit me once in sixteen years." She looked back at her husband. "I don't know what it was. It was like some kind of spell come over him after he read that letter. He didn't say anything right away, but I could tell something was wrong. That was yesterday, and I know he had a restless sleep last night. When we got up this morning, that's when all the trouble started. But he didn't get that bat and come after me until I told him I wanted to go to the county seat tomorrow to do a little shopping."

"I thought she was going to meet her...." He shook his head. "I don't know what I thought. I just got mad. It was like I was overcome." The sorrow in his eyes turned slightly suspicious. "Do you think it was like an evil spell or something?"

Maybe, Guthrie thought.

"Maybe you ought to go pray on it," his wife suggested.

"He can do that while he cools off overnight in my jail," Turner said.

"You don't need to do that...," Frannie began, but Turner cut her off.

"Yes, I do. You won't be here, anyway. I'm calling an ambulance to take you to County General so they can check out that arm."

She looked like she might object to that, too, but the pain was too much to ignore.

Turner put Slansky in the back of the Interceptor, then Guthrie waited with him for the ambulance to arrive. Mrs. Slansky was loaded aboard in short order, and Turner told her to call him when she needed a ride home. Then Turner drove to the police station, where he put Slansky into one of the station's two cells without booking him.

"We'll see what Frannie says tomorrow," Turner told him. "If she wants to press charges, you better get ready to spend a little more time in here."

"Honest, Chief, I don't know what come over me." Slansky looked about as hangdog as one could get. "But you're right locking me up here, at least for tonight. I need to ponder my sins."

"You need to ponder getting your temper in check, especially over something told to you by someone you don't know and don't even know is true."

"You're right, Chief. It was crazy what I did."

They left the small cell block, Turner shutting and locking the barred outer door behind them.

"Do you think our food is still there?" Guthrie asked.

"Bev'll take care of it," Turner said.

As soon as they sat down in the cafe, Bev came over to tell them Leo was replacing their meals, gratis.

"He says the police force can't investigate murders on either an empty stomach or an empty wallet," she told them. "Your food will be out in a few minutes." She gave Turner a peck on the cheek then returned to the kitchen.

This time, they managed to finish their meals without interruption, and by the time they were pushing their plates back, the hour was approaching six.

"I guess we ought to call it a day before something else happens," Turner said.

"Like that's going to stop anything," Guthrie said, and Turner gave a grunt somewhere between disgruntled humor and assent.

They went out to his SUV, and Turner drove them to the police station, where he parked in his spot, got out with Guthrie, and started toward the station's door.

"You're not going home?" Guthrie asked.

"I live right next door, remember? But Bev doesn't get off until eight, so I might as well get some paperwork done. No sense me sitting around the house, twiddling my thumbs."

"I'll be at the mobile home," Guthrie said. "Call if you need me."

Turner smiled wearily and nodded as Guthrie got into the Xterra. A few minutes later, he arrived at the state road, turned right, and drove the remaining distance to the trailer court. The Pit Stop was already lit up, and three cars were pulled up in front. Their drivers were inside, probably pumping Jerry for the lowdown on the holdup as much as they were pumping gas.

Inside the trailer, Guthrie stared at the walls and tried to organize his thoughts. But it seemed that nothing would be organized where Thorndike was concerned. Not until they found Freddie Jensen. He'd just fired up his laptop when his phone rang. The caller ID read, "Oakdale Police Department."

29

"GUTHRIE HERE," HE SAID AFTER he thumbed on the phone.

"Peters from Oakdale PD," came the detective's voice. "I hope it's not an inconvenient time to call."

"Not at all."

"First off, I want to thank you for finding Norm Telfor, and I can tell you Mrs. Telfor is grateful for the closure, even if it's not the outcome she'd have preferred."

"It was dumb luck," Guthrie said.

"Or not so dumb," Peters said. "The FBI agents told me you had the address all along and didn't share it with me."

"I apologize."

"That's okay. Nothing I could have done in Texas, anyway. Besides, I'm all about results, and you found Norm pretty quick when my bosses had written him off. That cuts a lot of slack with me."

"I appreciate the tolerance. Has the body been shipped to Oakdale?"

"Yeah. Jesus Christ. It arrived this morning, and the shape it's in is unbelievable. Mrs. Telfor wanted to see it, but I told her she didn't want to remember him like that. Our ME said he's never seen anything like it, and me, either. Mrs. Telfor is going to have him cremated, and everyone here agrees. That corpse has to be the worst I've ever been around, and not just because it looks like it does."

"It's pretty foul."

"Any idea why?"

"Not yet. Even the FBI lab's come up with nothing."

"We know he was shot at the sawmill, but do you have any idea what happened to him after that?"

"Only that he was transported here, probably with the sofa he was hired to deliver since we found him on one. I'm still in Thorndike, trying to find out."

"Still there? You already found him. Isn't your contract fulfilled?"

"You said finding Norm's body brought closure to Betsy Telfor, but that's not really so. She—and I—need to know what happened to him."

"That's dedication."

"You ought to know we've had a second unexplained murder here as well as another disappearance. I'm sticking around partly to help the local police chief figure out what's going on."

"Sounds like a mess. Let me know when you do. But listen. Thanking you isn't the only reason I called. I've found some...." Peters paused, as if groping for the right words."Some interesting information."

"Interesting?" Guthrie pressed.

"Well," Peters admitted. "Maybe a little bizarre. I don't know if any of it directly impacts your investigation, but I thought you'd like to know I located several people in Oakdale who formerly lived in Airla. I asked them about what happened to the town, and they told me that the place was fine until it suddenly wasn't. Sickness, fires, injuries, sudden or unexpected deaths, suicides, murder. You name it, it happened in Airla. The worst were numerous serious accidents, some fatal, at the sawmill. There was even a riot there right at the end, which would explain why the front offices and machinery were so torn-up. The riot drove the final nail in the coffin, and the mill shut down. After that, the population fell to just a few families who held on for another couple of months, but with nothing left of the town, they had to leave, too. No one's lived there for about two years before Telfor went there to pick up the sofa and go missing."

"Only two years? It's hard to believe the town deteriorated so much in such a short amount of time."

"Maybe," Peters said. "But remember it's located in a damp forest and was pretty poor and ramshackle to begin with. Places like that can fall apart real quick. Looks like the last official resident was the most recent owner of the sawmill, though I never saw a place that was hab-itable either time I was up there. Fella named George Rand."

"Rand?"

Guthrie's surprise must have been evident in his voice because Peters immediately said, "You know him?"

"He's in Thorndike."

"No shit? Odd that he owned the sawmill where you found Telfor's van."

"He denies knowing anything about the sofa even though Telfor was supposed to pick it up at the mill."

"Of course he does. Better watch out for him. Folks tell me he was a bad actor as well as a harsh employer, and things got worse after his father came to town and moved in with him."

"His father?"

"So he told people in Airla." Guthrie could almost hear Peters shrug at the other end of the connection. "This so-called father lived in Rand's house and didn't come out much, so no one ever talked to him, though they infrequently saw him with Rand."

"No first name on the father?" Guthrie asked, remembering that Rand had claimed—or at least implied—that he lived alone in the old Chaney house. "And why 'so called'?"

"No first name or last," Peters said, "but he couldn't have been Rand's real father. I did a little digging, and Rand's real father and mother were murdered six years ago in Baton Rouge. Apparently a burglary gone wrong. Both were shot to death about four months after Rand took out three life insurance policies on them totaling more than two million dollars."

"He told me he made a lot of money in business and real estate, but it certainly wasn't by selling the mill."

"The Baton Rouge PD were immediately suspicious of him, but they never could prove he was behind the murders. He openly admitted he'd been carousing with a pair of hookers in Houston, and that's a four- or five-hour drive from Baton Rouge. Houston PD queried the hookers, and they verified he was with both of them the entire night."

"Who was the so-called father?"

"No idea."

"You mind sending me the hookers' names?"

"You don't think they're telling the truth?"

"I'd just like to double check Rand's alibi."

"All right. I'll text them to you after we get off the phone. But back to Rand, he stayed in Baton Rouge for a couple more years, then he bought the sawmill and moved to Airla about four years ago. Everything seemed okay for a time, but soon his record was marred by a couple of sexual assault allegations from female office staff, later dropped. Then, according to workers at the mill, he started cheating his employees of pay, eliminating safety protocols, and not improving dangerous work conditions. There were so many accidents that OSHA got involved briefly, but that went nowhere. After the riot, Rand shut down the mill, cleared out the company bank account and payroll, and disappeared. And that's not all."

"As if that wasn't enough."

"It was rumored he molested several children in town—boys as well as girls. At first, he avoided prosecution by paying off their parents. Or maybe threatening them. Depends on who you talk to. But that seemed to be what sparked the riot. Apparently they were looking for Rand and probably would have strung him up if they'd found him, but he'd already gone. And now you say he's in Thorndike?"

"Unfortunately, though he seems to have lost his so-called father between Airla and here. Can't you bring charges regarding the payroll?"

"Not if nobody files a complaint, and so far, nobody has. Everyone I talked to seemed scared shitless of him."

"I've met him, and I can say for a fact he's off, but it's good to have some tangible background on him. So, we have a rich, corrupt individual who's destroyed lives but has used his money, position, and threats of violence to protect himself from prosecution."

"It's that same old story," Peters admitted. "But there's nothing we can do without someone filing a complaint."

After he hung up with Peters, Guthrie punched in Tereba's number from memory. It was too-important a detail to have in his phone's address book. Tereba answered on the second ring.

"Hello, Mr. Guthrie. Nice to hear from you."

"Nice, you mean, that I'm still alive?"

"I have great faith in your resilience," the old man replied blandly. "Besides, the Talisman of the Armor of Earth will help protect you as it has in the past. I assume you're calling to give me an update."

"More to help me clarify what's going on."

Guthrie described the circumstances of Telfor's disappearance and the discovery of his body, the murder of Jeff Mayfield, and the disappearance of Freddie Jensen. The condition of the sofa and the feelings Guthrie and others felt from it, not to mention the antics of the Kuei men, seemed to sober Tereba, as did the rot in the ditches leading to Chaney Marsh and the sensation of oppression that now lay over the wetland. Guthrie also told the old man about the desolation at Airla and detailed some of the incidents that had been occurring around town since the discovery of Telfor's body.

"George Rand, the former owner of Airla Lumber Company, is now living in Thorndike," he finished.

"I don't like hearing any of this," Tereba admitted when Guthrie was done. "It sounds like you're dealing with something like a veta-la—an evil spirit from the Hindu tradition that usually inhabits charnel grounds—and by extension, any place of decay. Certainly a dump would be inviting to it. A vetala enters and animates the bodies of the dead, much like the idea of the vampire in the West, and decay is halted until the vetala leaves the corpse for another."

"Could a vetala inhabit a living person? Like Rand?"

"I have heard of no instance of that, but to be safe, let's assume it can at least infect a living human and direct it to do its bidding, though I believe that person would have to be morally corrupt to begin with. In any case, a person, dead or alive, might not be the actual vehicle for a vetala—especially a powerful one—but merely a sort of peripheral puppet imbued with enough of the vetala's spirt to exert control over him or her. Perhaps Rand's inborn vulnerability to corruption is why the vetala—if it *is* a vetala—fixated on him and is using him as its human instrument."

"If it is a vetala, it might be aided by or controlling Rand, either willingly or unwillingly. Probably willingly. But I don't think it's inhabiting him. The Kuei men just don't react to him strongly enough. Not like they do to the marsh or even the sofa. What you're saying sounds basically right, though, but how does some evil Hindu spirit come out of southern Louisiana?"

"An excellent question."

"Is it possible that a vetala's influence can spread over a wide area instead of fixating on a single body? Such as a marsh or pond? Or even a small town like Airla or those two abandoned villages in Louisiana? Like Thorndike?"

"Anything is possible, I suppose," Tereba said after a moment. "If this is a vetala, perhaps it has grown too powerful to inhabit a singular human body and must resort to something larger, such as a charnel ground, a dump, a decaying town, or a marsh where much decay is present."

"I'm pretty sure whatever it is has infected the marsh and most likely the pond. What I want to know is how to kill it."

There was a long pause before Tereba answered.

"A force of nature such as a vetala cannot easily be destroyed," the old man said. "It does not have a body of its own but inhabits and feeds off the atmosphere, the odors, and the auras of places of corruption. But clearly this manifestation is not limited to such since it seems it managed to inhabit the sofa long enough to be transported to Thorndike. I think you'll have to isolate it from its current host, which seems to be the pond, and trap it in something that is more mobile. In the past, there has been some success in taking a vetala to a place where nothing, or very little, lives, such as a barren desert, and letting it starve to death."

"Yeah, well, there's not a lot of barren desert around here, and I'm not sure I could ride that far with that thing in the same vehicle. Besides, how would you transport it?"

"If it rode in on a filthy old sofa, apparently even an inanimate object will suffice. If you can entice it to take hold."

The old man paused, then said, "I continue to consult with my colleagues in Louisiana, but in any case, I advise you to proceed with great caution. Your Kuei men should afford some protection, but a vetala is a powerful spirit surrounded by a field of corrupting influence. Keep me updated."

"I will," Guthrie said, thinking, if I live long enough. "One last thing. Could you have someone track down the hookers who backed up Rand's alibi? I'll text you their names."

"I'll do that. Stay safe."

Yeah, right, Guthrie thought as he hung up, unable to still the restless thoughts churning through his mind. They were still churning away that night when he turned out the light, but he gradually fell into a restless sleep.

Sirens wailing down the state road toward town woke him.

30

THE SIRENS SOUNDED LIKE THEY came from fire trucks. Several. Thorndike didn't have its own fire department, so he knew they must have driven from the county seat. By the time he'd gotten up to groggily peer out the window, they were gone, but the sound of their honking sirens hung in the air, diminishing in the direction of town. He glanced at the time on his phone. Nearly two-thirty. Suddenly, the phone lit up as it rang. It was Chief Turner, his voice excited and a little breathless.

"The Baptist Church is on fire."

"I'm on my way."

Guthrie cut the connection, dressed quickly, and left the mobile home. In moments, he was heading toward town. Even though Thorndike's town center was more than three miles away as the crow flies, he could see a pulsing cherry glow lighting the dark sky above the intervening trees.

At this hour, the state road was empty except for a low night mist that spilled onto it from the fields on either side, so he stepped hard on the gas. The mist thickened the closer he got to the intersection with Main. He turned onto Main and raced down it but soon had to slow as he came upon tail lights embedded in fog ahead. This was the first time he'd been out at night in Thorndike, and he was surprised that the mist was this thick this far into town.

Several more cars pulled out from side streets behind him, their occupants drawn like moths to the scene of the fire. As he neared, he could see thick flames whipping billows of smoke into the darkness above. The church was the largest structure in town aside from the school buildings, and the whole thing was ablaze.

The intersection at Main where the police station was located was shut down, and more than a dozen cars clogged the block in front of Leo's. A crowd had assembled in the intersection, held back by Taylor, Tessa, Pete and Wally, and several street-work barricades. Guthrie parked a block down from Leo's and ran toward the intersection. Emergency lights from three fire trucks, an ambulance, and Thorndike's two police Interceptors flashed off the police station, the feed store, and Eli Carlin's Auto Repair, but they were weak competition for the flames, which clutched eighty or more feet into the air above the church.

"Glad you're here," Emmet said as he waved Guthrie through.

Guthrie hurried over to Turner, who was standing beside his SUV, watching the firemen doing their best to douse the flames. It looked like their best wouldn't be enough. Only two fire hydrants were nearby, and their jets of water were simply not enough to quench the massive blaze, even if they were supplied by the water tower standing only a block away. Already, the entire roof was on fire, and even at a hundred and fifty feet, the heat was intense.

"What happened?" Guthrie asked as he came up.

"Can't tell," Turner said, not looking at Guthrie but staring at the flames, a look of despondent futility in his eyes. "Gotta wait until they put it out and everything cools down. Problem is," he said, finally looking at Guthrie, "the fire department is half-an-hour away, minimum. Usually more like forty minutes. A fire can spread a whole lot in that time."

The two just stood then, silent, watching the building burn and burn. Another ten minutes, and a shout came from several of the firefighters, and they all moved quickly back. Seconds later, the roof collapsed with a creaking, muffled roar, sending gushes of smoke, sparks, and chunks of flaming fragments into the air. In moments, all that remained of the First Baptist Church was an empty shell of partial brick walls surrounding a crater of burning debris billowing acrid smoke.

Fires, Guthrie thought, as the smoke spread out and settled over the town, thickening and tainting the mist already there. You could tell what was burning by the odor: a nice camp fire with aromatic smoke, a barbecue pit of flavorful wood, a building fire reeking of burning furniture, rubber, plastic, and electronics.

He glanced around the assembled crowd behind them, faces dully lit by the flames. This was no accident, he thought. Very possibly one of the people in the crowd did this. He wished he could take their photos, but the light just wasn't good enough. He did note the absence of the Sanfords and their two cronies. Turning back to the flames, he saw a uniformed firefighter who wasn't tricked out in fire-fighting regalia approaching.

"Chief," the firefighter said, extending his hand. Turner shook it.

"Chief," Turner responded. "Any information for me?"

"I can tell you already it was no accident," the fire chief responded. "We can see it started almost simultaneously at several locations around the building. Probably an accelerant was used. Somebody wanted to make sure the destruction was total." He shook his head. "Even if we'd been in town when it started, it's unlikely the outcome would have been much different."

Luckily nobody had been hurt. The minister, Douglas Hansen, and his wife, Bridget, lived in an adjacent brick house, which remained undamaged. The minister had noticed the fire when he got up to urinate and immediately called 911. He and his wife were standing off to the side, bracing each other as they stared at the ruins of their church. Guthrie saw Mayor Acuff go over to comfort them.

"We probably ought to talk to them, too" Turner told the fire chief, who nodded. To Guthrie, he said, "Mind giving Emmet and Tessa a hand? I'll be over in a few minutes."

As Turner and the fire chief headed toward the mayor and the pastor and his wife, Guthrie strode back to where Emmet and Tessa were doing crowd control with Pete and Wally. They weren't having much trouble. Thorndike was a quiet little town, and most of its citizenry didn't seem prone to either violence or panic. But even if they were subdued as they stared at the dying blaze, Guthrie could hear murmurs of questions, speculation, and fearful disquiet.

"Hey, you," a man's voice rose above the rest. "The new cop. What's going on over there?"

"Yeah," came another voice. "What's happening?"

"Chief Turner and the fire chief are still discussing matters with the mayor," Guthrie said loudly enough for everybody to hear. "He'll be over in a few minutes to explain what they know."

The crowd was patient enough, maybe because they had the gradually dying fire that had been their church to entertain them. Human sight, Guthrie thought, is so easily captivated by flames. At last, Turner came over with the mayor.

"How'd the fire start, Chief?" a man in the crowd called out even before Turner and the mayor had stopped in front of them.

"We're not yet certain," Turner responded. "We'll let you know after a full investigation."

"Full investigation," another man snorted. "Sure. We all know how that goes around here."

"Do you, Roger?" Turner snapped. "I suppose you'd like to volunteer to help. Are you a licensed arson investigator?" That elicited no response, so Turner simply said to the crowd at large, "I know you have a lot of questions. We don't have the answers yet, but we'll let you know more when we know more."

"This has been a disaster for our community," Acuff said, taking charge. "But I have faith we'll come through this. Most of you worshipped in that church, and I know you're wondering what's going to happen now that it's gone. Let me assure you that we aren't going to leave you out in the cold. We haven't made it official yet by a council vote, but our plan is to let Pastor Hansen hold services in the high school gym until a new church can be built. For now, the fire's nearly out, and most of you have a full day of work ahead. Go home and get some rest."

Acuff left to return to the Hansens, and gradually the watchers drifted off until all were gone except for a reporter from the *The County Courier*, who took some photos and asked Turner for an interview. While the chief was occupied with the reporter, Guthrie joined Emmet, Pete, and Wally in moving the street-work barricades down the block to close off the streets immediately around the burned-out church. Tessa, too light for such labor, waited in the police station parking lot.

As he worked, Guthrie recalled that the church in Airla also had burned, as had a couple of other buildings. One thought rose paramount: Who started the fire? No, two thoughts. Why? The second question might be easier to answer: to disrupt the status quo, destroy social cohesion, and instill uncertainty and fear. The rodent infestation in Chaloupek's Grocery and the theft of Eli Carlin's tools were right in line with that. Obviously someone—or something—had an interest in seriously damaging Thorndike's equilibrium as well as its infrastructure. He wondered if the poison pen letters had a similar source. Unfortunately, those motives didn't draw an indelible line to anyone, though George Rand was at the top of Guthrie's suspect list. But he doubted Rand had been the one to torch the church. At least not personally. But there were the Sanfords, Miller, and Fitzgerald.

By the time Guthrie, Emmet, and the town service workers finished moving the barricades, dawn had come and gone. Turner left the reporter with the mayor and fire chief and joined them and Tessa in the police station parking lot. The fire was still smoldering, and the fire crew was squirting water on it, but the fire chief had told Turner it would be completely dead by the evening.

As they stood there, surveying the huge scar burned across the face of the town, Guthrie thought that none of Thorndike's little police force appeared to be much better off. Tessa looked weary, frazzled, and a little shell-shocked, Taylor withdrawn and sullen, and Turner stiff with pent-up anger.

"You two can get on with your day," he told Pete and Wally.

"We'll be at the dump if you need us" Wally said, and they left.

"What now, Chief?" Emmet asked.

"You all feel well enough to work?" Turner asked. They all nodded, but the chief said to Tessa, "Not you. I want you to go home and get some rest. Don't come back until tomorrow. Understand?"

"No way, Chief," she said, her slight frame drawing up straight. "Too much going on. You need me in the office."

"All right," Turner conceded, and as she started toward the station door, he looked at Emmet. "How you holding up?"

"I'm okay," Taylor said. "Any place you want me to check on?"

Turner snorted a bitter laugh.

"That would be everywhere." He shrugged. "I guess you can just go on patrol. Keep a sharp eye out. Report anything at all suspicious."

Emmet left in his Interceptor.

"I don't have any suggestions of what you might do since you don't have a police car and can't chase down speeders on the state road," Turner said to Guthrie. It was an obvious attempt at humor, but the exhaustion in Turner's voice belied the levity. "Why don't you drive patrol around town, if you don't mind."

"I don't, but we need to talk first." He wanted to tell Turner about the phone call from Peters the night before. He wasn't yet sure he'd say anything about the conversation with Tereba.

"Come on in the office. But first, I have to let Larry Slansky out of his cell. Frannie called from the hospital while I was talking to the mayor, and she wants him to come pick her up."

"Is she all right?"

"She has a fractured arm, but she doesn't want to press charges." Turner smiled. "Personally, I think she's kind of happy Larry is that jealous, especially since there's no reason."

They went into the station, where the chief released Slansky from his cell.

"What's going on out there?" Slansky asked.

"The Baptist Church burned down," Turner said.

"What?"

"You heard me. But right now, you have to deal with the consequences of your actions yesterday. You broke your wife's arm."

"Goddamn," Slansky said, voice subdued. "I didn't mean to do that."

"I hope you had a chance to think about what you did and why."

"I did, Chief." Slansky shook his head. "Like I said yesterday, I musta been crazy. I don't know what happened."

"I do. You didn't think, you just reacted. Poorly."

"You're right. I screwed up." Slansky hung his head.

"All right. Well, Frannie's not pressing charges. Go home and get your car and drive up to the hospital. They're releasing her this morning, and she's expecting you to pick her up. You think you can do that without causing more trouble?"

"No more trouble from me," Slansky said. "I ain't even gonna read any more mail."

"I'd be happy if you just quit giving Frannie shit over nothing."

"You're right, Chief."

Slansky headed for the door, pausing only to collect his personal possessions from Tessa.

"Okay," Turner said, gesturing toward his office. "Let's sit down, and you can tell me what you wanted to."

He started toward the office but halted as the front door burst open.

31

GUTHRIE TWISTED AND SAW A tall, middle-aged man with thinning dark hair and a prominent nose. The scowl on his face said he wasn't happy. Guthrie didn't know him, though he'd seen him among the crowd watching the church burn.

"Chief," the man said. "Am I glad to see you. I've been burglarized."

"Let's go look," Turner said.

Guthrie followed as the two hurried across the street to Havasau's Hardware. Inside, the man waved at the glass-topped display counter and the wall behind it. The wall was filled with empty rifle racks, and the shelves in the counter were empty of everything but pistol stands and price tags.

"You can see for yourself, Chief," Havasau snapped. "They took all my guns. Ammo, too. Fuckers musta done it while everybody was out watching the fire. I couldn't get in here until now 'cause of the fire and all the commotion, so I just found out."

"Didn't you have the firearms under lock and key?"

The hardware store owner gave a faintly sardonic chuckle and waved around the store.

"I had 'em chained up, but I think they had all the tools they needed."

The register drawer was open.

"Money, too?" Turner asked.

"Yep, they took that, but I don't leave much in there overnight. Most of it's in the safe in the office. Looks like they tried to get into that, too, but it was too strong or they didn't have enough time."

Havasau led Turner and Guthrie to the back of the store, where a door opened onto a short hall flanked by a small office and bathroom on one side and a larger room that served for storage on the other. The door to the storage area looked like it had been kicked in. At the end of the hall, a metal door to the alley at the back of the store gaped, hanging askew from the twisted top hinge.

"That's how they got in," Havasau said. "The safe's in here."

He led them into the office and pointed to a three-foot-tall safe set against one wall. The door and frame around the lock were scarred, but only superficially, and two drills, a power saw, and a grinder lay nearby.

"Like I said, they couldn't get into it," Havasau said, a touch of pride in his voice. "And they couldn't carry it out. Fucker must weigh five hundred pounds empty. The fellas who installed it had to bring it in with a floor jack."

"Why don't you go back up front and make an inventory of everything that's missing," Turner said. "Mr. Guthrie and I will do a little more investigation back here."

"Okay, Chief. I'll be up front if you need me."

Havasau headed toward the front of the store, leaving Guthrie and Turner to do what they needed to do. Out in the hall, Turner tilted his head toward the caved-in door.

"Let's look at that."

It was clear the door hadn't just been kicked in. It was metal, painted black, and its two locks were both substantial deadbolts reinforced by a two-by-four bar across the middle. The bar lay splintered on the floor. Whoever forced the door had to have used some sort of vehicle to burst it open like that. When Guthrie examined the outside surface, it was dented in and scraped just about the height of a tall pickup truck bumper. He said as much to Turner, who nodded.

"Yeah. Somebody pulled their truck down the alley behind the store and used it to push open the door. Then all they had to do was load the stolen merchandise into the bed." He looked at Guthrie. "What do you think?"

"I think you're right. I also think the burglars were amateurs."

"Why?"

"Anybody with skill would have known they couldn't break into that safe with conventional tools. Plus, everything they did would have made noise. Besides, how many professional safecrackers live here in Thorndike?"

"Not that noise would have mattered," Turner said. "All that commotion going on around the fire would have masked any sounds. And we had to cut power to downtown for several hours, so the burglar alarm would have been disabled." He gestured toward the other side of the alley, which presented the rust-mottled but seemingly sound corrugated sheetmetal wall of a long building. "Over there's Jack Herwitz's lumber yard, where Jeff Mayfield worked. Nobody there at night. Thank God they didn't burn *that* down, too."

"I think this was done by the same people who set the fire," Guthrie said. "It's too coincidental."

"Makes sense," Turner nodded.

They examined the outside of the building and the surface of the alley, which was dry dirt and gravel and held no distinct tracks. But it was the same alley that lay behind Chaloupeks Grocery right next door. Turner used a pocket knife to scrape flakes from the surface of the door's dented area, even though no obvious paint transfer had taken place.

"Anything else taken?" Turner asked Havasau when they'd finished and gone up front.

"A bunch of power tools are missing, and a generator. But Jesus Christ, Chief, they took enough guns and ammo to start a small war."

"I'm sorry for your loss, Buster," Turner said, stiffening. "But I have to ask why you think it's necessary to stock enough guns and ammo to start a small war in a town the size and character of Thorndike."

"People got their Second Amendment rights," Havasau said sharply. "I'm just making sure they can exercise them."

"And now we have some criminals running around town, exercising those same rights with your stolen guns."

"I don't have to take that kinda guff, Chief," Havasau said, drawing up. "I'm the victim, here."

"Wrong. You might not like it, but you do have to take it. I'm the law here, and your stolen guns just made my job a lot harder and Thorndike more dangerous. You aren't the victim. The town is."

"What am I going to do now?"

"I'll send Officer Taylor over later to take your statement, get the inventory, and collect the power tools to have them checked for fingerprints. In the meantime, I suggest you finish the inventory then repair that back door and reopen for business."

The chief turned and headed toward the front door and pushed through into the sunshine, Guthrie on his heels.

"I still need to talk to you," Guthrie said as they walked across the street to the police station.

"Not now. I have to file a report on the fire and the burglary while they're still fresh. Why don't you get a bite to eat? We'll talk later."

As Turner headed toward the station door, Guthrie walked over to Leo's. The air inside was fresher than outside, where the reek of smoke would taint the atmosphere for days. A coupe of dozen people were inside, among them the Slanskys, who were sitting in a booth by the windows, looking at menus. Mrs. Slansky's left arm was in a sling. The only other person at the counter was a thirty-something man in work clothes, who was just finishing his meal. Guthrie took a stool a discreet distance away, and Bev came over with water and silverware.

"How's your day so far?" she asked.

"Busy."

"Us, too. I think nearly the whole town came in for breakfast after the fire."

"I see Mr. Slansky picked up his wife."

Bev shook her head and gave a low chuckle.

"She won't be working for a while, which means that the women of Thorndike are going to look pretty frowzy until she starts up again. Need a menu?"

"I need something," Guthrie said. "But I'll take a menu."

She brought one, he ordered, and she took the order to the service window before returning.

"I guess you're missing home right about now, what with all the crazy goings-on around here."

"Yes, and that's both a blessing and a curse."

"How?"

"A blessing because thoughts of home are what keep me going, and a curse because when I'm there, all I can think about is the next case."

"Seems to me you need to develop a personal life."

"Yeah. When I get the chance."

"No," she said. "When you make the chance. Did you just come from the police station?" she asked, changing subjects.

"Yeah. Your husband's writing up reports." He didn't mention the burglary at Havasau's Hardware since the man at the other stool might have overheard. Everybody would know by sunset, but there was no sense in riling up more panic any sooner than necessary. "He can tell you about it tonight, if you haven't heard it from someone else before then." He grinned. "Which is likely."

She smiled back then looked into the room behind him.

"I need to tend to the Slanskys. I think they're ready to order."

As soon as she was gone, the man on the nearby stool said, "You're that new officer, ain't ya?"

"That's right."

"Any news on the fire?"

"Nothing until the arson investigators finish their work. I don't know when that'll be."

"How about them murders? You think the same person who killed that guy in the dump killed Jeff Mayfield, too?"

"I can't really comment...."

"Sure, I know the speech," the man interrupted. "I watch TV. But that don't help out the rest of us. Folks is scared."

"That's understandable. I assure you, Chief Turner is working hard to solve the murders, but when things like the fire this morning happen, it's a distraction."

"Maybe for him," the man said, "but my wife says if one more bad thing happens in town, she wants us to move up to the county seat."

"How about you?"

"Shit," the man said. "I work for Mr. Fuller, and his spread's south of town. I don't want to have to drive all the way down from the county seat ever day. That'd take me durn near an hour each way and make me a regular commuter." He gave a weak chuckle. "No, I like it here fine, but I gotta say, all this death and destruction is startin' to get to me, too. Maybe I'll do what the missus wants." He shrugged. "Life is hell, sometimes."

"That's the truth."

"I just hope you and the chief figure out what's goin' on around here before the missus makes us move."

"We'll do our best."

The man got up, went to the register, and paid, and soon after, Guthrie's food was ready. He ate absently, thinking about the events of the past few days but was unable to come to any firm conclusions. When he finished eating, he paid up and walked to his Xterra. He pulled out of the lot and began patrolling the streets, ending about five-thirty, coincidentally or not, at the entrance to the dump. The gate was shut and locked, but that wasn't what he was really here to see.

The rank water in the ditches looked much the same as before, filled with mucky rot that stank of death thanks to the small animals and countless insects floating on the scummy, umber surface.

He followed the ditches down the county roads, past Rand's house, the Audi parked out front. Just beyond, he turned toward the gate across the track leading to Jim Chaney's cabin. The closer he got to the gate, the worse the rot was, finally overflowing the edges of the ditch and encroaching on the margins beside it. He got out of his truck for a closer look at it and the woods beyond. It was dark in there. Very dark. And the space between the trees was already filling with mists that were slowly spilling out onto the grass-lands past the fence.

His Kuei men were kicking, but even if they hadn't been, Guthrie thought he'd have been able to tell something was very wrong in the marsh—something that had grown in power over the past few days. He could feel a repulsive, malign pressure aspirating through the woods, though not a leaf stirred on any of the branches. Which was odd, since the tall grasses on the pasture land on either side of him were rippling beneath a light but steady breeze.

He wondered if he ought to climb the gate and go down to the cabin to see how Jim Chaney was faring, but he decided not to. For one thing, night would fall soon, and he didn't want to be caught in the marsh after dark. It was menacing enough in the daylight. He could only hope Chaney's liberal use of garlic would help protect him.

Finally, Guthrie got into the Xterra and drove to the trailer. Only as he lay down in bed did he remember he hadn't told Turner about the phone call from Detective Peters. Tomorrow, he promised himself as he fell asleep. Tomorrow....

He was again awakened by the sound of sirens.

32

HE JUMPED OUT OF BED and glanced at the time on his phone. Just after three. He was already on the road by the time Turner called.

"The Methodist Church is on fire," the chief said, voice tense with anger.

"I'm on the way," Guthrie told him then thumbed off the phone and pressed down on the accelerator.

The Methodist Church had been a simple, rectangular frame building standing on a pier-and-beam foundation, and it was nothing but smoldering coals by the time Guthrie arrived on the heels of the fire department. Luckily, the firefighters managed to save the adjacent minister's bungalow, but nothing else. Even the trees shading the building had burned, flaming like huge torches.

Turner was talking to the fire chief, so Guthrie joined Emmet, Tessa, Pete, and Wally, who were again doing crowd control. Since the church was near the south edge of town, the crowd was smaller than the one that watched the burning of the Baptist church, but it was in an uglier mood.

"They's attacking our religion," Guthrie heard a man say, and several other people around him muttered assent. "I say we get some guns and go guard the Assembly of God."

The First Assembly of God, out on the state road just north of the gas station, was the third, smallest, and last church standing in Thorndike. Turner quickly dissuaded them.

"If you go out there, Carl, I'll arrest you."

"On what charge?"

"Organizing an armed vigilante mob, for starters. And I'm sure I can tack on other charges if you disobey a direct police order." He scanned Carl's cohorts. "All it takes is two of you to make a conspiracy case. Even if you don't do something stupid, which you're sure to do, you'll get time, a black mark on your record, and loss of income. Can any of you afford that?"

"Well, what are you gonna do about all this?" Carl demanded.

"Don't you have a job of your own to do, Carl? Go do it, and don't let me see you the rest of the day. All of you."

Grumbling, Carl and the others left. Only then did Guthrie notice that Emmet's Interceptor wasn't at the scene.

"Where's your cruiser?" he asked the officer.

"Somebody slashed all the tires."

"Right before this happened?"

"Yeah. I had to drive over in my own car."

By the time dawn brightened the eastern sky, the fire was out.

"The fire chief says it was definitely arson," Turner said, joining his little police department. He looked them over, concern on his face. "You two go on home," he told Emmet and Tessa.

"No way I can sleep, now," Tessa replied. "I'll be at the station."

"I have to call Eli Carlin to get my Interceptor and replace the tires," Emmet said.

Turner just waved them off tiredly, and both got into their cars and drove away. Turner faced the smoldering ruin of the church, eyes filled with anger, grief, and fear.

"What the hell is going on here, Clay?" he asked at last.

"It seems to me that someone or something is out to disrupt and demoralize Thorndike. Perhaps destroy it. Instead of making a frontal assault, it's attacking from the inside out."

"I still don't buy your unnatural monster theory. Someone living here set those fires."

"No stranger is writing those poison pen letters or tortured and murdered Jeff Mayfield, either. Besides, as you've already pointed out, there are only two strangers in town: me and George Rand."

"Well, I know it's not you," Turner said, a wry quirk twisting his mouth. "At least I don't think it's you. Rand, on the other hand...."

He paused thoughtfully then said, "You don't like him, and neither do I."

"Liking or not is meaningless. Evidence is what counts."

Guthrie told Turner about the phone call from Detective Peters, but he didn't mention the subsequent conversation with Tereba. Nor did he say anything about the two ruined villages in south Louisiana. So far, there was no direct link between them and Rand. But he did say he had someone checking with the prostitutes in Houston to verify Rand's alibi. The chief picked up on one important issue.

"So Rand isn't some successful businessman like he suggested he was. Essentially, he used the proceeds from murdering his parents to take charge of Airla, and now Airla is no more."

"In a nutshell."

"And now he's here, and things are going to hell." Turner's eyes narrowed. "Do you think this was him?" He waved over the smoldering remains of the Methodist Church.

"I don't think it wasn't him, though he probably didn't pour the gas and light the match."

"That's enough for me," Turner snapped, shoulders hunching. "Let's go roust him out of bed."

"We'll roust him, alright, but not yet. We need more to work with than what we have. We need Freddie."

"I don't need Freddie to question Rand. He's got to have something to do with the mess this town's become."

"Question him about bringing an invisible monster to Thorndike on a sofa?" Guthrie asked. "I'm sure he has something to do with it, but tell me: What's he actually done besides buy a house and some property? None of that is illegal, and if the Louisiana authorities can't bring charges against him, you certainly can't without accusing him of a specific crime committed in your jurisdiction. Besides, he's too canny. If you confront him now, he might sue you for harassment, which will give him power over us. We can't give him any sort of leverage."

"We gotta do something about him."

"That time will come," Guthrie said. "But we're not ready."

"Yeah," Turner said, calming down a little. "Besides, we know he can't be the one writing the poison pen letters. He just doesn't know enough about the people here to know what'll embarrass or rile them up."

"But he does know somebody," Guthrie said. "Remember, he was sitting with Wiley and his crew at the Lazy Q the day they attacked me. They all looked pretty friendly when I walked in."

"You said you thought he sicced them on you. You think they're in cahoots?"

"It took more than one person to burn the churches."

"You think Wiley and his crew are responsible?" Turner suggested.

"Likely, but I don't know if their arrangement with Rand is formal or not. Maybe Rand just convinced them he thinks like they do, and now they're all buddy-buddy. Or maybe he offered them something."

"Well, let's go roust them, instead."

"Probable cause, Chief?"

"Yeah, yeah." Turner shook his head. "Okay. I agree we need more evidence. Maybe the arson investigators will find something useful."

"We'll need something more than traces of accelerant," Guthrie said. "Anybody can pour gasoline and light a match."

Turner's shoulder radio suddenly hissed.

"Chief, come in." It was Tessa.

"Turner here."

"Dr. Hughes called just as I came in. He sounded bad and wants you to go over there right now."

33

"ON MY WAY," TURNER SAID, then looked at Guthrie. "Follow me?"

In three minutes, Guthrie pulled up behind Turner's Interceptor at the Canine Cottage. Both of the Hughes were outside on the front veranda of their home, seated in chairs, Dr. Hughes comforting his wife. She wasn't presently crying, but her red face and puffy, watery eyes, said she had been. A lot. Dr. Hughes rose from his chair as Guthrie and Turner approached, face also red, but with anger more than sorrow. His left hand was wrapped in gauze, blood spots showing through.

"What's the trouble, Dr. Hughes?" Turner asked.

"I'll have to show you," the vet said. He glanced at his wife.

"I can't go back in there," she said.

"Has something happened to one of your dogs?" Turner asked as Hughes led them over to the clinic building and through the front door. Just inside was the waiting room. It was empty of people and animals, but redolent of dog odor. And under that washed a scent Guthrie was too familiar with. Blood.

There was a lot of blood. In the back, past four small exam rooms, lay the kennel area for local pets. There were seven of them —five dogs and two cats. Both cats were alive, hissing and cowering in the backs of their cages, but every other occupied cage was a pen for slaughter. One stood open.

Hughes waved weakly at the carnage.

"They were alone in their cages. They must have bitten and torn their own limbs and flesh. Horrible, horrible." His head hung this time as he shook it again. "These animals were left in my care, and something terrible happened to them." He pointed to the empty cage with the open door. "That one was still alive when I came in. It was whimpering and quivering. A cocker spaniel. They're usually goofy, laid-back dogs, but as soon as I opened the door to see if I could help, it leapt out, snarling, and bit the crap out of me." Wincing, he held up his bandaged hand as evidence.

"I tried to slam the door shut, but it got out and ran over there." He pointed to the far corner of the room. A puddle of fur lay there, copper color barely showing beneath a caul of blood. "It chewed off its own back legs. I think it's dead, now." Hughes shuddered and turned away, face ashen, and after a moment, he looked at Turner, eyes filled with pain, fear, and guilt. "What am I going to say to the owners?" he asked, shoulders sagging helplessly.

"Your breeding stock?"

"Back there," Hughes said, voice heavy and helpless, gesturing toward a door in the back of the kennel room. "It's the same All dead."

He led them through the door, into the rear of the metal building, where he and his wife raised their Great Pyrenees. The dogs were together in a large space enclosed by a low chainlink fence. As the doctor warned, it too was a slaughterhouse. These dogs were the size of wolves, and Guthrie had once seen a video about a male Great Pyrenees who killed nine of eleven coyotes that attacked the herd of sheep he was protecting. Though he'd been severely wounded in the fight, he lived to bask in his glory. These dogs weren't easy to kill, he reflected, yet here were three adults and five pups, long fur no longer white but drenched with blood and gore. A couple of the pups were decapitated.

"Jesus Christ," Turner sighed. "What happened?"

"I don't know," Hughes said. "It must have happened while we were asleep. We came in this morning to feed them and found them like this." He shook his head. "Last night, nothing seemed unusual." He shook his head again, eyes avoiding the carnage around him. "Let's go back into the patient kennel. I don't think I can stay here right now. I loved these dogs."

He led them back to the kennel for the clinic patients. At least here, the blood was largely contained within the cages.

"Whatever happened to my dogs, the same thing must have happened to these, too."

"But not the cats," Turner observed. Hughes looked a little startled, as if just now registering that fact.

"You don't think it's some sort of infection or disease?" Guthrie asked, as much to reengage Hughes' clinical training as to gain an answer at this early stage.

"Nothing I know of can have an effect even close to this except rabies," Hughes said, straightening a little as his medical background took charge. "But none of these animals have the slightest symptoms of rabies except for irrational rage. And a rabid dog doesn't bite itself to death. Besides, they're all vaccinated, and even if they weren't, it's impossible for every single one of them to present with the same disease at the same moment."

"Poisoning?" Turner asked.

"We personally feed them all their meals, but not every one of them gets exactly the same food, especially the patients and boarders." He shook his head. "So not poison, though I probably ought to send some tissue and blood samples to A&M. If there are pathogens or poison, they'll spot it."

The last statement seemed to perk up the doctor a bit more and put him back into professional mode.

"Do you need help disposing of the bodies?" Turner asked.

"I'll call Freddie Jensen. He's got a pickup and a backhoe. Maybe he can haul them off and bury them more quickly than I can cremate them."

"Freddie's not going to be an option. Nobody's seen him for a week."

"Probably off on a bender somewhere," Hughes said, shaking his head. "I don't think Mabel will be much help, so I'll clean up the kennels, myself. I'll cremate my own dogs and freeze the patients and boarders until their owners tell me what they want done with the bodies."

"All right," Turner responded. "Let me know when the report on the samples comes back from A&M."

"I will."

"Call me if anything else happens or you notice something that might have caused all this. If anyone gives you problems, refer them to me."

"I will, Chief. Thanks for coming by."

They exited the clinic, but before Guthrie and Turner could leave, a green Chevy pickup pulled up behind Guthrie's Xterra. The cab held a man and a woman, but only the man got out. The woman was slumped in the seat, crying. The man, face darkened with anger mixed with shock and sorrow, didn't seem to be in much better shape.

"Dr. Hughes!" The man yelled from beside the bed of the truck. "You gotta see what happened to my dogs!"

Hughes hurried over, Turner and Guthrie following.

"That's Henry Richardson," Turner murmured to Guthrie. "He and his wife, Grace, own one of the larger farms just north of town."

Hughes reached the truck first and looked into the bed. He didn't recoil. Maybe he'd already seen too many torn up and dead dogs in one morning to have much reaction left. When Guthrie stepped up, he saw three dogs lying on a blue plastic tarp in the bed —one a Great Pyrenees and the other two hounds. All three were dead, mutilated with bite wounds and covered with blood. The Great Pyrenees was missing all of one foreleg and part of the other, and the throat of one of the hounds gaped open. The other hound's neck was bent at an unnatural angle.

"What happened, Henry?" Turner asked.

"I don't know, Chief. Last night they suddenly went berserk and got into a big fight. I don't know what got into 'em. They never done that before. The commotion woke us up about three, and by the time we got outside, they was all dead except Butch." He pointed to the Great Pyrenees. "But he didn't last long. Christ, Chief, he was bitin' off his own legs when we found him." Richardson might have been trying to shake his head sadly, but instead, his whole body quivered. "It was crazy. You don't think it's the hydrophobia, do you?"

"I see none of the common symptoms of rabies," Hughes assured him, "so you can relax about that. But we won't know more until I send some blood and tissue samples to A&M."

"How much is that going to cost me?" Richardson asked. "I ain't a rich man."

"Don't you worry, Henry," Turner said. "We'll call it a sort of health emergency. Any charges will be covered by the town."

Neither Turner nor Hughes mentioned that the Canine Cottage had become a canine abattoir.

"In the meantime," Turner went on, "Dr. Hughes will take charge of the bodies."

Richardson, who appeared to be functioning in a haze, helped the other three pull the tarp out of the truck bed. Carrying it like a blanket sagging with weight in the middle, they maneuvered it through the front door, down the hall, and into an exam room, where they laid it on the floor. Mable Hughes averted her face as they passed.

"We'll take it from here," Turner told Richardson. "You and Grace go on home, now. Dr. Hughes will call when he knows more."

Richardson looked glad to be relieved of both the burden and the responsibility for his dead animals. After thanking the doctor and the chief and giving Guthrie a nod, he left the clinic. The others followed him out and watched him start his truck and drive away.

"I'm leaving all this in your hands for the moment." Turner said to Hughes. "Keep me informed."

"Are you going to tell everybody what happened here?" Hughes asked pensively. "I don't want people to think I'm responsible. Especially after those terrible letters." He shook his head helplessly.

"We'll keep it quiet for the moment," Turner said, "though word's bound to get out. But now that the Richardsons have a similar problem, the issue obviously isn't just with you."

After that, Guthrie and Turner went to their vehicles.

"I'm having trouble thinking straight," Turner said. "I haven't been eating all that well the last few days. Let's go to Leo's. If I can stomach food after seeing all that carnage." He waved toward the Canine Cottage."

They got into their respective vehicles, and Guthrie pulled out after the Interceptor. Then he saw the chief glance in his sideview mirror and slow slightly. Guthrie peered in his rearview and saw a car pulling up in front of the Canine Cottage. A man and a teenage boy got out, and the man opened the trunk. The two of them reached into the trunk, and each lifted out a bundle wrapped in a bloody sheet.

We're going to see more of that, Guthrie thought. Or Dr. Hughes is. As if in agreement, another car pulled up in front of the vet's office.

As Guthrie followed Turner to Leo's, he couldn't help but reflect on the thick fog that had spilled out of the marsh the night before and inundated the town. It had been particularly dense along Main Street where the Canine Cottage was located, but it had extended several miles to the north, perhaps as far as the Richardsons' farm. Had some taint within it affected any canine within it's range?"

When Guthrie and Turner arrived at Leo's, the cafe was about half-full. Apparently the fire had kindled a lot of appetites. And talk. The room buzzed with angry and fearful murmurs, and almost everybody watched, some with trepidation, some with veiled hostility, as Turner and Guthrie entered and sat in a booth. Bev was out on the floor, taking orders. When she finished, she came over with two cups of coffee and silverware.

"You okay, Bill?" she asked, concerned expression on her face.

"Been better," he admitted. "I'll tell you later. Right now, food'll help."

She took their orders, took the ticket to the service window, then made the rounds of the room, a pot of coffee in one hand and a pitcher of water in the other. Guthrie saw Turner follow her movements, love and concern in his eyes.

"We'll get to the bottom of this, Chief."

Guthrie said it to Turner but maybe also to himself. He couldn't rid himself of the sensation of malignant decay imparted by the darkness growing in Chaney Marsh. More important, was there anything he could do about it? That last question wove a strand of doubt through his mind. Was it already too late? But he said nothing of this to Turner. The chief needed all the bolstering he could get. Now was not the time for Guthrie to waver in his resolve.

Turner's phone chimed, and he answered, face betraying anxiety.

"Turner." There was a pause as he listened. "You sure? Has anyone found his truck? Okay. Thanks."

"That was Dr. Bob," he said after he hung up. "Strange news. He says that the blood you found in the marsh is definitely Jeff Mayfield's, but there isn't enough to cause death by bleeding. He thinks Jeff was attacked and maybe shot down there but was killed elsewhere. They found traces of his blood along the path to the road, so it looks like he was carried out after he was subdued."

"That complicates matters. What about his truck?"

"Nothing yet."

"Even if he'd been shot first, it wouldn't have been easy to carry Jeff somewhere else."

"Yeah, we're definitely looking at more than one perp. You're thinking Rand accompanied by the Sanford brothers?"

"That's what I'm think...."

He was interrupted by a loud cry caught between pain and a bellow galvanizing the already tense air. It came from the kitchen, and Guthrie and Turner jerked their attention that direction just as Bev rushed to the service window and stared through it.

"Oh, my God," she gasped then bolted for the swinging doors to the kitchen.

34

LIKE EVERYONE ELSE IN THE cafe, Guthrie and Turner jolted to attention at the cry, and when Bev rushed into the kitchen, they hurried after her.

Inside, Leo was bent over, groaning and trying to wrap a dish towel around his left hand, which was bleeding profusely. A chef's knife lay on the floor, crimson blobs on its blade and the tiles around. His wife hovered like a nervous bird, wanting to help her husband but clearly frightened by all the blood.

"He's cut!" she cried as Bev, Turner, and Guthrie burst in. "Please, please, do something!"

Guthrie rushed to Leo and helped him wrap his hand, while Bev circled an arm around Martha's shoulders, half comforting, half supporting her. Turner looked on, helpless to do more.

"It's fucking bad," Leo gasped. "I need the doctor."

"I'll take him," Guthrie told the others. "Take care of Martha. I'll call when I know something."

In moments, he guided Leo across the restaurant beneath the shocked eyes of the diners. He got him into the Xterra and pulled off.

"I don't know what happened," Leo hissed between clenched teeth. "I never been that clumsy."

"Stay calm," Guthrie said. "We'll be at the doctor soon."

The drive to Dr. Williamson's office took less than two minutes, but the towel around Leo's hand was practically soaked by the time they arrived, and Leo was pale with shock. The small parking lot outside the building was completely packed, and several more cars lined the street in front. Guthrie double-parked. Inside, the waiting room was crammed with people, many of them parents with children, but as soon as the receptionist saw the blood-soaked towel, she ushered Leo and Guthrie to a treatment room then left. She was back moments later with Dr. Williamson and his nurse.

"Leo," the doctor said sympathetically. "What happened?"

"I don't know, Doc. My hands just went haywire while I was chopping up a lettuce, and the knife cut the fuck outta me."

"Here," Williamson said. "Let me take a look."

He gingerly unwrapped the towel, revealing a nasty slice running from the base of the forefinger to the base of the thumb. The knife had severed an artery, and blood pulsed from one end.

"Hemostat," Williamson snapped, and the nurse pulled one from a jar of disinfectant.

"We'll take it from here," the doctor told Guthrie as he clamped off the artery. "We'll to have to send him to County General."

"I'll drive him up there," Guthrie said. "I'll be out front. Let me know when he's ready to travel."

Williamson, intent on Leo's wound, simply nodded. Guthrie eased out into the hall and headed toward the waiting room. Just before he reached it, he glanced through the door to the receptionist's cubicle. She was busy checking in a woman with a burned hand. Guthrie waited until she was done then gestured for her to come out into the hall.

"What's with all the patients?" he asked. "Is it payday, or something?"

"Something," she sighed, brushing back a curl of light brown hair that had escaped her ear. "It's been like this almost all week, but today's the worst yet. Just this morning, we've treated cuts, scrapes, falls, a sprained ankle, sudden colds, headaches, and fevers. Even a broken arm, but we had to send that up to County General. It's crazy."

Almost like an epidemic of just about every bad thing that can happen, Guthrie thought as he went outside to call Turner.

"How's Leo?" the chief asked.

"The doctor's sending him to the hospital. I'll drive him up. What's the situation there?"

"I'm back at the station, but I'll let Bev know. Everybody was gone by the time I left. Nothing I could do there. Martha wants to close the cafe for the time being, but Bev promised she'd help out in the kitchen. Leo can supervise until he can work again. Emily can wait tables, and she has a couple of friends who can help. Folk'll understand, even if it shoots my home life all to hell." He snorted a laugh. "Like that isn't shot all to hell already. I'll tell Bev to take Martha to the hospital so she can be with Leo."

"Have her drive up in Martha's car so Martha can drive him home. I'll wait and bring her back. You also ought to know that the doctor's office is crammed with patients. He's already sent one patient with a broken arm to County General."

"This early?" Defeat was close to the surface in Turner's tone.

"Stay strong, Chief. I'll check in when I get back."

Guthrie thumbed off the phone and went into the waiting room. Williamson brought Leo out about fifteen minutes later. His hand was wrapped in a loose, bulky bandage and wrapped in a fresh white towel that was already showing spots of blood.

"I called the emergency room at the hospital, and they're expecting you. I've given him something for the pain, but not too much since I don't know exactly what they're going to do there."

"Thanks, Doc," Leo murmured.

Guthrie took Leo by the arm and steered him toward the door. In a minute they were on Main, heading for the state road.

"How you doing?" Guthrie asked.

"Hurts like hell, but that shot Doc Williamson gave me helped."

"Don't worry. We'll be at the hospital soon, and they'll fix you up. Chief Turner said Martha and Bev will take care of business until you can work again."

"That woman's a good wife," Leo said, "but she don't cook as good as me."

"It'll be good enough, and you can supervise until you heal. But you can discuss it at the hospital. Bev's bringing her up right after us."

Leo nodded then slumped in his seat, cradling his injured hand.

The county seat was a decent-sized town, but Guthrie found County General easily enough. He parked then helped Leo out and guided him through the emergency room entrance. The nurses inside took charge and led Leo to a treatment room. As soon as they had, he went outside where he wouldn't be overheard, pulled out his phone, and punched in Tereba's number. Tereba answered before the second ring.

"Mr. Guthrie, I'm glad you called. I was just about to call you."

"I hope you have something I can use," Guthrie said. "Things are getting pretty tense and weird around here. The whole town is going crazy. Have you found out any more about Rand or the vetala?"

"We have determined it is not a vetala, but my colleagues in Louisiana have discovered some significant information on what it is."

"What, then? I need something to work with here."

"I have to take you back several years, before the destruction of the two villages in Louisiana."

Each village, Tereba told Guthrie, had been inhabited by a close-knit clan who lived off fishing and crawfish farming. One was the Fortiers and the other the Dutetres, and between them was a long-standing and bitter conflict regarding territorial rights.

"About eight years ago," Tereba said, "two young Fortier men vanished while out in the swamps, and later, a teenage Fortier girl was raped by three Dutetre men. Claude, head of the Fortiers, wasn't one to sit around idle, so he gave his clan permission to retaliate against any Dutetre they might find vulnerable. This led to more bloodshed and destruction on both sides, none of which was ever reported to any police agency. Insular, tight-knit clans like those don't trust outside authority. They deal with matters their own way, often to their own detriment."

The feud escalated, and though the Fortiers held on for a couple of years, the attrition on their side surpassed the toll they'd taken on the Dutetres. This information, Tereba said, came from the remaining Fortiers and Dutetres still living in the general area. At last, in an attempt to cut off the head of the proverbial Fortier snake, several Dutetre men attacked Claude's house, hoping to catch him unawares. He was out in the swamp at the time, working his crawfish traps, but his wife and son were home. He found their bodies when he returned that night. His wife had been raped and slaughtered in their bed, and the son lay shot to death in his bedroom.

"When he discovered their bodies," Tereba said, "Claude abandoned any moral concerns he might once have had and developed a single-minded lust for retaliation and revenge. His surviving relatives called it frightening in its intensity. Claude, knowing that one man alone was not enough to exact the kind of revenge he desired, resorted to desperate measures by enlisting the assistance of a bòkò."

"A bòkò? What's that?"

"A vodou sorcerer," Tereba said. "Not to be confused with other sorts of vodou priests and priestesses, whose work is generally positive and uplifting for the community. But every patch of light is accompanied by one that is dark. Bòkòs are members of the Bizango secret society that is most active between midnight and dawn. Usually they are hired to lay a curse upon someone or to relieve a curse laid by another bòkò. This bòkò's name was known to two of the surviving Fortiers, and my colleagues in Louisiana tracked him down and got most of the rest of the story from him. He resisted at first, but a little severe distress amply demonstrated that his power was outmatched by theirs. He divulged that Claude Fortier had hired him to bring complete and total destruction upon his enemies."

To accomplish that, the bòkò would have to do more than lay individual curses upon the Dutetres. He would have to invoke something that would lay waste to their entire clan. After studying the Dutetres and the environs of their village, he discovered something he thought he could use. While a swamp can be a peaceful and even bucolic place, within many lie pockets of murky and foul decay, corruption, and disease inimical to the living. After finding such a slough near the Dutetre village, the bòkò believed he could infest it with a semi-sentient destructive power that he could set upon the Dutetre village. There, its corruptive and destructive influence and intent would suffuse the Dutetres, their environment, and the very air they breathed, worming its way into their thoughts and behavior and contaminating them and their village with discord, havoc, and devastation. It would then feed off the subsequent strong emanations of decay, pain, and suffering of those who would not or could not leave in time to save themselves.

"Think of it like a psychic amoeba that seeks to envelope food to consume. It does not have intelligence, only an instinctive drive to sustain itself."

"How was it created?" Guthrie asked. If he knew that, he might discover some clue to how to destroy it.

"All vodou priests, including bòkò, strive to invoke lwa, which are supernatural beings that vodou practitioners believe are present in all aspects of nature and are intermediaries to the higher power of the universe. Usually, single lwa are coaxed to enter the priest or to interact with humans for good or, occasionally, ill purposes. But to create a noxious force powerful enough to destroy the Dutetres, the bòkò invoked a composite of three lwa."

Two of the three, Tereba said, were Lasirenn and Gede. Lasirenn is a mermaid-like being who is the spirit of water. Most commonly, she is associated with seduction and wealth, but she also can animate the potential violence of water. Gede is the chief god of the dead, the digger of graves, and the god of derision. Connecting and overarching the two was Bawon Samdi.

"You might have heard of him in his human guise as Baron Samedi," Tereba said. "He wears a black top hat with a white skull and crossbones on the front. He's the one in charge of zombification and zombies. One of his subsets, Lakwa, is a ghoul and, also conveniently for him, keeper of graveyards.

"It was the union of these three lwa that the bòkò utilized to coalesce the foulness of the noxious slough into a cohesive, if amorphous, body filled with intent and destructive purpose. A miasma, if you will, an airborne psychic infection that can insinuate itself into the bodies, minds, and spirits of those it touches."

Taking substance from night mists, it settled like a cloud of psychic decay upon the Dutetre clan and proceeded to destroy them and their village by shrouding them in a pall of discord, self-destruction, and death and soaking up the resulting pain, fear, misery, and sorrow to fill the emptiness of its own hunger. The plan worked, and within a year, Fortier's enemies were no more, their village destroyed and the few survivors scattered.

But there was a hitch. To create the miasma, the bòkò needed a focus, and that focus was the the dark flower of hatred, violence, and corruption that had taken rooted in Claude's heart and soul. As long as the Dutetre village was viable, the hatred, violence, and corruption were directed at it, but once the Dutetres were destroyed and their few survivors scattered, the miasma sought to return to is progenitor like a dog returning to its master after a hunt. There was a symbiotic relationship between them more powerful than blood ties. The miasma was a mindless, insatiable darkness born from Claude's black fantasies had given purpose and direction. But with that purpose and direction gone, Claude was all that remained. Claude and the village over which he was patriarch.

The miasma gravitated to Claude and settled around him. And though it was bodiless, it remained cohesive. And hungry. It quickly sought fresh sustenance in Claude's own village, and after a number of deaths and other negative occurrences, the Fortier clan was on the verge of the same decimation that Claude had caused to be visited upon the Dutetres. Claude understood what was happening as soon as the miasma descended upon him and his village, but he was unable to stop or contain the force he'd commissioned because it was rooted in his own being, in the hatred and violence that still corrupted his soul. The social and economic structure of his village collapsed, and surviving inhabitants fled.

Desperate to save what little remained—and perhaps himself—Fortier contacted the bòkò who'd induced the lwa and brought him to the village to exorcise his creation. The bòkò was appalled at what his creation had become. He had assumed that once the miasma completed its task of destroying the Dutetres, it would gradually sub-side into the swamp and eventually fade away, just one more foul slough among many. But to his horror, instead of subsiding, it had sought out Claude because Claude's moral decay and corruption was the seed that the bòkò had employed to germinate it.

He also understood that while Claude was personally immune to its influence, his kinfolk had not been. Through subsuming the living energy of the Dutetres, and now the Fortiers, it had grown in strength and power. Worse, it had developed a sense of independent intent and purpose. Not an intelligence, exactly, but a powerful will to feed further. The nascent amoeba of corruption created to destroy the Dutetres had become a large psychic force capable of flowing over and consuming any food source in its vicinity and tainting every-thing around it with pestilent residue.

Fortier was now the last resident of the village and was still living in his house, though he no longer slept in the still-blood-stained bed he'd once shared with his murdered wife but on an old green velour sofa in the living room, around which the miasma settled and ingrained itself. The only reason the miasma had not moved on was because Claude seemed incapable of leaving the village he'd once ruled or the house where his family had been slaughtered.

"Fearing that Claude would eventually leave his ruined village and lead the miasma to fresh hunting grounds, the bòkò first tried to with-draw the three lwa from the miasma or dissolve it, but it had grown too powerful, too willful, and he was unsuccessful. He told Fortier he was unable to stop it and warned him that the malignancy coalescing around him as he slept each night would surely destroy the last vestiges of his humanity and cause further widespread destruction. Enraged, Fortier tried to kill the bòkò, who barely escaped with his life."

"Sounds like Fortier had already lost his humanity," Guthrie said.

"Any man willing to escalate a petty territorial dispute into wholesale destruction of his neighbors must have a malign sickness in his heart. The bòkò told my colleagues this: 'Fortier blame me for what he want done, but if you buy a bad dog for protection, don complain about gettin' bit.'"

"Only, this bad dog isn't through biting," Guthrie said.

"Apparently not. If you unleash a force of destruction on others, be careful that, once they are destroyed, it doesn't rebound on you."

"What happened after that?"

"Unknown," Tereba admitted. "The bòkò returned home and never saw or heard from Claude Fortier again."

"So, we know what the thing in Chaney Marsh might be, but not how it's connected to Rand."

"Actually, we do know that. Rand's murdered mother was Fortier's sister. We learned this from a Baton Rouge PD detective who went to the Fortier's village to query Claude about Rand while investigating the murders. That's probably how Claude learned his sister had been murdered and that Rand was the primary suspect."

"Did the detective have anything to say about the case?"

"Not much beyond that, though he's firmly convinced that Rand was guilty. But he did say he thought Claude had gone insane living alone in a decaying house sinking into a desolate, rotten, evil-smelling swamp. Somehow, the miasma must have aligned itself with Rand instead of Claude, though we have no idea how. But since it was focused on Claude, and Claude was anchored to the ruins of his village, it must have been getting hungry. Perhaps it sensed not only a greater personal corruption in Rand but more mobility. Clearly it was used to settling around Claude and that sofa every night, so it must have been able to imbue the sofa with its being long enough to be transported from the swamps to Airla then to Thorndike."

"Sounds like you have additional information on Rand."

"I do. The detective visited Houston to seek out the two prostitutes Rand claimed he'd been with, and they verified his alibi. But I had Li Wu do a little searching, and he learned that since then, both of their bodies were found in the area known as the Texas Killing Fields. You remember that, don't you?"

"A popular body dumping site east of Houston for several serial killers," Guthrie said.

"That's right, but the police believe that both of these women were killed by the same man because each was missing their right index finger."

"Sounds like a signature."

"The police in both Baton Rouge and New Orleans have been trying to catch a serial killer operating in their jurisdictions for more than a decade who also takes right index fingers from his victims."

"You think Rand is the culprit?"

"There's no direct evidence. Technically, Rand's in the clear for the murders of his parents, and he's not on the Baton Rouge or New Orleans police's radar regarding the serial killings. We can't find any solidly incriminating information or evidence on him except for what he did in Airla, but he seems to be a seriously dangerous man."

"But he is a man, not some amorphous pall like the one that's descended on Thorndike. We need to know how he came in contact with this miasma and why and how he apparently aided it in destroying Airla and now has set his sights on Thorndike. What about Claude Fortier? He might be able to shed some light on it."

"That's a dead end. He, too, has disappeared."

Or not, Guthrie thought. There still was the man Rand claimed was his father but who wasn't. Who'd maybe spent time sleeping on an old green velour sofa surrounded by an evil, corrupting force.

"We're counting on you, Mr. Guthrie," Tereba went on, "to provide some answers."

Why me? Guthrie's mind demanded.

He told Tereba about the rats in the grocery, and the other negative occurrences in town, including the self-cannibalization of the dogs.

"Could this thing control rodents?" Guthrie asked. "Avery Prentice could do that." He was referring to the leader of Fluxus from his first case for Tereba, who'd sicced a horde of hungry rats on Guthrie. "Or cause dogs to kill themselves?"

"Dark forces can find corruption and weakness in rats and several other types of animals—some people, included—and can easily control them," Tereba answered. "With people, the more corrupt, the more easily they are manipulated to serve dark ends. Not dogs, though, which are natural protectors closely allied to humanity. Maybe the dogs were compelled to kill themselves to eliminate that protection. It seems that the bòkò's creation is intent on destroying not only Thorndike's infrastructure, but its cohesion and safety. As for the cafe owner cutting himself and all the patients in the doctor's office, clearly the miasma has already begun to infect Thorndike's people. It might cause some to be be more susceptible to illness, some dangerously careless and accident prone, and some to become aggressive."

"I just want to know one thing more: How do I kill it?"

"Maybe it has vulnerabilities. It was born of water, so perhaps the opposite element, fire, would do the trick."

"It's not like I can set fire to a pond."

"I have faith in you. You'll find a way."

"If you haven't heard from me in the next few days, you'll know I haven't."

"Thank you for your dedication."

"I'll call when I have more news."

Guthrie thumbed off the phone, stuffed it into his pocket, and stared off into space, trying to get his thoughts in order. There were too many, all churning around. Soon after, Bev and Martha pulled into the parking lot in Martha's car. Bev had been driving, and when they got out, she handed the keys to Martha before they entered the emergency room. Bev emerged less than two minutes later.

"How's she holding up?" Guthrie asked after they were seated in the Xterra and he'd pulled out of the parking lot.

"Better now that she knows he's being taken care of." She was silent for a while—long enough for Guthrie to reach the state road and turn south. "What's going on, Clay?" she asked at last. "Thorndike's gone crazy."

Guthrie didn't know how much Turner had told her about the situation. Or Rand's unwelcome presence in the town and the state he'd left Airla in. And at this point, she couldn't even know about the dead dogs.

"Something not very nice," was all he could say, to which she just snorted.

"Okay, be like that."

"I'm not trying to be difficult. It's just that the situation is difficult. You ought to ask your husband."

"I have, but he's not saying crap to me. But he's worried to death, and that makes me even more concerned." She was silent for a moment then said, "You're not going to abandon him, are you?"

"No."

"You better not."

After that, they were silent until they reached Thorndike. Guthrie turned onto Main, and as he drove toward the town center, a stainless steel tank trailer wallowed out of the Stansic Oilfield Services compound, onto Main, driving in the opposite direction. He didn't think much of it except to note that Lonnie Sanford was at the wheel, Rob Fitzgerald riding shotgun.

"You can drop me off at the cafe," Bev instructed.

Guthrie pulled up at the curb beside Leo's, and Bev got out and leaned back in.

"We're closed for the rest of the day, but there's a lot to clean up. Tell Bill I'll be late tonight."

"I will."

She shut the door and went into the cafe. Guthrie drove the block to the police station and steered into the parking lot. He was inside the building a few moments later, and he went straight to Turner's office.

"How's Leo?" the chief asked.

"I didn't stay for the report, but Martha's up there with him. Bev's at the cafe and says she'll be home late."

Guthrie was about to excuse himself so he could go alone to confront Rand, but before he could, Tessa knocked and stuck her head through the doorway.

"Dale Stansic just called. There's been some kind of accident at the intersection of Main and the state road."

35

"WELL, GOOD GODDAMN," TURNER SAID heavily as he got to his feet. He retrieved his hat, and headed for the outer door.

"Call Emmet, and get him over there. Tell him we're on our way."

Guthrie followed Turner out to the parking lot.

"Maybe you ought to take your own vehicle," Turner said. "No telling what's going to happen next. We might need all the mobility we have."

Guthrie nodded, got into his Xterra, and followed Turner out of the lot and west on Main. They arrived at the intersection with the state road in just over a minute, and Taylor showed up right after. It was a single-vehicle accident, and there'd been no injuries, but the scene wasn't pretty. The tank truck Guthrie had seen exiting the oilfield services company parking lot just minutes earlier sat jack-knifed in the middle of the intersection. Its tank had split open, spilling its entire load of slimy drilling mud in the middle of the intersection, effectively blocking traffic on both the state road and Main Street.

Dale Stansic stood off to the side, away from the giant puddle of mud, talking to Lonnie Sanford and Rob Fitzgerald.

"Who was driving?" Turner asked after he, Guthrie, and Taylor walked up.

"I was," Lonnie said. "Rob was ridin' shotgun."

"You two wait here," Turner ordered, then he motioned for Stansic to move out of their earshot. Guthrie and Taylor followed.

'What happened, Dale?" Turner asked.

"Hell if I know. They loaded up the truck and left ten or so minutes ago. Next thing I know, Lonnie's calling to tell me this happened." He waved toward the thick pool of viscous slime oozing slowly across the pavement in an ever-widening circle around the ruptured truck.

"We need to get that rig out of the intersection and get that mud cleaned up. Will the truck drive?"

"I'm not sure. I'll get Lonnie...."

"I'd prefer that you do it yourself," Turner said.

Stansic gave him a questioning look.

"You think something funny's going on?" he asked.

"I don't think it's funny," Turner replied. "After you move it, I want you to go over that truck and make sure everything is as it should be."

"All right." Stansic was puzzled, but he also was angry about the accident, and he shot a look at Lonnie and Rob. "You think they deliberately did this?"

"I won't know what to think until you figure out what happened. Let me know what you find, then we'll discuss it. You have people who can help get this mess cleaned up?"

"Charlie Cummings got that vacuum truck he uses to clean out septic tanks and outhouses. Maybe he can suck up a lot of it. The rest we can wash off the road. But it'll take a couple of hours."

"Get it done. Tell Charlie the city will foot the bill. Make sure he clears at least one lane on each road first so we don't back up traffic."

Stansic nodded then waded through the mud and climbed up into the cab. A moment later, smoke belched from its stacks, and the truck shuddered then gradually pulled off to the sound of metallic grating and squealing from the torn tank. Blobs of mud still leaking from the rent dribbled in its wake. While Stansic parked on the shoulder of the state road a hundred feet south of the intersection, Turner directed Guthrie and Emmet to do traffic control though only two cars were backed up on Main Street and none yet on the state road. As Turner walked over to Lonnie and Rob, Taylor went to tell the drivers of the cars to take a different route. Guthrie stationed himself on the state road where he could intercept any traffic on it.

A short time later, Turner dismissed Lonnie and Rob, and the two began walking down Main toward the Stansic compound. Then Turner went to the ruptured truck, where he spent some time watching Stansic go over the vehicle. After that, they conferred for several minutes, Stansic pointing out this and that on the truck and tank. While they talked, the vacuum truck arrived, and the driver—Charlie Cummings, wearing tall black rubber boots—got out to survey the task at hand. Then he backed right into the slowly spreading pool, unlimbered the big hose, and started sluicing up the mud. Before long, he had one lane of the state road cleared of all but a thin coating. Then he left, driving down Main, presumably to Stansic's place to unload the mud before returning for another swipe.

Finally, Turner left Stansic and came over to Guthrie.

"What's Dale say?" Guthrie asked.

"He gave the truck a good going over. Looks like Lonnie and Rob were either mighty careless or they deliberately overloaded the truck then made such a hard left at the intersection that the tank split." Turner gave a rueful smile. "I admit I might have mentioned that the Sanfords and their cronies might be involved in some of the shenanigans going on in town, and Dale seemed to jump at the chance. He's going to fire the lot of them as soon as he gets back to the office."

"They won't like that."

"They don't like anything." Turner said. "But Dale can take care of himself."

By now, Charlie Cummings had returned and was clearing one lane on Main, and two of Stansic's employees arrived in a smaller tank truck laden with water. They parked, uncoiled hoses, and started spraying the mud still coating the asphalt, washing it into the roadside ditches.

More damaged ditches, Guthrie thought.

At that moment, an ambulance came down the south-bound lane, lights flashing.

"I didn't call for that," Turner said as the ambulance slowed at the accident scene.

He held up his hands, stopped it, and went over to the driver's window. A minute later, the ambulance pulled off, tires slipping in the mud still on the road, heading south.

"What was that?" Guthrie asked.

"Two of the employees at Johnson AgLime got into a fight, and one stumbled into some machinery and had his foot crushed." Turner looked distressed. "If this kind of shit keeps up, the ambulance drivers'll need to make hourly runs to Thorndike."

Johnson AgLime, Guthrie mused, was the southernmost viable business aside from the Lazy Q, not half a mile from the marsh and certainly within the miasma's range. Had it been responsible?

Turner went to tell Taylor to stay on the scene until the mud was cleared, then he directed Guthrie to follow him to the station.

"Anything new, here?" Turner asked Tessa, expression saying that if there was, he didn't want to hear it.

There was. Dr. Hughes had called to say that nearly everyone in town with a dog had brought it in, dead and mangled, wondering what the hell had happened to their pet or working dog. On top of that, eight people in town had their tires slashed or sand poured into their gas tanks.

"Looks like it's going to be a banner month for Dr. Hughes and Eli Carlin," Tessa remarked dryly.

"Not the kind of business they'd have preferred," Turner said.

The phone rang, and they all looked at it with dismay.

"Answer the damn thing," Turner barked after the third ring. Tessa didn't look anxious to, but she did.

"It's the mayor," she said, handing the receiver to Turner.

"Turner here," the chief said, then after a pause, "All right. We'll put out the word."

He passed the receiver back to Tessa, who hung it up and looked expectantly at him.

"Mayor Acuff is convening a town council meeting tomorrow at one to discuss the situation in town."

"Is that a good thing or bad?" Guthrie asked.

"The way things are going, your guess is as good as mine," Turner said, giving Guthrie a tired look.

By now, Guthrie was pretty tired, himself. And hungry. But he couldn't go home yet. He still had to confront George Rand. Alone.

36

GUTHRIE DIDN'T DRIVE UP THE long curving driveway to Rand's house. Instead, he stopped where the driveway intersected the dirt county road and parked across the driveway entrance, still on county property but effectively blocking access. He knew Rand was home because the Audi was parked in front of the house, but he didn't spot any movement in the yard or behind the windows.

He got out, shut the door, and made sure his pistol and badge showed prominently on either side of his belt. He had no doubt Rand would show up. The man couldn't afford not to. Guthrie was something he never imagined would happen, and he had to know more about this interloper who was disturbing his plans.

Guthrie leaned against the Xterra, facing the marsh. Even though the edge of the forest around the wetland was nearly half a mile away, and the malignant pond twice that, Guthrie distinctly felt the force of the bòkò's creation. The mists gathering beneath the canopy didn't seem to mask or hinder it, only give it substance. What was happening at night, when those mists spread across the pastures and into town? Was the miasma flowing with it through the streets of Thorndike and into the homes and businesses of its citizens? Into their hearts and minds?

He spent nearly ten minutes brooding on these and other questions before the sound of a vehicle crunching down the driveway made him turn, cautiously but casually. He loosened his pistol in its holster. Rand's Audi pulled up, bumper close to the Xterra's front passenger door, and stopped. A moment later, Rand emerged and walked around the Xterra's front end and up to Guthrie, his movements sharp and catlike.

"Mr. Guthrie," he said. "What brings you trespassing on my parcel of land?"

"That's Officer Guthrie. Your parcel of land? I believe this road is county property."

"So it is," Rand conceded. "I see you're looking at Jim Chaney's marsh. It's a lovely piece of property, don't you think?"

"It might have been. Two weeks ago."

"Yes, well, things can change quite rapidly."

"Yes, they can," Guthrie said pointedly.

"You should know that I'm in negotiations to buy the remainder of his property." Rand waved over the marsh.

"Is that right? That's not what Jim told me a couple of days ago."

"As I said, things can change rapidly."

"Maybe I'll pay a visit and ask him about it. See what he says."

"I understand he doesn't want any visitors right now. You probably ought to call first before you barge in down there and disturb his peace."

"Jim extended an open invitation to me," Guthrie said, "so I don't think he'd consider it barging in. And he told me it's you who's unwelcome. Besides," he reminded Rand, tapping his badge, "I'm now part of the Thorndike Police Department, and there was a murder down in the marsh a few days ago. I'm sure you know all about that. If I have to visit the crime scene or question potential witnesses, I'll barge in anywhere I want. Any time I want."

"I see," Rand said, stiffening, cold eyes turning frigid.

Guthrie took a couple of quick steps toward Rand, leaned in, and took an obvious deep sniff.

"Checking for something? Officer." Rand asked, contempt lacing the last word.

"Smoke."

Rand just gave a short, humorless laugh and backed off.

"It's not polite to get into other people's space."

"I think Jim Chaney has the same idea about you."

"You have anything more to say to me?"

The words came out easily enough, but Guthrie was intent on shaking the man's arrogant aplomb.

"I do. You said you live alone. If that's the case, where is your father?"

That definitely shook Rand. His shoulders stiffened, and his cold eyes deadened.

"My father?"

"That's right. The man you claimed was your father when you lived in Airla."

"I don't know what you're talking about."

"I don't see how you might get confused since your real father—and mother—were murdered in Baton Rouge under mysterious circumstances. Right before you collected the proceeds from the life insurance policies you took out on them just a few months earlier and used some of those proceeds to buy Airla Lumber Company. I understand you're the prime suspect."

"I don't have to take this kind of...."

"I asked you where the man you said is your father is."

"He's back in Airla."

"Nobody is in Airla. As you know because you ran the whole town into the ground before you hired Norman Telfor to haul that contaminated sofa to Thorndike. Why'd you kill him in the sawmill? I think it was because he wouldn't consent to drive that filthy and foul sofa anywhere once he got near it, so you killed him there. And afterward, you and your so-called father drove the sofa and Telfor's body here then took Telfor's van back to Airla to throw law enforcement off the scent."

"I don't know anything about a Norman Telfor," Rand said, face rigid. "I think we're done here." He made as if to turn to go to his car.

"We're done when I say we're done," Guthrie ordered, voice harsh. "I asked you where is the man you said was your father."

"And I told you, I left him in Airla. If he's not there now, he must have left. I don't know where he is."

"Who was he?"

"Just some guy I paid to pretend to be my father. To give me more credibility with the good citizens of Airla. He was a bum. I don't even remember his name."

"Let me remind you, then. It's Claude Fortier." Guthrie was striking blindly, but he saw that his words struck home. "He wasn't a bum but was the leader of the Fortier clan and brother of your mother. The mother you murdered along with your father to cash in on those life insurance policies."

Rand was visibly disturbed, but he tried to rally.

"None of that's true," he said. "All that's been thoroughly investigated by the authorities in Louisiana."

"Not quite. They're still suspicious and looking for anything that might incriminate you."

"I have an alibi."

"Those two hookers in Houston?"

"That's right."

"Dead hookers found in the Texas Killing Fields aren't good alibis. You might have thought getting rid of them after they'd lied to the police would cement their statements as fact, but frankly, it only makes you look guilty of their deaths as well as others."

"We're done here," Rand spat, and he turned, but Guthrie's voice, hard-edged, stopped him in his tracks.

"Take one more step, and I'll shoot you down like a mad dog."

Rand stiffened, and he turned back slowly, maybe trying to maintain his equilibrium, maybe getting control of his face, or maybe trying to figure out a response to whatever came next.

"Where is Claude Fortier?" Guthrie asked.

"Gone," Rand said. "He stayed in Louisiana."

"And why would he go back to a ruined and abandoned village decaying into the swamp? A village destroyed by the very thing he had the bòkò create to destroy the Dutetres. How did you gain an alliance with it? How did you get it to inhabit that nasty sofa long enough to transport it to Airla and then here?"

"I don't know what you're talking about." Rand tried to say it convincingly but failed.

"And speaking of Airla, I also want to know more about all those OSHA violations at your mill. And how you got away with sexually abusing your female staff, cheating your employees out of their pay, and molesting their children. Is that why a mob broke into the mill and trashed it? Were they looking for your blood?"

Rand's face tightened with rage.

"Those are unsubstantiated rumors."

"Heard straight from the mouths of those you wronged. You might have destroyed Airla, but you didn't erase the memories of the people who lived there. It's all coming to a head, Rand. I know all about you."

"You know nothing."

"Oh, so there's more? Tell me about it."

Rand was silent, so Guthrie went on.

"I know about your background, I know your intentions are corrupt, and I know about that." Guthrie threw a wave that took in the forest across the pasture. "I know you brought it here to feed off another town, and I'm telling you right now, I'm not going to let that happen."

For just an instant, Guthrie saw fear flash in Rand's eyes, but he quickly covered it up.

"I don't know where you came from or how you know about me and my friend, but if you start talking like that to anybody else, you're going to sound crazy."

"Maybe I already have believers."

"They can believe all they want, but can they, or you, do anything? Against what?" Rand wrinkled his mouth in contempt. "I think not. I think it's too late. For all of you. Now, are we done here?"

"Just one more question: Why?"

"Why?" Rand gave a short, sharp, humorless laugh. "Let's just say that the groans of men and the weeping of women and children are music to my ears."

Guthrie had to forcibly stop himself from drawing his pistol and shooting Rand on the spot. But that wouldn't eliminate the real problem. The real problem had seeped into the marsh and had taken hold, and the person of Rand was only peripheral to it. Killing Rand wouldn't eliminate the force squatting in the pond and might only complicate matters, though Guthrie probably could make a legal case for self-defense. A man like Rand didn't go around unarmed. He recalled that Telfor had been shot with a .380, a pistol easily concealed.

But even if Guthrie hadn't acted on his impulse, Rand crouched back, sensing he was, for a moment, close to death.

"Are we done?" Rand's tone was flat.

"For now. But there's always later."

"Yes. There's always later. Until then, I'll leave you to your investigations. Officer."

Rand returned to his car, backed up and made a three-point turn, then drove toward his house, trailing dust that glowed golden in the light of the dying day.

"Fuck," Guthrie muttered, relieved to have him gone. While he'd been in proximity, Guthrie's Kuei men had twitched even more than they had the last time he'd been near Rand. The main source of infection was down in the marsh, but Rand carried a good deal of it on his person, and the emanations from him were decidedly unpleasant, even if there'd been no odor of smoke.

He got into the Xterra and drove to the mobile home. After the confrontation with Rand, he didn't have much of an appetite, but he ate anyway, knowing he couldn't let himself knuckle under to the mental and emotional pressure. Later, he hit the sack early. Tomorrow would be the town council meeting, and he wanted to be as fresh as possible. It took him some time to calm his churning mind, but eventually he must have because the next thing he knew, he was waking to weak dawn light seeping through the thin curtains covering the mobile home's windows.

37

SATURDAY BEGAN BENEATH A CLOUD cover that, combined with the thick and only slowly dissipating night mists, gave Thorndike a dismal feel. The mists were gone from the town's streets by the time the town council meeting convened at one in the school gymnasium, but the overcast continued. The gym was set up with a couple of hundred folding chairs arranged on the floor in two sections separated by a central aisle. In front stood a low platform bearing a long table where the city council sat. Guthrie saw Segundo Yanez and another man setting up the chairs, but Segundo avoided eye contact.

After the doors opened at twelve-thirty, the chairs on the floor began filling up. By one, several hundred people were there, the overflow occupying the lower tiers of bleachers on either side. A steady nervous murmur hovered over the assembled crowd, and nobody looked happy. Most of the faces reflected a combination of anger, anxiety, and fear, and the tension in the room was palpable.

Many of Thorndike's leading citizens occupied the first two rows of seats, including the ministers of all three churches and their wives, Warren Fvers, Eli Carlin, Leo and his wife, Dr. and Mrs. Hughes, the Chaloupeks, and others. He didn't notice Frank Orman. Also conspicuously absent were Dr. Williamson, whose small clinic remained overrun with patients; Jerry Cantu, who couldn't afford to close his gas station; and Jim Chaney. That last didn't surprise Guthrie.

Scanning the people filling the seats, Guthrie recognized a few faces, notably the Sanford brothers and their two cronies. Several other rough-looking men were seated around them in the middle of the chairs on the right side of the floor.

"Big crowd," Emmet told Guthrie. "I don't think I've ever seen more than a couple of dozen people at these meetings." He leaned close to Guthrie and nodded toward the Sanfords and their group. "They never come."

"I doubt they're here out of civic pride," Guthrie commented, and Emmet nodded before moving off to flank the area where the Sanfords sat. Tessa was already on the far side of the gym.

It wasn't until Guthrie's gaze roved over the back of the room that he spotted George Rand, seated in the last row on the right, next to the aisle. Close to the exit. Rand's dark eyes were staring at Guthrie, and he didn't avert his gaze when Guthrie looked at him, though a faint, scornful smile twitched his upper lip. Guthrie met his eyes for a moment, but there was too much going on for him to engage in a pointless stare down.

Chief Turner wasn't on the margins with the rest of his small police force but was on the stage, seated next to Mayor Acuff, who occupied center spot at the table. Spread on either side were Thorndike's town council: Agnes Carpenter, Leland Fuller, Chuck Willis, Dale Stansic, and Roy Randall, the owner of the funeral home.

Acuff led off the proceedings by banging his gavel and calling the meeting to order.

"On behalf of the Thorndike Town Council, let me welcome you. I know a lot of you folks work on Saturday, and I'm sorry you have to be here, but it's the best day of the week for this sort of thing. And it'll give us all tomorrow, the Holy Day, to ponder what we discuss today."

"Just get on with it, Mayor," came a man's voice from the audience. Wiley Sanford. "Some of us got work to get back to."

"You mean you got to get back to drinking at the Lazy Q?" piped up a man on the left side of the audience. "Ain't that what you call working these days since you got fired?"

"Ain't none of your business where I spend my time, Greg," Wiley snapped. "And I ain't been fired. I quit that job for a better one."

By now, the room was in a semi-uproar, and Guthrie glanced at Dale Stansic. He was staring at the Sanfords, and the look in his eyes wasn't pleasant. Mayor Acuff stood up and banged his gavel hard and repeatedly until the hubbub began to subside.

"All right, Greg. That was uncalled for. We're here to solve problems, not create more." Acuff looked around the room before continuing. "We have several matters to discuss, today, but I know y'all are most concerned with the two murders, so we'll start off with that. Chief Turner will give you an update."

Guthrie figured politics would come into play here as much as anything. The mayor wanted to keep the murder investigations a local matter. Guthrie knew he was a proponent of modernizing Thorndike, and he believed that if the investigation went county-wide or, worse, statewide, it might stain Thorndike's reputation as the little town with two unsolved homicides.

Turner leaned into his mic and gave a rundown of the two murders without divulging details.

"Right now," he finished, "we don't have a suspect for either murder."

"You think they was done by the same person?" called out a man.

"There's no indication of that," Turner said. "The victim in the dump was murdered in Louisiana before his body was transported here."

That raised a further murmur from the audience.

"What about Jeff Mayfield?" the same man asked. "He was killed here. In Chaney Marsh. You think Jim Chaney done it?"

The murmur became a mutter, harsher in tone.

"Our investigation shows that Jeff was assaulted in Chaney Marsh, but he was killed somewhere else," Turner said. "We don't know where, yet. But in any case, we've completely eliminated Jim as a suspect."

Turner relayed this information with conviction, but Guthrie noted that his words didn't seem to mollify the audience. Enmity in Thorndike, he reflected, was strong against the old man hunkered down in the marsh.

"Surely you don't think someone in town is responsible," came a woman's voice. "Thorndike is a fine, upstanding community."

"I didn't say that, either," Turner responded. "Our investigation is ongoing, and when we know more, you'll know more. In the meantime, we're also investigating a number of other crimes, and the arson of our churches is at the top of the list."

"What are we going to do to protect the First Church of Christ so it don't get burnt down, too?" asked a man Guthrie recognized as Carl from the crowd around the smoldering Methodist Church.

"My department is keeping an eye on it during the daytime, and the state troopers are patrolling it at night. We've also set up several surveillance cameras. If someone tries anything, we'll know who they are."

"I still think we oughta post our own lookouts," Carl said.

"I might entertain that possibility if I didn't think you'd shoot someone who didn't need to be shot. Or maybe get shot yourself. Then we'd have three murders instead of two." Turner changed direction, but not much. "As most of you know by now, Buster Havasau's hardware store was burglarized, and all his firearms were stolen along with some power tools and cash. That crime also remains unsolved, so I urge you all to keep a lookout for any items that might look like Buster's stolen property. There also was a robbery at the Pit Stop, but those perpetrators were just passing through and were caught right away. They're in jail at the sheriff's office."

"What about all our dead dogs?" a man asked. "Now we ain't even got them to protect us."

"I'll let Dr. Hughes answer that." Turner took his seat, obviously glad to pass the torch to someone else.

Hughes stood, looking like the torch might burn him.

"I know you all have a lot of questions, but frankly, we don't have a lot of answers."

That started the crowd to muttering again, but Acuff's gavel banged it down.

"I've sent multiple blood and tissue samples to A&M for analysis," Hughes continued, "but so far, they haven't found any sort of virus or bacteria that might be the cause. They're as puzzled as I am. I know you're all worried, and I assure you I'll do everything I can to find out what happened."

With that, he sat, looking relieved to be out of the spotlight.

"All right," Mayor Acuff said, scanning the room. "If we're done with that, let's move on to the next order of business."

"What about all them other things?" a middle-aged woman near the front asked. "All them rats in the grocery store and all the accidents and sickness that keep happenin'?"

"Yeah," said the man next to her. "How the hell can so many things go wrong all at once? It's gone plumb crazy around here."

Guthrie deliberately stared in the direction of Rand. He wasn't surprised to see the man staring back, eyes cold, smile twitching the corners of his mouth. Apparently, he was here to soak up the sounds of men moaning and women and children weeping. Guthrie wished he'd gone ahead and shot him when he'd had the chance.

"We know the rodents got into the store through the back door, which was accidentally left open," Turner said. "That situation has now been rectified, and as you all know by now, Leland Fuller generously donated enough meat to restock the grocery."

He gestured toward Fuller, who smiled and looked like he might get up to give a speech, but Acuff laid a restraining hand on his arm, and he subsided.

"There is one more matter everybody needs to be aware of," Acuff said. "Someone has been writing poison pen letters and sending them to people in town. Chief Turner has had nearly two dozen reported to him, and some of you might have received such letters and have been too embarrassed to come forward. They all have a picture of an eye at the top. I want to state one thing unequivocally: Whoever is writing this trash is telling nothing but unfounded lies designed to damage lives and ruin reputations. Do not believe a word in them. Chief Turner's working to find the source of these letters, but that's not an easy task. I'm asking everyone who's received one to bring it to the police station as soon as possible. Everything in them will remain strictly confidential. The more evidence we have regarding these letters, the faster we'll be able to stop them. Thorndike has enough problems right now without this kind of thing stretching us to the limit.

"Finally, I want to introduce you all to Clay Guthrie." He pointed, and all eyes turned on Guthrie, making him feel like a condemned man facing a firing squad. "For those of you who don't know, we've hired him to help out during this time of crisis. He's a former Houston police officer who now works as a private investigator. He has the credentials and experience, and he's willing to stay and help us solve these crimes."

"Ain't he the one who brung all this crime to Thorndike?" Wiley called out. "We know none of us around here done it. Must be some stranger. A stranger like him." He thrust a forefinger at Guthrie. "Ain't you the one who found that body in the dump? We didn't have no trouble until you come to town. You're the one we oughta be investigatin'."

A nasty mutter rose from some in the assembly, mostly from those surrounding Wiley.

"Wrong, Wiley," Turner snapped. "You and your crew cause plenty of trouble nearly every weekend, and plenty of other times, too."

The unpleasant mutter turned a touch more pleasant as heads nodded in agreement. A few nervous chuckles and titters rose but quickly subsided.

"May I remind you" the mayor said sharply, "that if Mr. Guthrie and Chief Turner hadn't found the body, it would probably still be out there, and we'd be none the wiser. Chief Turner intends to find out who did it and who killed Jeff Mayfield, and Mr. Guthrie has volunteered to assist in his investigation, with my full support and authority."

"Yeah," came Lonnie Sanford's voice. "And look how that's workin' out." He smiled.

"That's enough," Turner said forcefully. "As Mayor Acuff said, Mr. Guthrie might have been the one who brought it to our attention, but the first homicide had already taken place before he arrived and in a different state."

"We don't know who's responsible," the mayor put in. "But with one dead man in our dump and Jeff Mayfield killed, too, I, for one, am grateful for Mr. Guthrie's help."

"And just who's payin' him?" asked a man in the Sanford's group. "And how much?"

"I am," Turner said. "Mr. Guthrie agreed to help with the case in exchange for a one-dollar bill."

That brought laughter from most of the attendees.

"I've already been paid by the insurance company who employed me," Guthrie spoke up. "I don't have another case right now, and I'm willing to help."

"Why?" a man asked. "What's Thorndike to you?"

"As the lady pointed out earlier, Thorndike is a fine, upstanding community. I want to help you preserve that. And personally, it's not enough for me to have found the man I was looking for." He stared straight at Rand. "I want to know why he died and who killed him. His wife will get an insurance settlement, but you all know that's not enough. She needs answers, and I'm going to help find them for her."

"Fine words…," Wiley started, but the mayor cut him off.

"You wouldn't recognize a fine word if it did a naked dance in front of you. This meeting will be conducted in an orderly manner."

"Yeah, we all know what that means," Wiley sneered. "Keepin' us folks quiet while you ramble on about bullshit."

"That's right, Wiley," Acuff said, face clouding in anger. "Just like everybody knows why you might feel that way since the only thing you've ever contributed to this town is the fines you pay after getting into drunken brawls."

That brought a fresh round of laughter from the majority of the audience.

"Alls the same," Wiley said, uncowed, "that Guthrie fella was lookin' for Jeff just before he was killed. Maybe he done in Jeff, just like he done in that other fella over at the dump."

"If he'd done in that fella in the dump, Wiley," Turner said, "and come in to report it and help me locate the body, he'd be as ignorant as you. And Jeff was killed *before* Mr. Guthrie came asking about him at the Lazy Q, where you and your brother attacked him without provocation and got the crap kicked out of you."

Wiley's face reddened as the audience laughed, this time louder, though the handful of men around him glared at the rest.

"It's all the fault of these newcomers," Johnny Miller grated, and there was a scattering of agreement and nodding heads. "Ain't none of this ever happened in Thorndike before they started comin' in."

"And just how many newcomers have you actually seen, Johnny?" Acuff asked.

"What about him?" Johnny waved toward Guthrie.

"Mr. Guthrie isn't a newcomer. He's a visitor who will be gone after he helps Chief Turner solve this case."

"How about that guy who bought Crazy Chaney's house?" someone else asked.

"That's one," Turner said. "He's in the back, if you want to ask him."

Guthrie glanced where Rand was sitting, but the chair was empty. Rand had left unnoticed before attention might be brought to him. Or maybe he just didn't want to hear the town council trying to improve the town he was trying to destroy.

"Well," Acuff said. "Looks like he skipped out. Any others?"

"What about all them people workin' for Grant Industries?" Lonnie asked. "We like Thorndike just the way it is. We don't want 'em comin' in and takin' our jobs."

"Exactly what job have they taken from you, Lonnie?" Acuff said. "The one you just got fired from for incompetence?"

"What's that supposed to mean?" Belligerently.

"It means," Dale Stansic snapped, "you deliberately wrecked my truck and cost me and the town tens of thousands of dollars."

"It means," Acuff said in a level voice, "you have nothing they want."

"Oh, yeah? And what's it they want?"

"For you to leave them alone, for one thing."

"I'll leave 'em alone when they stop flooding our town and costing us more" Wiley said. "Hell, this new gym probably cost the town a fortune."

"If you paid the slightest bit to what goes on, you'd know it didn't cost us anything. All the funds were donated by Miss Agnes."

"Well, they oughta be since she's one of the main ones wantin' to bring in newcomers and change things."

"Change is going to happen, Wiley, whether we like it or not," Miss Agnes spoke up. "Sometimes we don't like it, but there it is. I remember, for example, that once upon a time you were a cute little kid."

That brought a fresh burst of laughter.

"You're always so high and mighty, Miss Agnes," Wiley sneered. "Maybe someone needs to take you down a notch."

"Perhaps, Wiley," she said. "But it certainly won't be you."

"I don't gotta sit here and take guff from the high and mighty," Wiley snarled, standing abruptly, chair scraping the floor. "Y'all ain't nuthin' but a bunch a whiney, bitchin' housewives. Fuck all y'all. Y'all deserve what you gonna get."

He bullied his way to the aisle, followed by his brother, Fitzgerald, and Miller, and stalked out of the gym. The men around them watched them go but didn't make a move to follow. In a moment, the door closed behind them.

"Now that we have some peace and quiet," Acuff said, "we'll move on to the next order of business, which is voting to allocate funds to expand our water and sewer system."

"What do we need that for?" asked a man on the right side of the audience. "What we got works fine. I don't see why we need to spend money to expand nothin'."

"If I may address that, Mr. Mayor," Leland Fuller said. "What we have has worked well enough until now, but as you all have seen, it was inadequate to save our beloved churches, even in town."

Almost everybody nodded at that.

"As you all know, I'm expanding my business to include a meat processing facility, and like it or not, that's going to bring new faces to Thorndike. And more people means we need more of everything, and that'll bring others. The world outside Thorndike is marching onward, and if we don't keep pace, we're going die and dry up like so many other small Texas towns. The time to plan for the future is now, not when it's too late to do anything about it."

A fine speech, Guthrie thought. Self-serving but true none-the-less.

"That's all well and good," the man replied. "But I think we oughta hear from Miss Agnes. We all know she's gotta do somethin' with her spread. The rest of us are entitled to know what. Are you sellin' out to Grant Industries, Miss Agnes?"

Miss Agnes stood and smoothed her dress before she spoke.

"I wasn't ready to make this announcement, and neither were Leland and Chuck. But if I don't, I suppose you all will make a public scandal of me. I've thought long and hard on this matter since Eddie died. And this is what I intend to do. Some of you might not like it, but this is the way it's going to be. Thorndike is ideally situated between Dallas and Houston, and while we're a little too far from either to be a place where commuters live, we're not too far from the future to take advantage of our situation. When Leland expands his stockyard and builds his meat processing plant, that'll give a lot of you who lost jobs to Grant Industries a place to work. But there aren't enough of us to do that, so we're going to see new people come in. And there'll be jobs in all the stores that must come with an increased population."

"Does that mean you're selling out to some developer?" another man asked.

"I'm not selling out. I'm partnering. And most of my profits will be plowed back into the town. You all have heard that we need to upgrade and expand our water and sewer systems, but we need a lot more than that. We need our own fire department."

That brought murmurs of agreement.

"And how about our own post office?" chimed in a woman, bringing more agreement.

"That, too," Miss Agnes said. "And a pharmacy."

"What about Chuck Willis?" asked the man named Greg. "You selling out?"

"Miss Agnes, Leland, and I have had many long conversations about Thorndike's future," Willis said. "My decision is that, yes, in a sense I am selling my ranch. But not to Grant Industries. I'm going into partnership with Leland and Miss Agnes. We intend to make Thorndike the largest meat producing region in this part of the state. As Miss Agnes points out, we're ideally located between Dallas and Houston, which gives us direct access to the two largest markets in the state."

This time, the murmurs that rose in the audience were more positive than negative.

"Thorndike is on the top of the fence," Willis went on. "It can fall one way or the other, and Miss Agnes, Leland, and I intend for it to fall on the side of prosperity. For all of us. Leland and I will create the jobs, and Miss Agnes will build the houses for our newly prosperous citizens to live in. Between the three of us, we'll provide seed money to jump-start improvements to the infrastructure and the construction of our own fire department. And we'll work with the county, state, and federal governments to bring in outside funding. And our own post office."

This time, the murmuring was accompanied by nodding heads.

Willis sat, and Acuff banged his gavel.

"If there's no more discussion, I suggest we take a vote on improving the infrastructure. All in favor...."

The vote passed unanimously with only a scattering of dissent from the audience, and after that, Acuff adjourned the meeting.

Guthrie watched the audience file out. A few seemed stunned by the proceedings, but most looked excited. He saw Turner coming over to him.

"I guess that worked out well enough," the chief said.

"It's hard to argue against greater prosperity, even in the abstract," Guthrie said, wondering how that push for prosperity might stand up against the corrupting miasma lurking in Chaney Marsh. Would it just add more fuel to the fire? "But I have to say, Wiley's parting remark gives me cause for concern."

"You're right. We need to watch him and his crew."

38

SOMETHING WOKE GUTHRIE. A SOUND? A movement of air where
it shouldn't be? Instantly aware, he reached for his phone. A little after
three. Thorndike's new witching hour. If this kept up, he was going to
have to start setting his alarm for 2:30. The Kuei men weren't twitching, so whatever it was wasn't supernatural. The sound came again: a
stealthy movement outside the back wall of the mobile home.

As silently as he could, Guthrie swung his feet off the bed,
dragged on his trousers, and slipped into his sneakers, foregoing
socks. His next movement was to pick up the S&W from the bed-
side table. He stepped quietly into the narrow hall separating the
bedroom in the back from the living room and kitchenette at the
front. Flanking him on the left was the tiny bathroom, with the
closet on the other side. The closet was about as much protection as
he could hope for. Its flimsy walls wouldn't be a barrier for bullets,
but at least it was visual cover, and it gave him a clear view of the
the living area and kitchen. Both were only dimly lit by green light
filtering through the trailer's thin curtains from mercury vapor fix-
tures atop several poles scattered around the mobile home park.

The sound came again. No. Two sounds, now. Maybe three.
Maybe more. Moving from the back of the mobile home to the
front. People sneaking around outside his trailer at three in the
morning didn't give him much confidence he'd be able to go back to
bed anytime soon. Unless it was permanently.

A metallic sound came from the front door, and in the green light, he saw the doorknob wiggle a little. It wasn't much of a door-knob, but it was locked. The wiggling stopped, only to be replaced a moment later by a metallic scraping. Somebody was sticking a pry bar or screwdriver into the door frame to pop the lock. It worked, sending out a sharp snap. The movement of the men outside held its breath as they waited to see if the sound had awakened Guthrie.

It hadn't, he thought with a grim smile as he silently slid the closet door aside, backed into the space, and crouched beneath the clothes hanging from the bar. In the darkness, he'd be invisible to anyone peering down the hall toward the bedroom. Now it was just a matter of waiting.

It didn't take long. Apparently the men outside had little taste for patience. They were exceedingly stealthy, though, as two of them came in the door. Not as stealthy as special ops guys. More in the manner of experienced hunters. As they crept past, intent on the bedroom, Guthrie thanked his foresight in backing into the closet because they wore night-vision goggles. And both carried AR-15-style carbines.

Guthrie couldn't afford to wait. In another second, they'd see his bed was empty and would start looking for him. And he could hear more footsteps outside, so making a dash for the door while the intruders' backs were turned wasn't an option. As soon as the lead man entered the bedroom, the second, heavier man stepped just past the closet door.

"The fuck's not here," the lead man snarled, stopping suddenly. The second guy bumping into him with a grunt, and Guthrie lifted the barrel of his pistol and shot him in the left cheek of his ass.

The guy bellowed and lurched heavily against his partner's back, spasmodically squeezing off a three-round burst that went through the ceiling before he dropped his carbine and clutched his gluteus maximus. Both men fell into the room, the first guy bouncing awk-wardly off the corner of the bed. He was lucky the bed didn't have a footboard, but the force threw him over onto his back next to the bed, his carbine lying on the floor past his head. Guthrie put a bullet into the top of his left thigh to discourage him from reaching for it, and he cried out and jackknifed into a sitting position, clutching the wound. Next Guthrie took the sidearm from the guy he'd butt shot.

"I wouldn't shoot in here, Wiley. Your buddies are still alive, and you might hit them before you hit me."

He knew it was Wiley out there, and probably Lonnie, too, because the two cretins lying on his bedroom floor were their buddies: Johnny Miller and Rob Fitzgerald. But Guthrie heard no reply, only quick, fading footsteps followed by the distant double-slam of car doors a few moments later. A big engine cranked, and a vehicle sped off with a roar and spewing of gravel. Guthrie flipped on the light and turned his full attention on his two moaning guests, seeing for the first time that they were dressed in special-ops camo. He almost laughed.

"If you do one thing I don't like," he said, keeping the humor out of his voice, "I'll shoot you again. And I'll be completely justified, even if I kill you. Remember, I'm part of the law in Thorndike. Understand?"

The groans from the two men turned compliant for a moment before returning to the pain at hand.

Guthrie fully disarmed them under the barrel of his S&W, tossing their various weapons—sidearms, backups, knives, and even brass knuckles in addition to the carbines—onto the bed.

"Quite an array," Guthrie said after he'd divested them of their armaments. "You must be true patriot warriors."

"Fuck you," Miller spat. He was the one with the leg wound. Fitzgerald was groaning too much to speak. No wonder, Guthrie thought, with a bullet lodged in his butt cheek. He'd have a hard time sitting on a toilet for quite a while.

Ignoring Miller's jibe, Guthrie picked up his phone and called Chief Turner.

"This better be good," Turner growled, voice clouded with sleep.

"So bad it's good," Guthrie answered. "Wiley and his crew just attacked my trailer."

"What?"

"They broke in, fully armed, intending to kill me."

"Obviously they didn't." Turner's voice now sounded slightly labored, and Guthrie could hear the sounds of him dressing. "What's the situation?"

"Two wounded, two escaped into the night. Unseen, I might add. Also, you might want to radio for an ambulance. I had to shoot both of them."

"Since you're asking for an ambulance instead of a hearse, I assume they're both alive."

"Their wounds are painful but not life-threatening."

"That's just great," Turner said. "I'm on my way."

Guthrie forced his prisoners outside, both moaning, groaning, and complaining. There was a bit of mist outside, but this far north of the marsh, it was thin and close to the ground. In a couple of minutes, Miller was sitting on the dirt while Fitzgerald lay on his uninjured side. Guthrie didn't bother to tie them up. Neither one could walk much less run. By then, most of the trailer park's residents were up and out, goggling at Guthrie and his prisoners, Warren Evers among them. Guthrie went over to reassure him that the gunfire was finished. As Guthrie returned to the prisoners, Evers did the same with his tenants, who all edged closer for a better look.

Back at the prisoners, Guthrie surveyed them for a moment, then shook his head.

"I know Wiley and Lonnie put you up to this," he said. "Why do you do their dirty work?"

"What's it to you?" Miller grated through his pain.

"I'm the guy you came to kill on their orders, and I didn't kill you in return."

"Yeah, but you shot me in the leg and Rob in the ass."

"You'll live. I wouldn't have. So again, why do their dirty work?"

"We wasn't doin' nothin' for them. We was doin' it for us. But we're tight with 'em 'cause they're good guys to have as friends and bad guys to have as enemies."

"Looks like your friends have left you in the hands of their enemies."

At that moment, Turner pulled in behind the spectators and hooted his siren, parting them as he pulled forward and parked. Guthrie glanced at the time on his phone and smiled. The chief must have torn up Thorndike's empty nighttime streets to get dressed, get to his Interceptor, and drive to the mobile home park in less than seven minutes.

"What the hell is this? Johnny? Rob?" Turner asked after he emerged from the SUV and came over to Guthrie and the prisoners. He looked back and forth between the two.

"We ain't sayin' nothin' 'cept we come to rob him," Miller said. "Just us. Nobody else."

"You two don't have enough brains to act on your own," Turner said. "I know Wiley put you up to this."

"Wiley ain't got nuthin' to do with it," Fitzgerald insisted. "That man," he pointed at Guthrie, "brung trouble to our town, and we was just tryin' to make things right."

"Attempted murder of a law enforcement officer isn't any way to make things right, Rob. Now you're going to prison for a very long time."

Fitzgerald and Miller turned sullenly silent except for their groans. Maybe, Guthrie thought, Rand ought to be here to hear it.

At that moment, Emmet Taylor pulled up behind Turner's car, got out, and came over.

"You okay, Clay?" he asked.

"Better than them," Guthrie responded, gesturing to the prisoners.

Emmet went over to the prisoners, and he and Turner spent a couple of minutes cuffing and searching them again.

"I've called an ambulance," Turner told Taylor. "Watch these two miscreants until it gets here. DPS should be coming with it, and they'll secure the prisoners in the hospital. Give them a preliminary report, then go back to bed."

"Bed?" Emmet snorted. "Hell, Chief, these days I'm practically sleeping in my car."

Turner gave a sour chuckle then looked at Guthrie and jerked his head, motioning for them to move away from the prisoners.

"You said Wiley was out here," Turner said when they were out of earshot. "Maybe Lonnie."

"I have to admit that's a guess," Guthrie said. "I heard what sounded like two more people moving outside, but after I neutralized Miller and Fitzgerald, they fled. I heard two car doors slam and a vehicle drive off. It sounded like a big pickup, but I didn't actually see that, either."

"Too bad. We can assume it was Wiley and Lonnie, but unless we can get Johnny or Rob to open up, we're stuck with assumptions. But we can go roust Wiley and Lonnie and confront them. We'll see if they've been asleep or if they're wide awake. They won't fess up, but they'll know I'm about to make their worthless lives a lot harder."

"Mind if I go inside and get my socks and comb my hair, first?"

Turner drove them to the place Wiley and Lonnie called home. Guthrie had seen it before, though he hadn't known who lived there. It lay on a dirt street three-quarters of a mile from downtown, in Thorndike's most southerly and poorest area. Farther south, even, than the mobile home where Segundo and Marielle Yanez lived, but not as far out as Jeff Mayfield's trailer. Guthrie couldn't really call it a neighborhood. The lots were an acre or more in size, and most were empty of anything but weeds, saplings, and trees. Only about a quarter of them held a ramshackle house or trailer accompanied by the sheds, junk, and debris usual in this part of town.

In the darkness, the Sanford house was barely visible behind its wall of trees and brush. The only clear place was the rutted dirt driveway that curved around the trees before ending in front of the structure. To Guthrie's eyes, the property rivaled Freddie's ramshackle home, but the yard around it was even more cluttered and littered. At least Freddie's place was graced by the pole barn and the well-maintained backhoe parked inside. The Sanford house looked barely better than some of the homes Guthrie had seen in Airla. The only neat and new thing about the place was Wiley's white, lifted dually Chevy pickup, mud and dust spewed up along its sides. The house's windows were dark, and the porch light was off.

"I don't expect too much trouble," Turner said. "But these two are pretty volatile. Stay vigilant. You still armed?"

"I am," Guthrie affirmed.

They got out of the Interceptor and waded though the knee-high mist to the front door. As they passed by the truck, Turner laid a palm on the hood.

"Warm," he said.

Meanwhile, Guthrie inspected the heavy, tubular steel bumpers in the light from his phone. Both were painted dull black, and the back right corner was slightly dented and scraped, as if the truck had been used to push something heavy or resistant. Guthrie pointed it out to Turner.

"You think this is from forcing open the door at Buster's hardware store?" Turner asked, running fingers over the dent.

"It's a distinct possibility."

Turner straightened and went up to the front door, Guthrie on his heels. The windows lit after Turner's third knock, then the bare bulb over the porch flared on, and the door opened to reveal Lonnie. He was wearing a stained green t-shirt, blue striped boxers, and a pair of well-worn pull-on work boots. Neither his hair nor his Fu Manchu were mussed.

"What the fuck?" he asked, rubbing eyes that didn't look at all sleepy.

"You always wear boots to bed, Lonnie?" Turner asked.

Lonnie glanced down at his feet then up at Turner.

"What do you want?" he asked.

"I need you to get Wiley and come back out here."

"Wiley?" Lonnie gave a look he probably thought made him look puzzled. Instead, it only made him appear complicit. "He's asleep."

"He's not asleep," Turner said. "Get him. Now."

"I'll get him," Lonnie said. He tried to close the door, but Turner pushed it wide with his foot.

"You better come back with empty hands," he said, laying a hand on the butt of his .40.

Anger flared in Lonnie's eyes, but he said nothing as he turned and disappeared into the house. A few moments later, he returned, Wiley coming up behind him.

"What's this about?" Wiley began, but Turner cut him off.

"Shut the fuck up, Wiley, and listen to this. You and your buddies chose to attack a law enforcement officer in my town...."

"We didn't do nothin'," Lonnie said.

"I told you to shut the fuck up, Lonnie," Turner said. "If you didn't do nothing, you must have done something."

"Huh?"

"Shut up, Lonnie," Wiley snapped. "You got somethin' to say, Chief, say it."

"You got your two stooges to try some heavy lifting they weren't capable of. Now, I have a shit storm on my hands on top of a bunch of other shit storms. Johnny and Rob are on their way up to County General as we speak, and after that, they're going to prison for a long fucking time for assault with intent to murder of a law enforcement officer. That's a long stretch."

"So, Johnny and Rob done somethin' they shouldn't. That's not on us. We was sleepin' here in our beds and dreamin' nice dreams."

"You never have nice dreams, Wiley," Turner said. "I know you put them up to it because those two have shit for brains and don't do anything without your say-so. I also know you were driving your truck sometime within the past half-hour. The engine's still warm."

"That's your evidence?"

"That's an affirmation of your guilt. As soon as Johnny and Rob come out of surgery, I'm going to make sure they realize they can out you two assholes in a second for reduced sentences. Dream on that nice dream when you go back to bed. And from now on, you better toe the line, or I'm going to lean on you. Heavy."

"That sounds like a threat," Wiley said, hackles raising.

"You hear a threat, Officer?" Turner asked Guthrie.

"What threat?" Guthrie said.

"So that's how it's gonna to be," Wiley said.

"You dealt the hand," Turner replied. "Now you're going to play your crappy cards. Stay out of my way. Understand?"

"Is that all?" Wiley asked.

"No," Turner said. "I want to know about your relationship with George Rand."

"Who's that?" Lonnie asked.

"If you speak one more time, Lonnie, I'm going to arrest you."

Lonnie looked like he might be about to respond, but Wiley backhanded him on the arm, and his mouth snapped shut.

"You ain't got no reason to…," Wiley began.

"I asked you about George Rand," Turner interrupted harshly.

"What's it to you?" Wiley asked, face screwing with anger. "We barely know the guy."

"Barely know, as in how? How do you barely know him?"

"He come in the Q a few times and bought us a few rounds of drinks and chatted us up. Asked if we wanted to do some work for him at his place. Said Jim Chaney let it go all to hell. So we been over there, helpin' him fix it up. Remodelin'. Gotta do somethin' after you got that bastard Stansic to fire us. Is that a crime?"

"Remodeling?" Turner stepped back a few paces and let his eyes wander over the front of the Sanfords' house, its ramshackle nature dimly revealed by the bare bulb over the porch. Then he looked back at Wiley. If sarcasm produced tears, Turner would have been weeping. "Right. You know, Wiley, any kind of remodeling work you'd do probably *would* be a crime. Now you two listen, and listen good. I'm going to be looking for either of you to take one more wrong step. Take it, and you're done."

Neither of the Sanfords replied to that, but Guthrie was certain they got the picture. Turner spun and strode back to the Interceptor, Guthrie following. In a few seconds, they were out on the dirt street.

"Can't take you back to the trailer," Turner said. "It's now a crime scene."

"If you'll let me go in and get my stuff, I'll drive up to the county seat and get a motel room."

"The hell with that. Ethan's off at college, and his room is empty at the moment. We'll get your stuff, and you can bunk there until we can let you move back into the trailer."

"I don't want to impose."

"No imposition. I insist."

Turner drove them to the mobile home park. State troopers and sheriff's deputies had arrived with the ambulance, and they stood around with Emmet Taylor as the paramedics gave Miller and Fitzgerald preliminary treatment. Dr. Bob and his team were ten minutes behind the ambulance. Dr. Bob didn't look at all happy, even when Turner assured him there were no corpses to deal with, only bullet holes and fingerprints.

"I swear, Bill," he said before he directed his team to get to work. "Would you please get your townsfolk in line enough to commit their crimes during regular working hours?" Latimer followed his team into the trailer.

Most of the residents were still outside, watching, and so was Warren Evers.

"I'm sorry about all this, Warren," Turner told him.

"It sure was a scene, Chief," Evers replied. "But when I saw him," he waved at Guthrie, "haul Rob and Johnny out, I knew it had something to do with Wiley and his brother. You go talk to them?"

"I can't comment on an ongoing investigation," Turner said. "But I want to assure you there won't be a repeat. Mr. Guthrie's trailer is a crime scene, and he'll be moving in with me and Bev for the time being. I'm going to put up some crime scene tape, and I'll let you know when you can take it down."

Evers nodded and went back to his residents to further reassure them. While Turner strung crime scene tape around the trailer, Guthrie went in to retrieve his gear. Inside, he found the crime scene techs photographing and collecting all the weapons Guthrie had taken from his assailants.

"Damn," Dr. Bob said when Guthrie came into the bedroom. "They sure were loaded for bear. I'm surprised they could afford all this."

"Maybe they didn't buy it."

"You think this is part of the haul from Buster Havasau's store?"

"Very possibly some of it. The chief said I could get my gear. I'll be staying there until we can open this up again."

He left Latimer and his people to their tasks, got his gear together, then went outside and put it in the Xterra. After that, he followed Turner to his house. Dawn was just breaking, and Bev was already up, preparing to help Martha open the cafe. Turner explained the situation to her, and her concerned expression gave way to a bright smile.

"I'm so glad you're all right," she told Guthrie. "Wiley and his boys have been begging for comeuppance, and I'm glad you gave it to them."

"Just the boys," Guthrie reminded her. "Wiley and Lonnie are still at large."

"Well, you just make yourself at home. Let me show you Ethan's room."

Guthrie followed her to a bedroom typically outfitted for a teenage boy interested in sports and pop stars. Guthrie didn't recognize any of the musicians and singers on the posters, which made him feel even more tired than he already was.

"I'll leave you to get settled," she told him "I have to get to Leo's. Since he's out, there's a lot of extra work before the Sunday breakfast crowd. The second bathroom is down the hall." She smiled. "You'll have to share it with Emily, and I'm afraid she's feminized it since Ethan went off to A&M."

She left the room, and after Guthrie dumped his stuff on the bed, he took his toiletries to the bathroom, which, as advertised, was decorated in teenage-girl style. The shower curtain was pink, and makeup and other beauty products littered the counter around the sink. He found space on top of the toilet tank for his kitbag then returned to the kitchen, where Turner handed him a key.

"This is good for both the front and back door locks. Come and go as you please."

"Thanks," Guthrie said.

"No thanks necessary. I've been trying to do something about Wiley and his boys for a long time, and you've presented me with the best opportunity I've ever had."

"Even if I was in danger?"

Turner snorted a laugh.

"Wiley and his boys might give you some trouble, Clay, but I doubt if the likes of them can be a danger to someone like you."

"I appreciate the confidence, Chief, but I'm only flesh and blood. The smallest microbe could take me down."

"But we're not facing microbes here, are we?"

"No, Chief, we're not." But the danger, he thought, was an infection, nonetheless.

"It is mighty peculiar, don't you think, that they attacked you right after the town hall? Almost like they suddenly realize you're more of a threat to them."

"Not them."

"You're thinking Rand?"

"I am. I had a heart-to-heart talk with him last thing Friday, and he didn't like what I had to say."

"And what was that?"

"That I suspect him of bringing whatever it is that's lurking in Chaney Marsh here. And more."

"You seem pretty sure something's down there."

"I'm positive."

"Well, I'm not convinced about that, but I can't help but think that everything was all right in Thorndike before Rand came to town. After destroying Airla. You think he incited the attack on you?"

"I'm certain of it. I made it obvious I'm not leaving until we get this thing sorted out, and I'm a wild card he wasn't expecting. I know too much about him, but he doesn't know anything about me. That makes me a clear and present danger to him and his plans. But there's no way to prove a connection between him and the attack without corroborating evidence or incriminating testimony."

"Which we're not likely to get from the Sanfords or their cronies." Turner paused thoughtfully, then said, "So Rand is the cause of our problems?"

"He's a lot more dangerous than we've given him credit for. He might not be the nexus, but he's closest to it."

39

IT WAS SEVEN BY THE time Guthrie finished filling out the police report on the foiled attack and handed it to Turner. The chief barely ran weary eyes over it before tossing it onto his desk.

"I wish we could have nailed the Sanfords," he said. "That would have cleaned up at least part of what's infecting this town."

"Removing them would simply be treating symptoms," Guthrie said. "We need to excise the infection itself."

"Is there such a thing? It's crazy to think that some unknown force could move into Thorndike and proceed to destroy it from within."

"You know what happened to Airla after Rand moved there."

"And you think the same thing is happening here?"

"I've learned a little additional information. Before Airla, two villages in southern Louisiana were similarly destroyed."

"What's that have to do with Airla or what's going on here?"

"Rand. His uncle, Claude Fortier, was head of one of the villages, and his village was in a bitter blood feud with the other."

"Just stop right there," Turner said, shaking his head. "This is all too much for me to think about right now. I haven't had a decent night's sleep all week, and I've been living on caffeine, adrenaline, and anger."

"It's Sunday," Guthrie pointed out. "Church is about to start. Go over to the school and try to relax. The worst is probably yet to come."

"Can't," Turner replied. "I checked the weapons you took off Miller and Fitzgerald, and the serial numbers are on Buster

Havasau's list. That was enough for me to get a warrant from the county judge to search their house. A sheriff's deputy drove it down while you were filling out that." He gestured to the report.

Miller and Fitzgerald were cousins, Turner told Guthrie as they drove toward the southeast quadrant of town. They both lived in the same house, about four blocks from the Sanfords. It had been left to Miller on the death of his parents, and Fitzgerald had moved in shortly after. It once had been a fairly well-built brick ranch style home, but its roof was splotched with tar repairs and several substantial cracks in the brick siding showed that its slab needed leveling. The lot might have been grassy once but now was weed choked and strewn with the usual sorts of debris typical in this part of town. Miller's pickup was parked on the cracked cement driveway in front of the pulled-down two-car garage door.

"Looks like they had a ride out to your trailer," Turner said as they approached the front entry. Turner pulled a set of keys from his pocket. "Took these off Miller when I searched him."

The ring held only the keys for the truck and the door, and in a moment, the door was open, and they stepped inside. Guthrie expected to see a mess, and he wasn't disappointed. Two shabby easy chairs were set up in front of a new-looking TV, their side tables littered with candy wrappers and beer cans. One had an overflowing ashtray, the other a plate of food scraps. They went through the house, which had a layout similar to Freddie Jensen's house and was shabby but unremarkable. Except for the garage. In the middle of the floor sat for four large fold-out gray plastic tables butted together in a rectangle, four folding metal chairs painted gray haphazardly scooted under them.

On top of the tables lay a variety of firearms—about three dozen, from several AR-style carbines to hunting rifles, shotguns, and sidearms. One side wall had several workbenches with metal working and gunsmithing tools. Two partially disassembled ARs and their receivers lay on the bench tops.

"Looks like they're reworking the receivers to make these ARs fully auto," Turner said after he bent for a closer look.

Cases stacked along the wall at the back bore labels for ammunition, and boxes against the other side wall held a variety of power tools. Piled next to them were four stout tool chests filled with well-used mechanic's tools, and next to those was a green tackle box and white plastic bucket.

"Well, well," Turner said, surveying the room, his voice holding the most satisfaction Guthrie had yet heard in it. "This must be the contraband stolen from Buster Havasau. And Eli Carlin's tools."

"That fishing gear belonged to Jeff Mayfield," Guthrie said.

"Johnny and Rob are never getting out of prison," Turner replied, nodding. Then he wrinkled his lips. "I guess we'd better get a little help."

Turner radioed Tessa to tell Emmet to bring the list of Havasau's stolen merchandise to the house. Taylor was there in less than fifteen minutes, and together, the three of them went through the stockpile of arms, ammo, and tools, taking numerous photos and notes. Almost everything on the list Havasau provided, including boxes for the night-vision goggles, was there, but conspicuously missing were several pistols and AR-style carbines and a couple of crates of ammo. Among all the new weapons was one that didn't fit: an old S&W .38 Special.

"That looks like the gun Jeff had in his waistband," Guthrie said.

"Since it's not on Buster's list, it probably is. We'll have the ME's office check it for Jeff's fingerprints."

Finally, they were done and had everything loaded in the trunks and seats of the Interceptors,. It barely fit, and both vehicles sagged on their tires from all the weight. They drove to the police station, where they started carting it inside.

"Buster's missing stock?" Tessa asked as they brought in the first load.

"Yeah," Turner said.

"Thank God," she breathed. "I'm not the only one nervous about all those missing guns."

"Call Buster and let him know we have most of his stock, but he can't reclaim it until all this is over."

Tessa didn't question what "all this" meant. She picked up the phone and called the hardware store owner at home.

The station's evidence closet was too small to hold all the booty, so they piled everything in one of the two cells and locked it. Turner glanced at his watch.

"Sunday services aren't over yet," he said. "I probably should go over to the school to help reassure everyone." He snorted. "Like the blind leading the blind. You, too, Emmet. What about you, Clay?"

"I'll keep an eye on things while you two are at church."

"Thanks," Turner said, Taylor echoing him. They left.

Guthrie told Turner he was going to keep an eye on things, but he didn't say where. Chaney Marsh. He drove to the gate across the entrance to the dirt road to Jim Chaney's gate. As he passed Rand's house, he noticed the Audi was in the drive, but he ignored it. He parked in front of Chaney's gate, got out, and stared down the track into the marsh. As usual, the forest was filled with mists that clogged the undergrowth and clung to the branches of the trees with unnatural stillness despite the gentle breeze ruffling the adjacent pasture. The mist was more dense than ever, and he could barely see a hundred feet into the forest. And it was dark under the trees. Darker than the only slightly overcast day warranted. The woods seemed to billow with unseen warning, like a hostile, malignant emanation that's enveloping touch promised disorientation, fear, and panic.

The Kuei men buzzing beneath his belt buckle, Guthrie climbed the gate and headed down the road, into the misty, tree-lined tunnel, bucking the force pressuring him to turn and flee or succumb. The air was dead still, with no sound or sight of any animal or movement except his own. But it was redolent with the odor of death, as if every small animal who'd called the marsh home was now decaying beneath the blanketing mists, and every bit of low foliage was rotting into the same kind of muck that filled the ditches. He didn't see the tree until he'd passed a couple of bends in the track. It wasn't a large tree—trunk only six or so inches at its base. Though it was fully leafed, it lay neatly across the road, effectively blocking vehicular traffic.

Perhaps it was simply a natural tree fall, but the barely wilting leaves said the tree hadn't been sick. A glance told Guthrie that the trunk hadn't rotted through but had been cut with a chainsaw. Most likely, it was a warning as well as a blockade. Guthrie ignored both possibilities, climbed through the branches, and forced himself onward through the fog.

This early, mists or no, the marsh should have been alive with the sounds of insects and birds and maybe even creeping critters or the plop of a turtle going into the water. It had been the first time he'd come down here with Chief Turner. But now there was nothing. No sound, no movement except for Guthrie's feet shuffling down the track, their scuffling muted by the thickening mist. The temperature dropped steadily as he advanced, turning chill. But that wasn't all Guthrie felt. The air seemed heavy and dense, like it had the last time he'd come down here with Turner, but now the sensation was amplified, and he almost felt like he was having to push against a wind, though not a leaf stirred on the surrounding trees. Nothing stirred, and even the swirls caused by his legs swishing through the mist faded the instant he passed.

The farther he walked, the more the pressure became a seeping, creeping, clinging, cloying sensation that threatened to deaden his limbs, enervate his body, and sap his will. Usually the Kuei men were a sort of Geiger counter for the uncanny. On rare occasions, they'd helped protect him when such forces turned malign. It might feel like they were twitching or even giving small kicks when the going got tough, but right now, they were doing something they'd never done before—they were vibrating, the sensation like a hive of angry bees buzzing in his belly. Far from being annoying, the vibration sent a warming sensation though his body and limbs, strengthening his sense of purpose as well as solidifying his sense of being.

He needed every ounce of that protection because his inner resolve, even bolstered by the Kuei men, didn't entirely halt the psychic pressure, and the closer he got to the cabin, the greater its force became, pushing at him with gusts that almost drove him back to the Xterra. Something really didn't want him here, and it would be all too easy to cave in, return to his vehicle, and drive home to Houston.

He shook himself to rid himself of the idea. That would only delay an inevitable that surely would only grow worse. Besides, no way he could afford to think in distractions that would weaken and defeat him. Best to concentrate on the task now before him, which was walking down to Jim Chaney's cabin to check on the old man. He hadn't thought that any case could be more dangerous than his last assignment for Tereba or any end worse than having a glowering monster gleefully eat you alive from the feet up, but maybe there was. This wasn't some tangible creature, but a taint in the air that insinuated itself around and into the unprotected. Hell, he thought, beneath the tree cover and this close to the broad pool of water at the heart of the marsh, the taint *was* the air.

Finally, almost stumbling, he reached the spot where Chaney parked his truck and started down the path toward the cabin. Abruptly, as the pungent odor of garlic filled his nostrils, the malignant psychic pressure slacked off. The aura of the garlic seemed to be keeping the foul force at bay around the cabin, as if the cabin sat in a bubble of protection. But how long before that bubble burst or was squeezed out of existence?

Beyond the cabin, the pond's once bright, sparkling water had become a foul dark slough reeking of decay. The streaks of diseased green he'd seen before were broader, now taking up half the expanse, and rotting fish and bird and animal carcasses floated on the scummy, slime-slicked surface. The stink of death was strong enough to cut through the smell of the garlic festooning the cabin, and the light breeze out on the pastures did nothing to reach into the center of the marsh to sweep away the stench. The once-bucolic marsh had become a dismal, fetid, and diseased swamp.

"Jim Chaney!" Guthrie yelled. "It's Clay Guthrie. I'm coming down to the cabin. Don't shoot."

Chaney cracked the front door of the cabin instead of coming around the back corner from the deck. He was holding his shotgun.

"It's you. Comin' down here to make sure I ain't gone down to your crime scene?"

"I came to make sure you're all right. Mind if I come in?"

"You bring anything with you?" Chaney's furtive eyes bored into Guthrie then darted around the forlorn landscape behind him.

Strange choice of words, Guthrie thought.

"I'm alone," he assured Chaney.

"Alright, then. I guess you can come in."

Chaney stepped back into the cabin, admitted Guthrie, then shut and bolted the door. With three deadbolts, two of which looked brand new. It seemed as if he'd taken Chief Turner's advice and bathed, shaved, and changed his clothes, but other than that, he looked terrible. Sagging shoulders beneath a washed-out face said he'd endured maybe more than a man can handle. But it seemed his stubbornness had given him strength. Or maybe his guilt was more powerful than the malign force squatting in the marsh, at least so far. Breathing as much as he could through his mouth, Guthrie thought that the almost overpowering odor of garlic hadn't hurt Chaney's situation.

Chaney propped his shotgun beside the back door, and Guthrie saw that it, too, had triple deadbolts, two gleaming of new brass. Then Chaney gestured to a chair for Guthrie and took a seat of his own. As Guthrie sat, he glanced around the cabin. It was very basic: one large room that contained the living, kitchen, and dining areas. Two open doors in the righthand wall revealed a bathroom and a bedroom with a tousled bed. Windows were set into almost every exterior wall, but all had wooden shutters closed over them.

"I'm surprised to find you inside," Guthrie said.

"Ain't nothin' nice goin' on out there I can see," Chaney replied, staring at Guthrie with a mixture of belligerence and resignation.

"Want to talk about it?"

"Talk about what?"

"You know what I mean. You can't feel it inside here. I guess your garlic is working pretty well, but outside…." He let the statement dangle, and Chaney took the bait.

"I can't fight it no more," he said, the resignation taking over. "It's all around. That's why I'm inside. It's safer in here. At first, I thought it was Enid come back to me. I even thought I seen her walkin' through the woods a few times. starin' at the pond, watchin' the water. But it wasn't her. It was just something that ate up my memories of her and spit 'em back at me."

"What is it?" Guthrie asked.

"I ain't actually seen nothin', 'cept what I thought was Enid wanderin' around. But you're right. I can feel it." Chaney paused a moment, shook the absent look from his eyes, then altered tack. "Did you see the water? It changed. All the fish died. Bunch a animals, too. Birds, squirrels, possums, and coons all floating out there."

"I saw."

"Hell, maybe it's me that's changed. I ain't been right in my head since Enid died." Chaney looked at Guthrie, loss opening beneath his stubborn belligerence. And fear. "I know somethin's out there, though I don't see or hear nothin'. Nothin' but that damn fog. Don't know where it comes from, but I ain't never seen it so thick. And it stinks and has a greasy feel." He leaned forward and clutched at Guthrie's arm. "You believe me, don't you? It's strong and all around."

"I feel it," Guthrie said, tugging on Chaney's arm. "Let me get you out of here."

It wasn't so much that Chaney resisted as that he just didn't budge.

"I can't," he said. "It ain't go holt of me yet, but it won't let me leave. I tried already. Tried to drive out. 'Spect you saw the tree across the road."

"I did," Guthrie said, and Chaney shook his head and stared sadly at Guthrie.

"Tried walkin' out, too, but it wouldn't let me. I ain't strong enough, and it just drove me back here." He shook his head and gave Guthrie a sad look. "I'm mighty sorry, young fella, that I got you into this mess."

"Wasn't you, Jim. I was chasing this mess and just found it here." He pulled on Chaney's arm again. "Come on, I can get you out."

"I can't. Don't you see? It's my memories of Enid. They got me tied here. Trapped. They're my fate." He pushed Guthrie away. "I gotta fight it with everythin' I got. My garlic keeps it back, and I got my shotgun for them others. I got plans for this marsh, and no goddamn person or thing is gonna move in on 'em."

"What others?"

"That bastard George Rand."

"Has he been here again?"

"Every goddamn day. I told him the first time I wasn't gonna sell. If I was, I'da sold it to Grant Industries. But he keeps coming back and offerin' more money. Yesterday, he brung them Sanford brothers, and the bastard actually threatened me."

"With harm?"

"It wasn't so obvious. But he said bad things can happen to old folks who live isolated and have little contact with their neighbors. He didn't say it like he was concerned about my welfare, and he had the Sanfords to back him up, so I took it as a threat."

"Did they have any trouble getting down here?"

Chaney was a bit taken aback.

"No," he said after a thoughtful pause. "It don't seem like they did. Hell, them city shoes Rand was wearing wasn't even dusty. Fact is," he gave Guthrie the once-over, "can't rightly say how you managed it."

"I have some protection," Guthrie said without amplification.

"That may be, but it better be powerful stuff. I can't even go out on the back deck any more. Almost don't matter, though. Even if I could, I don't want to see all them dead animals rotting in the water. But I gotta stay and fight it. This marsh is all I got left. Five generations, and this is all that's left of me and my life. My family. My history. I ain't givin' it up lightly. But you go, now, young fella. Get the hell away from this cursed place."

"I'll go," Guthrie said. "But I'll be back with help."

"You can try," Chaney said, "but it probably won't do no good."

As Guthrie trudged up the path toward Chaney's truck, he almost agreed. As soon as he emerged from the cloud of garlic odor, the psychic pressure ramped up. Only instead of inhibiting his forward momentum, now it pushed him away, squeezing him out of the thick tension overlying the marsh.

Determined not to let the force control him, Guthrie kept his pace deliberate, which proved difficult because he had the distinct sensation of being stalked. He paused and listened intently, but the mist-laden air was still, as still as a predator preparing to pounce. So still he should have been able to hear the movement of anything that might have been out there among the mist-hazy trees and underbrush. But there was nothing. No sound at all, and the not hearing was worse than the not seeing, making it seem as if he was hemmed in all around by some great but silently milling crowd sulking toward mindless mob violence. In the end, the force was so powerful, so fearsome, that he thought he'd have to stop. But he couldn't stop. Not here. He had to go forward or back, and he couldn't return to the cabin. He had to go forward, so he forced himself along, half afraid to take his eyes from the track and half afraid not to scan the surrounding forest.

A sudden rustling from just off the track to his right froze him in place just an instant before a snake slithered out not five feet in front of him. A big one. Close to six feet. He saw by the shape of its head and its muddy color that it was a water moccasin, normally the least volatile of pit vipers. But this one lunged off the ground at him, and he leapt back to avoid being struck. In seconds, the snake had driven him back a dozen feet and was still coming. Guthrie drew his pistol and shot off its head.

Holstering the pistol, he set off again, but horribly, more snakes emerged from the surrounding underbrush on both sides of the track. Way too many to shoot. Dozens of moccasins, and they weren't the only ones. An almost equal number of brown-patterned backs writhed among them, and ominous rattles vibrated the air. He even saw a couple of coral snakes. It seemed like every damn poisonous snake in the marsh had slithered out onto the road in front of him. How could there be so many? They obstructed it so much that Guthrie couldn't find enough spaces between them for his feet. But there was no way he was stepping off the track into the rotted ditches or the sullen, glowering marsh. At least out here, he could see the damn things.

He had to get past them, get to his vehicle. Almost mindlessly surging forward and picking up speed and his feet, he raced across the serpents. Step after step smashing down on muscular tubes writhing, coiling, and snapping with dripping fangs. Several caught his pants legs, but he was moving too fast for any to make contact with his flesh.

The mat of snakes was still thick, and he gave a quick glance over his shoulder. To his horror, all the snakes he'd passed were slithering after him. He cast ahead and saw he was nearing the fallen tree. His Xterra was just a couple of bends farther on. Could he make it?

He had to.

Darting, dodging, and hopping to avoid the snakes as they went for his legs, he broke free of the main part of the—herd? What the hell do you call a mess of snakes all bunched up and working together? he wondered inanely. Dropping the thought, he ran flat out, the narrow track directly behind him so completely covered by a writhing mat of serpents that, in the dim light and fog, it almost could be mistaken for a rippling stream.

Gradually, he began to pull ahead, and at last he reached the fallen tree and clambered desperately through it, losing a little ground. But he raced on and, moments later, flung himself at the gate and climbed it. Only when he stared at the road from his perch did he see that the mass of snakes had stopped at the hazy shadow line. Not a single one came out into the watery sunshine beyond the canopy. Nor had the mists enveloping the diseased marsh.

Breathing heavily—and not just from exertion—Guthrie jumped to the ground and quickly got into his vehicle. He sat there for several minutes, calming himself and staring through the bars of the gate at the snakes beyond. Writhing and coiling, they still carpeted the road like a nightmare come alive.

Looking down that dark track, Guthrie knew it was going to be a difficult task getting back to the cabin. And once he got there, he had to somehow eliminate the miasma. If he didn't, there was no way he was making it out of the marsh alive.

He started the Xterra and drove back to town. Time to convince Turner, once and for all, of the magnitude of the problem in Chaney Marsh.

40

CHIEF TURNER HAD JUST COME come from church services at the school, but he wasn't in the best of moods when Guthrie found him in the police station. Guthrie couldn't get in to see him right away, though. Leland Fuller was visible through the chief's big office window, and the door was closed.

"What's going on?" Guthrie asked Tessa.

"I don't know. Leland was waiting here when the chief came in, but he wouldn't say. All I know is he brought a box with him."

Turner and Fuller conferred for about fifteen minutes longer before they rose and Turner ushered Fuller out of the office. Fuller strode across the outer office to the front door. He didn't look at all happy, and merely nodded his white Stetson curtly at Tessa and Guthrie as he passed. As the front door shut behind him, Turner waved Guthrie into his office.

"Leland have a problem?" Guthrie asked as they sat.

"Looks like he might." Turner gestured toward a small cardboard carton containing four mason jars of water. The water in two was clear, but the water in the others was murky. "He wants me to have these analyzed. He claims Jim Chaney is poisoning Steele Creek before it leaves the marsh."

"Why would he do that?"

Turner shrugged.

"Could just be spite. Jim and Leland have been at each other's throats for as long as anyone can remember. Probably even them."

"I take it that the ones with the murky water are from the downstream side of the marsh and the clear ones are from upstream."

"Leland said he collected them over the last couple of days."

"Jim wouldn't poison the marsh," Guthrie said.

"You know him that well after just a few visits?"

"Well enough to know he'd never do anything to damage the marsh. It's too precious to him. It's all he has. Besides, he complained that something was poisoning his fish. He wanted to take water samples himself, but the ME was at the Mayfield assault site."

"I remember, but maybe he was just trying to cover up his own guilt."

"Nearly a week before he was accused? Jim might have plenty of things to feel guilty about, but poisoning the marsh isn't one of them."

"You sure?"

"As sure as I can be. I was just down there, talking to him, and he also believes the pond is poisoned. And he's got a lot stronger proof than those." He waved toward the jars of water. "Lab analysis might not show anything obviously wrong, just like with the sofa, but something definitely is. The pond has become lifeless. The water's scummed over—nothing but fish, bird, and animal carcasses floating in it."

Turner stared at Guthrie for a moment.

"Like the blight in the ditches."

"That is now in the woods. And perhaps in the pond."

Turner didn't look happy.

"Leland also says that nearly twenty of his herd died on his north pasture in the last week," he said at last. "That's just off the south edge of the marsh. He brought Dr. Hughes out to see them, but the doctor is just as puzzled by that as by all the dogs going crazy."

Guthrie didn't say anything but just stared back, and Turner slumped in his chair and wiped his face with a weary gesture.

"I don't know what to think anymore. The whole town is going to hell, and there doesn't seem to be a damn thing I can do about it."

"No, Bill, there is," Guthrie said earnestly, leaning forward in his chair. "But first you need to better understand our enemy."

"How do I do that?"

"We go out to your Interceptor, drive to Jim's gate, and then walk down to his cabin. Something's going on down there, even if you can't accept it. You need to feel it for yourself."

"Do you think Jim's in danger?"

"If we don't help, something bad is likely to happen to him. Soon. And maybe worse for the town."

"But what can we do? About what? Some ditch rot and a creepy feeling in the woods?"

"You know it's more than that, Chief. But I'm not going to convince you with words. Come on, let's go."

Turner rose reluctantly and went to the hat rack.

"This better be good," he said as he put on his Stetson and they emerged into the outer office.

"It's not, Chief. It's bad. Very bad. We'd better bring along shotguns."

"What for? Jim's not going to take potshots at us."

"No, he's trapped down in the cabin," Guthrie said, thinking they probably wouldn't be able to make it that far. "The shotguns are for something else."

"What do you mean 'trapped'? And what something else?"

"You'll see what I mean."

Turner shot Guthrie a jaundiced look then pulled two pump shotguns and two boxes of shells from the gun safe in the outer office and handed one set to Guthrie before leading the way out to his Interceptor. Tessa, open-mouthed, stared after them.

"I don't know why we have to go to Jim's cabin," Turner said as they buckled up. "Weren't you just down there?"

"Yes. And now it's your turn."

Turner started to say something else, but his lips tightened, and he just pulled out of the parking lot and onto Main. On the way, Guthrie loaded both shotguns. In fifteen minutes, they were on the county road, passing Rand's house. The Audi was parked in front. Seconds later, Turner steered onto the dirt track leading to Chaney's cabin. Even before they arrived, even without the twitching of the Kuei men, Guthrie could sense that the dark force was now extending its influence into the pasture beyond the fence. He also noticed Turner growing visibly nervous and anxious as he pulled up to the gate.

"What now?"

"We get out and walk down to the cabin."

"What's down there?" Turner seemed reluctant to leave the SUV.

"This isn't about what's down there. It's about the journey there."

"What the hell does that mean?"

"It means we get out and walk down to the cabin."

"I called Gilbert Espinoza," Turner said. Maybe he was stalling, trying to delay getting out of the apparent safety and security of his vehicle. "He wouldn't tell me exactly what you did for him, but he told me to trust you, no matter what you said." He snorted. "A complete stranger telling me to believe anything you, another complete stranger, says." His face grew grave. "He tells me, Miss Agnes tells me, even Bev. Why can't I accept what you've said?"

"You have to trust yourself," Guthrie said. "Trust your sensations, not your preconceptions."

"How do I do that?"

"Walk down this road with me."

To emphasize the point, Guthrie unlatched his seatbelt, opened the door, and grabbed his shotgun as he got out. He didn't shut the door behind him. He didn't want to have to fumble for the door handle with a bunch of poisonous snakes swarming around his feet. Turner got out heavily and uncertainly, eyes darting sharp, nervous glances at the dark, foggy forest beyond the fence. It wasn't a good look on the stalwart cop Guthrie had met when he first came to Thorndike. Guthrie only hoped that Turner, unprotected by Kuei men, wouldn't break down somewhere along that dark track.

"Leave your door open," Guthrie advised.

"Why?"

"You'll see. Don't forget your shotgun."

"Still don't see what we need shotguns for."

"Bring it, anyway."

Turner retrieved his shotgun then followed Guthrie to the gate, where they stared down the dirt road into the fog and darkness that suffused the marsh. Guthrie noticed the chief's knuckles whiten as he unconsciously gripped the shotgun tight.

"Jesus Christ," Turner said. "What's that smell?"

"I told you. The pond and woods are full of dead animals. Probably every animal that lived here. Well," he amended. "Almost every animal."

"It's dark in there." Turner shook his head. "I don't feel right."

"No, you don't, and it's not going to get any better. Come on."

Guthrie climbed the gate, and after a moment, Turner followed.

"I don't know about this," Turner said as they stood on the other side, hunching his shoulders as if bearing a weight.

"Don't know about what, Chief? We've been down here a couple of times together, and I've come alone."

Guthrie knew perfectly well that the marsh's malignant psychic pressure was what bothered Turner, but he couldn't say so. Turner had to acknowledge it on his own.

"It's mighty foggy in there for this late in the day," Turner said, waving at the woods spread on both sides of the track. "I've never seen it like this."

"Come on," Guthrie said, leading off down the road. "I'll show you one of the reason's Jim's trapped in the cabin."

The second they stepped out of the sunshine and into the gloom beneath the tree canopy, Turner almost staggered.

"You okay, Chief?"

"I'm a little light-headed," Turner said, shaking his head as if to clear it. "Must be coming down with something."

Guthrie gave him a moment, though he couldn't help but wonder how much good that did. The foul psychic emanation didn't let up, and the longer they were enveloped within it, the worse off they'd be. And while Guthrie had some protection from the buzzing Kuei men, Turner was completely exposed. Finally, the chief straightened, shook himself, and glanced guiltily at Guthrie.

"Sorry," he said, then he waved down the track. "Show me what we're here to see."

After they struggled against the intangible headwind for a couple of the track's sinuous turns, the fallen tree came into view.

"That's one reason Jim can't get out," Guthrie said, voice sounding dull in his own ears.

They approached the tree, Turner with faltering curiosity, Guthrie with caution as he scanned for serpents in the underbrush on either side of the road.

"It's been cut down with a chainsaw," Turner said, vague hope blanketed by a dull resignation. He looked at Guthrie. "Is this what you think is trapping him? Heck, he could cut this up in no time."

"If he had the opportunity. But who cut it down? And why? Let's go on."

Turner stared through the branches of the fallen tree at the track beyond. Guthrie couldn't see his eyes, but his body language said he didn't want to take one step farther.

"What's the matter, Chief?"

"I don't know."

"Just a little farther," Guthrie urged. "Come on. Follow me."

He worked his way through the branches of the fallen tree, walked on a dozen paces, then looked back. Turner was still on the far side of the tree.

"You have to take that step," Guthrie said. "If you don't, you might as well go home, pack up all your belongings, and move your family to some other town, because if we don't stop what's down here, Thorndike and everybody in it is doomed."

"Those are mighty strong words," Turner said defensively. "Why should I believe anything you say?"

"I'm not asking you to believe me," Guthrie said. "Believe yourself and ask why you can't come over here. Why you doubt me when you can feel what I'm talking about. I know you feel it."

"What? I don't feel…."

"Then prove it!" Guthrie snapped. "Come over here."

Finally, Turner forced himself to take the step, and he clambered through the branches and walked over to Guthrie. The furtive look in his eyes almost shocked Guthrie.

"Not much farther," Guthrie said.

He knew they wouldn't be able to easily penetrate the marsh, and they probably couldn't actually get to the cabin. Perhaps he could, alone, but not the chief. But he had to make Turner try and fail.

As they slogged down the track, the pressure of the foul psychic wind thickened, slowing their walk to a halting shuffle. Or at least Turner was shuffling, his face taut with effort and fear. The vibration of the Kuei men sent protective thrills though Guthrie, shielding him from the brunt of the oppressive force. It was almost, he thought, like the Earth's magnetic field protecting the planet from solar winds. Turner wasn't so lucky. His faltering steps caused him to lag behind Guthrie as they pressed on another two hundred feet. Suddenly, Guthrie heard his companion rack a shell into the shotgun's chamber. He looked back at Turner, who seemed completely dazed and confused. His eyes were glazed over, and he was gradually lifting the barrel of the shotgun in Guthrie's direction as if the action took great effort.

"Fight it, Bill," Guthrie said as forcefully as he could, though his words seemed muted in the thick, still air.

Turner had the barrel raised about half way when he trembled and collapsed to his knees, the shotgun held in listless hands. His head bowed, and his Stetson fell off onto the ground.

"Get up," Guthrie said, stepping to the kneeling man and dragging on his arm. "We can't stay here."

"I need to go," Turner gasped as Guthrie helped him stagger to his feet.

"Not yet. Just a little farther," Guthrie urged, picking up Turner's hat and handing it to him. "Stay close to me."

He didn't know if the Kuei men's protection would extend beyond him to help shield Turner, but even if it didn't, he had to force the chief to go deeper into the marsh. He had to rub his face in the wrongness surrounding them and make it impossible for Turner to deny the reality of the corruption that lay all around, suffusing the fog like a pall of toxic fumes. But they didn't make it much farther. Just when Turner seemed on the verge of collapse again, the serpents appeared. Guthrie had been watching for them along the margins of the track.

"Here they come," he called out, raising his shotgun.

"Here come what?" Turner said, but then he saw. "Holy fucking shit!"

The sudden danger galvanized him. He unlimbered his shotgun and cranked the entire magazine though the receiver, blasting the leaders of the oncoming wave. Guthrie did likewise before slapping Turner on the arm.

"Let's get out of here!"

Now the foul psychic wind did not impede but pushed them along. They reached the tree, crashed through it, taking scratches on their arms, and dashed on, barely keeping ahead of the snakes. At last, they rounded the final bend and raced out into the sunlight, and the carpet of pursuing serpents halted. Seconds later, Guthrie and Turner nearly vaulted the gate, scrambled into the Interceptor, and slammed the doors.

"What the fuck was that?" Turner gasped, staring through the windshield at the mat of serpents writhing and coiling on the shadowed track beneath the tree line.

"I told you something's down there," Guthrie answered. "Now you know I'm not just blowing smoke. That was its warning to keep out."

"Jesus Christ, Clay. I was going to shoot you."

"No, *it* was going to shoot me."

"Yeah, but I was the one about to pull the trigger." Turner's shoulders sagged. "What the fuck is it?"

"Call it an infection, a contagion, a moral sickness. It was created to destroy a village in southern Louisiana, and it destroyed a second one before moving to Airla and destroying that, too. And now it's here, courtesy of George Rand."

"But why? What possible motive could it have? Or Rand."

"Friday afternoon, Rand told me that the moans of men and the weeping of women and children are music to his ears. He's a psychopath who's already murdered several people we know of, and there are probably more we don't know about. A man like that is never satiated and is always looking to up the ante."

"What about the thing in the marsh? You think it likes the same things that Rand does?"

"I think it's similar in nature but different in motivation."

"How?"

"When we're done for the day, what are you going to do?"

"Go home, I suppose."

"To do what?"

"Eat supper, obviously. And see if I can get some sleep, though I doubt that's possible."

"Pay attention to the first part of what you just said."

"You mean eat? You think that thing feeds off of towns? You mean Thorndike is just another meal for it?"

"It seems so. It was created to consume the energy of a small village, and since then, it's moved on to other towns. Unsuspecting towns. Towns where there might already be strife."

"It doesn't even have a body. What does it need to eat for?"

"It's a living thing, Bill. Maybe it's sentient, maybe it's mindless, but either way, a living thing has to take in energy to survive. But apparently it doesn't consume vegetation or flesh."

"What, then? The soul?"

"Don't know about the soul. Call it the spirit. Maybe the spirit of a person, or maybe that isn't enough. Maybe it needs to consume the spirit of something larger, like a small town. Or maybe it feeds off the emanations of fear, turmoil, and discord it spawns and the moral and physical decay that ensues. Whatever it desires, it was created to destroy a village, and now it's here in Thorndike."

"That sounds like bullshit."

"That's your preconceptions talking, not what's actually happening. Look around and think about what's been going on in

Thorndike and tell me it's all normal. All the usual course of events. Tell me you didn't witness what you just witnessed and felt what you just felt. Tell me those, and I'll go home right now and wash my hands of the matter."

Taken aback, Turner's shoulders drooped.

"Okay," he said. "Like some kind of spirit vampire without a body. It's completely insane, but even if I don't have your background with these kinds of things, I've seen everything you have, and I have to admit what you say sounds as plausible as any other explanation for the total shit show Thorndike's become. Or what I felt—and almost did—down there."

Turner nodded toward the marsh then gave Guthrie a long, hard look that mixed denial and fear. But beneath it was growing anger. Turner wasn't a man to be pushed around, even if he didn't know what was doing the pushing, and he was desperate enough to find out and eliminate it.

"I hate to think of Jim down there in the thick of all that," the chief said.

"He's safe enough for the moment. The garlic seems to be keeping the force at bay around the house. But that won't last long. The force has allies in human form, and they'll do what they can to eliminate him."

"As in Rand. And Wiley and Lonnie."

"There's at least one more," Guthrie said.

"How do you figure? Rob Fitzgerald and Johnny Miller are locked up, and they're about the only men I know around here who closely associates with the Sanfords."

"Do you think any of them know enough about the people in town to send those poison-pen letters?"

"Maybe, but not likely," Turner admitted.

"So the next logical question is, who knows just about everybody in town?"

"Lot of folks know lots of folks," Turner said. "But I guess not many know nearly everyone."

"And who among them associates with Wiley and Lonnie?"

Turner didn't have to think about that for long.

"Hetty Mruska."

41

WHEN GUTHRIE AND TURNER ARRIVED at Chaloupek's Grocery, Hetty was at her usual spot at the checkout line, scanning groceries for a youngish Hispanic woman shepherding three young children. She glanced up as Guthrie and Turner came into the store but dropped her eyes as soon as she noticed them looking at her.

"Let's find the Chaloupeks," Turner suggested, and he headed toward the back of the store. They passed Kevin, who was spritzing down the vegetable bins, which had been replenished since the rat raid.

"Hi, Kevin. Where's Todd?:" Turner asked.

"He and Laura are in the back taking inventory," the clerk said, nodding toward the swinging doors at the back of the store.

They found the Chaloupeks in the storeroom. Laura was making notations on a digital tablet while Todd went through the many boxes and cartons half filling the room. They both glanced up at Turner's knock.

"Chief," Todd said, straightening. "You come to see how we're recovering from all that damage the rats caused? This shipment," he waved his hands over the stacked boxes, "will help get us back on track. That and Leland's generous donation."

"We're here about something else," Turner said. "I need to talk to Hetty. Laura, would you mind getting her and meeting us in the office?"

"What's this about?" she asked.

"I can't say right now. Just get her."

Laura glanced at her husband, who nodded.

"I'll get her and do the check-out until she comes back," she said.

They left the storeroom, and while Laura headed toward the front of the store, Todd led them into the office across the hall.

"You better wait outside," Turner told him.

Chaloupek, obviously curious, reluctantly left.

"Since we don't have any direct evidence against Hetty, anything we learn probably won't be admissible in court."

"This case is never going to court," Guthrie told him. "You and I are going to take care of it in any way we must."

"I'm the chief of police. I need to worry about legalities."

"We'll worry about legalities later. Right now, your duty isn't to the law but to the people of your town. You have to realize that if you and I don't do something, Thorndike is as doomed as Airla." He gave a sardonic snort. "If you think differently, tell me exactly why, not half an hour ago, you couldn't walk down the road to Jim' cabin, and you just about unwillingly shot me. What words would you use to explain that to a judge and jury? But if you're worried about legalities, here." Guthrie unclipped the badge from his belt and held it out to Turner. "I resign. Now I'm a private citizen who can't be accused of police overreach. You can arrest me later for assault if you feel the need."

Turner was still staring at the badge in Guthrie's hand when the door opened. Hetty came in, eyes darting furtively from Turner to Guthrie then around the room, as if she didn't want to face them.

"Put that back on and close the door," Turner told Guthrie then said to Hetty, "Have a seat, Hetty."

As Guthrie shut the door, Turner pulled out the desk chair and scooted it toward her.

"I don't wanna to sit," she said. "What's this all about?"

"I think you know," Turner said.

"I ain't gotta listen to this," Hetty snarled, and she turned toward the door as if to leave.

"You do," Guthrie said, stepping between her and the door.

She flailed her arms at him, raking her nails at his face, but he easily trapped her limbs and, with a gentle shove, sent her plumping down into the chair, surprise almost wiping away her anger. She started to rise, but Turner laid a hand on her shoulder and kept her in the seat.

"You're going to be in a lot of trouble if you don't cooperate with us," he said.

"I ain't done nothin' wrong," she snapped.

"Making terroristic and slanderous threats is a crime. And so is obstructing a police investigation."

"I ain't sent no letters," she said, voice still harsh.

"I didn't say anybody sent any letters," Turner said.

"What else could they be?" she asked, belligerence tempered with a note of panic.

"Nobody sends letters anymore. You know that. Most people use text or email, but you know those can easily be traced, don't you? But letters not so much. Now, suppose you tell us about them."

"Even if I did send some letters, they wasn't nothin' but the truth."

"Your personal truth, maybe, but not the factual truth."

"I ain't sayin' nothin' else." She folded her arms, her face falling into a stubborn frown.

"We'll see about that," Turner said. To Guthrie, he said, "Watch her while I talk to Todd."

Turner left the room, closing the door behind him. Guthrie perched on the edge of the desk, looking down at Hetty, who stubbornly refused to meet his eyes.

"You should talk to us," he said. "Things will go easier for you."

Finally, she looked at him, face reddening as it screwed with anger, hatred, and fear.

"I wish to hell they'd killed you the other night."

The vehemence in her voice was so tight that Guthrie had to chuckle, which made her madder still.

"Go on and laugh," she snarled. "You won't be laughin' much longer. Not after Wiley and Lonnie take care of...."

She shut up, realizing she was saying too much. But she already had.

"After they take care of what?" he asked. Or who?

She didn't answer but just sat sullenly, eyes downcast.

Guthrie casually pulled out his phone then said, "Look at me Hetty."

She raised her head and gave him a look of pure hatred that quickly dissolved into panic as he leaned forward and snapped a photo of her eyes.

"What the fuck you do that for?" she shrilled.

"I see *you*, Hetty."

"You fuckin' bastard!"

She made as if to rise, but a sharp shake of Guthrie's head and a stern look of warning made her sink back, though she remained as tense as a severed live wire.

Turner came back into the room with Todd, who looked sadly at Hetty for a moment.

"I can't believe you'd do this to us, Hetty," he said. "We took you on and treated you well, and you repay us by spreading lies about us?"

She remained stoically silent, eyes again downcast.

"What about the rats and mice," Guthrie asked her. "Are you the one who left the back door open that night."

"I say it was *you*," she snarled. "I saw you sneak back there and open the door."

"If that's so, why didn't you close it after?" Turner asked. "Why didn't you say something to the Chaloupeks?"

"I ain't gotta answer your questions."

"I know I checked the door right after we closed," Chaloupek said. "That's been bothering me ever since. Mr. Guthrie was nowhere around at the time. There are only four people who could have opened it after, and that's me and Laura, Kevin, and you."

"It musta been Kevin…."

"It was you," Turner said. "I could charge you with malicious tampering with the intent to cause property damage in excess of…." He glanced at Todd. "How much do you estimate the damages at, Todd?"

"Leland replaced all that meat…."

"There was still property damage, no matter who paid for it. Including the meat, about how much?"

"Probably in the area of six or seven thousand."

"You hear that, Hetty?" Turner said. "That's felony territory. I could arrest you right now, and you'd be facing a couple of years at least in prison, not counting what a federal judge might hand down on the terroristic threat charges over the letters."

"You can't prove none of it," she spat, but she didn't look so certain. "There ain't no fingerprints on any of 'em."

"I took a photo of her eyes while you were out," Guthrie said to Turner. "We can take a better one if necessary. I think it'll match what's on the letters."

Turner looked at Hetty again.

"You ever hear of DNA evidence?" he asked with a predatory smile. "I bet you licked the flaps, didn't you?"

That shut her up, and she seemed to shrink within herself.

Todd, whose face had darkened with anger, calmed himself a moment then said in a strained but level voice, "I'm going to have to let you go. And I'd appreciate it if you didn't come back. You'll have to do your grocery shopping elsewhere."

That brought her around.

"You can't do that!" she shouted, rising.

Turner stepped between her and Chaloupek.

"This is his store, Hetty. He can say no to anyone he wants. But it probably won't matter. As soon as the rest of Thorndike learns you're the one writing those letters, how do you think they're going to feel? Everybody will be out for your hide, and I'm going to make sure everybody knows."

"We'll see about that," she said. "There's some who'd say no to him and you and everbody else, and mighty quick."

"Is that a threat?" Turner asked.

"A promise," she retorted, then she looked past him at Todd. "You owe me last week's pay."

In answer, Chaloupek went to the safe, opened it, and counted out a sum of cash on his desk, in full view of Hetty, Turner, and Guthrie. Then he wrote out a receipt and handed it and a pen to Hetty.

"I'm paying you for the full week, even though you only worked four days."

She snatched the receipt from his hand, scrawled her name, then threw the paper and pen at him and scooped up the short stack of bills.

"You'll regret this," she said. "I have friends."

"You and your friends will regret it even more if you try to make good on that threat," Turner said. "Now get out of here, and if you cause one more iota of trouble, I'll lock you up and charge you."

She huffed and went out of the door, followed by the others. At the checkout lane, she shoved a surprised Laura Chaloupek aside to retrieve her purse from a shelf beneath the moving belt before looking at the small group watching her leave.

"Fuck all y'all," she yelled, face a red scowl, shooting the bird at them with both hands.

The next second, she stormed out of the store. If the grocery hadn't had automatic sliding glass doors, she'd probably have slammed whatever door was there.

Guthrie looked at the Chaloupeks. Todd's face remained angry, while Laura appeared to be in shock. So was Kevin, who had no idea of what was going on.

"I'm sorry this had to happen," Turner told them after Todd briefly explained the situation to the others. "But you're probably better off with her gone."

"You really think she's the one who left the back door open and let in all those rats?" Laura asked.

"Not many other people had access," Turner pointed out.

"*I* didn't do it," Kevin said defensively.

"How could she know about the rats?" Todd asked.

Guthrie didn't respond, but he thought that Rand—or the miasma—might have had a hand in that, as with the snakes.

Todd heaved a sigh of relief and said to Turner, "Tell the truth, I'm kinda glad it was you who brought this about. I was beginning to suspect she was not only pilfering but short-changing some of our customers, and I was trying to work up the nerve to confront her. Not so much because of her, you know, but Lonnie. And Wiley. They wouldn't have taken it kindly, even if I was in the right."

"Especially if you were in the right," Turner said. "Well, you can relax since it was me who got her canned. But you be sure to tell me if either of the Sanfords even looks at you sideways."

With that, Guthrie and Turner left the grocery store owners to get on with their business. Out in the late afternoon sunshine, Turner glanced wearily down the street toward Leo's Cafe. Maybe missing a meal, maybe missing his wife. Guthrie couldn't tell. They walked across the street to the police station, where Turner paused to look at Guthrie.

"It's been a long day," he said. "I need sit down for a while and try to wrap my head around what's going on. And write up a report." He shook his head ruefully. "On Hetty, not on our little trip down to the marsh. Send me that photo of her eyes, would you?"

"Sure thing," Guthrie said. "I'm going to grab a bit to eat at Leo's. I'll see you at the house."

Turner nodded wearily then headed toward the police station door.

42

DESPITE THE HEAVY ACTIVITY OF the day before, Guthrie woke with the dawn. He couldn't say he was refreshed, but at least he'd rested. Showering and dressing as quietly as possible so as not to disturb the Turners, he wondered what he might be able to find for breakfast in the kitchen pantry. Considering how the last two days had gone, he wished Leo's was open so he could have a solid breakfast. But the cafe didn't open until eight, even when Leo was at the griddle, which he wouldn't be for at least another two weeks according to Bev's update the night before.

He needn't have wondered what he might scrounge. As soon as he opened the bathroom door, the odor of frying bacon sifted into his nostrils. He dumped his dirty clothes in his temporary bedroom then headed down the hall to the kitchen.

Bev was at the stove, and Turner was seated at the table, scanning a sheaf of papers. His face looked drawn, as if he either hadn't slept well or had too much on his mind. Probably both, Guthrie thought.

"Morning," Guthrie said.

"Grab yourself a cup of coffee and have a seat." Turner nodded toward an empty chair.

Bev pointed to the drip coffee pot, next to which sat an empty mug. Guthrie filled the mug and joined Turner.

"I'm just finalizing my report on the Havasau burglary," the chief said, waving the sheaf of papers. "At least we solved one case."

"Two," Guthrie reminded him. "Hetty and the letters. Or does she make it three, counting the rats?"

"I'd like to say I can't believe she'd do something like that," Bev said, "but unfortunately, I can."

"We might have solved those issues, but there's plenty of others," Turner said morosely.

Guthrie noticed that Turner didn't openly refer to the miasma suffusing Chaney Marsh. He didn't know how much the chief had confided to his wife, and he didn't want to put him on the spot, so he simply said, "We'll deal with it."

"Want to have a look?" Turner asked, passing over the papers.

The report itself only occupied two single-spaced pages on which Turner had outlined not only the Havasau burglary, but the attack on Guthrie's trailer and the subsequent search of Miller's house. Next came Havasau's list of the weapons and other items stolen from his store, and after that were a number of photos of the weapons and other contraband in situ in Johnny Miller's house.

"Looks about right to me," Guthrie said when he finished.

"Well, you boys can put that down for the moment," Bev said. "Fuel is on the way."

She set a plate in front of each of them: scrambled eggs piled high, bacon, grits, and a biscuit.

"It's not Leo's Number Three," she said, "but it should do."

"Dig in," Turner said and immediately followed his own instruction.

"Better than Leo's Number Three," Guthrie said when he finished.

He got up and carried his dirty dish and silverware to the sink, then poured a second cup of coffee.

"What now, Chief?"

"We finish our coffee then go over to the station to see what other crap's come up."

"Dad!"

Emily had just entered, wrapped in a long robe, hair disheveled.

"Sorry, sweetheart."

She just laughed as she went to the stove to dish her own plate of food.

While Guthrie and Turner finished their coffee, Bev and Emily, thankfully oblivious to the intangible danger surrounding Thorndike, talked about Emily's friends who were going to help out at Leo's. Guthrie heard them but didn't really listen. He was anxious to do something. What, he wasn't sure, but surely there was something. Apparently, Turner was feeling the same, and as soon as he drained the last of his coffee, he jerked his head toward the door.

"Time to get to it."

They left the house, Turner grabbing his hat from a peg by the front door on the way out. They didn't have to drive to the police station since he'd left his Interceptor, as usual, in the station parking lot. Guthrie had followed his example, and his Xterra was parked next to the chief's vehicle. But as they approached the steps going up to the police station's front door, Turner abruptly stopped. He stared at Guthrie, eyes lit.

"Well, good goddamn," he said, looking like he might facepalm if he wasn't wearing his Stetson.

"What?" Guthrie asked.

"Freddie. I should have guessed it."

"Guessed what?"

"Where he's probably hiding." Turner shook his head then amplified, "I bet he's out at the old Dixon quarry."

"The place he worked back in the day?"

"I didn't think of it earlier because it's in the next county and twenty, twenty-five miles away. It's been shut down more than twenty years, but I think a couple of shacks are still out there—an office and a tool shed. Maybe Freddie's holed up there."

"That's a long way for him to walk, especially considering he's been back to his house at least once," Guthrie said. "But he doesn't seem to be anywhere else. What are we waiting for?"

"For you to get your ass into my vehicle," Turner said, digging the keys from his pocket.

On the way, Turner radioed Tessa to let her know where he and Guthrie were going and to have her keep Emmet on patrol.

"I'm way out of my jurisdiction, here," Turner admitted as he pulled to a stop in front of a rusty iron-barred gate that was chained and locked across a disused dirt road.

A shredded plywood sign mounted on rusting metal poles next to the gate might once have indicated that the sandpit lay down that road, but now it said nothing. The metal sign bolted to the aluminum gate was a different matter. Its red letters, peeking from beneath blooms of rust, read, "No Trespassing," and it didn't look to Guthrie like anyone had violated that directive recently.

Past the gate, the wide dirt road had once supported heavy traffic of heavy trucks bearing heavy loads, but now the surrounding weeds and brush were squeezing its sides, and its surface was mottled by patches of weeds and clumps of grass. It curved out of sight around a bend and over a rise that masked the quarry from the paved road. Turner got out, signaling for Guthrie to do the same. He opened the Interceptor's back hatch and pulled a pair of bolt cutters from the toolbox of equipment in the back.

"To hell with jurisdiction," he said, gesturing for Guthrie to follow.

Turner cut one of the chain links free, and Guthrie swung the gate wide.

"After I pull through, shut the gate after me," Turner said. "No sense advertising we're in here."

Turner went to the Interceptor, tossed the bolt cutters into the toolbox, slammed the hatch, got into the driver's sear, and pulled through the opening. Guthrie swung the gate shut and draped the chain around it and the post to keep it tethered, then he joined Turner in the SUV. Turner pulled off and drove slowly, the scrubby growth on the road scraping the vehicle's undercarriage. Within two minutes, the quarry came into view two hundred yards ahead. It might have been a booming business in its day, supplying sand and gravel to help build the nearby cities and roads between, but now it was a mini-desert carved out of a grass- and tree-covered rolling landscape that, even two decades later, had only barely begun to reclaim its own. The lower portions held brackish pools surrounded by fringes of weeds and saplings.

"How big is this place?" Guthrie asked.

"I'm not sure. Hundreds of acres, surely. There's a couple of larger operations southeast of here that are still going strong. All this area is part of the ancient Navasota River floodplain, though the river's east of here, now. Some places, the river left the kind of silt farmers love, and some it left sand and gravel. Dixon finally dug everything useful from this site then shut it down."

The chief eased to a stop.

"Let's walk," he said. "If Freddie's here, I don't want him to hear us and get spooked. I'm in no mood to run him down."

They got out and closed the Interceptor's doors quietly so as not to make telltale sounds.

"Where are those shacks you mentioned?" Guthrie asked.

"Back in here somewhere," Turner said. "Like I said, it's been a while since I've seen the place."

They didn't stay directionless for long. As soon as the road opened into the quarry's staging area, they spotted a couple of wooden shacks off to the right. If they'd ever been painted, it had long since worn off, leaving bare wood to turn silver-gray beneath the harsh Texas sun and weather. One of the shacks was half-collapsed, but the larger one, obviously the quarry's main office, was better built and still intact. A trickle of smoke issued from a black stovepipe poking through the rusted tin roof. An old, red, men's single-speed bicycle with a front basket was propped against the wall next to the door.

"At least we know how he's getting around without his truck," Turner said, waving toward the bike.

They headed toward the shack. When they were about twenty feet away, Turner yelled out.

"Freddie! It's Chief Turner. Come on out, now."

At the first sound of Turner's voice, a clattering issued from the shack, and a voice cried out in dismay. A shadow passed behind one of the grimy windows, and a moment later, the door opened a crack. A face with a bushy gray beard peered through the gap. Then the door swung wide, and the whole, dirty, disheveled man stood in the opening. The lower right leg of his jeans and the boot below were covered with some sort of lumpy brown substance.

"You scared me, Chief Bill," Freddie said. "Made me drop my pan a beans. Now I got nothin' to eat and a big mess to clean up." He gestured down at his soiled leg. "And it's all over my britches and boot, too, and I got nowheres to wash 'em 'cept in that dirty water down there."

He waved at the closest of the pools.

"We've been looking for you, Freddie."

"You and him? Who's he?"

"This is Clay Guthrie. He's a private detective from Houston assisting me on a case."

"What's that got to do with me?"

"Come on out here, Freddie, so we can talk."

Freddie reluctantly stepped to the ground, stomped his right foot several times to shake off most of the beans, and walked over to where Turner and Guthrie stood.

"Why are you hiding out here?" Turner asked.

"I ain't hidin'." Freddie's voice was vehement, but his eyes betrayed anxiety, as did his twitchy body language.

"You left your truck at the dump two weeks ago, you took off your boots and pants and ran to Jim Chaney's place, where you spent the night. Jim said you told him some wild story about being attacked by a black fog. In the morning, you went into town without getting your truck, bought some supplies at the grocery, then walked all the way out here."

"I didn't walk," Freddie said indignantly. "I ain't disrespectable. I got my bike."

"We know you've been home at least once, so why are you out here if you aren't hiding from something?"

"I admit I told Mr. Jim some crazy shit that night," Freddie said. "But I was just drunk and seein' things."

"You don't seem drunk now."

"I ain't had a drop since I come out here," Freddie said defensively.

"A man like you doesn't stop drinking just like that for no reason. You might have been drunk that night, but you weren't just seeing things. Mr. Guthrie and I know that for a fact."

"What you mean?"

"I mean something really was in the dump that night."

Freddie shuffled uncomfortably, staring at his feet.

"I tole you I ain't seen nothin'."

"We know you did, and I'm going to need you to come back to Thorndike and tell us all about it."

"I ain't never goin' back there."

"Let's not make this difficult, Freddie," Turner said, voice both soothing and commanding.

"Fergit it, Chief." Freddie stood defiantly, arms folded across his chest. "I already tole you I ain't never goin' back there."

"What about your job? Your house? Your friends?"

Freddie snorted at the last.

"A job in the dump? And what friends are those?"

"Didn't Jim Chaney take you in and give you shelter and clothes? Didn't I get you your job?"

"I guess you're right about all that," Freddie admitted. "But that don't mean nothin'. I still ain't goin'. We ain't in Thorndike. Hell, we ain't even in the same county. You're all out of your jurisprudence and can't do nothin' to me."

"You're right, Freddie. I am out of my jurisdiction. But Mr. Guthrie doesn't have a jurisdiction. If the welfare of the town you grew up in isn't enough to make you come with us, I'll just have to ask him to take you against your will."

"Him?" Freddie looked Guthrie up and down, upper lip twisting his mustache with disdain. "And who else?"

"I think he'll be enough."

"Well fuck him and the horse he rode in…." Freddie began, but his words were cut short when Guthrie abruptly stepped forward.

Freddie reacted clumsily, raising an arm against an attack that wasn't really an attack but a feint designed to give Guthrie a lever, and Freddie's raised arm was ideal for the purpose. In two seconds, Freddie was on his knees, groaning in an arm lock, and a moment later, Turner snapped handcuffs on his wrists.

"I'm sorry we have to do this to you," Turner said as he and Guthrie hauled Freddie to his feet, "but you're coming back to Thorndike whether you like it or not."

"Well, I don't fuckin' like it," Freddie spat. "You let me outta these cuffs right now."

"You coming peacefully?"

"No! You're fuckin' kidnappin' me!"

Freddie began struggling. He was strong from a lifetime of hard work, but he was in handcuffs and against two men who also were strong. Even so, Guthrie and Turner had to drag him, yelling and writhing, to the Interceptor. When they finally shoved him onto the back seat, Turner slammed the door. Freddie complained loudly as Turner drove out of the quarry to the county road, where the chief stopped while Guthrie got out and opened the gate. After Turner pulled through, Guthrie shut the gate and draped the chain around the post so it would't swing open, then he rejoined the two in the Interceptor.

By now, Freddie, realizing he was definitely going back to Thorndike, settled into sullen silence. The drive was brief, and after Turner parked in the police station lot, he and Guthrie got Freddie out of the vehicle. The moment Freddie emerged, he saw the charred square block that once had been the Baptist Church.

"What the fuck?" he breathed, eyes wide.

"That's right, Freddie," Turner said. "What the fuck?"

They took the prisoner into the station. Tessa stared as they practically dragged Freddie toward the cellblock. Guthrie thought he caught an expression of concern mixed with relief on her face as they passed. One of the cells still held the contraband stolen from Buster Havasau, so Turner removed the cuffs from Freddie's wrists and gently pushed him into the empty one.

"What the hell you lockin' me up for?"

"For your own protection."

"Hell, there ain't no protection in this town," Freddie spat. "'Sides, you can't just keep me in here without a lawyer. I know my rights."

"You aren't under arrest," Turner said as he locked the door. "Besides, do you have a lawyer? In fact, does anyone even know you're in here except me, Mr. Guthrie, and Tessa?"

That sent Freddie into a sulk that seemed equal parts anger and fear.

"You spend some time thinking about what you want to tell me and Mr. Guthrie. We'll be back in a little while to hear all about it."

"Chief!" Freddie yelled, impotently shaking the bars. "You can't leave me in here! I ain't even et!"

Turner and Guthrie went back to the front office, trailing shouted invectives from the prisoner. The chief paused at Tessa's desk, where he told her to do her best to ignore Freddie. Then he looked to Guthrie.

"I'm going to Leo's to get Freddie something to eat. Mind waiting here until I get back?"

In answer, Guthrie pulled the chair from the knee well of the unused desk next to Emmet's and settled into it. His desk, he supposed, smiling slightly.

Turner left.

"He was out at Dixon sandpit?" Tessa asked.

Guthrie nodded.

"My word," she said. "That's a long way for him to walk."

"He had a bicycle."

"He sure is mad, but he doesn't seem drunk." She sounded hopeful.

"He claims he hasn't had a drop since he disappeared."

"That'll be the day," she commented dryly, though her voice was tinged with sadness.

Freddie's protestations ceased after a few minutes. Maybe he'd just gotten tired of shouting at the bars and walls.

Turner was back in less than half an hour, one hand bearing a styrofoam box that smelled like breakfast, the other holding a bottle of water. A cellophane packet with plastic utensils and a paper napkin protruded from a shirt pocket.

"We'll fatten Freddie up a little before the slaughter," he said.

He carried the food through the outer cellblock door, upon which Freddie resumed his yelling.

"You gonna use your mouth to complain?" Guthrie heard Turner say. "Or eat? I even brought you pancakes."

After that there was silence, and Turner came out of the cellblock, a smile on his face.

"I don't think he's had a decent meal since he disappeared."

They waited fifteen minutes, then Turner said to Guthrie, "We've fattened up the prisoner. Ready for the interrogation?"

43

THE POLICE STATION DIDN'T HAVE an interrogation room, so after
Turner retrieved Freddie from the cell, he took him into his office,
Guthrie following. Tessa watched them, obviously wishing she'd been
invited, too. After they were seated, Turner led off.

"Okay, Freddie. We've fed you good, now it's time to talk."

"I don't know, Chief. I ain't really sure...."

"You better be sure," Turner said. "I'm depending on you. The
whole town is depending on you."

"That's hard to believe."

"Let me just say that, at the moment, you might be the most important person in Thorndike. You saw the Baptist Church, didn't you?
The same thing happened to the Methodist Church. I've got two dead
bodies, one of them Jeff Mayfield, and that's only what's obvious."

"Jeff's dead?" Freddie's eyes widened.

"Yes, and another man who was lying on that sofa you found at
the back of the dump. If you'd pulled off the moving quilts, you'd
have found him. And there's more. Every dog in town is dead, the
Chaloupeks' was infested with rats, and there were burglaries at Eli
Carlin's and Havasau Hardware. And those are just scratching the
surface of what's been happening here since you skipped out. Clay
and I are doing what we can, but we need you to tell us what happened to you in the dump."

"You ain't gonna believe me."

"We'll believe you," Guthrie said. "Just tell us what happened."

Freddie had driven to the dump on Tuesday morning as usual to open the gate and take his post in the shack near the entrance. He was armed with a baloney and mustard sandwich, a pack of smokes, and a bottle of cheap bourbon, all of which would be gone by quitting time. He also was hungover from the bender he'd slipped into over the weekend. He was going to have to watch that, he thought. I don't need to get *that* plastered every night.

But he had last night, and this morning he intended to do as little as possible. Luckily, he might expect only two or three customers on any given day, and his only contact with them would be to collect the twenty-dollar fee and direct them to the appropriate place to dump whatever it was they were dumping. Town garbage pick-up was tomorrow, and that would be even better since Pete and Wally never needed to disturb him in his cracker-box palace at the dump's entrance. But Thursday would be busy since he had to bulldoze all the garbage Pete and Wally dumped.

But this morning, bleary or not, Freddie noticed right off someone had been messing with the chain fastening the gate. He might be a ne'er-do-well and a drunk, but he knew for certain that there hadn't been two padlocks on the chain when he'd locked up late Saturday afternoon. He lifted the chain to examine the new lock and saw it was a brand-new brass MasterLock unlike the old-style MasterLock of graying metal he'd been unlocking and locking nearly every day for the past three years. Somebody had cut out a link and replaced it with the second lock.

Looking at the second lock, Freddie felt his ire rising. Who the fuck was encroaching on his territory? Freddie didn't have much, but he had his pride—though even that had lost some of its luster as he'd shuttled from one job to another over the last decade, each one worse than before. Until Chief Bill had gotten him hired on to supervise the dump. At least that was a step up from begging.

"I mean," he said to Turner, "you got me that job 'cause you knew I could do it, but mostly 'cause I needed it bad. And I appreciate it, Chief Bill. Don't never think I don't. So when I saw that second lock, I admit I got kinda testy."

He dropped the chain and stared over the gate into the dump. Had somebody been in there over the weekend without his knowledge? But who? And why?

To dump something they shouldn't, of course. He wondered if he ought to call Chief Bill, but it was early. Besides, he was afraid if he called the chief about every little problem, Turner would think he couldn't handle the job. So he unlocked the gate, swung it wide, and drove to his parking spot next to the shack. He made a quick tour of the dump's main tracks, half expecting to find a large animal carcass, but he didn't notice anything unusual aside from the uncharacteristic quiet of the morning. Nor were any buzzards circling around, which there would have been if a dead animal was present.

But he did notice how quiet the dump was. Usually by this time, insects were buzzing about, and birds chirped and hovered, looking for bugs or bits of garbage to eat. Not to mention the rats and mice that constantly scurried through the debris, searching out morsels, and squirrels in the branches of the surrounding trees. But this morning, everything was still. There even seemed to be less of a stink.

Just as well, he mused, hoping for a quiet day, himself. Besides, he was tired of walking around the dump. He needed a drink, so he returned to the shack, went in, took his seat, lit a smoke, and tugged at the bottle. The day passed with almost no customers, giving him time to brood over the second lock. All day and a bottle of bourbon, and when the bottle was drained and the daylight seeping out of the sky, he left the shack and staggered to his truck to do one last patrol of the dump before he went home.

He fumbled the key into the ignition, started the truck, and drove veeringly down the main lane that led into the dump, scanning to either side with bleary eyes. The late spring days had been warm, but the nights had been cool, and already a mist was beginning to form along the lanes between the mounds of debris as the sun dropped below the no-man's landscape of the dump.

Considering the mist and his condition, it was a miracle he noticed fresh-looking tire tracks in the soft dirt of a lesser lane leading toward the back of the dump. He stopped, got out of the truck, and swayed over the tracks as he examined them. They were definitely fresh. Only three people had come to dump trash today, and drunk as he was, he knew he hadn't sent any of them this way. He got into the truck and steered onto the lane, toward its end, where mounds of debris and earth a dozen or more feet high were piled near the dump's rear cyclone fence.

He got out and swayed as he stared at the ground. The tire tracks didn't end but led around the back, between the last mound and the fence. Some vague warning echoed in his brain, but the thick alcohol haze dampened it and let his curiosity get the better of him. What could be so bad back there that he hadn't seen its like before? Even if there weren't any buzzards, it probably was a farm animal carcass some cheap, lazy rancher didn't want to take the trouble to bury. They coulda hired me, he thought. I could use the dough.

Staggering, he followed the tracks around and was surprised to see what looked like a large, lumpy green sofa mostly covered with ratty and stained blue moving quilts, sitting in an open area behind the mounds of earth, garbage, and debris.

It hadn't been here when he'd last bulldozed this area a couple of weeks before , and it shouldn't be here now. He thought back, trying to remember letting anyone in with a load like that. Surely he'd have remembered, but he couldn't. That didn't really surprise him. He didn't always examine the loads people dumped, especially later in the day when the alcohol had taken him over. He forgot a lot of stuff these days. It was the drinking, he knew. Drinking that he should stop. But he couldn't. Or didn't want to. Drink and fixing up old furniture were all he had since Jim Chaney had sold out and let him go. Thank goodness Chief Bill had gotten him this job. It was close to his house, and now he didn't have to sneak in Sundays and Mondays to see if there was anything he could salvage. Maybe the drinking had erased the memory of someone bringing that sofa, but faulty memory or not, he certainly wouldn't have told them to dump it back here.

Then he remembered the second lock on the gate chain. So this is what that was about. Somebody trying to save the fee and trying to hide the evidence way back here. No telling who. He didn't care. But it really pissed him off they hadn't paid. He really needed this job, and he was afraid if Chief Bill found out people were getting in and dumping for free, he might fire him. Also, if this was what the unknown dumper had dumped, why the secrecy? Whoever it was could have just paid the dump fee, and everything would be hunky-dory. In fact, Freddie probably would have had them leave the sofa for free next to his shack so he could take it home and fix it up.

Well, hell, he could do that anyway. Plus, he'd often found many dollars in change fallen into the gaps behind and beside the cushions of sofas and easy chairs brought to the dump. Maybe there was some cash in this one, too. If the sofa looked salvageable, he could bring his truck around and load it up, though it looked heavy as hell. Must have taken at least two men to unload. But he ought to check it out for money first.

He approached the sofa, but the closer he got, the more reluctant he was to get closer. The alcohol haze suffusing his brain might have dulled his sensations, but even at twenty feet, the sofa was repulsive and stank of death. Not big death or new death but death just the same. And foulness and filth. Way worse than anything else in the dump. Almost like he could feel it more than smell it. The stink didn't smell exactly like decaying flesh, but maybe it was, anyway. Maybe an animal had crawled up under the quilts and died. He hoped not. He didn't want to have to move some rotting raccoon or opossum to check the cushions for lost change.

If he could get past the stench of corruption and death that seemed to hang above the nasty blue quilts covering the sofa. Halting, he peered at it in failing light and felt a chill shoot through him. Or had it wafted over and around him? Fuck, he thought with more vehemence than usual, staring at the lumpy, mounded moving quilts. Breathing through his mouth, he edged forward, each shuffling step harder than the one before, as if he was forcing his body through molasses.

At last, he stood next to the sofa, swaying with drunkenness, staring down at the lumpy quilts. Preparing himself to see something bad, he reached for the edge of one of the quilts to drag it off the sofa when he felt something stir across the exposed flesh of his arms. Something—some feeling—like a snaking chill creeping over him. The skin on his arms and neck goosefleshed, and a shiver shot up his spine.

"Fuck!" He jumped back a pace, certain he'd felt something moving at the hem of his worn jeans.

He stared at the ground along the bottom edge of the sofa. Was that a snake under there? It had to be…something. But despite the uncertain light and the growing night mist now blanketing the ground, he could tell nothing was there.

Or was there? What was that, wavering just at the lower edge of the sofa? Some big damn black snake creeping slowly along or just weirdly undulating in place, was his first thought, and he glanced around for some sort of weapon. Despite that he was in the dump, everything was so smashed and chewed up that nothing on the ground offered help except a broken wooden chair leg, which he snatched up to use as a club. But as he stepped forward to look for his target, he felt more plucking at the hem of his jeans. He jumped back again and, fearing a bite, kicked out, but encountered no resistance. And when his boot retracted, it looked like its toe was smeared with some sort of oil. In a panicked fluster, he stomped his foot, and the darkness on the toe rolled off like water off oilskin before seeping back into the undulating darkness beneath the sofa.

Then he saw more of the darkness coiling out—not like oil but like some thick, dark vapor. It began oozing across the ground like a liquid that wasn't a liquid, a darkness that was there but wasn't. A darkness that seemed to absorb what little light remained in the dump. Panicked, he stumbled back. His heel caught something, and he fell backwards, barely keeping his head from smacking the ground. From his supine position, he could see all the way under the sofa. Nothing but a pulsing blackness met his eyes. And in that instant, he saw the oozing darkness begin to merge with the growing ground mist, diffusing rapidly into the mist like whiskey into water, darkening the mist like a spreading stain, darkening it faster than the failing daylight.

As the roiling blackness crept toward him like a sluggish inundation of water, he scrambled to his feet. More of the blackness spilled out of the sofa, thickening the mists with its taint. But the worst of it was the terrible feeling that crashed over him like the waves at Galveston, where he'd sometimes gone as a boy. Only this wasn't a physical wave but a wash of dread battering every fiber of his being.

Freddie had no more thoughts. He simply turned and tried to run toward the gap between the last mound and the fence. But, the blackness now boiling out of the sofa and blending with the mists carpeted the ground along his escape route. Abandoning all thought of wading through the black fog, he clambered up the piles of mounded earth and garbage behind him and scrambled across them until he reached the dirt lane some twenty feet behind his truck. But he was too late. The black mist had flowed around the last mound and now swirled almost sentiently around the truck's tires and lapped at the door sills. And fuck, it was spreading in his direction! Fast! Before he knew it, it was all around his legs. He ran until he was well out of it then looked down. To his horror, his boots and pants hems were stained black, and the blackness was creeping up his pants legs.

Freddie plumped down in the dirt and tore off his boots, then standing, unbuckled his pants, jerked them down and off, and dropped them beside his boots. Thank God his hands and legs didn't look contaminated. He shot another glance at his truck, but his eyes couldn't linger because the terrible mist had almost reached him again. Fear ballooning in his chest, he took off down the track, heading for the front gate. At the first junction, he threw a hasty backward glance and saw the black fog flowing down the track toward him like a slow-moving flash flood imbued with intention.

The last dregs of alcohol haze vanished beneath Freddie's panic, and he wished he could run faster. He still had strong muscles, but not for running, and smoking had worn out his lungs. But he made it to the gate ahead of the black roil, then he was through and out on the county road. He stared at the dump and saw the blackened mist spill through the margin of trees and brush between the dump and the road. Turning, he went as fast as he could up the road toward his own house, but the black mists poured onto the pavement ahead of and behind him like sluggish pincers trying to grab him. With little other choice, he staggered into the far ditch and up the other side.

Somehow, he made it through the barbed wire fence that bordered Mr. Jim's former pasturage. He lurched a couple of hundred feet across it before he had to stop, bent over, leaning on his knees, gasping for breath. His terrified eyes ranged over the grass, but the mists out here in the open were wispier and lighter and weren't moving. He turned to stare back in the direction of the dump and saw the dark thing using the fog as a vehicle flow across the road and spill into the near-side ditch. There, it rose over the lip of the ditch a little, but stopped suddenly and sank out of sight, as if it sloshed back. Maybe it didn't have enough energy to crawl up a slope, only flow flat or downhill.

Freddie didn't care what stopped it as long as it stayed back and he got away from it. Whatever it was. All he wanted right now was to be as far from the dump as possible. But he couldn't get past the mist to his home. It was all over the road, and no telling how far it had spread. The only place he could go right now was Jim Chaney's cabin, maybe a mile and a half away over open ground, directly away from the terrible fog.

With one last desperate glance at the now distant dump, he set off across the darkening pasture, fear giving him fleet feet considering he was nothing but a broken-down drunk old before his time. Who smoked way too much, he realized as his burning lungs gasped for air. But if he slowed some, he didn't stop to catch his breath until he reached the gate across the track to Mr. Jim's cabin. Then the gasps came rapid and deep until they finally slowed to about twice normal. The whole time, he leaned on his knees and scanned the field spread dimly before him in the last of the twilight.

The air was dead still, as if it held its breath. The mist was still low out there, though it was thickening and rising in the woods behind him. It looked normal—beautiful, even—in the glow from the rising gibbous moon. But he knew the calm and beauty were shallow, a surface that could be undermined all too easily by a horrible creeping darkness.

I'm quittin' cigarettes, he thought. I'm quittin' booze. Fuck all that shit.

He climbed the gate and set off down the track. It was almost pitch black beneath the tree cover, with only glimmers of moon glow to light the way. But Freddie knew the road well. Many a time, Mr. Jim had him bring supplies down to Miss Enid. Freddie knew what was going on between them. Most people in town did. The only two people who didn't know that everyone else knew were Mr. Jim and Miss Enid, themselves. He'd often thought that maybe things might have been different if they had. And then he felt guilty. He could have been the one to say something. He could have let the word slip. Sure, Mr. Jim might have fired him, but hell, he eventually did, anyway. But at least not out of rancor, only necessity. There were no hard feelings between him and Mr. Jim. After all, he'd worked for him, off and on, going on fifteen years and especially toward the end. Surely Mr. Jim would give him shelter for the night. Maybe in the daylight, with the mists burned off, he'd be able to get back to his truck.

Hell, no, he thought. No way he was going anywhere near that sofa. He didn't know what the hell was in it, but it wasn't something he ever wanted to deal with. In fact, he had no plans to return to the dump. Ever. First thing in the morning, he was walking to town to talk to Chief Bill. The chief might not believe him, but at least he'd get the terrors of the night off his chest. And maybe the chief would help him get his truck.

But right now, Freddie just hoped Jim Chaney was home. He was, and he was surprised to see Freddie, but he let him in. Freddie hadn't intended to tell Mr. Jim anything, but hell, he had to tell him something. Some reason that he had to spend the night in the cabin. Some reason he didn't have his britches or boots or truck. Something that didn't make him look crazy or drunk or like he was having the DTs. But in the end, he couldn't help blurting out he'd been chased out of the dump by something that looked like a black mist with a thousand fingers.

Maybe Mr. Jim believed him, maybe he just thought Freddie had reached his drunken bottom. Whatever he thought, he agreed to let Freddie stay the night, and gave him a pair of pants and old boots and the sofa to sleep on.

The next morning, Freddie told Mr. Jim he was walking to get his truck. That's what he wanted to do, but he was afraid to go to the dump by himself. Mr. Jim offered to drive him to the dump, but Freddie didn't want to admit he was afraid of the dump and wasn't going there, so he said he'd just walk. But he waited in the cabin long enough for the morning sun to burn off the night mists. Mr. Jim let him go, but only reluctantly since he'd been so upset.

Freddie walked to the dirt county road that served the Chaney ranch and was only a couple of hundred yards from its intersection with the paved road going to town when he heard a vehicle approaching from behind. Thinking it was Mr. Jim come after him anyway, he turned, but what he saw was a black Audi driving down the road at a good clip, dust spuming in its wake.

Freddie recognized it as belonging to that Mr. Rand fella who'd bought the last of Mr. Jim's ranch. Freddie knew the former Chaney place well and knew it needed a bunch of work. Work he'd be willing to do cheap if he could just get the man to hire him. So Freddie had gone to see if he might have any work, but the man had just said, "Not around here." Then he laughed—kind of nastily, Freddie thought—and rudely shut the door in his face.

That kinda pissed Freddie off, but not really. He was used to that from folks. Only a few people around town treated him with any kind of respect due a human being, no matter what his circumstances. But it had been easy enough to laugh off Rand's rejection.

After all, he had the dump job to back him up, and his furniture restoration business, as he liked to think of it. He didn't need to be humping for some city slicker, especially not at his age. It was a lot easier to bulldoze a few piles of earth and garbage a couple of mornings each week and spend the rest of the time relaxing in the shack, pulling on a bottle, feet up, staring at the trees, and doing as little as possible except listen to bird cries and watch squirrels scamper through the trees around the shack.

Or had been, he thought, a sinking feeling in his gut. Now all that was done with.

Freddie stopped and waved at the car, but instead of slowing down, it suddenly sped up. Shocked, Freddie realized the driver was aiming the front bumper right at him! He was closest to the south side of the road, and he turned to leap across the ditch, but a dark glimmer lurking in the shallow water there brought him to a stumbling halt. It was something he felt more than saw, some vague subconscious warning. The darkness that had pursued him the night before was down there in that ditch. He could feel it, even through his panic. There was no way he was going into that ditch.

With an almost superhuman leap born of pure existential fear, he sprang to the other side of the narrow road and threw a glance into the ditch there. Water, but no darkness. Another leap carried him across most of the ditch, just as the Audi brushed by. Had he been standing in the road, he would have been killed instantly. If he'd gone into the other ditch, well, no telling, but he remembered the oily darkness that crept up his pants legs and the creeping black mists. He scrambled over the lip of the ditch, through the barbed wire fence, and onto the pasture beyond.

Behind him, he heard the Audi grind to a stop and its door open. Then came a pop and a whining a couple of feet to his right. A fucking bullet! The fucking guy had tried to run him down or feed him to the darkness, and now he was shooting at him! Freddie did the only thing he could do under the circumstances. He ran in a broken zig-zag. The gun sounded like it was small, and Freddie was gaining distance. More pops came but he only heard one of the bullets. How much ammo did the guy have, anyway? Hell, he could have a bunch, and so far, he'd only shot seven. Or maybe more if Freddie had gotten far enough away that he couldn't hear the pops anymore over the sound of his labored breathing.

He risked a glance over his shoulder. Back on the road, the Audi was pulling off, heading for the paved road. There, it turned toward town. The guy would be up there somewhere along the road, waiting to intercept him. Well, the hell if that was gonna happen. And even if it didn't, who was gonna believe who? Would Chief Bill believe him over the word of the Audi's driver? After all, what motive could Rand have to wantonly run him down or shoot him? And Freddie's only defense was he'd been chased out of the dump, near naked, by some creeping evil darkness. Fuck that. The chief would just chalk it up to Freddie's drunkenness, which he'd dealt with all too often.

For the umpteenth time since he'd fled the dump, Freddie swore he was going to give up booze and smokes if it was the last thing he was gonna do.

But now, Freddie couldn't even go to Turner. Not with his wild story. Nor could he go to the dump to get his truck. Not yet. No way he wanted to encounter that darkness that crept into the ground mists. It might still be hanging out in the dump. But he thought he might be able to go to his house. Surely, Rand didn't know where he lived. Freddie was without his truck, but he had a plan—a place to go where creeping mists and Rand couldn't find him. It was a long way away. Too far to easily walk, but he had that old bicycle he'd salvaged and fixed up but rarely rode.

"I went home and got my bike, but I was too afraid to stay right then and get any of my stuff except for some cash. I really didn't plan, much. I just wanted to get the hell outa Dodge. After that, I rode to town on some cow paths along the edge of the Grant property to get supplies at the grocery. Then I hightailed it out to the sandpit. I been back to the house a couple a times, but mostly I been out there, sweatin' the booze outta my system. It was pretty rough that first week, and I nearly broke down with the shakes and bad dreams, but I pulled through and feel better, now. At least I thought I did since I thought I was safe, but it looks like you found me, Chief." Freddie leaned forward in his chair. "Now I done told you everything, though I know you ain't gonna believe a word of it. Can I go?"

"The thing is, Freddie, we do believe you," Turner said. "And I'm afraid you can't go. Not yet. You'll have to spend the night here. You'll be safe in jail for the time being."

Freddie went pale, his eyes lit with fear.

"If you believe me, Chief Bill, you know there ain't no place safe in this town."

Guthrie silently agreed with that.

But Freddie let the chief lead him out of the office to the cell-block without protest.

"What now?" Guthrie asked after Turner came back.

"Now we have probable cause to roust George Rand. You armed?"

44

TURNER TORE UP THE PAVED county road as he drove south, though he didn't turn on the Interceptor's lights or siren. Guthrie could feel tension radiating from the chief, and he was seriously tense himself. It didn't take long to reach the dirt county road that led to Rand's house and Chaney Marsh, and once Turner swerved onto it, he slowed to a more reasonable pace.

"No sense making Rand more wary than he already is," Turner said.

"I don't think wariness will be an issue," Guthrie replied.

"Meaning?"

"When he came here, he thought he'd find anonymity and easy pickings like he did in Airla. He wasn't counting on someone like me coming in, knowing too much, and disrupting his plans. But now he knows we've got him in our sights, and a confrontation has to come. He won't be wary, he'll be watchful and waiting."

Whether Rand was watchful or not was moot because he wasn't waiting. As Turner pulled up the long dirt drive to the house, the Audi was nowhere in sight. They got out of the Interceptor, both loosening their pistols but not drawing them, and mounted the porch. Turner banged loudly on the door with his fist

"Thorndike police, Mr. Rand," he yelled several times and banged some more. But the house remained silent. And the Kuei men weren't twitching, which told Guthrie more certainly than the silence that Rand wasn't home.

"He's not here," he said.

"You think he skipped?"

"I doubt it. Let's look around."

Turner nodded, and they descended to the ground and walked around the corner of the house.

"You take the garage, the coop, and those sheds." Turner gestured toward the several smaller outbuildings scattered between the house and barn. "I'll check the barn."

They split up, and Guthrie went to the garage and pulled open the side-hinged doors. The space was half filled with junk, old furniture, and two rusted-out riding lawn mowers, and half with a nondescript gray Ford sedan with Louisiana plates that was several years old. It wasn't dusty, though everything else in the garage was. Guthrie tried the door handles, but the car was locked. He didn't see anything unusual through the windows, though the presence of the car was curious. The chicken coop was empty except for racks of roosts still littered with old hay and feathers. Apparently the coop hadn't held any chickens for quite some time as even the odor inside had faded to a musty shade. After that, he looked in the first shed, which held an assortment of shovels, rakes, picks, and other hand tools. The second shed was completely empty, the dust on the floor testifying it hadn't been used for a long while.

He left the shed and was walking toward the barn, from which Turner had not yet emerged, when he noticed the pump house. A small, square wooden structure, it sat near the old stone-rimmed well. He headed toward it just as Turner came out of the barn. As he got closer, something warned him that things weren't right, but it wasn't the Kuei men twitching. It was his nose. The distinct odor coming from the pump house was the effluvium from a corpse.

"Over here!" he called to Turner.

"Something dead," Turner said after he came close. "Something big."

They approached the pump house door, both of them bracing themselves as Guthrie opened it. But the only thing inside was the water pump.

They stepped back and simultaneously stared at the old stone well. It looked bucolic, with its little ramshackle roof held up by two support beams, only wanting an old wooden bucket to complete the scene. But there was no bucket, and the well opening was covered by a square of warping, weather-stained plywood. Turner levered the plywood off, and as it clattered to the side of the well, the stink of putrefaction billowed into the air.

"Jesus," Turner gasped, stepping back and averting his head.

"You have a flashlight?"

"In my vehicle."

As Turner hurried to the Interceptor, Guthrie backed off thirty feet to remove himself from the worst of the cloud of stench enveloping the well. Turner returned in moments with two flashlights and two pairs of nitrile gloves. The flashlights weren't as powerful as the instrument Guthrie had saved from his last case for Tereba, but they were powerful enough.

Both men donned the gloves then covered their mouths and noses with their handkerchiefs as they approached the well, leaned over the opening, and shone the lights into its depths. The water table was shallow here, only thirty or forty feet down, and their lights clearly showed a bloated and decaying naked human corpse floating in the dark water.

"Fuck," Turner said, stepping back. "Not another one. Who do you think it is?"

"Detective Peters in Oakdale said he heard Rand had an older man with him in Airla. Someone he called his father, who wasn't actually his father but his uncle, Claude Fortier. The head of one of the villages destroyed in southern Louisiana."

"You think that's him?"

"We haven't seen him here. I can't think of anybody else it might be."

"Damn. I guess I'd better call Dr. Bob."

"Not now," Guthrie said. "Later."

"We can't let this go."

"We're not. But he's not going anywhere, and we have more important matters to attend to."

"Such as?"

In answer, Guthrie waved toward the house.

"We need to look inside there."

"I'll need another search warrant."

Guthrie didn't immediately respond but went to the well, holding his breath, and slid the plywood back on top. Then he started toward the house, Turner reluctantly following. They went up the steps, and when Guthrie reached the front door, he paused for just a moment, gathered himself, then slammed his foot against the door next to the lock. The door frame splintered, and the door jolted inward.

"Oh, look, Chief," he said. "Somebody kicked in the door, and there's a body in the well. Maybe we ought to check to make sure the owner's okay."

"That's probable cause enough for me," Turner said.

They both drew their guns and entered the house. Inside, the place looked like just another old farmhouse filled with old farmhouse furniture and decorations—not much different than Miss Agnes's home. But the surfaces were dusty, and the air was musty and stale, as if the windows hadn't been opened in a long time.

"You look down here," Turner said. "I'll take the upstairs."

They went their separate ways, the old stairs creaking as Turner ascended. Guthrie went through most of the lower floor, noticing that the only two rooms Rand seemed to have used much were the kitchen and a parlor that had been converted to an office with a desktop computer and printer and a stack of file boxes. There wasn't even a TV in the living room. The kitchen sink was empty of dishes, though several sat neatly in a dish drainer. There was no kitchen table, but four old wooden chairs with cracking dark blue vinyl seats were roughly arranged around a space where a table might have been.

Suddenly, he heard a yell from upstairs. He hurried up and found Turner in one of the bedrooms. Only it was no longer a bedroom. It was a torture chamber, empty except for an old black iron bedstead holding a bare mattress, a wooden table next to it that matched the chairs in the kitchen, and a five-drawer chest painted dull green against one wall. Plastic sheeting covered the floor under the bed and the wall behind it, and two rolls of plastic sheeting lay on the shelf of the small, open closet. A pair of folded photographic tripods leaned against the back wall beneath the shelf.

From the bloodstains on the mattress, it had seen use, but the blood wasn't excessive. Probably the mattress had been covered with plastic sheeting during use. Pairs of handcuffs were affixed to the headboard and footboard, and a bondage mask with a red rubber ball gag lay on the table along with a variety of surgical instruments, knives, pliers, tin snips, and small power tools. The tools looked clean, but the tabletop was spattered with dried blood and gave off a mild but foul odor.

Guthrie opened the dresser's top drawer, and Turner joined him. Several objects were inside: two wallets and cell phones and two digital cameras, one for stills, the other for video. Next to them was a thick, black scrapbook binder with the word, "Memories," embossed in gold on the cover. Turner picked up the wallets one by one and looked inside. The first belonged to Norman Telfor and the other to Jeff Mayfield.

"I'd guess the phones are theirs," Guthrie said.

Turner replaced the wallets and pulled out the binder, laid it on top of the dresser, and flipped back the cover. Four photos—old Polaroids—were affixed to the first page, all showing young women in various stages of being tortured, a name and date neatly typed on a small label affixed beneath each. About two thirds of the other pages held more of the same, though after a dozen pages, the Polaroids were replaced by clearer digital images printed on photo paper. There were dozens of photos, dozens of victims. Only the last two pages were different. In the several photos spread across them, Jeff Mayfield was chained to the bed, obviously in pain and distress. More than one set of arms had done the work, and the tattoos on one of them looked like the serpents that twined around Wiley Sanford's forearms. The last two photos showed the castration, clearly performed by Rand himself.

"Jesus fucking Christ," was all that Turner could say.

Guthrie closed the binder and put it back in the drawer. He'd seen enough, and apparently so had Turner. Certainly all they wanted to see. He shut the drawer and opened the second one. It held cases of various sorts of video media, from tapes to DVDs to sim cards.

"I don't want to see what's on those," Turner said, voice heavy.

Guthrie didn't either. He shut the drawer and opened the next. It contained a great number of small objects: rings, necklaces, and other mostly cheap jewelry, all jumbled together. The fourth drawer held dozens of small plastic ziplock bags, each with a typed label. A close look revealed that each bag contained a severed, almost mummified, finger. The most disturbing item was a glass jar holding two small bloody spheres in a clear liquid tinged red.

"You think those are Jeff's…?"

Turner couldn't finish, but Guthrie nodded anyway.

"Who the fuck is this guy?" Turner said softly, stepping back as Guthrie closed the drawer and opened the last one. Thankfully, it was empty, but it gave Rand plenty of room to expand "He must have killed all those women? And Jeff, too."

"And probably Norm Telfor and whoever is in the well," Guthrie said. "Remember that the two prostitutes who gave him an alibi for the murder of his parents were later found dead, both with missing fingers. I've learned that the police in New Orleans and Baton Rouge have been looking for more than a decade for a serial killer whose signature is to take a forefinger from his victims." Guthrie shook his head, filled with a mix of sorrow, disgust, and anger. "Looks like Rand's been a busy boy, but he probably didn't do much of it here. He hasn't lived here long enough." He waved around the room. "But a setup like this wasn't created and used by an amateur. It seems George Rand is more of a predator than we gave him credit for."

Turner surveyed the room, obviously aghast, then he gave Guthrie an almost helpless look. Guthrie could sympathize, but not right now. Right now, they had to act. But Turner couldn't quite abandon his training.

"Now we call the coroner. And the sheriff and DPS."

"Not yet."

"But we have to...."

"Listen to me, Bill. That will only complicate matters, and it won't stop what's killing Thorndike. Destroying that thing is what we have to do. As soon as possible. Hetty said Wiley and Lonnie were about to take care of something. That can only be helping Rand take legal possession of the marsh. He's been down there nearly every day, trying to force Jim to sell., and he took the Sanfords with him yesterday to threaten Jim with violence. You know what a stubborn coot that old man is, and he's resisted so far, but Rand knows we know about the thing in the marsh. He also knows I'm onto him about the serial killings. He doesn't realize we've seen the proof, but he knows I won't stop. His time is growing short, and he needs to hold legal title to the marsh so he can take full possession of Thorndike before we can corner him. I think he's down there right now, closing the deal. Besides, the miasma has grown too powerful to ignore. You felt its power. Can you imagine that flowing over town, infecting it even more than it already has? We can't wait another day, or Thorndike will be lost. We can deal with all of this later."

Or maybe not, he thought, if they didn't have a later.

"I need some air," Turner said, shaking his head. "I'm not used to this. I can't think in here."

"Nobody's used to this," Guthrie said, "except those who commit such atrocities."

The chief clumped down the stairs and out into the daylight, Guthrie following. They stood beside the Interceptor for several minutes, neither one speaking. Turner couldn't stop glancing between the well and the house. Guthrie, though, stared across the overgrown pasture south of the old Chaney house, eyes taking in the edge of the marsh's forest.

The malignant force had been born in a swamp and now occupied a marsh, and in between, it had resided in a damp forest. It could perhaps occupy something like the old sofa, but only briefly, like a human could endure sitting in a coach airline seat for a few hours but not permanently. It needed dark, damp space to live in and rot, cruelty, chaos, and misery to feed off and empower and extend its corrupting influence.

But maybe there was a way to take all that away from it, he thought, as a plan began to form in his mind.

"I think I'm beginning to see we might have a way of getting rid of it," he said.

Something in his tone sparked some life into Turner. Some hope. But it was a bare glimmer.

"How, when we can't even get down there?"

"You can't get down there, Bill, but I can if I go alone."

"Alone? Fuck that. I can't let you go down there by yourself. Look what almost happened the last time."

"And what happened? You almost shot me. What's going to happen now that it's even more powerful? Besides, I have some protection."

Apparently, Turner no longer questioned what Guthrie meant by "it," but he still wasn't satisfied.

"Your sixth sense? You think that's going to do you any good?"

He'd never show his talisman to anybody, but maybe he had to reveal it to Turner.

"It's more than a sixth sense. I'm sure you've realized that by now. I want you to look at this."

Turner stared as Guthrie lifted his shirt and tugged down on his belt buckle it to expose the Kuei tattooed beneath his navel.

"A tattoo?" Turner sounded skeptical.

"Not just any tattoo. It's a talisman called the Armor of the Earth. It was put there over my power center by a powerful sorcerer to help protect me from supernatural forces."

Turner was silent for a moment, then he nodded slightly.

"Okay," he said. "It guess it's no crazier than everything else that's been happening, and you're the only one who hasn't been affected by the thing in the marsh. You got me out when I could barely function. But what about me? I can't just sit around twiddling my thumbs while you and my town get destroyed."

"You'll have plenty else to do. It'll be a two-pronged attack. But we're going to need help."

"As in who? Nobody's going to believe a word of this. Hell, I do only because you've walked me through it. Walked me down the road to Jim's cabin. Or tried to."

"There is one person who will believe us. And he's just the person we need."

45

"You want to take the sofa, too?" Dr. Bob asked as he dropped the keys to Freddie's pickup into Turner's hand. He didn't sound serious, though his voice held a hopeful note.

It was well after hours, but Turner had called the ME at home and asked him to meet them at the coroner's office.

"Yeah," Turner said curtly, tossing the keys to Guthrie. "We're taking that, too."

"I'm not sure...." Latimer began but Turner cut him off.

"We're about to put a lid on this case. We need that sofa."

"Are you bringing it back?"

"No."

Latimer was obviously puzzled, but he held up his hands and shook his head.

"Like I said, I don't want to know."

He led them outside to the lighted compound behind the building, where the shed holding the sofa stood. Freddie's pickup was parked next to it.

"Can't say I'm sad to see it go," Latimer said as he unlocked the shed door. "I didn't really want the damned thing around, anyway."

Guthrie and Turner donned leather work gloves they'd brought along, dragged the sofa out of the shed, and loaded it into the bed of Freddie's pickup. It was still nasty and foul, though not quite as pungently as before, and the kicking of the Kuei men was much reduced. But it was heavy as hell. Then Guthrie drove the pickup onto the street through a side gate Dr. Bob held open. He waited for Turner to go back through the building to the front lot where his Interceptor was parked, then he followed the SUV's taillights through town and south to Thorndike. Guthrie had hoped he would be able to withstand the foul aura exuded by the sofa long enough to make it to town, and he didn't have too much trouble. It probably helped having it in the bed of the pickup and not right behind him. That would come all too soon.

In Thorndike, they pulled into the police station parking lot and emerged from the vehicles.

"I still think you shouldn't go to Jim's cabin alone," Turner said. "If Wiley and Lonnie are with Rand down there, that's too many."

"There's no other way. You know you can't make it, and I can't be worrying about you the whole time. I have to go alone. We need to stick to the plan. As soon as they realize what's going on, one or more of them are sure to come your way."

"I still don't like it. It's way past dark, and from what you say, this thing is strongest at night. We can't wait until morning?"

"We can't wait at all," Guthrie said. "If Rand is down there now, he's not coming out until he's taken legal possession of the marsh. But you're right. Our enemies have plenty of firepower. Maybe we could use an extra hand."

"Who? Emmet? I can't pull him into this mess."

"Who else? He's already involved. He's seen most of the mayhem that's been going on, and he's already suspicious something's out of the ordinary."

"But what am I going to say to him about that...thing in the marsh? He'll never believe any of it."

"He doesn't have to believe, just help you."

"And what's going to help us?" Turner asked, trepidation in his voice. "You know what happened the last time I tried to go into the marsh. I don't want Emmet and me to start shooting each other."

"You won't be going all the way in," Guthrie said. "Just to the edge. And I think the thing will be more concentrated on me since I'll be attacking Rand. It won't realize what you're doing even if it can realize anything. But maybe we ought to hedge your bet."

"How? So far, you're the only person it doesn't seem to affect. You have that talisman?"

"I can't transfer any of its protection to you, but remember all the garlic around Jim's cabin? It helped keep the thing in the marsh at bay, so it ought to help you, too."

"Where are we going to get that much garlic? You heard Jim say he'd bought all he could in town and everywhere around."

"Bev works at a restaurant. I can't believe Leo doesn't have a supply on hand."

So they drove to Turner's house to get Bev to open up the cafe.

"You want what?" she asked, incredulous. "Why?"

"I can't tell you right now, sweetheart," Turner said. "I'll tell you everything later, but right now, we need all the garlic you can find."

"This have something to do with what's going on down at Jim Chaney's place?"

Turner looked surprised.

"How'd you know about that?"

"Really, Bill?" She gave him a severe look. "You and Clay are always going down there, and that's where poor Jeff Mayfield was attacked. But you said you were in a hurry."

She went to the kitchen and came out with a few cloves of garlic and a shaker of garlic powder. Then the three of them hurried over to Leo's, where she found a dozen cloves of garlic in the kitchen and three shakers of garlic powder. She put it all in a plastic grocery sack.

"Does Leo have a garlic press?" Guthrie asked, taking the sack from her.

Bev nodded, found it, and handed it over. Guthrie dropped it into the sack with the garlic.

"Just tell me one thing true, Clay," Bev said, face stiff with worry. "Did you bring this here?"

"I did not."

"He was sent here to fix things, Bev," Turner said.

"You sure of that?" Her eyes shifted to her husband.

"Dead sure."

"Is that right?" Her eyes turned back to Guthrie. "You're here to fix it?"

"I am."

She stepped back and nodded.

"Then go fix it, whatever it is."

"Thanks, sweetheart," Turner said. Then he gripped her by the shoulders. "I love you more than I can say. Now please go home and lock the doors."

"You stay safe." She looked at Guthrie. "You, too, Clay." Then to Turner again, "I'll see you in the morning." It was a statement, but it just as easily could have been a question.

"Bill will tell you everything when it's all over," Guthrie assured her. At least he hoped so, because something would be all over for sure. But would it be the miasma and Rand or Guthrie and his makeshift band?

Bev stared at Guthrie for a long moment, then she turned and embraced her husband.

"You better tell me everything," she said, "or there's going to be hell to pay."

The three of them left the cafe, and after Bev locked up, she walked up the block to the Turner's house. Guthrie noticed she didn't look back.

"You have a hell of a wife," he told Turner as they entered the police station.

"Yeah," the chief said.

Inside, Turner called Emmet, who arrived fifteen minutes later, obviously puzzled.

"What's going on, Chief?" he asked.

"Listen, Emmet. I'm going to ask you to do something without a whole lot of explanation. You can go home, if you want, but Clay and I will proceed. We have to. The whole town of Thorndike is at stake."

"Does this have to do with all the weird, ugly shit that's been going on?"

"It has everything to do with it," Guthrie said. "We're going to end it. Tonight. But it'll be very dangerous."

"Chief?" Emmet asked, looking at Turner.

"Look, we don't have time to convince you of something you're not likely to believe right off. It's taken Clay nearly two weeks to make me see the truth, and he had to rub my nose in it. But if we don't succeed tonight, Thorndike is doomed. I need you to trust my word for that, because we need your help."

"All right." Emmet said, obviously stressed by what Turner said. "I've always trusted you before, so I'm not stopping now. And Clay's solid. I'll help. Besides, my family lives here. I'm not letting anything happen to them."

"You'll probably feel and see things that won't seem pleasant or real," Guthrie said. "But you won't be in the thick of that. Your job will be to help Chief Turner protect Freddie."

"Protect him from who?"

"The Sanford brothers are down in Chaney Marsh with George Rand, and they're armed with some of Buster's stolen weapons. Once they realize what Freddie's doing, they'll try to stop him."

"What's Freddie going to be doing?"

46

"WELL, I AIN'T," FREDDIE SAID after Turner got him out of his cell, brought him into the office. "I ain't goin' down there. Ever."

"Yes," Turner said. "You are."

"I can't."

"Where you going to go?" Turner asked. "Back to Dixon sandpit?"

"At least I'm safe out there."

"No," Guthrie said. "If you go out there, you'll never be safe from the knowledge that your inaction helped destroy the town you've called home your entire life."

"Thorndike never give a shit about me...."

"Jim Chaney cared about you, and he's down in his cabin right now, fighting a losing battle for his life. When the evil that's down there is finished with him, it will finish off Thorndike. People will get hurt. People will die. You want that on your conscience?"

"I can live with that," Freddie said.

"You can't, and you won't," Turner said harshly. "You grew up here. You played football for the high school. This town sustained you until you lost yourself, and then Jim helped you. I helped you when you needed it most. You're going to do this for me and for Jim, but most of all, you're going to do it for yourself—to prove that you're more than what you've become. Remember the black fog that drove you out of the dump? Drove you away from everything you ever knew?"

Freddie nodded hesitantly, eyes fearful and downcast.

"When it attacked you, you ran to Jim, and he helped you. Now it's now down in Jim's marsh, and he needs your help. All of Thorndike needs your help. And I'm telling you this: If you don't do what we're asking you to do, I'm going to drag you down to the marsh and personally feed you to the darkness because that's where you'll belong."

Freddie was already scared, but that threat made fear rise into his eyes like a dark flame.

"You wouldn't do…."

"I would, and I will. Mr. Guthrie isn't even from Thorndike, yet he's risking everything he has to help save us. And so is Emmet, and so am I. Now it's your turn to step up and help us make a touchdown, just like you did when we became regional champions. You remember that, don't you? How it felt to be needed and important?"

"I can't go anywhere near that," Freddie said. "I don't think my heart can take it."

"We're not asking you to go into the marsh," Guthrie said. "We just need you to do something nobody else in town can. And Chief Turner and Emmet will be with you every moment."

Emmet had been watching the exchange among the other three, eyes wide, mouth half open.

"I'm not sure I'm getting all of this, Chief," he said, voice tentative. "Are you saying there's some kind of evil thing down in Chaney Marsh that's been causing everything to go wrong? And we're going to get rid of it?"

The way the other three looked at him shut him up. He blinked, as if doing so might erase what was beginning to look like a bad dream, but the others were still looking at him the same way.

"I said you have to trust me," Turner reminded him.

Emmet didn't look convinced, but he nodded.

"Okay, Chief. There's some weird shit going on in town, some of it in proximity to the marsh. Tell me what you want me to do."

Guthrie quickly outlined the plan he'd come up with it while he and Turner stood beside the Interceptor at Rand's house. Turner agreed it might be the only thing that would work, but it was risky, especially for Guthrie, who'd have to enter the marsh alone. There was no way Turner or Emmet could go into it, now. The force lurking there had grown too powerful. No doubt Rand and the Sanfords were in sync with it somehow, but Guthrie knew that an unprotected man wouldn't be able to make the journey. Even shielded by the Kuei men, maybe even he couldn't. And he knew he wouldn't just be facing the cursed miasma that clung like a pestilence to the rotting marsh.

"I'll do it, Chief Bill," Freddie said at last in reluctant agreement. "But you gotta be with me. You and Officer Taylor. I ain't doin' it by myself."

"We'll be with you the whole time," Turner assured him. Then he opened one of his desk drawers, removed the baggie holding Freddie's wallet, pocketknife, and change, and handed it over. "Here. If you're driving, you'll need your license."

The absurdity of the statement made all four of them laugh, but it wasn't merry laughter, and it didn't last long.

"One last thing," Guthrie said, holding up the plastic grocery bag holding the garlic. "We need our repellent. Hold out your hand, Emmet."

"You want us to smear that all over our skin?" Emmet asked after Guthrie had squeezed a garlic clove through the press, dropping the wad of garlic goo into the officer's hand.

"I know it sounds crazy," Turner said. "Just do it." He held out his own hand.

In short order, all four of them reeked of garlic. Guthrie might have the Kuei men to protect him, but he figured he'd hedge his bet. Then he opened one of the shakers of garlic powder and shook some in his hair and over his clothes. The others followed suit.

"I hope this shit wears off pretty quick," Freddie said, nose wrinkling. "I stink as bad as a skunk."

After that, they went out to the parking lot. The second that Freddie saw the sofa sitting in the bed of his truck, he shied back.

"What's this, Chief Bill?" he shrilled. "You never said nothin' about that sofa. I ain't goin' near that."

"The thing that was in it isn't there anymore," Guthrie assured him. "You won't have to drive it, anyway We're moving it to my vehicle. It'll stink and feel bad, but only while we're handling it. Remember, you're protected by the garlic."

"Here." Turner passed pairs of work gloves to Freddie and Emmet.

Together, the four of them dragged the sofa off Freddie's truck and maneuvered it into the back of the Xterra. Guthrie had to lay down the back seats to make the interior space longer, but even so, the sofa protruded several feet past the bumper. He tied the back hatch down with rope and looped more rope around the end of the sofa to anchor it in place. The three gallon can of gas he'd bought earlier at the Pit Stop when he'd filled the Xterra's tank went on the floor of the front passenger seat, right next to a chainsaw that had been part of Buster Havasau's stolen merchandise.

Then they went back inside to arm themselves. In addition to carrying their handguns, Turner, Emmet, and Guthrie chose ARs with pouches of extra magazines from the stockpile in the cell. Turner handed a .38 revolver to Freddie, who took it gingerly.

"I ain't shot much," he said.

"If you see anybody who isn't one of us or Jim Chaney," Turner said, "You shoot him."

In addition, Guthrie. Turner, and Emmet each took a night-vision headset. After that, they all went outside to the vehicles.

"How long will it take you to get ready?" Guthrie asked Freddie.

"An hour," the man answered. "I can drive up the road to the old cemetery with the truck. That'll get me real close, then it's only another half mile across the pasture and through the trees, but it'll be easy goin'. I know just how to get there."

"I'm holding you to it," Guthrie said, glancing at his watch. "One hour, Chief."

"We'll be there."

Then Guthrie watched as Freddie got into his pickup and pulled off, Turner and Emmet following in Turner's Interceptor.

"One hour," he muttered to himself.

He got into the Xterra and pulled out after the other two vehicles. By now, it was nearly one AM, and the streets of Thorndike were deserted, but he had to drive slowly because of the load in the back. The taillights of Freddie's pickup and Turner's Interceptor vanished in the fog in just a couple of minutes. At last, he reached the dirt county road that led to Rand's house on one side and the marsh on the other. There, he stopped and cut his headlights so he wouldn't betray his approach. He donned the night-vision goggles and pulled off, scanning ahead and to the sides as he eased down the road, keeping the crunching of his tires on the gravel to a minimum. Inside two minutes, the green glow from the goggles revealed the entrance to the track to Chaney's cabin. He turned down it and, a few moments later, saw that the gate that normally barred the track from unwanted visitors stood wide open.

47

GOOD, GUTHRIE THOUGHT. THAT MEANT someone had driven down here, which also meant that the fallen tree might no longer be an obstacle. He'd been afraid he might have to cut it up with the chainsaw, exposing himself to human attack as well as to the miasma. And snakes. But it was too early to drive farther. He stopped, put the transmission into park, and checked his watch. Thirty-five minutes to go.

He switched off the engine, removed the night vision headset, and got out of the vehicle so he could breathe easier. The sofa might have been partly rid of its foul residue, but even with all the Xterra's windows down, it still exuded stench and a nasty feeling. The reek of the garlic in the enclosed space didn't help. Also, he wanted to hear the sounds of the night. But there were no sounds. No sounds at all. Even beneath the nearly full moon illuminating the pastures around, the dark woods across the fence line seemed almost solid with billowing, pulsing menace. The only movement was mist preternaturally oozing blackly across the pastures toward town. That and the Kuei men buzzing beneath Guthrie's buckle.

His eyes roved over the ground around, and he noticed a lumpy something embedded in the dark mist. On closer inspection, it proved to be a black trash bag. He couldn't smell the contents because of the reek of his own skin, but it proved to be garlic. A whole lot of garlic. Rand and the Sanfords must have removed all the garlic from around Chaney's cabin and deposited it here, just outside the confines of the marsh. That didn't encourage Guthrie. With the garlic gone, the miasma had nothing to stop it from invading the cabin, allowing Rand to focus it on Chaney. He remembered that Chaney had said he'd eaten a lot of garlic too, and Guthrie could only hope that would help protect the old man from the miasma, if not from the human predators confronting him.

Leaving the bag where it was, and more reluctant to let the mists envelop him than he was to endure the smell of garlic and the foul emanations from the sofa, he got back into his truck, donned the night-vision headset, and tried to breath shallowly.

The minutes crept by. The mists rose and darkened even more, almost opaque to the moonlight. The Kuei men buzzed, filling Guthrie's belly with warmth and energy. So far, the green glow of the night-vision goggles betrayed no movement in the trees or along the road. He checked the time again. Five minutes.

And then the five minutes were gone. Hoping like hell that Turner, Emmet, and Freddie were in position, Guthrie fired up the engine, rolled up the windows, and eased through the gate. Just beyond, the billowing darkness enveloped him.

He'd wondered how powerful its repulsive energy had become, but driving through it was different than walking. Walking was like pushing through water, but driving wasn't much different than feeling a slow, steady acceleration. Apparently, the force affected and worked against the movement of living flesh, not against that of machines. Or maybe it was now too extenuated in the direction of town, weakening its influence in the marsh. Plus, the Xterra's cab was filled with the odor of garlic and Guthrie's belly with the vibrations of the Kuei men.

But that didn't mean Guthrie didn't feel malign and sinister oppression pressing in from all sides around his protective cocoon. To prevent the pressure from seeping into him and decaying into panic, Guthrie kept his speed low and deliberate. He didn't want any snags at this late stage.

The first two bends passed, and then he saw the fallen tree. Or what had been the fallen tree. It was now cut into pieces that had been dragged far enough to either side of the track that vehicles could pass. Thank goodness for that, he thought.

He drove through the gap, branches scraping the sides of the Xterra and peered ahead to see if the road would be inundated with snakes. But none appeared, and the bodies of the ones he and Turner had shot were absent. Maybe they'd been eaten by the still-living snakes since there was no other prey left alive in the marsh. But even if they'd swarmed out onto the road, they'd have been no deterrent and would be easily crushed beneath his tires. He looked off to the left, hoping to catch a glimpse of light or sounds coming from the far-eastern end of the marsh, but there was nothing. Had Freddie miscalculated the amount of time it would take him to prepare? Surely, Turner would have urged him on, made him comply. Guthrie contemplated stopping, then decided against it. He had to believe they were in play. Stopping would only make things worse for him. He was in motion, and now the only thing to do was to remain in motion.

Then he had to stop as the hammering of a fully-automatic weapon ripped the air, and four rounds smashed through his windshield. He threw himself awkwardly across the console, feeling the gear shift grip grate his ribcage. Ignoring the pain and praying that none of the bullets hit the gas can, he used his left hand to throw the transmission into park while the fingers of his other hand snagged the handle on the passenger door. The door opened, and he crawled out, groping for his AR as he fell onto the ground. Just in time as more automatic fire tore through the driver's door, ripping into the seat back.

He crouched behind the front right wheel for a moment, the malignant black mists swirling more forcefully and purposefully around him, clutching and dragging at him but failing to get past the Kuei men's shielding. His mind recalled Freddie's description—a thousand black fingers—but he tried to ignore the sensation, trust the Kuei men's protection, and ease his breathing. He wanted to lie prone and peer beneath the truck, but the black mist was too thick that close to the ground, impossible to see through. And he sure didn't want to breathe any more of it than he had to. Instead, bucking the pressure growing around him, he moved to the rear, where he could look over the butt-end of the sofa protruding from the bed. More fire came, and this time he saw muzzle flashes from the left as the rounds punched into the Xterra, taking out half the windshield and perforating the doors and body. Two shooters. Probably the Sanfords. The night-vision goggles showed one as a dim man shape among the trees about a hundred and fifty feet into the woods, but he couldn't spot the other.

So far, Guthrie hadn't revealed that he might still be alive, and he kept still, observing the man shape move closer to the road, darting from tree to tree.

Guthrie's own AR was only a semi-auto, but it would have to do. Taking careful aim and tracking the figure, he was about to squeeze off as many shots as he could before either man returned fire, but a sudden flare of light shone dimly through the mists and trees at the eastern end of the marsh. It was accompanied by the muted but heavy growl of machinery.

The light and sound galvanized the men in the woods, who sent more bullets into the Xterra before racing toward the road, the second man rising from behind a clump of brush. They must have intersected the road around the next bend since Guthrie couldn't see them after that. But they were certainly headed for the cabin to warn Rand that something wasn't going to plan. Hopefully, they'd also report they'd killed Guthrie, or at least disabled him.

After keeping still for a few moments to make sure the men weren't just hiding, waiting for him to emerge, Guthrie shut the passenger door then hurried around and opened the driver's door. Considering how many rounds had gone through it, he was amazed the mechanism still worked, though it was stiff and the door wouldn't close properly. The back cushion was shredded, and the seat was strewn with glass. He brushed the worst of it off, slid into the seat, and used the butt of the AR to hammer out enough of the remains of the windshield that his vision wouldn't be obstructed. Also amazing, most of the bullets had been aimed at the cab, and the truck's engine was still running, though he could hear a hiss of steam and smell the stink of hot oil and radiator fluid.

He put the transmission in gear and, not wanting to advertise that he was still alive and approaching, pulled off, keeping his speed low. In two minutes, Jim Chaney's pickup came into view. Parked close by were Rand's Audi and Wiley's truck. Guthrie pulled behind them, got out, bringing the AR, and scurried over to Chaney's Ford. From there, he looked down the slope at the cabin. It hulked darkly in the green light, bright slivers fluorescing around the doors and shuttered windows. Light also flared from the corner at the rear of the cabin, indicating that the lights over the deck were on. He could hear shouting coming from inside. Then the front door opened, and Lonnie Sanford and Frank Orman emerged carrying carbines and wearing night-vision goggles. So, Orman had joined the Sanfords in helping Rand subdue Thorndike. He'd been the one with Lonnie, shooting at the Xterra from the woods, not Wiley, who was framed in the bright green rectangle behind them.

"Go see what's goin' on," Wiley ordered. "I'm stayin' with Mr. Rand."

Lonnie and Frank levered the night-vision headsets over their eyes and headed toward the path that wound east along the edge of the pond. From that direction, lights, bobbing and weaving, still shone, and a heavy machine at work still sounded. Wiley slammed the door, and Guthrie heard the three deadbolts being shot home.

Guthrie waited two minutes to give Lonnie and Orman time to leave the vicinity of the cabin, then he turned the Xterra around, aimed it down the short slope toward the pond, and pressed the accelerator. In a second, the vehicle was bouncing backward toward the pond. Guthrie jammed on the brakes, slewing to a halt at the edge of the water. In another second, he was out of the truck and ducking behind it. The lights under the deck cover were too bright for the night-vision headset, so he tore it off and dropped it, all the while keeping an eye on the cabin's back door. A moment later, it opened a crack, and Wiley, holding an AR, took a cautious look outside. Guthrie shot at him, but the rounds splintered the door frame instead of Wiley's head as he quickly withdrew.

Guthrie churned up the short slope, the pressure of the miasma slowing but not completely hindering his progress. At the corner of the cabin, he peered around at the deck and back door. The door was shut and probably bolted, but Guthrie had been inside and knew the location of all three bolts Chaney had installed in a futile attempt to keep out unwanted visitors. Guthrie eased around the corner and onto the deck, hoping the boards wouldn't creak beneath his weight. He managed to get to the door without making much noise, and there, he aimed and quickly shot out all three locks then pivoted to the side and jumped several feet away, doubting that the cabin wall could withstand AR fire. It couldn't, but the door was the main recipient of bad luck as Wiley emptied his whole magazine through the panel, smashing a ragged hole through its middle. Wood splinters flew onto the deck, and Guthrie could hear slugs smacking the black water beyond. Then came a pause. Wiley had to be reloading.

Guthrie pivoted and kicked in the door.

48

THROUGH THE OPEN DOORWAY, GUTHRIE saw Wiley in the foreground, slamming another magazine into his AR. Off to the side, Rand stood next to the kitchen table, a small black pistol in his hand. Beside him sat Jim Chaney, bloody and beaten and bound in a chair. Hetty Mruska, snarling, crouched behind Chaney, holding a large kitchen knife to his throat. Then Wiley, reloaded, jerked the barrel of the AR toward Guthrie, who spun away from the door frame and threw himself to the side. An instant later, the frame shattered, and a line of holes splintered the wall next to it.

Guthrie had to get some traction, had to neutralize Wiley and get to Rand. That might be difficult. If he hadn't seen Jim Chaney tied to the chair, he'd have stepped back and emptied his own magazine through the wall and given Rand and Wiley a taste of their own medicine. But he didn't want to hit the old man. Collateral damage, though, was no impediment to Wiley, who could shoot through the walls anywhere he heard the sound of Guthrie's voice.

"It's over, Rand," Guthrie called out.

In anticipation, he'd already crouched, and a good thing, as a three-round burst slammed through the wall where he'd been.

"Stop shooting!" Rand yelled. "I want to know what he knows, and I can't do that if he's dead. He's not getting out of here alive, anyway. If we don't get him, my friend will."

"So you say." Wiley growled. "But it ain't got him yet."

"Patience, Wiley. You'll have your chance. Remember how I let you help me with our black trespasser?"

"Okay, Guthrie," Wiley called out. "I won't shoot until Mr. Rand tells me to. Then I'll blow out your guts one round at a time."

The sound of gunfire erupted from the east end of the marsh.

"Hear that, Wiley? That's your brother and Orman being taken out by Chief Turner and Officer Taylor."

At least Guthrie hoped that was the case, but more gunfire from that direction dimmed his hope. The muted clamor of Freddie's backhoe didn't stop, though, giving Guthrie courage. He needed all he could get right now, facing murderous, well-armed foes inside the cabin and the billowing darkness crashing in all around him, somehow sentient to his assault on its being and closing in with the implacable intent of self-preservation. The fierce buzz of the Kuei men turned into a throbbing energy in his belly, cocooning him and giving him strength, but how long could their vibrations withstand the power of the miasma saturating the pond and marsh and now seeming to flow tangibly over the edge of the deck toward and around him?

What the fuck was taking Freddie so long?

"There will be no more shooting for the moment, Guthrie," Rand said, ignoring the sounds from the east end of the marsh. "So, why don't you tell me what you know? Don't you want to tell me how clever you were in sussing me out?"

"There isn't much sussing out when you're following the path of a bulldozer through a forest. You and Uncle Claude have left a psychic path a mile wide and reeking of corruption. You didn't think somebody would notice and send someone to deal with it?"

"The police?" Rand's voice was filled with scorn. "The police know nothing."

"Not yet, but they will. I'm not talking about the police."

"Who?" Was that genuine curiosity—and perhaps concern—in Rand's voice?

"You'll never know."

"You'll tell me eventually. You might as well do it now."

"I'd rather learn about you," Guthrie said, sarcasm tight in his voice. "So tell me. Tell me all about how mommy and daddy fucked up your life so badly you had to murder them and become a psychotic monster."

"You bastard!" she shrieked, clawing at his face and eyes. "You fuckin' killed my Lonnie!"

He stepped forward, turned, and slammed her against the wall. She let out an oomph and slumped a little but recovered in an instant and attacked again. Guthrie, hampered by the AR, couldn't bring his tai chi fully to bear, but he used the weapon to lever her off then shoved her away. Her back to the slope down to the pond, she stumbled, fell backward, and tumbled almost to the water's edge, next to the Xterra, stunned. Guthrie quickly turned and saw the barrel of Wiley's carbine poke around the corner just a second before a sliver of Wiley's face appeared. Guthrie jerked up his AR and fired, not hitting Wiley but driving him out of sight.

Guthrie knew his own position was untenable. Wiley was armed with a fully-automatic AR, and Guthrie's was only a semi-auto. And he and Rand could shoot at him through the wall or around either corner. He had to move, and the only place to go was the vehicles. He let loose three more rounds at the corner where Wiley hid then darted toward Wiley's pickup, hoping Wiley would be reluctant to fire on his own truck. When Wiley looked to see where he'd gone, Guthrie shot at him again and missed again.

As he'd hoped, Wiley did not immediately fire back.

"You fucking bastard!" Wiley bellowed.

Wiley was now more exposed than Guthrie, and Guthrie let loose with as many shots as he could before his weapon clicked on empty. Wiley ducked back, and all that Guthrie's shots shattered was the corner trim. If Guthrie'd hit him, it didn't show. Wiley popped out again and fired, probably figuring that one dead Guthrie was worth a few holes in his vehicle.

But by now, Guthrie had moved to Chaney's Ford, reloading as he went. As soon as Wiley received no response from the direction of his truck, he stuck his head out a little farther for a better look then ducked back again before Guthrie's bullets could take him. Guthrie watched the shadow Wiley cast from the light over the deck diminish and vanish as he retreated into the cabin.

A second after that, Guthrie straightened, preparing to run to the front corner of the cabin, thinking to shoot out the locks and kick in the door, further exposing the enemy inside, but a voice behind stopped him in his tracks.

"Freeze, asshole, or I'll blow you open."

49

THE VOICE BELONGED TO FRANK Orman. He'd either heard the gunfire at the cabin and realized the significance and come to help or had survived the shootout at the east end of the marsh and fled. Since he was the only one here, Lonnie must have bitten the dust. Or rather, damp dirt. Whatever the case, Orman had seen Guthrie make the move from Wiley's pickup to Chaney's Ford.

"I got him!" Orman yelled excitedly. "I got him, Mr. Rand! Want me to kill him?"

He sounded eager to follow up on that suggestion.

"No," Rand yelled. "Take his guns and bring him inside."

"You heard the man," Orman told Guthrie. "Drop everything you got on the ground. Easy, or I'll shoot your foot off. That way you'll still be alive for Mr. Rand but won't be no trouble for me."

Guthrie laid down the AR, then removed the bandoleer of ammo magazines and unholstered his S&W and set them next to the carbine.

"Now turn around and back up ten feet, nice and easy, hands on the back of your head."

Guthrie did, and Orman kept him covered while he picked up Guthrie's weapons.

"Walk over to the deck," Orman gestured with the barrel of his AR. "Slow."

As Guthrie rounded the corner to the deck, Wiley loomed in front of him. Wiley laid a heavy hand on his shoulder, turned him around to face the door, and jammed the muzzle of his AR into Guthrie's back, just to the right of his spine.

Guthrie could have tried something when Wiley grabbed him and spun him around. For a bare moment, the barrel of the AR wasn't pointed at him, and Wiley was more off balance than Guthrie. But this close, Wiley's weight and strength were advantages, not to mention the AR and the pistol on Wiley's hip. Tai chi was good at medium to very close ranges, but not when a bear has you in a bear hug. Li Wu probably could easily handle Wiley that close, but he had nearly thirty years of real-world combat experience at his disposal.

And Frank Orman was only eight feet away. He might have been armed with more weapons than he could possibly use quickly, but surely he'd be able to find one during any scuffle Guthrie initiated with Wiley. Even if Guthrie defeated Wiley, Orman would gun him down. Guthrie was alive for the moment. He had to turn that moment into a much longer period of time.

"We got you now, motherfucker," Wiley hissed in his ear, ramming the barrel into Guthrie's kidney. "I want to blow you away so bad, but Mr. Rand wants another word with you. I'm sure it'll be fun. For him. Get your fuckin' ass inside." He grated a laugh and shoved Guthrie toward the door.

Orman, cradling Guthrie's weapons and his own, followed. Hetty, who'd recovered from her tumble down the slope, came up behind them, growling curses. During the brief firefight between Guthrie and Wiley, she'd crouched beside the Xterra until Orman got the drop on Guthrie. Inside, she got another kitchen knife from a drawer and resumed her place behind Chaney, holding the knife to his throat.

"Put his weapons over there," Rand directed Orman as soon as the three of them were in the room, gesturing with his pistol to the sofa in the main living area. Far out of Guthrie's reach. "Well, well, Mr. Guthrie. It seems that something truly is all over for someone."

"Where's Lonnie?" Wiley demanded, ignoring Rand.

"He's back there." Orman jerked a thumb toward the east end of the marsh. "At the dam."

"Let me handle this, Wiley," Rand said. Then to Orman, "What's going on over there?"

"It's Freddie Jensen. He got his backhoe, and he's tearin' down the dam."

"What! Why aren't you back there, stopping him?" Rand's voice was harsh but tinged with panic.

"Chief Turner and his nigger officer are protectin' him. We couldn't get close enough to stop him."

"You two get over there and finish them off. Right now!" Rand ordered Wiley and Orman. "We can't let them drain the pond. I can handle Guthrie."

"Fuck your pond," Wiley growled, turning on Orman. "Where the fuck is Lonnie?"

Orman's expression sagged.

"I think they shot him."

"Shot him?" Wiley grated. "What the fuck does that mean?"

"We was tryin' to stop 'em, but I saw him fall. It was Turner who done it."

"What!" Wiley shouted. "You left my brother there to die?"

"He was way far off, Wiley. I couldn't a done nothin'."

"Yeah? Well I can do this." Wiley pivoted and fired a short burst into Orman's chest.

In the two seconds that took, Rand jerked toward him.

"No, you fool!" he yelled.

And in those two seconds, Guthrie moved. He didn't bother going for either of them since both were armed. He had only two seconds to get out of the way of their bullets, and to do that, he needed to get out of the cabin and find some sort of leverage. And he knew exactly what that leverage would be.

It was what everyone had forgotten. Something so usual that it seemed a permanent fixture, just like the back door's deadbolts, now chunks of twisted metal lying on the floor. So usual that Rand and the others hadn't even noticed it, but Guthrie had. It was Jim Chaney's shotgun, propped in its usual place against the door frame. Thankfully, the bullets Wiley had stitched through the wall and door had been on the opposite side of the door and hadn't touched it. A pump shotgun holding more shells would have been better, but Guthrie was sure Chaney, always wary of danger, kept the weapon loaded.

Orman staggered backward, jerking with the impact of the bullets, and fell heavily onto his back, unmoving but bleeding profusely, chest a shattered mangle. Guthrie didn't really see it happen because he was flinging himself through the back door. His left hand snagged the shotgun as he passed, and he spun and landed on his back, facing the doorway, and fired. The upper barrel went off, and the recoil, added to his momentum, helped push him onto the deck. Wiley and Rand both shot back, but their rounds went over Guthrie. Guthrie's shotgun blast, fired rapidly from his off hand, also went high, over Wiley's right shoulder. Too bad it hadn't been over the left because that was the location of Rand's head, but at least one of the pellets gouged Wiley's shoulder, and he grunted and staggered back.

Guthrie didn't have time to think about Chaney or assess Wiley's wound. He was too busy rolling to the left, switching the shotgun to the lower barrel, and getting to his feet. He wasn't quite up when Wiley stormed out onto the deck, shoulder bloody, AR seeking Guthrie's anatomy. Guthrie swung the shotgun barrel upward, catching momentarily beneath the forward part of the handguard of Wiley's weapon, deflecting the barrel upward.

Both weapons bucked as each man tried to force his aim toward the other. Now the empty shotgun was more of an impediment, and Guthrie dropped it and grabbed the barrel of the AR. It seared his grip as the the last rounds in the magazine punched harmlessly through the deck's tin roof. Then the bucking ended in a dry click.

Wiley jerked away, ejecting his magazine and groping for another. Guthrie desperately surged forward and kicked the hand holding the fresh mag. As the mag clattered to the deck, Wiley tried to club Guthrie with the carbine's barrel, but Guthrie managed to ward off the blow without taking much damage. Wiley groped for a fresh mag, but he was fresh out. He dropped the AR and went for the pistol at his waist.

Guthrie wished he had his own pistol, but it was inside. Fortunately for him, Hetty intervened. While Guthrie and Wiley locked horns and discharged their weapons, she'd chased after Wiley, still holding the knife. Whatever her intentions, they proved as misguided as ever. As Wiley drew his pistol, she flung herself at Guthrie, trying to stab him in the gut. Guthrie swept the knife hand aside and instinctively twisted her around to throw her off and push her away. The rounds from Wiley's pistol, intended for Guthrie, smashed into her chest as she spun. Emitting only a wet sigh, she sagged backward against Guthrie, who shoved her collapsing body at Wiley.

Wiley fired twice more, the bullets smashing into Hetty instead of Guthrie, before she slammed into him, her flopping left arm tangling his right. Her dead weight caused him to drop his pistol, which skittered off the end of the deck, into the black water below with a thick splash. Casting Hetty's body aside as she fell, Wiley recovered fast and charged Guthrie.

Guthrie was wary of fighting with Wiley. He might be a brawler with little finesse, but he was strong and had practical fighting experience. During the encounter in the parking lot of the Lazy Q, both Wiley and Lonnie had been at least partly drunk, and they'd misjudged Guthrie as an easy target. And he'd had ample room to operate. But now Wiley knew Guthrie wasn't a pushover, and worse, Wiley was maddened with the heat of battle. And more with the loss of his brother. Unfortunately, the pellet wound in his shoulder, though bloody, didn't seem to hamper him but only enflamed his rage.

The two wrestled for a moment, and Guthrie knew he had to disengage. Wiley's size and strength would play well in a grapple, and he'd eventually gain the upper hand. Without enough space to redirect Wiley's force, Guthrie did the only thing he could. He stomped hard on Wiley's instep.

The man howled and loosened his grip enough for Guthrie to shake free and back off. But in doing so, he was framed by the open door. A split second later, the sound of a gunshot came from inside, and a bullet whined by his head. He jerked away from the opening as Wiley came at him again. The suddenness of the multiple moves left Guthrie vulnerable, and Wiley slammed him to the deck, reared back, and sent a haymaker right at his face. Guthrie twitched his head to the side just in time, and Wiley's fist grazed by his head and slammed against the wooden planks. Wiley bellowed and recoiled, giving Guthrie just enough room to smash him in the face with the heel of his right palm. Wiley grunted and jerked back, blood spurting from his nose, and Guthrie used his backward motion to shove him off and scramble to his feet. Damaged hand and broken nose or not, Wiley was up in an instant, and he faced Guthrie, rage contorting his features.

"I ain't drunk, this time, motherfucker," he snarled. "And now I know you got tricks. I'm gonna tear you to shreds and wring your fuckin' neck."

But he didn't charge forward. Maybe he'd learned from his previous attempts. This time he came on slow, though he was limping. He must have heard the shot come from inside the cabin, because his steady approach was calculated to drive Guthrie within sight of the doorway.

Guthrie wasn't having it. He veered away from the doorway and onto open deck. But there wasn't much room left, and Guthrie couldn't afford to get backed up against the rail. Then Wiley came on strong, aiming a right at Guthrie's face followed quickly by a left to his gut. Guthrie managed to ward off the right, though the left caught him solidly. But he didn't absorb much of the shock. Tai chi had taught him that incoming energy can be turned back on an attacker. Guthrie redirected the power of Wiley's and drove his right knuckles, bent into a panther fist, into Wiley's exposed throat.

Wiley's eyes went wide as he gagged and clutched at his neck. Blood choked out of his mouth, mingling with the red already coloring his grimacing teeth and staining his beard. He lurched back, and Guthrie used the lurch to shove him hard against the rail, which splintered. Wiley crashed through, into the water below, where he clawed at his crushed larynx and writhed and thrashed, roiling the black, scummy surface.

"Wiley?" Rand yelled out. "You get him, Wiley? What's going on out there?"

"I'll tell you what's going on, Rand. Either you come out with your hands up, or it's the last moments of your life."

"Not a chance. Chaney already signed over the marsh to me. It's mine, and you're trespassing and attacking me on my own property. I shoot trespassers. And when your friends come looking for you, I'll shoot them, too."

"What about Wiley and Lonnie and the others? Everyone dead but you. How are you going to explain all that?"

"All your doing. I was fortunate enough to have been in Dallas while all this was going on. Imagine my shock when I returned to discover you perpetrated a massacre in Chaney Marsh, my recently acquired property."

"You're not going to miss your minions?"

"Who cares about them?" Rand said with a sneer. "People like that are too unpredictable and are a dime a dozen. So what if they're dead? I'd probably have killed them myself, eventually. You just saved me the trouble. I'm sure their deaths gave my friend a little more power, especially if they died painfully."

Suddenly, the whole pond shuddered, convulsed, and writhed beneath the full moonlight as a heavy sound of rushing water came from the east end of the pond. Almost immediately a wind began blowing through the marsh. Or rather, into it from all angles. The miasma was forcibly withdrawing into the pond from the surrounding terrain, abandoning its reach and retreating in the interests of self-preservation. The temperature dropped as the black mists rushed through the trees to settle into the water.

"What's that?" Rand cried out, panic in his voice.

"It's time to say goodby to your little friend," Guthrie said. "We're draining the pond."

He couldn't help but stare at the water. Freddie had finally broken through the earthen dam there, and almost instantly, the level of the water began to subside. It probably would take the rest of the night to fully drain the swamp, but Guthrie couldn't think of that right now as he heard a scraping coming from behind him. He spun and saw Rand appear in the doorway, pistol raised.

"You've ruining everything, you bastard!" Rand screamed, firing.

Rand was right handed, and Guthrie was several feet to the left of the doorway, so Rand had to almost completely emerge to aim properly. And he was so enraged that he fired prematurely. One of the bullets went wide, and while the second connected, it merely gouged Guthrie's upper right arm. Guthrie, charged with adrenaline and the throbbing buzz of the Kuei men, barely noticed as he took two long, bounding steps toward the the door, making the angle too acute for Rand to hit him. That didn't stop Rand from firing off two more rounds, but before he could withdraw his arm, Guthrie snatched the wrist and elbow and flung him out onto the deck. The pistol clattered to the side.

Rand rolled to his feet and, snarling, leapt at Guthrie. He was no Wiley or Lonnie in size and strength, but he seemed possessed by a demonic energy that surged out of the pond and around him, simultaneously smashing down on Guthrie and sending him reeling. A switchblade snicked open in Rand's hand and snaked toward Guthrie's gut. Guthrie jerked back, and Rand struck again and again, thrusting at Guthrie's belly and slashing at his arms and face, his own face a twisted mask of rage, eyes wild with madness.

Guthrie took a cut on his left forearm. The damned knife seemed to have a mind of its own. Then the thought vanished as Rand's sharp steel snaked and slashed again and again, Guthrie barely keeping away. The miasma's oppressive pressure bore down on him, making the air around him seem thick and his movements sluggish, even while it flowed around and into Rand, empowering his actions with powerful, agile cunning. Guthrie took a second cut.

Abruptly, the vibration of the Kuei men went incandescent, so fiercely that it inflated Guthrie with a power that settled a great calm over him and seemed to oust him from the seat of conscious control over his own body. He seemed outside the fray, as if he was simply an observer, watching events unfold. But even if he wasn't in control, he didn't stop moving, and as he moved, he watched Rand move, watched the knife move, and found himself capable of anticipating its every angle and target.

In the end, there was no contest between Rand's blind rage, no matter how empowered by the malignant pressure of the miasma, and the movements of calculated training. Rand was vicious and enraged, but he was used to using a knife on those bound and gagged, and his combat repertoire was limited. The battle ended after Rand stabbed once more at Guthrie's face. Guthrie snatched the incoming wrist, spun on his axis, and pulled Rand to the side and down, simultaneously twisting the wrist. Rand flipped over and crashed down onto his back with a woof, though he managed to keep gripping the knife. He scrambled to his feet, but Guthrie was already on him, sweeping the knife hand aside as Rand thrust and delivering a sharp, penetrating punch to Rand's chest, right over his heart. The energy went deep, and Rand dropped the knife and clutched at his chest, gasped for breath that wasn't there. Taking advantage of his dropped defenses, Guthrie arced both fists up, driving the first two knuckles of each into Rand's temples. Rand's eyes rolled up in his head, and he collapsed to his knees then fell onto his back, limbs twitching. Guthrie snatched up the fallen pistol.

"You called it," he said and shot Rand through the heart.

Rand might have been dead, but the miasma wasn't, and it seemed to coalesce around Guthrie and crush in from all sides as if attempting to squeeze itself into his flesh. Guthrie could feel it, but the incandescent field emanating from his belly repelled it. Dropping the pistol, he forced himself forward through the thick air to the edge of the deck and glanced over. Wiley had stopped moving, though his body was drifting slowly toward the middle of the pond as the draining water created a current flowing downstream. Guthrie sure wasn't about to go in there to drag him out.

The crushing pressure around Guthrie suddenly eased as the pond shuddered again and the miasma withdrew into the water. Almost immediately, a viscous black mist exuded from the surface like diseased sweat. With the pond draining out, the bòkò's creation no longer found sanctuary. It required stillness and stagnation, and if it tried to stay, it's density and cohesion would be attenuated and diffused beyond reorganization as it was swept downstream along ever-widening waterways to the Gulf of Mexico.

But Guthrie desired a more definite resolution, and as he'd hoped, it sensed the presence of its old temporary home: the decrepit and foul sofa protruding from the back of the Xterra just a couple of yards up the bank. Rand said it was powerful but mindless, and desperate mindless things always seek familiar shelter, even when that shelter is a trap.

Mindless or not, the miasma oozing out of the pond coalesced at the edge of the bank below the Xterra like an immense bodiless slug of malignant energy. Guthrie couldn't see it, exactly, at least not as more than a darkly increasing density of the air. But it was there, a huge coagulation of corruption. Then, as the water level dropped even more, it flowed like a dark cloud into the Xterra's interior, part of it sinking into the sofa like water soaking into a sponge. But it was too large, now, to subside completely into the sofa, and the excess filled the rest of the vehicle like dense clot of black, foggy shadow.

Suddenly, everything in the marsh seemed cleaner and brighter beneath the moonlight, though the tainted water remained scummy and diseased looking in the moonlight. But it was draining out and eventually would be gone. There remained one final act—one that Guthrie regretted but accepted. He approached his vehicle cautiously, the Kuei men still incandescent in his belly. The truck was so inundated with the foul, oily, roiling force that Guthrie could barely get close. But he had to. Steeling himself, he opened the front passenger door, quickly hauled out the gas can, and flipped the cap off its spout. With only a momentary pause of regret, he thoroughly doused the sofa with gas through the hatch and open windows. Then he twisted off the truck's gas cap and sloshed gas around it and on the tire and quarter panel below it. He hated losing the Xterra, but it was too riddled with bullets now to be worth salvaging, and anyhow, it was fifteen years old. Time to say goodbye. In spectacular fashion.

He backed off and used the last few ounces of gas to make a torch with a branch he found nearby. Digging the lighter he'd brought along out of his pocket, he lit the torch, and tossed it onto the end of the sofa sticking out of the hatch. He moved quickly away as the gas ignited with a powerful whoosh. Flames blew out of the open windows, and more gushed through the hatch, flaring into the night, lighting up the ground all around. Guthrie beat a hasty retreat up the bank to the deck. The truck's gas tank was full, and he didn't want to be close when it blew. It did seconds later, lifting the entire vehicle two feet off the ground. More flames erupted through the windows, the hood ripped askew, and the hatch cover snapped off and splashed into the pond a dozen feet from the bank.

All Guthrie hoped now was that the burning would be effective. Apparently it was, because almost immediately he could sense a diminishing of the corrupting force emanating from the flaming Xterra. He didn't know what to expect from the miasma as it burned with the sofa. Some plaintive sound perhaps? Some wail? But no sound came from it.

No matter, he thought, as long as it burned. He could see it squirming in there, like a crumpled piece of black paper tossed onto hot coals, writhing and twisting as it shriveled, turning to black, dissipating steam carried upward by the rising heat into the night air. The longer the sofa burned, the better Guthrie felt, and as it did, the fire of the Kuei men gradually subsided to a buzz, then to a few twitches. Then there was no movement from them at all.

Feeling as burned out as the Xterra, he watched it long enough to make sure the flames weren't going to catch the deck or trees on fire, though what he might have been able to do if they had was beyond him. He turned from his erstwhile vehicle and rushed into the cabin.

Jim Chaney was barely conscious, only the bindings holding him to the chair keeping him upright. Those and the knife rammed through his left hand into the tabletop. Guthrie could see that several of the fingers were broken, and Chaney's face was so battered that one eye was puffed shut. He had a deep gash in his throat slowly pulsing thick blood, and blood pooled all around his chair. Hetty had cut his throat before she'd come out after Guthrie. Guthrie jerked the knife out of Chaney's hand, used it to cut the ropes, then eased the slumping man to the floor, only then noticing several bloody teeth lying there. He tried to staunch the blood pulsing from Chaney's neck, but he knew it was useless.

"Did you get 'em?" Chaney gasped at last, blood bubbling from his mouth.

"I did."

"I couldn't help it." Chaney waved feebly toward the table with his right hand. "I couldn't help it. They finally got to me. I done signed it over." He choked more blood.

Guthrie looked at the table and saw a piece of paper on it. He was reluctant to ease the pressure on Chaney's neck wound, but maybe something was more important now than a futile effort to keep Chaney alive. He picked up the paper, Chaney's blood on his fingers smearing the document. It was a deed assigning Chaney Marsh to George Rand.

"Look, Jim," he said, crouching and holding the deed where Chaney's good eye could see it. He deliberately tore it in half, then quarters, then eighths. Chaney eye lit as he watched what he'd done become fragments. "The marsh is still yours."

"Ain't," Chaney gasped, then he choked again as more blood spilled out of his mouth. Guthrie raised his head, hoping to help. "It's Enid's," Chaney whispered. "It was always Enid's. Tell Bill Turner Eldon Smith has my will."

Then the light faded from his eye, and he slumped. Guthrie felt for a pulse and found none. Jim Chaney was dead.

A sound at the door galvanized him, and he jerked upright, groping for a pistol that wasn't there. But it was only Turner, Freddie, and Emmet silhouetted against the orange glow from the burning Xterra, faces smeared with stress and shock. Emmet was limping with a wound in his outer right thigh, crudely bandaged with a blood-soaked handkerchief.

"Jim?" Turner asked as they came into the room.

"Gone."

"And the force?"

"Do you feel it?"

"No."

Suddenly, Guthrie was too tired to stand. He slumped into the chair where Chaney had been bound.

"Lonnie?" he asked.

"I had to shoot him. I saw Rand and Hetty on the deck, and Frank Orman's over there. What about Wiley?"

"He's in the pond," Guthrie said wearily. "Someone ought to retrieve him before he washes downstream."

50

"HOW ARE WE GOING TO explain all this?" Emmet asked.

"We can't tell what really happened," Guthrie said. "Nobody would believe it, and we'd just look crazy and culpable. But we have to tell as much of the truth as possible. And you and Chief Turner will go down as heroes."

"How do you figure?"

Turner told Emmet and Freddie what they'd found in Rand's house.

"You two caught an interstate murderer who turned out to be a prolific serial killer," Guthrie said. "You'll be famous."

"What about me?" Freddie asked.

"Do you really want to be famous?" Turner asked. "I'm not sure I do." He looked at Guthrie. "What's the story we tell?"

Guthrie told them. Jim Chaney and Leland Fuller had separately complained about the quality of the water in the marsh. Fuller thought Chaney was poisoning the marsh, but Chaney suspected it was Rand, who was trying to force him to sell the wetland. Chaney already had complained on several occasions about Rand and the Sanfords intimidating him and threatening violence if he didn't sign over the property.

With that information, Turner and Emmet went to Rand's house to tell him to stay off of Chaney's property and quit making threats or there would be legal consequences. Rand wasn't home, but they found a decaying body in the well and the front door was kicked in. Fearing violence had occurred in the house, they entered, only to discover the torture chamber upstairs.

"Me?" Emmet asked. "It was you and the chief."

"I need to stay in the background," Guthrie said. "I can't be the public hero, but you can. And the heroism is real enough. We probably won't get a chance to take you into Rand's house before we call in the higher authorities. We're too messed up. We'd leave trace evidence all over the place that might contradict our story. But the chief and I can describe what it's like."

At that point, he went on, Turner and Emmet knew Rand was a vicious serial killer. They left the house but before they could report the scene, they heard gunfire from the direction of Chaney's cabin. They drove there, and called Guthrie to join them in his own vehicle, which was carrying the sofa on which Norman Telfor's body had been found. Guthrie was going to take it to the dump as a favor to Turner but had gotten the call from Turner before he could.

There, they discovered George Rand and his local cohorts torturing Jim Chaney to make him sign over the marsh to Rand. Chaney had previously complained about Rand harassing and intimidating him, and now Rand had become violent. The presence of Jim Chaney's body and the bloody and shredded deed gave proof to that.

When Turner, Emmet, and Guthrie confronted Rand, he ordered the Sanfords to attack them with weapons they'd stolen from Havasau's Hardware. During the ensuing fight, Hetty fatally sliced Chaney's neck then got in the way of Wiley's pistol. Orman, too, had been shot down by Wiley after Orman killed Rand with Rand's own pistol. Who knew what the reason was. Maybe he'd protested Chaney's torture or been trying to protect him. Wiley had then been killed in hand-to-hand combat with Guthrie, while Lonnie had been killed in the gunfight with Turner and Emmet.

"What about me?" Freddie asked. "And the backhoe? I can't get it out of there until daylight, and there'd be obvious tracks, anyway."

"And what about the pond?" Turner asked.

"Chaney wanted to drain out the polluted water, so he hired Freddie to tear down the dam with his backhoe." He looked at Freddie. "You finished about three and went straight home, cleaned up, ate dinner, and watched TV until bedtime. All you have to do is stick to that story. You were at home, sleeping after a hard day's work, and didn't see or hear anything and don't know anything."

To make all that credible, they used a wheelbarrow they found propped against the cabin's front wall to cart Lonnie's body from the east end of the marsh to the cabin. There, they arranged it near the vehicles as convincingly as they could. That left Rand's body. Guthrie wiped Rand's pistol clean of prints, then used Rand's right hand to simulate a grip, printing the stock and barrel. In the cabin, he did the same with Orman's out-flung hand and left the pistol on the floor right beside it.

They all understood that's what the story had to be. It quickly would be public knowledge that Rand had been a truly evil man. Everybody would learn about the serial killings and the murders in Thorndike and Airla. But those were evils everybody had seen before, though not often on that scale. Something that seemed all too human and could be understood. That's who Turner and his little police force had caught. But just how evil Rand had been probably would remain just between the four of them, or maybe a select few others. Outside of that group, there could be no mention of a creeping, evil miasma that had spread corruption, discord, and destruction across the town of Thorndike.

After they settled on the story and arranged the scene, Freddie and Emmet went back to the east end of the marsh, Freddie to get his truck and drive home and Emmet to retrieve Turner's Interceptor and drive it around to the entrance to Chaney Marsh and down to the cabin. After that, Turner called the state police and county sheriff.

"And send an ambulance," he finished.

The state police captain and three of his squad cars arrived first, followed soon after by the county sheriff, two more squad cars, and the ambulance.

Turner walked Guthrie and Emmet up the slope to the ambulance.

"I'm sorry we didn't let you in on this earlier," Guthrie told Emmet.

"No problem," Emmet said. "You and the chief did all the heavy lifting. I probably wouldn't have believed it, anyway. At least not right off. All I had to do was shoot off a few rounds."

"You did get shot," Guthrie pointed out.

Emmet glanced down at his roughly bandaged thigh.

"Oh, hell," he said with a wan smile. "That's nothing."

Turner waited at the ambulance while the paramedics tended to Emmet's leg and the two slashes Guthrie had taken on his left forearm, the graze wound on his arm, and the stab wound in his shoulder. That last one was starting to hurt now that the flush of adrenaline and deadly encounter was draining from his system.

"I need to tell you" Guthrie said to Turner, wincing as the paramedics rinsed his shoulder wound, "that Jim wanted you to talk to someone named Eldon Smith about his will."

"Eldon's an attorney up in the county seat," Turner said. "I'll call him later."

The paramedics told Guthrie and Emmet they were lucky. Their wounds were only superficial, though Hetty's knife probably had left a nick in Guthrie's shoulder blade. They ought to go to County General, the paramedic said, but both declined the ride.

"I think you'll already have a full load with all the bodies down there," Emmet said, nodding toward the cabin.

Dr. Bob arrived while Guthrie and Emmet were being stitched and patched. The coroner looked grumpy and sleepy, but his eyes turned sharp as he took in the scene.

"Why does all the bad stuff in Thorndike have to happen in the middle of the night?" he groused.

"It's worse down there." Turner nodded toward the cabin. "And there's a body in the water."

"There's a boat on the bank," Guthrie said, trying to be helpful.

"I see you burned the sofa," Dr. Bob commented dryly. "Is that Mr. Guthrie's vehicle it's in? Why's it down there by the pond? And why do y'all stink like garlic?"

"You might find a few irregularities," Turner told him. "Maybe you could find a way to overlook them."

Dr. Bob gave Turner a long, hard look.

"Has justice been served?" he asked.

"On a silver platter," Turner assured him.

"Okay. If your irregularities are as irregular as Mr. Telfor's body and that sofa, I suppose I've overlooked those. But I'm going to want answers later. No. No. Wait. I don't think I do. Keep 'em to yourself. I have enough shit to think about." He glanced over his shoulder and waved his techs forward. "Okay, let's get to it. We have a whole lot to process."

As he left, the state police captain and the sheriff came up.

"Okay, Bill," the sheriff said. "What happened here?"

Turner took the lead in telling their story, Guthrie and Emmet nodding and saying, that's right, at appropriate moments.

"Looks like Rand made good on his threat to harm Mr. Chaney," the captain said when Turner finished.

"Yes. I'm just sorry we were too late."

They had to repeat the whole story an hour later when the county district attorney showed up. He seemed a little miffed he hadn't been informed of the magnitude of the case earlier, but Turner assured him that even he hadn't known until just this evening. Eventually, Turner, Emmet, and Guthrie would have to write up reports, but with the scene now in the hands of others, there was nothing for them to do but go home. Thankful that they could. Turner drove them in his Interceptor.

"You going to be okay, Emmet?" the chief asked as he pulled up in front of Emmet's house.

"I'll never be the same again," Emmet said. "But I'm okay."

"I'll tell you about all the rest of it later," Turner promised.

Emmet nodded soberly then got out, limped to his front door, and went inside. Turner pulled off and drove to his house. Bev was up and waiting, radiating anxiety. But her tension released as soon as the two came through the door.

"Bill!" she cried, rushing over and embracing him.

"Don't worry, sweetheart," he told her. "It's all over now except for the explanations."

She hugged him a moment longer then released him and looked him up and down.

"Those can wait until tomorrow," she said at last, convinced that her husband was unharmed, though perhaps not unscathed. She looked at Guthrie. "I'm so glad you're okay, too, Clay." She noticed the blood on his shirt and the bandages on his shoulder and arm. "But you're hurt."

"It's nothing," Guthrie said. "The paramedics took care of it."

Actually, the wound in his shoulder ached pretty badly. He needed to take one of the painkillers the paramedics had given him.

"Well, you two had a long night. Are you hungry?"

"And how," Turner said.

Suddenly Guthrie realized how famished he was. The harrowing last few hours piled on top of the stress of the past two weeks had played havoc with his food intake. He could swear he'd lost a belt notch.

"Me, too," was all he could say.

"Well, you both need to get cleaned up," she said, then she grinned. "I guess there's a good reason ya'll smell like you've been rolling in a garlic patch."

The two men spent the next forty-five minutes showering, Guthrie as anxious to rid his skin of the miasma's oily residue as of the odor of garlic. He did his best to keep the shoulder wound out of the spray, though he couldn't help getting the bandages on his arm wet. No matter. The cuts were shallow. He didn't feel like a new man after he put on clean clothes, but he felt a hell of a lot better, though he thought he still exuded a faint odor of garlic. By the time he and Turner were done cleaning up, Bev had a massive breakfast waiting. They ate rapidly and in silence, and after that, as the food suffused him, Guthrie felt suddenly tired. Too tired to stay awake. Excusing himself, he went into his bedroom and slept until late afternoon. If he moved during his sleep, it sure wasn't much.

51

AFTER HE WOKE, GUTHRIE MOVED out of the Turner's house and back into his trailer.

"You don't have to do that," Turner said when Guthrie told him.

"Yes, I do. I need to get out of your hair for the time being. You and Bev have a lot to talk about, and she'll have a lot of questions. You need your space."

Right now, Guthrie needed his own space, too.

"I'm not sure how to tell her what happened."

"Be completely forthcoming with her," Guthrie advised. "You can't damage the good thing you two have by holding back. But I wouldn't spread the story any farther, otherwise they'll be putting you in a loony bin instead of back in office. Don't even tell Emily all of it. Let her believe Rand was a heinous serial killer that you brought down. You'll always be that hero to her. The rest will only disturb her, whether she believes it or not. I know Emmet will play it close to the vest, and I hope Freddie toes the line, too."

"I think he will. His story is simple. But it's more than that. It seems to me he's a changed man."

"I hope so."

"Are you going to tell me the rest of it?" Turner asked. "Considering the shit we've been through, I think I deserve to know."

So Guthrie told him. Most of it.

"That's some deep shit, Clay. I can't believe all of it wound up here."

"It had to wind up somewhere, and Thorndike was ideal."

"Was?"

"Not any more," Guthrie said. "Now your town has a new lease on life. I hope it takes advantage of it. Say, you mind driving me over to Evers'? I seem to be without wheels at the moment."

"No need." Turner said, fetching a key ring from a rack near the utility room door. "Believe it or not, we do have a regular car. It's in the garage, but we hardly ever use it. It's yours for as long as you're here."

Guthrie drove his gear over to the mobile home park. The crime scene tape was still up, so he pulled it down, wadded it up, and carried it in to the trash. After that, he spent the rest of the day washing his clothes and resting, feeling relaxed for the first time in two weeks.

FBI agents Wilson and Aznar returned the next day, and Turner, Emmet, and Guthrie reiterated their story. That wasn't hard to do since they'd already told it several times, and each time, it became more solidified in the minds of those they told.

The agents were more conciliatory, now, considering all their obvious questions were answered and a seriously deranged serial killer had been taken down as thoroughly as possible. They only seemed disappointed they'd jumped the gun and written off the case and hadn't been the ones to solve it. But they were on the periphery and, they swore, would have cracked the case if Turner hadn't lucked out. Guthrie was glad they'd stayed out of it. They'd only have complicated matters.

"The forensics on this case could take years," Wilson said, sounding happy. "But I suppose it's a good thing Rand is dead. Nobody wants or needs to see what's on those videos—certainly not a jury."

Dr. Bob didn't have a chance to do the gritty work of processing Rand's house. Wilson and Aznar took over and brought in an FBI forensics team. There might have been some inconsistencies in the evidence of the confrontation at the cabin, but not at Rand's house, which was where the FBI investigation centered. The battle of the marsh was left to Dr. Bob and his team, who'd already done most of the work at the cabin and its surroundings.

Not having to deal with the house probably was a relief for Dr. Bob and his techs who were nearly overwhelmed with the mass of evidence already collected at the cabin. It also meant they weren't tasked with retrieving Claude Fortier's body from the well. However, the FBI lab did release the two small red spheres floating in the pickle jar to him. They'd been positively identified as belonging to Jeff Mayfield and were returned to his body before it was buried in the town cemetery.

Guthrie hoped that Dr. Bob had muddled inconsistent evidence around the cabin enough to conform to the story he, Turner, and Emmet told. Apparently, the coroner had, and the few inconsistencies left were overlooked considering the enormity of the crimes Turner and his little police force had uncovered and brought to a close. Everybody seemed less interested in the details of the battle at the cabin and more interested in the contents of Rand's torture chamber. Those were farther-reaching. As with all the statements given by Turner, Emmet, and Guthrie, Guthrie's role, by choice, was downplayed as much as possible, giving the lion's share of the credit to Turner and Emmet. Guthrie was, he assured everybody, just a johnny-come-lately who had very little direct participation in Turner's investigation into Rand until the very end.

Every morning while he was still in Thorndike, Guthrie went to Dr. Williamson's office to have his wounds checked, and the doctor said they were healing well. Gratifyingly for Williamson, the mad crowding of his office just days earlier had abated. And the case against Rand and the Sanfords was going just as well, with evidence mounting over the next few days. With all the perps dead, there would be no trial, though there would be the inevitable inquest.

As the days passed, the FBI didn't make regular reports to Turner, but Dr. Bob kept him apprised of the developments. FBI forensics IDed blood, hair, and fibers found in the trunk of the car in Rand's garage as belonging to a number of women he'd killed. Shoe impressions from Rand and the Sanfords matched those found at the Mayfield attack site. Later, a farmer some twenty miles southeast of Thorndike noticed tire tracks running across a field, headed straight for the Navasota River. He followed them and found Mayfield's truck mostly submerged in the water, bloody clothes in the cab.

"We'll probably never know exactly what happened to Norm Telfor between the time he left home and when you found him," Dr. Bob told Guthrie and Turner on one of their visits to the coroner's office to get an update. "But we do know for certain he was killed by Rand's pistol. Ballistics match it not only to the bullet that killed Norm, but to the two slugs they dug out of Claude Fortier. At least the blood in the sawmill places Norm's murder there, so we don't have to deal with that, too. One more thing to leave to the feds." He chuckled and leaned toward Guthrie while giving Turner a sly look. "He's already getting famous. The news agencies have all the motel rooms in the county seat booked solid for the next two weeks, and network news vans are in the parking lots. Let's hope the Thorndike Chief of Police doesn't get a swell head."

"I think Bev'll keep me on the straight and narrow," Turner chuckled.

Somehow, Guthrie managed to remain obscure, though he couldn't be completely forgotten or ignored. He bore the scrutiny and stuck with his cover story and pretended to bask briefly in the periphery of the spotlight. But he hadn't done anything, really, he insisted. It had all been Chief Turner and Officer Taylor. So he managed to fade quickly from the scene, leaving Turner and Emmet to shoulder the burden of fame.

On the third day, Guthrie was summoned to the inquest, where he reiterated the story. And on the fourth morning, he received a mysterious invitation from Turner to come to the police station. There, he found not only Turner, but Miss Agnes, Mayor Acuff, Leland Fuller, Chuck Willis, Roy Randall, and Dale Stansic. Most of the powers that be in Thorndike. There were too many of them to crowd into Turner's office, so they were in the front room, Miss Agnes seated in Emmet's chair and a man Guthrie hadn't seen yet at the empty desk. A briefcase lay on the desk, a file folder next to it. The men either perched on desktops or lounged against the counter. Tessa was in her usual place behind the counter, attentive but trying to shrink into the background, as if she didn't want to be noticed and asked to leave.

"Who's he?" Guthrie asked Turner, nodding toward the seated man. "What's going on?"

"Eldon Smith. Seems like we're about to hear the reading of Jim Chaney's will. The rest of us were summoned by Mr. Smith, but I thought you'd like to be here."

The news surprised everyone. Chaney had bequeathed the marsh, in trust, to the town of Thorndike as a park to be named the Enid Chaney Nature Preserve. Included was a considerable bank account—presumably from the sale of most of his ranch to Grant Industries and the rest to George Rand. The funds were more than enough to set up a trust fund to keep the marsh and cabin in good shape in perpetuity and to fund a full-time caretaker position. Most surprising to Miss Agnes, the will gave her complete oversight of the facility for as long as she desired, with management to be turned over to the Thorndike town council upon her retirement or demise. Though the will didn't specifically name either Leland Fuller or Grant Industries, to ensure that the marsh would never fall into their hands, a final proviso stipulated that if the town no longer wanted to possess the property, the trust, including the funds that went with it, would would be turned over in its entirety to Bill and Bev Turner or their heirs.

"Well, damnit to all," Fuller snorted. "That bastard snookered me right up until the end."

"Cheer up, Leland," Willis said, slapping his shoulder. "We have plenty to do and plenty to do it with."

"I guess you're right." Fuller looked at Miss Agnes. "I guess it's all yours for now."

"No," she said. "It belongs to Thorndike."

Then all the questions were answered for the time being, and Guthrie was free to leave, though he'd eventually have to return to the county seat to testify at Miller and Fitzgerald's trial. And it was time to leave. He no longer had a car, so he called Li Wu.

"Mind driving here tomorrow morning to pick me up?"

"What happened to your truck?"

"Burned up. I'll tell you when I see you."

"What time?"

"Nine should do it. I'm at Evers Mobile Home Park on the state highway just north of town"

He hung up, drove into town, and parked the Turners' car in their driveway. Then he walked to the police station and went inside. Tessa looked up at him, her thin lips cracking into a bright smile. She didn't know everything that had gone down at Chaney's cabin, but she knew enough to be Guthrie's friend for life.

Turner looked up as Guthrie came into the office, and he seemed disappointed when Guthrie dropped the car keys into his hand.

"You leaving?"

"Got to get back to it," Guthrie said. "Someone's picking me up in the morning. I've had a call to take on another case."

"Another case like this?"

"I hope not. I'd like something easy for the moment, like a violent extortionist or murderous embezzler."

Turner laughed.

"May all your cases work out," he said.

"I need a ride back to the trailer."

"I'll drive you."

"Let's go over to Leo's first. I want to eat there one more time and say goodbye to Bev."

He was going to simply say goodbye to Tessa on the way out, but she got up and hugged him.

"Thank you for all you did," she said as she released him.

"Thank Chief Turner," he said. "He's the hero."

"Yes, he is, but he's not the only one."

"I didn't tell her anything," Turner said as he and Guthrie walked across the street. "And I'm not going to. But she's sharp enough to see what's been happening in town and know you had a big hand in making things right, even if she doesn't know exactly what went on."

Inside the cafe, they found a booth some distance from the few other diners, all of whom smiled at them. Bev came over, also with a big smile but no menus.

"Leo saw you come in," she said. "He's fixing chicken-fried steaks for you two at no charge."

"That's nice," Guthrie said. "But I came to say goodbye to you as much as I did to eat."

"Ask Leo if you can sit with us a while," Turner said.

She nodded, went to the kitchen, and came back a few minutes later with their silverware and water.

"He said everything's good," she said as she slipped onto the seat next to Turner. "He'll call when the food's ready."

"I told her everything," Turner said.

"It's incredible," Bev said. "If I hadn't watched some of it unfold, I'd never have believed it."

"Believe it," Guthrie said. "But don't spread it around."

"We cafe waitresses are in the business of taking in information, not giving it out," she said, grinning.

"I want to thank you, Clay, for everything you did," Turner said. "You saved our asses when we didn't even know we needed saving."

"It wasn't just me," Guthrie said. "It took all of us. We had a chance to destroy that thing together, and we took it. Just the luck of the draw that it all worked out."

"It was mighty generous of you stepping back and letting Emmet have credit. I told him about all of it, too, and it was a lot for him to swallow. But he felt that horrible thing same as me, and there's no denying it once you've felt it. He knows what went down that night, and he was glad to be part of it." He chuckled. "Just the public aspect of it's given him a big boost around here."

"Just hope he doesn't accept some bigger job in Dallas or Houston. He's a good man, and I'd hate to see you lose him."

"Can't say I'm glad to see you go, either, Clay. You're a handy man to have around."

"Got to get back to my own life. Besides, after what happened—and the mystery around what happened—folks might be wary of me. To most of them, I'll always be the stranger who brought trouble to Thorndike."

"They might not know you saved all our asses from that thing, but they know you helped clean up and square away some bad apples. As far as the Sanford boys and their crew go, most everybody's glad it went down the way we said it did. I think you'll always be welcome in Thorndike. But I know you have other things to deal with."

"Got to keep busy or I'll start chewing on myself."

"Luckily you won't have to do that right now," Bev said as Leo called her over to the service window. She was back in a minute with steaming plates heaped with chicken-fried steaks, mashed potatoes, and green beans.

While Guthrie and Turner ate, there wasn't a lot of talk, and when they'd finished, there wasn't much left to say.

"Ready to take me to the trailer?" Guthrie asked.

"No," Turner said. "But let's go."

They all stood, and Bev gave Guthrie a warm hug.

"Goodbye, Clay. Come back sometime."

"Thanks," Guthrie said. "Bye."

He and Turner were mostly silent as the chief drove him to Evers Mobile Home Park.

"You'll be coming up to testify at Miller and Fitzgerald's trial," Turner said as he pulled up in front of Guthrie's trailer. "Be sure to stop by when you do."

"I will," Guthrie promised.

"Just tell me one thing," Turner said. "Is Thorndike going to show up as another bank deposit from a mysterious law firm?"

"I told you," Guthrie said, smiling. "I'm being paid by the insurance company." He got out of the Interceptor and leaned back in. "You keep your town safe."

Turner nodded, and Guthrie shut the door and watched him pull out of the trailer park and disappear down the state road. Then he went into the trailer.

The next morning, Guthrie dropped off the keys and thanked Warren Evers for his hospitality and all the trouble.

"Don't you think a second thought about it," Evers said with a laugh. "The residents are still talking about how you got the drop on Miller and Fitzgerald. Heck, you made my little trailer park famous."

After that, Guthrie sat on the trailer steps, his bag by his side, waiting for Li Wu to pick him up. Li arrived not long after in a brand new Ford Maverick hybrid pickup painted a dusty blue.

"All done?" Li asked as Guthrie settled into the passenger seat.

"All done here. Let's go home."

Li pulled out of the parking lot and headed south toward Houston.

"Nice ride," Guthrie said, looking around the cab. "But a pickup is more my style than yours."

"Glad you like it," Li said. "I told Master Tereba your old vehicle was destroyed, so he bought this one for you. Free and clear. If you don't like it, trade it in for another." He grinned. "But I'll drive us back to Houston. You look beat."

52

INSTEAD OF TAKING GUTHRIE HOME, Li Wu drove to a parking garage behind a bank on Kirby. After corkscrewing up the entire building to the roof-top level, he pulled up next to the boxy cement structure covering the stairwell head jutting up at one corner of the building. Only a few cars were scattered among the spaces, one of them Wu's.

"His door's around there," Wu said, gesturing toward the back of the stairwell head. He dropped the keys to the Maverick into Guthrie's hand. "It's a hybrid. You don't crank it, just switch it on."

"He's not using the back of the mall in Bellaire?" Guthrie asked as they got out and he locked the Maverick's doors.

"That location has been compromised. Too dangerous right now. He's moving the door around. He's inside, waiting. I'll see you at practice next week."

Wu went to his car, got in, and drove toward the down-ramp. Guthrie watched him go then walked to the stairwell head and glanced around the back corner. Indeed, Master Tereba's door was there, heavy wood carved with arcane lacquered symbols. Guthrie noted that it couldn't be seen from the parking lot or adjacent building. One would have to know it was there. And when it was there. He stepped to it, pulled it open, and went inside.

No matter where the door appeared, the apothecary shop was always behind it, never changed except for the levels of plants, powders, and assorted nastiness in the jars on the racks lining the walls. Those and Master Tereba, who was perched as usual on a stool behind the simple dark wooden counter. Guthrie walked the worn parquet floor to the counter and sat on a stool there.

"Nice to see you, Mr. Guthrie," the old man said.

"Nice to be here. I suppose you want to know what happened."

"Every word of it." Tereba reached under the counter, produced a bottle of water, and set it on the counter in front of Guthrie.

Guthrie told him. It took some time and most of the bottle of water.

"The situation was pretty tight for a while," he finished. "But we prevailed."

"In every change there is friction," Tereba said. "Friction and heat. And a temporary sticking. But in the end, no person can stand up to the flow of reality. It always moves on, bearing him or her with it."

"You seem to do pretty well standing against the flow of time," Guthrie said. "You never said exactly how old you are, but…."

"I'm not sure exactly how old I am," Tereba responded a little tartly. "My date of birth was so long ago, I've forgotten."

"Yeah, right. I doubt you ever forget anything."

"Your success is indicative of the nature of reality," Tereba said, ignoring Guthrie's remark. "Rand was trying to control and alter the flow of reality, and most of the time someone tries to do that, the results produce effects opposite those intended. Take Tomas Midgely Jr. He developed leaded gasoline to solve the problem of engine knock. It proved toxic, but not before the health of billions worldwide had been affected. As if that wasn't enough, he then helped develop freon, and you know what that did to the ozone layer. He was trying to solve problems, but lack of knowledge and foresight not only negated his efforts, but led some to call him a one-man environmental disaster who killed more people than anyone else in history. He even killed himself accidentally with an elaborate rope and pulley system he designed to help him move around after he contracted polio. Most of the time, it's much better to work to restore the natural flow rather than go against it."

"I hear you, but what if Rand had succeeded? We'd have had a terrible world to live in. And I have to wonder what would have happened after he died. Would the miasma lose its direction and thus weaken and finally dissipate? Or would Rand have gathered a coterie of men and women whose venality, corruption, and lust for power would encourage them to keep it constantly fed, self-perpetuating, and growing in strength?"

"Who knows what evil lurks in the hearts of men?" Tereba said.

"It's amazing how an essentially minor feud could result in a situation that could endanger and ruin countless people."

"Sadly, all too common in humankind's long and sordid history. Yet try as he might to do something awful, Mr. Rand failed because you were there to help restore the natural flow. And in the end, he accomplished something good by becoming the motivating force of reality that caused friction and heat but that finally caused momentum."

Guthrie couldn't argue with that.

"Li said you might be in some danger," he said, changing the subject.

"Perhaps some. It is inevitable in my business."

Guthrie couldn't argue with that, either.

"Anything I can do?"

"Later, perhaps. Right now, I'm sure you need a rest. Go home."

Guthrie did, but a call from Detective Peters the next afternoon told him the loose ends of the case weren't yet tied up.

"I don't know if you're still in Thorndike or if you're available," Peters said, "but Betsy Telfor is having a memorial service for Norm tomorrow afternoon at one at their house. Thought you might like to be there."

"I'm home," Guthrie said. "I'll be there."

"Maybe I'll see you," Peters said then hung up.

Early the next morning, Guthrie rose, got into his new truck, and drove to Oakdale. He liked the way the Maverick rode on the road, but the front-wheel drive was going to take a little getting used to. As he pulled up in front of the Telfor home a few hours later, he noticed Norm's van was parked in the garage next to the yellow Nissan pickup.

A woman Guthrie didn't recognize let him in, giving him a big smile when he told her who he was.

"I'm Angie," she said, taking his proffered hand in both of hers. "Norm and Betsy's daughter. I know who you are. Thank you for coming. And thank you for finding Dad. It meant a lot to all of us, especially Mom."

"I wish the outcome had been better."

"It is what it is," she said sadly.

There were perhaps thirty people in the living room, dining room, and kitchen. The furniture in the living room was arranged the same, but it looked like a cleaning crew had come through, vacuuming, dusting, polishing, and straightening things up. It almost looked like a new house. He glanced at Norm's chair, and saw a simple pewter urn sitting on the seat, an unopened can of beer next to it. A photo of Norm was in the formerly empty gilt-edged frame, now leaning against the seat back behind the urn. Norm was back home in his favorite chair.

Betsy was sitting in her own chair, looking at the urn, but she saw Guthrie come over and immediately stood and embraced him. Then she stepped back, but kept a hand on his arm.

"You found my Norm," she said, clutching his arm tight. "I know it was you. Them other men, that police chief and his officer are gettin' all the credit, but I know it was you. Please stand with me for a few minutes here by Norm. You give me strength."

He did, but he could tell she had her own strength to rely on. Despite the tragedy that had occurred, she would come out all right. And all the people in the house showed she had a lot of support. As they stood there, looking down on the urn. Guthrie didn't know what was going on in Betsy Telfor's mind, but he was wondering if the Kuei men would react to Norm's cremated remains. Thankfully, they were as still as death.

"The man who killed Norm was an evil man, wasn't he," she said at last.

"A very evil man."

"It's sad that Norm died, especially at the hands of a man like that. But it turns out Norm was what brung you into things. He was the pebble that started the landslide that buried that bastard."

"Norm was the one," Guthrie said. He reached into his jacket pocket and came out with the photo she'd loaned him. "I want to give this back to you."

He handed it over, and she looked tenderly at it for a moment before propping it on the chair next to the framed photo.

"I think I'm gonna leave him there on that chair and turn on the Cowboys games every week. Maybe he'd like that."

"I'm sure he would."

"I just can't believe Norm took out that insurance for me," Betsy said. "And just two weeks before he died." She looked Guthrie in the eyes. "You think he had some kinda premonition somethin' was gonna happen to him?"

"I think he loved you enough to provide for you, whatever the circumstances."

Out of the corner of his eye, he saw Detective Peters come in the front door.

"If you'll excuse me for a minute, Mrs. Telfor. I'd like to have a word with Detective Peters."

She nodded, and he left her and walked over to the detective.

"I want to apologize if I stepped on your toes," he said.

"No worries. I told you I'm results oriented. Besides, there was no way I could have cracked the least part of this case."

Not the real case, Guthrie thought, no matter how good a detective Peters might be.

"You and Oakdale PD did your part," he said. "That's what counts."

They shook, and Guthrie went back to Betsy.

"I'll be running along now," he told her. "I'm sorry things didn't work out better."

She embraced him again then stepped back.

"You couldn't help what happened to Norm, but you brung him home to me and found justice for him. I'll never forget that."

"Goodbye, Mrs. Telfor. And best of luck."

He drove home. It had been a long round trip for a thirty-minute stay, but it had been worth it to see Betsy coping with her loss.

Three months later, Guthrie had to drive up to Thorndike's county seat to testify at the trial of Johnny Miller and Rob Fitzgerald. He took the state road east of Thorndike but didn't stop on the way up. Nothing seemed changed except for a new building going up almost across the road from the Pit Stop. A sign in front proclaimed it was the new home of the Thorndike City Hall and Police Station. He also noticed a sign at the entrance to the road that angled off through Miss Agnes's property stating that Thorndike Hills, a new subdivision, was going up somewhere down there.

During his testimony, the DA linked Miller and Fitzgerald to the Sanfords and thus to Rand and the deaths of Norm Telfor, Jeff Mayfield, and Claude Fortier. Not to mention to the weapons stolen from Buster Havasau and the tools stolen from Eli Carlin. Apparently, Chief Turner had testified the day before about those matters. The two were toast, Guthrie thought, though he didn't hang around to hear the verdict. Instead, after spending the night in a motel, he drove home, pausing in Thorndike on the way south. His first stop was Leo's Cafe. As he parked in front, he noticed that the Baptist Church was being rebuilt and that the formerly boarded-up brown brick building across the street was now the Thorndike Post Office.

"Clay!" Bev said, coming over as soon as he entered. "So nice to see you. I don't know whether to take your order first or call Bill and tell him you're here."

"I'll have a Number Three," he said, grinning. "Now you can call Bill."

He took a seat in a booth, noticing that the several other diners in the room all smiled and nodded at him. Bev pulled out her phone and called her husband as she headed to the service window. She was back in just a couple of minutes with coffee, water, and silverware, and she'd barely set them on the table when Turner came through the door. He spotted Guthrie, a big smile on his face. Guthrie rose and shook his hand, then the chief took the seat across the table, and Bev slipped in next to him.

"I guess you've been testifying at the trial," Turner said.

"Yesterday. Thought I'd drop by on the way home to see how things are going here."

"Couldn't be better," Turner said. "Seems like business is back to usual now that all the hubbub has died down. Better than usual, actually."

For a time, he told Guthrie, it seemed that everybody had a story to tell reporters about the case, maybe hoping to see their names in print or winding up in an episode of some true crime TV series. He'd even had a few requests himself, though he'd declined.

"I've had enough microphones stuck in my face to last a lifetime," he said.

But all the excitement faded following the departure of the reporters. For most people in town, the only remembrance was of those crazy, dismal couple of weeks when a serial killer had lived in their midst and it seemed like everything in town had gone to hell. There was some lingering talk over the news that the Sanfords, Orman, and Hetty had been in cahoots with Rand, but most folks were glad they were gone. And happy to forget about them as soon as possible.

"Life goes on," Guthrie said.

"And how," Bev said. "There've been a lot of positive repercussions. You can't see much from the state road, but there's a lot of excitement going on here."

"I saw the new town hall," Guthrie said. "With a new police station."

"I'm even getting funding for a third officer," Turner said. "Emmet and I are the town heroes, and the council's going to do whatever it takes to keep us happy."

"That's great," Guthrie said. It seemed that Thorndike had returned to some sort of normalcy and was even beginning to flourish beneath the late summer sun and the ferment and fever of revitalization.

"How about Leland Fuller and Chuck Willis's enterprise?"

"Construction is underway on the meat-packing plant as we speak, and that's already providing jobs. Leland accepted the idea that it was Rand who poisoned the marsh in an attempt to drive Jim out, and the deaths of the cattle in his north pasture was a result."

"Thorndike is on the upswing," Bev said. "Did you see the sign for Miss Agnes's new subdivision?"

"I did."

"Just the first," Turner said. "With the projected growth, the Chaloupeks are building a big new store on one of the vacant plots of land between the Canine Cottage and the state road. A pharmacist is interested in buying their old building."

And Jim's marsh?"

"Now the Enid Chaney Nature Preserve," Bev said. "Just like Jim wanted. Miss Agnes spends most of her time down there now that she doesn't have to manage her ranch. She hired Freddie as the full-time caretaker."

"Who's going to manage the dump?" Guthrie asked.

Turner chuckled.

"That's something we haven't figured out for the long term, but Pete and Wally are doing it until we can hire a full-timer."

Leo called from the kitchen, and Bev went to pick up Guthrie's food and bring her husband a cup of coffee. While Guthrie ate, the Turners talked about this and that. Dr. and Mable Hughes had purchased a well-conformed pair of Great Pyrenees and resumed their breeding program. The deaths of all the dogs remained unexplained, even after the EPA was briefly involved. And though the weapons used in the final confrontation in the marsh had been confiscated, Buster Havasau had recovered the rest and been reimbursed for the confiscated guns by his insurance company. But after seeing how they'd been used against Jim Chaney and the Thorndike police, he drastically reduced his stock to sporting arms. Guthrie's burned-out Xterra had been hauled off to a junkyard in the county seat. The same one that was now home to Jeff Mayfield's truck. The vehicles belonging to Rand, the Sanfords, and Johnny Miller were in the sheriff's impound lot for the time being.

None of them talked about what had gone down in the marsh.

At last, Guthrie finished his meal, and he sat with the Turners through a second cup of coffee, but now that talk of Thorndike's revitalization was done, there didn't seem to be much more to say. It was as if what they'd gone through together had said enough. It was time to go. Bev hugged him, and Turner shook his hand.

"Don't be a stranger," Turner said.

Guthrie left, but he didn't immediately drive home. Instead, he went down to Jim Chaney's cabin to visit Freddie and Miss Agnes. On the way, he stared at the old Chaney place. It was boarded up. He also noticed that the formerly diseased ditch looked nearly normal.

The gate to the cabin road was open, and a rustic but artful sign was mounted beside it. The words, "The Enid Chaney Nature Preserve," were etched into the heavy dark wood and painted white. As he wound down the narrow lane, he noticed that the blight in the ditches was clearing up here, too.

At the end of the road, he found Miss Agnes's car and Freddie's pickup. At the cabin, the siding and trim that had been damaged by bullets was repaired, and most gratifying, the pond was full once again with clean, sparkling water, a few birds flitting over it, seeking buggy meals. Apparently, the miasma hadn't inhabited it long enough to impart a long-lasting stain.

He heard someone whistling on the back deck, and he went around the corner to find a clean-cut stranger sweeping the floorboards.

"Excuse me," he said. "I'm looking for Freddie and Miss Agnes."

"Clay!" The man stopped sweeping, leaned the broom against the wall, and came over to shake Guthrie's hand.

He was Freddie. A much changed Freddie. Guthrie hadn't immediately recognized him now that his bushy gray beard was gone.

"You're looking well," Guthrie said. "I see you shaved."

"Yeah," Freddie said, rubbing a palm across his cheek. "I ain't used to it yet, but other than that, I'm doin' great. I ain't been drinkin' or smokin', and I feel a thousand percent better. But what about you? How's the shoulder?"

"All healed up."

"I guess you know Miss Agnes give me the job of caretaker, here," Freddie said. "Pays pretty well, too." He noticed Guthrie staring over the pond. "Nice again, ain't it? First thing I did as soon as all that fouled water drained out, I rebuilt the dam. Reinforced it, too, to make sure it'll last. And did you see our sign? Made it myself."

"You've done a lot of good work, Freddie, and I don't just mean on the dam and the cabin."

"That Rand was an evil man," Freddie said. "I'm glad he's dead."

"Me, too. And so are all the women he never got a chance to kill, even if they don't know it."

"Ain't that the way it is? You can do all the great good you can do, and most people who benefit from it don't even know who you are or what you done."

"It doesn't matter if everybody knows, only that the right people do."

"Ain't that the truth. But it wasn't just him, was it, Clay? It was that thing that was in the pond, causing all the fear and destruction in town."

"It was that thing most of all, and we couldn't have gotten rid of it without you. Don't you ever forget that."

Freddie laughed.

"Ain't much chance I'll ever forget none of it. But don't you worry. It's our secret: you, me, Chief Bill, and Emmet Taylor. Like a special club, with you and me the silent partners nobody ever knows about. I'm happy with that. I ain't even said nothin' to Miss Agnes, though she keeps pumping me for information. I keep tellin' her I wasn't down here, but even if she believes that, she knows I know more than I'm tellin'." He laughed again. "I normally wouldn't go against Miss Agnes, but this might be one of them times. Say, you know who's also pumping me for the lowdown? Tessa."

"So that's why you shaved your beard."

Freddie chuckled, lowered his voice, and leaned close.

"I think she's sweet on me now I quit drinking and have a respectable job."

"I think she knows you played a big part in saving Thorndike, so you're not quite the unknown hero you think you are."

"Might be, but I ain't never gonna tell her, either. Don't want her to think I've gone plumb crazy and spoil things. We spent a couple of nights at her place, watchin' TV and, you, know...." His voice trailed off in embarrassment.

"I say go for it. Life isn't gettin' any longer."

"Ain't that the truth." Freddie straightened and nodded his head toward the door. "Go on in. She's in there, probably back in her office, doing some paperwork or something."

Guthrie opened the door and went inside. The interior of the cabin's main room was largely the same, but Guthrie could see through the bedroom door that it was no longer a bedroom. Miss Agnes was in there, sitting behind a desk, reading a document. She looked up and saw him, and a smile brightened her face. As he walked across the living area to the office, Guthrie had to smile, too, since the scene was so similar to the first time he'd met her when she'd been sitting behind a table in Leo's as he approached. And so dissimilar too. Circumstances since then had flip-flopped more times than he could remember.

"Clay," she said, rising and coming around to greet him. "So nice to see you."

She embraced him then held him at arms length. The look she gave him was something akin to the affectionate and proud one she'd given Bill Turner. It made Guthrie feel good.

"You have my deepest gratitude," she said. "I don't know what happened down here, but it must have been terrible." She dropped her arms. "I can't even get Freddie to tell me anything."

"That should tell you all you need to know," Guthrie said, smiling.

"I know George Rand wasn't responsible for everything that happened. There was something more. Just tell me it wasn't because of us. Some evil quirk of our own nature?"

"Not you. Thorndike had discord, as any town is apt to have. But the evil that took root in the marsh was spawned elsewhere. George Rand simply brought it here, seeking vulnerable prey."

"Well, he's gone, and so are those who helped him. Things are better now. I can feel it in the air. Thordike's a better place, thanks to you."

"Wasn't just me, Miss Agnes. Bill and Emmet were right there. And Freddie. Don't forget about him."

"I won't, but you were the one who chased the evil here and put an end to it. I won't ever forget that, either. But even if it's best I don't know, I still wish one of you would tell me something. I don't like not knowing what's going on in my own backyard."

"Why, nothing, Miss Agnes. Nothing's going on. Except maybe that subdivision I hear is going up on your land. And the new city hall. And all the other things happening in town." He waved around the room. "And all this."

"Yes, this," she said. "This is perhaps the most surprising of all. To think that Jim left this property to the town of Thorndike and gave me complete oversight for as long as I'm able. I hope that's a long time now that I have a whole lot less ranch to worry with. It's almost unbelievable Jim would do something like this and put me in charge. He didn't much like how close Enid and I were until we finally quit seeing each other. That was a heartbreak for me."

"He told me that you and Enid were best friends until he drove you apart. That's one scratch in the surface of his guilt. I guess he was trying to make up for everything with one act."

"He had a lot to make up for considering the way he treated Enid."

"I have to tell you he said he never physically abused her, even if everybody thought he had."

"And you believe him?"

"Yes. He admitted he abused her psychologically and emotionally. But a physical abuser would never allow his wife to live away from him, out of his direct control."

"All right. Maybe I misjudged him on that count and jumped to conclusions like everybody else. Whatever the truth, I certainly wouldn't have wished his terrible death on him."

"I can guarantee he died happy in leaving this resource to Thorndike and giving you the opportunity for it to bear your mark. He did all that in Enid's honor."

"Now that your work is done here, I suppose you'll be leaving us for good."

"I have plenty of other work to do."

"Well, you go on and do it. But you come back here sometime. I have a spare bedroom with its own bath, and I'd love to have you visit. So would Bill and Bev."

"I'll do that," Guthrie said, though he knew fate might not permit him to come this way again. "Bye for now."

She touched his arm and smiled, then he was out the door and heading across the cabin's main room. He could have gone out the front, but he went out the door to the deck. Freddie was still sweeping.

"Bye, Freddie," he said. "Good luck with Tessa."

Freddie gave him a smile and a wave.

"Bye, Clay."

Guthrie's final act in Thorndike was to visit Jim Chaney's grave. He drove around to the paved county road and turned south. The entrance to the nondescript dirt road leading to the old cemetery was just south of the dump. The road wound across gently rolling pastures for half a mile before ending at the graveyard. Guthrie could see the churned-up path Freddie had blazed when he'd driven his backhoe from here to the dam and back.

The cemetery was small, containing only about thirty graves, and Jim Chaney's wasn't hard to find. It was the only one with newly turned earth. Right next to the one for Enid Chaney.

He stood there for several minutes, looking at the mound where Chaney's misspent life and guilt were buried with him. And no differently, the events of those two weeks Guthrie had spent in Thorndike were fading into the past, reminding him that the actions he took today would not only shape his life in the future, but would become his later memories of this time. He resolved to make those memories count toward something good.

He got into his new truck and drove home.

Phosphene Publishing Company
publishes books and DVDs relating to literature,
history, the paranormal, film, spirituality, and the
martial arts.

For other great titles, visit
phosphenepublishing.com